# DECANTED

*Linda Sheehan*

Hope you enjoy
my story!
cheers,
Linda Sheehan

Black Rose Writing | Texas

The author grants the final approval for this literary material.

First printing

This is a work of fiction. Names, characters, businesses, places, events, and incidents are either the products of the author's imagination or used in a fictitious manner. Any resemblance to actual persons, living or dead, or actual events is purely coincidental.

ISBN: 978-1-68433-703-3
PUBLISHED BY BLACK ROSE WRITING
www.blackrosewriting.com

Printed in the United States of America
Suggested Retail Price (SRP) $19.95

*Decanted* is printed in Palatino Linotype

*As a planet-friendly publisher, Black Rose Writing does its best to eliminate unnecessary waste to reduce paper usage and energy costs, while never compromising the reading experience. As a result, the final word count vs. page count may not meet common expectations.

Cover design- Susan Faiola
Author photo- Nicola Parisi

This book is dedicated to the real-life Samantha whose sense of humor, thirst for adventure, and ability to create delicious wines continues to astound me.

praise for

# DECANTED

"A captivating story of a young woman following the example of her avant-garde aunt to find her own passion in life. There's love and heartbreak, unexpected success and near disaster, and through it all, an insider's view of the art and craft of winemaking."
**–Pamela Taylor, author of *The Second Son Chronicles***

"From the first sip to the glorious finish, author Sheehan has woven a compulsively readable story of love, passion, wine, and true grit, for all who savor a tale well told."
**–David Noonan, author of *Memoirs of a Caddy***

"A highly enjoyable tale of love, wine, and passion with juicy deft plotting. Readers will receive an enjoyable education on winemaking as Sam learns and works. Indeed, the emphasis on Sam's dreams give the book an admirably feminist bent."
**–*Kirkus Reviews***

"Fascinating . . . intriguing . . . fresh and appealing....able to hold the readers' attention until the final sentence. The author's clear expertise in the wine industry—conveyed through eloquent use of wine terminology and descriptions of growing and harvesting grapes—sets the work apart."
**–*The Booklife Prize***

"Sheehan tells her story in evocative prose that makes your reading of her novel a bit surreal, a little bit magical, and totally absorbing. If you have ever been to France, you'll feel like you're back. If you haven't: welcome...You'll get a feel for the wine region's unique, romantic atmosphere. Alternating between the past and present, friendships and romance, hope, and despair, *Decanted* becomes a novel about finding oneself through passion, history, acknowledgment, grief, and love. *Decanted* is women's fiction at its best."
**–*Authors Reading***

"…wonderfully realistic and intelligent…revealing a well-researched wine culture that's effortlessly entertaining. I enjoyed the rich and detailed explanations of the natural views and taste or smells of the food and drink in the book. This book is a paradise for the gastronomically inclined. I highly recommend this as a light and refreshing read to any who dreams of the French campagne, soleil, et bon vin."
–*Literary Titan*

"A well-penned celebration of womanhood, wine, and the wisdom of age. The prose is smart and the relationships believable, and the story is rich with conversation and authentic dialogue, which drive the plot forward, while also touching on global culture, travel, love, music, and wine. Sheehan is a careful and patient storyteller, making this novel a fun and easy escape."
–*SP Review*

"This very well-written novel succeeds in doing many things. It tells the story of a courageous, intelligent, adventurous woman who leaves behind all with which she is familiar to turn her dream into a reality. It also delivers an appealing love story. And it introduces us to the intricacies of winemaking, both in France and in California. However, that is not all. It does all of these things in duplicate, because deftly woven into the story is the sub-story of Vivian, Samantha's great-aunt, who lived her own adventures in the 1930s and passed down her courage and passion for wine to Samantha, two generations later. This novel is well worth the read."
–*Sublime Book Reviews*

"Author Sheehan has gathered multiple threads to weave a vibrant tapestry…with well-researched detail and two gutsy females in the limelight. Each chapter opens with a dictionary definition of vintner's terminology relevant to the story. One in particular beautifully symbolizes the necessary inner transformation that guides and enheartens the novel's heroines: to "decant" is to pour wine from its confining bottle to a more open container, giving it needed air and releasing its hidden flavors and fragrances. In *Decanted*, author Sheehan demonstrates this magical process with her well-chosen words and evident *joie de vivre*"
–*A Woman's Write*

# DECANTED

# prologue

---

*Montmartre, Paris June 1936*

Marciel erased the asymmetrical portion of the figure model's right breast and corrected it with his pencil. Though he'd been studying nudes since his first days at *L'Académie*, it still surprised him how few women had two bosoms that matched each other in size and shape. But the model's anatomy wasn't the reason he'd sent her away the previous day before her session had ended. It was rather that she lacked that special something—that elusive *élément magique* that would inspire him to take his sketch to canvas. Between touch-ups of the drawing, he checked his watch for what seemed like the hundredth time in the past hour. Phillipe had assured him that his new model would be there at two p.m., and it was already half-past three. He decided to give her ten more minutes, before he'd pack up his pastels and easel and head to the *Place du Tertre* to take advantage of the waves of tourists that flocked to Montmartre in summer. His gift of capturing the outer beauty, as well as what lay beneath the surface of his subjects made him one of the more successful portrait artists on the hill. Those commissions put food on his table, but did nothing to further his chances of getting recognized by the only people that mattered to unknown artists like himself—the dealers at the galleries on Paris' Rue Laffitte. Another look at his watch reminded him that while time was running out for the model, it was running out for him as well. He'd turned thirty last month and had yet to get one of his paintings up on a gallery wall. Picasso was a celebrated artist by age nineteen. Chagall made a name for himself in his early twenties. Marciel had shown exceptional promise while a student at *L'Académie*. He received high praise by his professors for his painting style that, by adding in a tilt of the head or a smoldering gaze, could turn an ordinary looking woman into a mythological heroine, a sinister creature, or an object of unbridled desire. Then . . . maybe it was the ever-growing stench of human waste on the city streets, or his anxiety caused by the Nazi cloud that loomed over Europe, or perhaps the talent and creativity of his youth had passed its shelf life. Whatever the reason, the passions within him that had ignited the canvases of his earlier works seemed to have vanished over the past two years. And unless they reappeared soon, his only recourse would be to return to his family's domaine in the south of France to join his father and sister in the cave making Grenache and Syrah.

Gaining attention as an artist in Paris was becoming harder all the time as Montmartre continued to be a magnet for aspiring painters who flocked to the district with dreams of becoming the next Cézanne, Matisse, van Gogh, or Degas. It also made it harder to get suitable models who would take their clothes off for under ten francs. The ones in demand worked for artists with bigger names and fatter wallets, leaving the prostitutes and gypsies for those struggling like himself. The last girl Phillipe had sent him was as skinny as a chicken carcass pecked over by buzzards. The one before that was over forty and fat as a Yorkshire pig. But the agent had assured him that this girl, though young, would set his brush on fire. Now, he'd give his friend hell for her being a no show. He put the cork back in the bottle of the Burgundy he'd opened to use as a prop for the painting, and hoped the wine would keep its character for a few more days. While he returned the bottle to the shelf, there was a gentle rapping on his door.

# one

New York City, three years ago

A dome of unyielding heat and humidity blanketed the Manhattan skyline, unseasonable even for mid-August. But as I sat with my friends at the dark mahogany bar of Spence's Fines Wines & Spirits, the cool air that rose from the cellar below Columbus Avenue made that summer evening feel like a crisp fall morning.

"Here's a wine well-suited to toast a grand lady on what would have been her ninety-sixth birthday," Spence Walker said as he climbed up the cellar steps, emerging with a bottle in his hand. "A Tannat from Gascony." He flipped the blade from his corkscrew and ran it around the lower lip of the bottle's neck to remove the top of the tin capsule. After twisting in the screw and popping the cork, he poured the deep purple liquid from the grapes of Southwest France into four glasses. I rotated mine on the counter and raised it high in the air.

"To Great-aunt Vivian! Who encouraged me to trust my instincts, to take chances, and to taste."

"To Samantha's Aunt Vivian," Spence, Stephanie, and Cameron said as their glasses met mine then touched each other's.

"Some great-aunts teach their nieces to knit and bake cookies. Mine taught me how to tell the difference between a Grenache and a Syrah," I said before taking a sip. "*Whoa!*" I licked my lips to negate the intense drying sensation that had taken over my mouth. "She might have loved this wine, but it's sure not my style."

"Let it wake up a bit," Spence suggested. "You'll be surprised by how it develops. It's bold, but Vivian once told me it has the power to take you to unknown places."

"That sounds like my aunt," I agreed.

"Yup. That lady had one adventurous palate," Spence said. "Wasn't she considered a bit of a rebel back in her day?"

"Yup. A rebel with a mind of her own." I gave the wine another swirl. "After she finished high school in the 1930s, her parents assumed she'd attend Mrs. O'Grady's secretarial school for women. *Wrong!* Instead, she took her savings and booked passage on the *SS France* bound for Paris. Thought she could make a living by selling her clay sculptures. When that bubble burst, she enrolled in art school with the money she earned as a life model."

"A *life model*?" asked Cameron. "You mean a *nude* model? That *little old lady* was a *nude model*?"

"She wasn't always a little old lady. You've seen her on that canvas hanging over my mantle. The artist who painted it thought her face and form expressed a complex range of characteristics that seeped onto the canvas: sexuality, innocence, bitterness, sweetness, softness, acidity —"

"Just like great wine," said the willowy and beautiful Stephanie.

"Yeah, just like great wine. She told some radical stories about her life in Paris right before the war," I said. "The nightclubs, the fashions, the artists and writers she hung with, the fear that their world was about to come crashing down. But it was strange that she never talked about her life when the Nazis took over the city."

"It had to be a nightmare," said Stephanie.

"I'm sure. I just know that after the occupation, she moved back here and became a stylist for Vogue. She also wrote a nationally syndicated column about food and wine."

"That Vivian was quite the Renaissance woman," Spence said as he took another sip of the Tannat and let it linger on his tongue. "And she sure knew her French wines." While he spoke, he kept his eyes on the shop's front window as if waiting for Vivian to walk in with her determined but abbreviated gait. "With just one whiff, she could name what was in the glass and where it was from, be it a Petit Verdot from Bordeaux, a Syrah from Provence, or a Chenin Blanc from St. Émilion."

Though my great-aunt had died six months before, it was still hard to believe she was gone. When I graduated from college and took a job at Weatherhouse Accounting, Vivian invited me to move into her co-op on the Upper West Side. I was soon making enough money to share a decent space with my friends in Bed-Stuy, but I just wasn't comfortable with a lady that age living alone. The reality that she wouldn't be around forever hit when she handed me a list of what would go to whom upon her death. The apartment she got for a steal in the 1970s would go to my parents, the funky art deco jewelry would go to my mom, and the furniture, the painting, and a case of some wine she'd been storing would go to me. Not long after, I got a call on my cell from the NYPD. Vivian's heart had stopped beating while she was selecting her favorite salad mix of Russian kale and curly endive at the Seventy-ninth Street market.

"I sure hope I'm as spry as Miss Vivian was when I'm ninety-five," Spence said while he held up his glass of the almost-black wine to look through it. "Fat chance of that though. My eating habits are awful. Coffee for breakfast, no lunch, tasting wine all day long, fast food for dinner. Did you know I used to surf? All summer long. But the only exercise I've done for the past twenty years has been shuffling cartons and stacking bottles on these shelves."

"I can remember being in shape. Great shape, too." I felt the waistband of my jeans cutting into my belly and silently cursed that new hire Austin for leaving those Krispy Kremes on the coffee counter each morning. "When I had time for a five-mile morning run, evening spin classes, TRX—"

"You still have a primo body for a girl who rarely sees the light of day," the always supportive Cameron said. "And that face still looks pretty, even under those office lights. If I had even the slightest interest in the feminine sex, I'd never let you leave the house." While speaking, he looked my way with eyes puffy from lack of sleep. Those bags and his ever-increasing slouch from being affixed to a computer made the guy who was once the captain of his Varsity diving team look far older than his twenty-eight years.

"You'd never let me leave the house? That's creepy, Cam. *Creepy*."

"Where's your sense of humor, Sam? You need to chill. Or what you really need is a good—"

"I know what I need. But who has time for sex after working from seven in the morning 'til eleven at night all week long? Of course, my mom neglected to mention that I'd be working these hours when she convinced me to major in accounting. I guess I'm just destined to look like an overweight cadaver after thirty-five."

"Seems like it's only a matter of time before we all look like cadavers after enough of these eighty-hour weeks crunching numbers," added Stephanie, who was new enough at the firm to still have her sunny glow. She took another sip of the wine. "Spence was right about this getting yummier though." While we were talking, she'd been entering her tasting notes on the Tannat into one of her favorite wine-sharing apps. Then she added a picture of the vintage's label and tagged us as her drinking partners.

I checked the time on my cell. "Playtime's over for me. Another late night awaits. Got that bear of a presentation tomorrow for the Bannex Box Company. I've already created thirty-two schedules and sixteen spreadsheets. Getting close though."

"Wait. Isn't Bannex *Favia's account*?" asked Cameron. "She's all over those folks."

"Favia's on vacation, so Van Ness gave the assignment to me. He likes what he's seen with my plan to expand the firm's reach. So instead of schlepping to Duluth and Cleveland to audit paper pulp and carton factories, I'll be traveling to wineries in Sonoma and châteaux in France. It'd be a great way for me to parlay myself, *and maybe all of us*, into the wine industry. After all, how many times have we heard him say he wants his hires to think outside the box?"

"Only maybe . . . three times?" asked Stephanie. "A day, that is."

"More like three times an hour," Cameron said with a yawn.

"See you in the morning, guys," I said.

"*You go, girl!* Knock the socks off those carton kings!" Cameron called out as he held up a glass of a crisp white from the Phelz region in Germany.

"Will do. Bye, Steph. Here, you take the Tannat, Spence. I shouldn't be drinking tonight anyway," I said as I slid my glass down the bar in his direction.

"Hey, Sam, I've got the distributor for Domaine LeMont in Beaujolais stopping in around seven tomorrow evening," Spence said. "I haven't carried their wines for years, but since *Wine Snob* named them the best in the region, I've been getting calls for it. So come on by. I'd like your young taste buds to try them."

"Wild horses couldn't keep me away," I said as I unlocked the door and let myself out of the shop.

.　　.　　.

"To sum things up, we're confident the offshore subsidiaries you'll be creating can provide close to three hundred million in tax savings for Bannex by the year 2020. And with the way the codes read now, it's all perfectly legal." I had what I hoped looked like a sincere smile frozen onto my face as I stood at head of the Weatherhouse conference table in my serious dark suit with my wild mess of blonde curls blown straight and pulled back into a too-tight pony tail. On my right, our firm's managing partner Michael Van Ness hung on my every word. "With no foreseeable end to the exponential increase of online sales, as Amazon continues to take control of the universe, your company will enjoy the same degree of unprecedented growth. And we're taking our job of protecting your profits very seriously." My wrap-up for my two-hour presentation received chants of "*Hear-hear!*" and a burst of applause.

When the meeting ended, Tom Bannex put his hand on my shoulder and turned to Michael Van Ness. "You do know this lady is worth her weight in gold, don't you, Van Ness?"

Michael thrust out his chest and smiled at me like a proud papa. "Samantha is one of our brightest stars here at Weatherhouse. She's an outstanding example of an accountant who really, as I like to say, *thinks outside the box!*"

"That's rich!" Tom answered with a chuckle as he extended his hand toward me. "Samantha, it's been a pleasure. My team will be in touch. Likewise, Van Ness," he said to Michael as the two men shook hands.

After we saw the clients off in the elevator, Michael turned to me. "Need I say that you did a splendid job in there, Samantha?"

"Glad to be of service, sir."

"Perhaps tomorrow you and I could have a chat about your future here at Weatherhouse and how we can best utilize your impressive talents."

"Sure! I've already got some ideas about exciting new avenues for the firm to explore."

"Well then . . ." He pulled out his phone. "Looks like ten a.m. would work for me."

"Works for me too, Mr. Van Ness!"

"My office? That good by you?"

"That'll be great! See you then. Have a nice evening, now."

•　　•　　•

"*Yes!*" I cried out as the elevator doors shut and I began the fifty-two-floor descent to the lobby of the building called 'The Box' by those in the accounting industry. "*I did it! He loves me! He trusts me! It's gonna happen!*" Over the past few months, I'd been planning my pitch, and was now perfectly primed to help take Weatherhouse Accounting outside of the box business and into the wine industry. When the elevator doors opened, I traded my heels for my running shoes, squirmed out of my wool suit jacket, and slid the clothes into my briefcase. Despite the ninety-five-degree heat and what seemed like one hundred percent humidity, I felt a surge of energy as I joined the throng of commuters, tourists, and locals, as they rushed to restaurants, subways, theaters, museums, and a million other places. I smiled, knowing that after working my butt off as an analyst at the most excruciatingly boring job I could ever have imagined, I'd be traveling to exciting wine regions like Napa and Sonoma.

Walking up Central Park South, I patted the neck of one of the carriage horses as it waited to carry customers on a ride through the park. While I looked around for a fruit stand to buy the animal an apple, I got a text from my dad who owned a small PR firm in the city. He was leaving his office on West Thirty-third Street and would head to Aunt Vivian's co-op. Even though it was technically my parents' place now, it would always be Aunt Vivian's to me. My folks were allowing me to continue living there provided I take care of the two thousand a month maintenance, which is why I had my eye out for a roommate to split the costs. But though finding someone to share a two-bedroom two-bath apartment on the tenth floor of an elevator building was easy, finding someone I could trust not to bring a string of hook-ups home, blast music while I tried to work, or leave dirty dishes in the sink, was hard.

When I neared the front of the co-op, I saw the elderly lady who lived in 7C struggling to unlock the door while maneuvering her handcart filled with bags from our neighborhood grocery store. "Here let me help you with that, Mrs. Cranston," I said.

"Thank you, dear," she said in a voice worn thin by time. I took the cart and wheeled it into the lobby and pushed the elevator button for us both. "So nice to have young ones like you around to lend a hand to us relics from another era."

"No problem, Mrs. Cranston. I always enjoy seeing you."

She looked up at me through slightly watery eyes that drooped — the right more severely than the left. Arched lines above them created by a cosmetic pencil served as eyebrows. "I know you were a bright spot to your aunt at the end of her life. And time does march on, Samantha. It seems like it was only last week that I was a high-energy honcho like you. Catching a cab at the crack of dawn in my pantsuit and pumps. Coming home after dark with a briefcase full of memos that kept me occupied for the evening."

"Sounds like me. Only a laptop is my briefcase."

"Our secretaries did our typing on those IBM Selectrics. No email or cell phones either. Can you *imagine*?"

"I can, after watching *Mad Men*." The elevator stopped on her floor. "Here, I've got this," I said as I wheeled the cart out and started down the hallway to her apartment.

"Most of my entire younger adult life was just one big race to get to the finish line." She sounded a bit winded as she sped up her step to keep up with me. "And now that I'm just a mass of arthritis and dissolving bones, all I've got is a mountain of regrets for not enjoying the ride." We reached her door, and she opened the lock.

"Can I bring this in for you, Mrs. Cranston?"

"No, thanks. I can manage," she said as she wheeled the cart through the door. "But you *could* do something else for me, Samantha."

"What's that?"

"You can make sure you enjoy your ride. Your great-aunt sure enjoyed hers."

"I'm working on it, Mrs. Cranston."

I bounded up the stairwell that felt like a sauna and hit the switch on the air conditioning unit when I walked into the apartment. Then I changed from my skirt, nylons, and a silk blouse that had sweat marks under the armpits into a gauzy white peasant shirt and jeans that seemed to be getting tighter by the week. Just as I finally snapped them shut, the doorbell buzzed, followed by a *"bam, ba bam-bam... bam-bam!"*—mine and Dad's special knock.

"Coming, Dad! It is you, isn't it?"

"It's me, Sam," he called out.

"This is an impromptu vis ... it," I said as I opened the door and saw that he had a suitcase in each of his hands.

"Hi honey! I was going to call first but wanted to tell you in person."

"Tell me what, Dad?"

"I prefer that you call me Greg. You're an adult now."

"No, that's weird. You're Dad, and that's what I'm calling you. Now what's with the bags? Is Mom coming to meet us?" I leaned out the door and looked down the hall toward the elevator.

"Can I come in and put these down?" He made his way through the door.

I had that all-too-familiar feeling that my stomach was twisting into a knot. "Oh no. You cheated on Mom again, didn't you?" His affair the year before had almost destroyed their marriage.

"No, I didn't. Not really. But she threw me out of the house anyway. I think it's for good this time."

"What does 'not really' mean?"

"It means I can see how it looked like I was planning to cheat. But I wasn't. I downloaded this app for networking. Our graphics guy Oscar was going on about it." He pulled his phone from his pocket and showed me an app on the home screen. I took the phone from him. "I was curious to see what it was all about. They've got them for everything: job sourcing, finding golf partners, even scouting out wine-tasting friends. You say there are no interesting guys at work, maybe you should try—"

"This isn't for networking, it's for hook-ups," I said as I tapped on the app. "Mom found this, didn't she? How *could* you, Dad? After all the problems that crazy Deleenda woman caused for you guys last year? Making a scene in Mom's store? Showing up at the house? And after Mom gave you another chance, you put something like this on your phone?"

"I know. It was stupid. There was no activity on it. I tried to show her, but she didn't care. She wanted me out. Your mother will stay at the house, and I can move in here. At least for now. I'll even cover the maintenance for the next few months. How's that for a good roommate?"

"It's terrible! I don't want you paying my bills. I want you to stop breaking Mom's heart. And I'm stressed out enough by my job without having you and your hook-up app living right under my nose."

"I'm sorry to add to your stress, honey. But you've gotta find a better way to manage that anxiety. Are you still on those meds? That Lorazepan stuff?"

"I'm trying to cut back on the pills. They can't be healthy. Plus, they make me drowsy."

"Stress isn't healthy either. You and your mom are two peas in a pod. Both type A. I couldn't wait to get her out of the firm. She was great with the finances, but way too rigid."

"I'm sure she ran a tighter ship than you're running now."

"Maybe so. But morale is better without her. I thought the store would be the perfect project for her. Now she's a nervous wreck about that."

"All the small retailers are hurting, Dad."

"I know, but it's no fun living with someone that tightly wound. She's a totally different woman from that wild-and-crazy girl I married. She used to think I was the uptight one. Bet she never told you about that mooning-from-the-back-seat incident she got ticketed for in college."

"*Mom? Mooning?* No, she sure didn't."

"How about the fact that she subbed for the captain of our school's streaking team sophomore year?"

"What? Mom? A streaker? Oh, c'mon!"

"Yup. She was quite the character. People change though." He looked around the apartment. "Speaking of characters, I see you've still got that stuff from Aunt Vivian. That old nude of her. Plants are looking good. I'll just put my bags in the other bedroom."

"Please don't get too comfortable here, Dad. You and Mom need to work things out."

"Sure, honey. Hey, how about I pickup a bottle of wine later on and that Thai you like? We can watch one of those British mysteries and chillax."

"Nope. Got a night of prep ahead of me. I'm headed to Spence's place now. Be back in an hour."

• • •

"How was your big meeting?" Spence asked when I walked into his shop. I'd tried calling my mom, but she hadn't answered her phone.

"Meeting? Which meeting?"

"The Bannex thing." He furrowed his brow in concern. "You okay, Sam? Something wrong?"

"Only that my mom kicked my dad out of the house and in with me. Besides that, I'm fine."

"Gosh, I'm sorry. That must be upsetting for you."

"Yeah. But back to Bannex. I got a score of . . . hmmm . . . 98 points? And from what the others in my department say, the boss is a pretty tough critic."

"Congrats! Never a doubt on this end! Speaking of 98 points . . ." He handed me one of the bottles he'd opened that were next to a row of wine glasses on the bar. "Here's the Beaujolais we'll be tasting." The wine's label was printed on what looked like ancient paper. There was a family crest with a design of a lion on a feudal banner above a pen and ink illustration of a stately château surrounded by vineyards. "The LeMont distributor had his samples delivered early this morning so they wouldn't cook from shipping in the heatwave. He should be here any min—"

Spence froze as he looked through the locked door of the shop where a man and woman stood. Spotting us inside, the man smiled and rapped on the glass. After taking a deep breath, Spence marched forward and opened the door.

*"Bonjour, mon ami! Comment vas-tu?"* the man, who looked to be in his mid-thirties, exclaimed as he embraced Spence and gave him a kiss on each cheek.

"Hello, Henri! I didn't expect to see you. Thought the rep was stopping by," Spence said before he slowly turned toward the woman. She looked close to his age, was slim with wavy dark hair and a heart-shaped face.

"Change of plans," Henri said. "We flew in last night. I'm joining Patrice for a week's worth of appointments in the next three days. And you've met my *maman* before, no? She joined me on the trip to see some friends and family."

"Nice to see you, Sara," Spence said after a moment's pause. The woman moved to embrace him, but he abruptly offered his hand.

"Great to see you, Spencer." She took his hand and held it for a moment. "It's been a long time."

"So it has," he said, avoiding her gaze.

"Seems things haven't changed much in here though." She looked around at the mahogany shelves lined with bottles of wine from France, Germany, Italy, Portugal, Spain, Argentina, Napa, and Sonoma. Then she pointed to the bare wall next to the register. "And you never did put those pictures up."

"Nope. The roll of film is still in that camera." He took his hand from her and turned to Henri. "So, how's this year's crop looking? You've had a nice rainy winter."

Spence's dismissive attitude toward the woman stunned me. Here was a guy whose impeccable manners were key to the success of his business while he opened amazing bottles for influential wine critics, legendary chefs, and celebrity clients. His extensive knowledge of the industry and his engaging personality were a major reason *New York Magazine* had named his shop one of Manhattan's ten trendiest wine stores for the past three years. But now, his indifference toward the mother of an acclaimed wine producer was making me cringe.

"Yes, our grapes are looking *beau*," Henri said, showing no notice of the slight to Sara. "And who is this beautiful lady?" He walked over to me, picked up my hand, and kissed it.

"Oh, jeeze! Do they still do that in France?" I asked through my giggles.

"They do when meeting a woman so *magnifique* as you," he said, fixing two blue eyes on me that had flecks of lavender sprinkled through the irises. Though the guy dressed beautifully and was quite handsome, he was coming on too strong for my tastes.

"This is Samantha Goodyear," Spence told him. "She keeps me current on what the millennial generation likes to drink."

"*Enchantée, Henri!*" I attempted a playful curtsey. Then I caught Spence's eye and tilted my head toward Sara for an introduction.

"And this is Henri's mom, Sara," he said. "She used to live in New York. In fact, she's from Larchmont, same as you."

"Sure am," Sara said with her blue eyes twinkling. "Grew up in one of those old Tudors near Manor Park."

"Wow . . . from Larchmont to Beaujolais." I loved meeting people from my tiny hometown that was a short commute from Manhattan. "Did you go to Mamaroneck High too?"

"Yup! Good ole MHS! Then to college here in the city. Did a semester abroad at the Sorbonne in Paris where I met my husband and bid New York adieu. Though I sure do miss it." Her eyes shifted toward Spence, who was showing Henri around the shop.

"Spence is going to tour me through his underground cave before we taste," Henri told his mother. "Do you care to climb down with us?"

"Nope, you go ahead, baby. I've been hoofing it all day to those appointments. Maybe Sam will keep me company. We Larchmont girls have to stick together."

"'Cause we're the coolest!" Sara met my fist bump as we took a seat at the bar.

"So, tell me, Sam . . ." She slid her bar stool closer for our tête-à-tête. I loved her energy and enthusiasm. She seemed like a free spirit compared to my mom. "Is 'Blinky' Warnakey still at the high school?" she asked. "The tall assistant principal with the tic? He used to hide behind cars in the parking lot and jump out when he caught us smoking during lunch."

"*Ha ha!* Is that what you called Mr. Warnakey? *Blinky? Oh, that's mean!* He was our head principal when I graduated, but that was seven years ago. And he sure couldn't do much jumping by then."

"I can't believe he got promoted," Sara said, shaking her head. "He was always the butt of our jokes. Poor man. For a senior prank, some kids trailered in a cow from God knows where, led it up the stairs and left it in his office overnight. Besides the piles of poop, the animal wouldn't go down the stairs, and they had to hire a crane to lift it off the roof of the building! We were all outside having conniptions while the cops blocked traffic and the school officials stood fuming!"

"*Oh, my God!* You guys were *evil!* They must have been happy to see your class go!"

"If you two can stop your chatter for a moment, we're ready to taste," Spence told us. His stern expression again surprised me as he gave each of us a pour from the bottle labeled Old Vines Designate. While I twirled the dark, cherry-colored wine in the long-stemmed glass, I looked at Sara, then at Henri, and felt a tingle of excitement in my belly to be sampling the wine made from grapes grown in their vineyards, crushed in their cellars, and aged for over a year in their wooden barrels. I closed my eyes as the aroma of the bouquet floated up and transported me to a region where the sun, the rain, and the earth came together to create this offering. When I took a sip, and rolled the liquid across my taste buds, the realization struck. I didn't want to work in a job that was just somehow *related* to wine . . . I wanted to *make* wine someday. No matter how long it would take me. No matter where I had to go to learn my trade . . . I wanted to create something as beautiful as the wine in that glass. Still reeling from the impact of my epiphany, I vaguely heard Spence telling Henri that the wine was lovely, and the finish was silky soft. "What's your take on it, Sam," Spence asked. "Sam? *Sam? Sam? Earth to Sam!*"

"Huh? Oh, sorry Spence!"

"I was asking for your thoughts on the wine."

"Well . . ." I began, hoping not to sound foolish to the experts. "I taste violets, red berries, and an aura of black tea. It's flavorful. Incredibly flavorful. And it's got a bright acidity too." I took another taste and looked up at Henri and Sara. "Congratulations to you both on producing an amazing and delicious wine!"

"Oh, no," said Sara, waving me away with her hand. "I had nothing to do with it. The wine is all Julien's baby. He's—"

"My brother Julien is our winemaker," Henri interrupted. "He's in charge of the cellar and has taken our wines in some new directions. Some say he's breathed new life into a very old domaine."

"A very old domaine in a very beautiful region," Sara added. "Hey Sam . . . if you ever come to France, would you pay us a visit? We can do some more reminiscing about growing up in Larch—"

"Better yet, how about joining us for dinner? Here in Manhattan? *Tonight?*" Henri asked. "Or joining *me* for dinner? I think my *maman* has plans, *oui, Maman?*"

"I don't, but maybe Spencer has time for a bite at that little Mexican place around the corner. Is it still there, Spencer?"

"Yes, it is, and no, I don't have time," Spence said.

"Well, thanks for your offers, Sara and Henri," I said, trying to break up what was fast becoming an uncomfortable silence. "But I've got a long night ahead of me and a big meeting tomorrow. I'd love to visit your domaine sometime though. I want to learn everything I can about wine and making wine."

*"Hold on!"* Sara said. "Our harvest begins next month. Is there any way you could escape your job for a few weeks? It's not at all glamorous and can be pretty labor intensive. But if you're serious about what you just said, many excellent winemakers have learned or honed their skills by working harvest with Julien."

"No, *maman*, don't even suggest. This beautiful young woman is not a *vendangeur* to slave from the dawn 'til the dusk in the damp air and the blistering sun while breaking her backside lugging baskets of grapes up hills, pushing pulp into tubs, and sleeping over the cellar. And even if she *was* crazy enough to do that, Thierry can't issue checks to non-EU residents without prior approval from the Ministry."

"I know that, my love. And I wasn't suggesting—"

"You don't have to pay me!" I said with heart racing. "I could use a break from the city. Seeing sunrises that aren't blocked by buildings, waking to chirping birds instead of screaming sirens, inhaling fermenting wines instead of fumes from city buses. That wouldn't be work!"

"But hey, Sam. I didn't mean for you to be busting your pretty butt like a field hand or a cellar rat," Sara said. "I was inviting you as a guest. To stay in the château where you'll be comfy and can dabble at whatever suits you."

"I don't need to be comfy. I want to get down in the trenches and learn what making wine and working a vineyard is all about!"

"The reality is that working harvest means long days," Henri said.

"I work long days now."

"Long days and very hard work," he added. "So perhaps you'll come out when I return to the domaine after Beaujolais Nouveau Day. Then the work will be done and I can be a proper host."

"That'll be too late. Harvest will be over," said Sara. "Sam's telling us she wants to—"

"The problem is . . ." Henry began. "The problem is, I don't recommend you going into the cellar with my brother. Though he has great skills, he is what we call a *coureur de jupons*—a skirt chaser. He takes every advantage of the ladies who come to work harvest, and the groupies that follow our nation's acclaimed young winemakers."

"Oh, Henri, that's rubbish!" Sara scoffed. "You're just jealous that Julien's younger and prettier than you! And when are you two going to stop acting like you're still—"

"Tsk-tsk," Henri clucked with a shake of his head. "You can see my *maman* prefers her baby boy to me. To her, he is still as pure, as kind, and as innocent as the—"

"Well, whatever he is, it's all a moot point anyway," I said, now returning to reality. I had a good-paying job that others would kill for, and I couldn't risk losing it. "Because I can't take any more time off work. We have to put in for vacation in December, and I took my two weeks in April. But the good news for me is that I'm planning to take another route into your industry. That is, if tomorrow's meeting goes well. So I can't accept your dinner invite. Thanks, Henri. Thanks, Sara." I offered my hand to mother and son. "I really love your wine."

"Please, take my *carte*, and let me know if you can spare a moment for a glass of Champagne or a café au lait before Thursday. Then I go to Chicago, Texas, Colorado, North Carolina, California, and wherever our sales force needs my help," Henri said as he handed me his business card.

"Here's my cell number. Keep it. You never do know!" added Sara. She jotted her number on a napkin. "And friend me on Facebook. I've posted some silly high school shots!"

"Will do! And it was great meeting you both!"

"*Au revoir*, Samantha!" Henri gave a salute.

I turned to Spence. "I'll be stopping by tomorrow night with Cam and Steph to grab a bottle before closing. We're doing a picnic in Riverside Park."

"I'll be here," Spence said as I opened the door and walked out into the still-light night.

•   •   •

"Here she is, the brightest new star of our century-old firm!" Michael Van Ness boomed as I walked into his office on the fifty-fourth floor of The Box.

"Good morning, Mr. Van Ness! And thanks for fitting me into your busy day."

"Good morning to you too, Samantha! And you're most welcome! Please take a seat." He got up from his desk and motioned for me to sit at his conference table, where I opened my laptop to pull up the spreadsheets I'd created to show the projected growth of the wine industry over the coming decade. "I'll begin by saying that I always have time for those who show initiative," he continued. "It's important that we're all fired up about what we're doing here. To channel our creativity and passions into what *could* be just another job. That's why you *might* have heard me say that I want my hires to *think outside the box*, if you'll pardon the pun!"

"Ha ha! Yes, I have heard that!" I said. "Now to give you a bit of background, I'd like to mention that I'm a bit of a wine geek. I love reading about the role of wine in civilizations throughout the ages, how it's a must for every tradition and celebration, and most important to *our* business, the way wine consumption is exploding across the world, resulting in a steady increase in sales year after year. So, what I'm proposing is for Waterhouse to consider setting up a division that specializes in catering to wine producers. I've been poring through the codes for these businesses . . . they're extremely complicated and they're in constant flux. Most of the financial folks for the wineries I've contacted have said that the relatively few firms that specialize in the field are too busy to take on new customers. And we'd be the only one of the big four—"

"Excuse me, Samantha, if I *may* interrupt? What exactly does this have to do with boxes? Maybe you're talking about going after the companies that manufacture *wine* boxes? That might prove to be an avenue worth—"

"No, that's *not* what I'm talking about, sir, not at all."

"Labels then? Wine labels? Let's go after those folks! There must be hundreds of firms making auxiliary products that can slip into our model and take us *out of the box!* I've read about several companies in the Midwest specializing in Styrofoam inserts! And is 3M the only company that makes cellophane shipping tape?"

"No labels, no plastic shipping supplies! I'm talking about servicing the people who make *wine!* The beverage made from *grapes!*" My chest started heaving, and I felt short of breath.

"I appreciate your efforts on this, Samantha. I do." He gave an apologetic smile. "But wineries are way too far in left field for us to go after anytime soon. They're subject to an entirely unique set of laws. Now, if you've got any other makers of non-perishable shipping-related goods besides boxes to suggest, I'm all ears." Like I said, "I want our hires to—"

"I know, I know . . . to think outside the box." The image of Mrs. Cranston's unevenly drooping eyes started flashing before me. Then my own eyes watered as I looked up at the florescent lights in the ceiling and envisioned spending the rest of the day, the rest of the week, the rest of the month, the rest of the year, the rest of my *life*, underneath those pulsating electrons. A surge of anxiety exacerbated by a lack of sleep and a plethora of frustration sent my heart racing as the walls of the office started closing in on all sides of me. I stuck my hand into my bag and fished around for my meds, but remembered I'd left the vial of Lorazepan on my bathroom sink. *It's just a minor panic attack, Sam. Breathe slowly . . . in and out, one, two, one, two. Visualize a babbling brook, picking grapes at dawn, marching up green mountains, tasting the new wines of harvest.* Then I heard a voice echo up from my larynx and felt my jaw move and say those words. "In that case, I'm submitting my resignation from Weatherhouse, sir. I'm happy to stay two more weeks to tie up any loose ends. And I can't thank you enough for giving me the opportunity to work for this wonderful company."

•    •    •

"Michael Van Ness called me a bit ago, Miss Goodyear. He said you've given us your resignation and wanted you and me to have a brief chat about that." I'd been organizing my umpteen files of schedules, records, and tax forms to ease the transition for my replacement when I got the call from our regional vice-president, Steve Bowen. Though it had only been an hour since my meeting with Michael Van Ness, I'd already messaged Sara and Henri LeMont to tell them I'd decided to take Sara's offer of working harvest at their domaine. Both had gotten back to me within minutes to express their delight and to give me a link to follow for details. And now, I was sitting in Steve's office to explain why I was quitting the company. "Michael said you did a bang-up job with the Bannex team yesterday," Steve continued. "He says you're resourceful, hard-working, and have gotten top reviews from Favia Moss since you started here. If you need a little recharge after the Bannex pitch, I'll be happy to get you a req from HR to take a few personal days." He scanned through my personnel stats on his laptop screen like a physician reviewing a patient's chart. "And you seem to be thriving here from what I see. You've got a nice little start on your 401K plan, and you'll be up for your three percent merit increase by year-end." He snapped down the screen of his computer, took off his reading glasses, and looked me in the eye. "So, what's the problem, Samantha? How have we as a firm failed you?"

"You haven't . . . the firm hasn't failed me, Mr. Bowen. I will say that I didn't do well this morning in my meeting with Mr. Van Ness. I'd had the idea of Weatherhouse setting up a division to take on wineries as clients, but he had absolutely no interest in my plan. And that frustrated me."

"First of all, Samantha, you must understand that Michael doesn't have the authority to make that call. Even *I* don't have the authority to make it. Neither does my superior, our East Coast President, Josh Hardy. The only person who has the power to submit a proposal like that to Chairman Morton Drydock would be our President of Worldwide Operations, Brett Newmark. And Brett's made it clear down the line that Weatherhouse will never veer from its core business of servicing the makers of shipping-related items. But that shouldn't be the reason for you to just walk away from a promising future with a solid company."

"It is the reason, Mr. Bowen. Because I'm determined to get into the wine industry. I'm thinking that I could even make wine myself someday. And if I had even a sliver of hope that my plan to service wineries might come to fruition, I'd have stayed and worked my butt off to make that happen. Because if I'm going to spend twelve hours a day here, I want to be working on something I'm passionate about. So, I'm putting my accounting career on hold to work harvest in France, and learn everything I can about wine and making wine."

He paused for a moment, then rocked back in his tufted-leather swivel chair and folded his arms across his chest. "So . . . you're just chucking everything you've built here to run off and chase a dream. Is that it?"

"I don't see it as chucking everything, Mr. Bowen. I've got some serious business experience under my belt, and I believe I've made some good contributions to the company in the time I've spent with you all. Now, I hope to get some quality experience in Beaujolais."

He returned the chair to its upright position, and his eyes lit up with interest. "Beaujolais, huh? Home of the Gamay grape, Beaujolais Noveau, wines like Louis Jadot, Morgon, Paul Janin, and the producers on Mont Brouilly."

"Sounds like you know your wines, Mr. Bowen!"

He stood and walked over to a credenza near his desk and opened its doors to reveal a row of wine bottles and several glasses. "I've been waiting for the right moment to open this Fleurie from Le Vissoux." He set two glasses down on his desk and uncorked the bottle. "I admit I'm a bit of a wine geek myself. Been on some buying trips to Burgundy and Bordeaux. Can tell a Malbec from a Merlot," he said as he poured the wine into the glasses.

"Then maybe you could put yourself in my shoes and try to understand why it's time for me to take the leap."

"Understand? *Understand?*" He picked up the glasses and handed me one. "Not only do I understand you. I envy you!" He clinked his glass against mine. "And I've gotta toast you for having the guts to get out of this fucking boring-as-hell prison to follow your dreams! 'Cause if I wasn't forty-seven years old with three kids in private school, sky-high real estate taxes, and a wife who wears fucking Fendi to Whole Foods, I'd do exactly that in a heartbeat! Best of luck to you, young lady!" He touched my glass with his again and took a sip of his wine. "And be sure to keep me posted on your endeavors."

"I sure will, Mr. Bowen!" I breathed in the floral aromas of the wine and took a sip. "Thanks for everything. Including the wine. It's really elegant and should pair well with whatever you're having for lunch."

"I think it will." He took another sip. "And please . . . put me down for a case of your wine when you start making it."

•   •   •

"You look happy, miss!" the security guard told me when I waltzed through the sliding glass exit of The Box that evening. I sailed down the steps of the building toward Fifth Avenue, pulled off my suit jacket, and felt the stress that had been balled up inside me drift away in the warm summer breeze. All my life I'd done as I was told. Get good grades in high school, major in accounting in college, take a job at a big four firm, work as many hours as needed to stay on schedule. Now, the only voice I was listening to was mine. Quitting Weatherhouse *was* a risk. I had twenty-five thousand dollars in savings. And with no idea of where I'd be going or how to find my way in the wine industry after my harvest stint, that money could be my sole support for a long time. But I knew that if I was ever going to take the leap, I had to do it then. After crossing Fifty-eighth Street and navigating my way through the swell of Asian tourists snapping selfies in front of the glorious Plaza Hotel, I pulled out my phone to make the call I'd been dreading.

"Hi, Mom! How're you holding up with Dad being such an asshole?"

"So, he told you what I found on his phone, did he?"

"Yeah. That was childish of him. But he swears he only downloaded that hook-up app to see what that guy Oscar was talking about."

"It wasn't *that* hook-up app," my Mom said. "It was *those* hook-up apps. Four of them. He'd also filled out his profile on one. On the line that asked what nationalities he was most interested in, he checked Indian, Laotian, Punjabi, Filipino, and Mongolian. On the line that asked if he was interested in a low, moderate, or high level of experimentation, he checked high."

"Dad did *that*?" Again, that stomach clench. *"Wow!"*

"So besides boring the hell out of him all these years, I'm also from the wrong side of the world."

"Maybe he was just messing around with his friends at work, Mom."

*"Yeah, sure.* Anyway, Greg's the least of my problems." Her voice sounded like a taut cello string about to snap. "Business is awful! For all the retailers in town, not just us. Customers come in and try on every size and color of our garments before they toss them inside out on the benches of the dressing room. Then they walk out the door, or even stand in the shop, and order the same clothes on their cell to save ten bucks. Used to be I couldn't keep enough inventory in stock. Now the shop's overflowing with stuff I can't sell. And I'm stuck with a five-year lease here! My only solace is that you've got a steady job with a

healthy firm. Especially one that has all those box companies as clients."

I took a few deep breaths, closed my eyes, and spoke at a ramped-up pace. "Actually, I just quit my job, Mom. I'm going to France to work harvest in three weeks to learn everything I can about making wine. That's what I want to do with my life. And I know Aunt Viv would approve."

"What? *What?* Are you *crazy?* And who cares if the family kook would approve?"

"She wasn't a kook, Mom. Aunt Viv was a very accomplished woman."

"*Whatever!* You just march yourself right back into HR tomorrow morning. Tell them you didn't mean it. Tell them you were just overtired. Tell them you have your period! Just *do* it!"

"No. I've made my decision. And you sound like a wreck. Maybe you should play more bridge. Weren't you going to try some yoga to help you relax?"

"Nothing can relax me. Especially with *this* news. *Oh, good God!* I'm feeling some chest pain."

"Just take some deep breaths, Mom. Maybe pop a Lorazepan. Better yet, have a glass of wine. I'll be out to see you this weekend."

• • •

Cameron and Stephanie had beaten me to Spence's shop to buy a bottle for our picnic in the park and were sitting at the bar typing emails.

"So, you're getting out of Dodge, are you?" asked Cam when I walked in.

"I am, and I'm sure you're both welcome to join me. If not at Domaine LeMont, plenty of other wineries in France are happy to accept harvest help, from what I've seen online."

"I'd go in a heartbeat if I had your courage," Stephanie said. "And if I wasn't saddled with thirty-plus years' of student loans." She put her elbow on the bar, rested her chin on her palm, and let out a deep breath. "I'll be past menopause by the time I've paid them off."

"It's a colossal risk for me too." I said. "As my furious mother just reminded me. And with all those accounting majors trotting around with degrees from the Ivies, I may not be able to get back into Weatherhouse, or any other big firm, if I go bust."

"They'll take you back. They love you there," Cameron assured me.

"But here's something weird. Henri LeMont, who sells the family's wine, warned me about his brother, Julien, the winemaker. Said he didn't recommend me going into the cellar with him. Called him a *coureur de jupons*—a skirt chaser."

"Oh my, that's not good," Cameron said. "If you think sexual harassment is a problem here, just—"

"Could be bogus info though," I said. "Sounds like those two guys have some major sibling rivalry going on. And Julien's a serious winemaker. Not a playboy."

"Yeah, but we're talking about France," Cameron said as he checked his phone. "Let's see . . . Julien LeMont images . . . he we go. Julien LeMont, *Paris Match*. Oh boy! He looks like a young French Hugh Hefner." He held the screen up for Stephanie and me to see a photo of a twenty-something guy with dark curly hair, an impish smile, and three very young, very hot blondes draped over him at what looked to be a restaurant.

"Looks like he's got some other interests going on there besides making wine," Stephanie said. "And he sure is cute."

"Well, I'll just make it clear from the get-go that I'm there to learn—not party." I looked over at the bag of wine on the counter. "So, what'd you two pick out for us? Some nice bubbles to help me celebrate?"

"Spence suggested we try something new from Napa. It's a sparkling rosé," Stephanie said as she rose from her bar stool and picked up the wine from the counter. "Thought we'd grab some fresh oysters, cheeses, and maybe some prosciutto to pair with it. Our treat since you're about to be unemployed."

"Thanks, guys. And how 'bout you, Spence?" I called out. "Can you close up early and join us?"

"Don't think so," he said while slashing the top of a carton with a box cutter.

I walked closer to where he'd surrounded himself with cartons as he restocked his shelves. "Hey, you've been awfully quiet today, Mr. Walker. Was it something I said?" I'd texted him along with Stephanie and Cameron to tell him my big news, and he surprised me when he hadn't responded right away like the others had. In fact, he hadn't responded at all.

"It's just been a busy day. I'm kind of beat." He didn't look beat to me. He looked sad.

"You guys go ahead," I told my friends. "I'll meet you in the park in a few."

"Okay. By the marina. Same as last time," Cameron called as they walked out the door.

I turned to Spence when the other two were gone. "I know you never talk much about about your personal life, but—"

"It was thirty-three years ago," he cut in as he turned toward the bare wall by the register. "From the back of the shop, I heard the jingle of that bell over the door. It took me a minute to come out, but when I did, I saw the most beautiful girl my twenty-two-year-old eyes had ever seen."

"I had a feeling this was about Sara," I said.

"She was staring at that wall with a bottle of Negretti in her hand. When she heard me come near, she said, 'You need to fill this spot.'

'Excuse me, miss?' I asked. She didn't turn around. Just kept talking.

'How about three large photos? Black and whites. Maybe an establishing shot of a French vineyard? A closer shot of the vines with grapes? Then a close-up of purple berries?' She turned and gave me that smile . . . those two dimples . . . that heart-shaped face. 'Sorry if I seem kinda pushy,' she said. 'I'm really into art and interior design.'"

"She had some good ideas," I said. "Why's the wall still bare?"

"I told her I'd run it by my boss. Then I looked into those blue-green pools she had for eyes and suggested that she and I go to France together to take the photos. Told her I had a decent camera. She cocked her head without saying a word at my indecent proposal. Then she let out a laugh of pure joy. I hope she still has that laugh after all these years."

"So, what happened? Did you go?"

"We did. A year later. And we took a slew of photos. I never got them developed. Never even took the film out of the camera. Seems like we just got back when she returned to France for her junior year abroad. I'd already bought my ticket to visit her. Was packing my bag when her letter dropped through my mail slot. She'd met and was marrying the heir to the LeMont kingdom." He reached over toward the bar and picked up an empty bottle of the LeMont Beaujolais that he'd left there. "I bet she did a bang-up job restoring that castle," he said as he stared at the label.

"Was she the reason you never married?"

"She was. She still is. When you've been drinking something as elegant, as complex, as subtle and surprising as Romanée-Conti, anything else tastes like Two Buck Chuck."

"I liked her from the get-go," I said, now understanding why Spence, who met lots of cool women in his shop every day and wasn't bad looking for an older guy, was still single.

"Last night was the first time I'd seen her since she left," he said. "I've carried the domaine's wine from time to time over the years, which is how I know Henri. I've never met the other son, the winemaker, though I've heard he's very talented. I'm glad you're going, Sam. And when you see Sara, please apologize to her for my rudeness."


### Montmartre, Paris June 1936

Marciel pulled the door of his garret open and wondered why the young woman was standing there. In a white lace blouse, a red gathered skirt cinched with a wide leather belt, and with hair held taught in a thick braid behind her back, she reminded him of one of those tiny dancers that spin on top of a child's music box. "*Puis-je vous aider, mademoiselle?*" he asked while he shoved a pile of shaggy brown hair away from his eyes. He'd hoped that the model he'd been waiting for had finally shown up. Instead, he'd have to waste precious moments giving directions to another tourist searching for the garret of some distant relative they planned to meet up with on their pilgrimage to Paris.

The girl hesitated and handpicked her words before speaking. *"S'il vous plaît, excusez-moi pour le désagrément, monsieur."*

"What are you doing here, little lady?" he asked, recognizing an American accent through her too formal French. *Probably wandered away from her tour group*, he thought. *Mummy and Daddy, or Gran and Poppi, must be frantic!*

"I'm Vivian. Vivian Goodyear. The model," she answered, relieved that the artist, though visibly annoyed, spoke good English. Though she'd been working hard on her French and had aced it at her high school back in Brooklyn, becoming conversational was harder than she'd expected.

"The model?" the artist barked, his annoyance now bordering on anger. Nothing seemed special to him about this girl.

"Yes. And please, I'm sorry to be late. It won't happen next time. You are Marciel Duprée, I trust?" She now wondered if Phillipe had jotted down the wrong address in his haste. But one glance through the door told her that this was the painter whose work she'd fallen in love with during her art classes at *L'Académie*. "Phillipe did tell you I'd be here, *oui?*"

*"Oui, mademoiselle,* but he said two o'clock. And he knows I require an experienced figure model."

"Yes, *monsieur,* and I apologize again for the delay. Now, may I please come in?" the girl asked while she stepped through the doorway and inhaled the smell of the oils, pigments, and solvents that had been a staple for the generations of artists that had occupied the space over the past two centuries. Taped to the walls and spread out on a drafting table were dozens of penciled sketches of one woman in different degrees of undress. But none of the sketches appeared to have made it onto a canvas. And though Vivian recognized Duprée's unique style in the drawings, she wondered why the fire that sent her heart pounding in the paintings of his she'd seen on the walls of *L'Académie* was nowhere to be found in these works. She pointed to a privacy screen that had a red robe slung over it. "I suppose I should change into the cover-up, *monsieur?*"

"I suppose," he said, wondering if it would be just as well to send the child away.

She went behind the screen and kicked off her walking boots. Then, trying to ignore the pangs of fear that gripped her belly, she slowly unbuttoned her blouse, removed the belt, stepped from her skirt, shimmied out of her camisole and knickers, and wrapped the silk garment around her otherwise naked body. "Now where will you position me?" she asked with a voice cracking from nerves.

"Over there. In the corner." He pointed to a chaise upholstered in purple velvet.

She reclined on the piece and forced the corners of her mouth to turn upward, like a child following orders from a parent to smile for a photograph. The stuffy old chaise smelled like mothballs. Her eyes went to the wretched-looking man behind the easel who hadn't yet touched his pencil to the paper. "Shall I keep the robe on?" she asked.

"Might as well," he said, having little interest in what lay beneath it. *Another night wasted,* he thought. It was already too late to make it up the hill with his paints and easel before twilight. He walked over to where he'd left the bottle of wine, uncorked it, poured the Burgundy into a glass, and took a long sip.

"Would you pour me a glass, *monsieur*?" the girl asked, hoping that the wine would relax her. Her audacity shocked him. He'd already wasted good money on her fee and Phillipe's commission. He wasn't about to waste excellent wine.

"No, I won't. It's only for me to consume. Anyhow, I hear it's illegal to drink before twenty-one in the States."

"I'm eighteen and change. More than old enough to drink wine in Paris. But I don't want the glass for drinking." She rose from the chaise and walked to the room's large window that opened to the *Arènes de Montmartre* garden. "Could I suggest an alternate pose? If you don't like it, I'll go back to the chaise."

"Go on then." He rolled his eyes and shook his head. The girl's impertinence seemed to have no limits.

She positioned herself on the window's wide ledge. After sliding her arms from the robe, she pulled the fabric through a loop created by her fingers, and fashioned it as a drape that meandered through the peaks and valleys of her form, revealing the mounds of the breasts but masking the nipples, exposing one of her hips and a portion of her belly, before it floated down between her legs that were bent at the knees. Then, she undid the braid behind her head to release a torrent of auburn curls that tumbled around her shoulders. "That glass of wine might add a nice element to the pose," she told Marciel. "What are your thoughts?"

"My . . . my . . . thoughts are . . ." he began as he felt a good portion of the weight that had encumbered his spirit over the past year lift from his shoulders. "My thoughts are that you might be right." He poured a second glass of the wine and brought it to her. "And do taste it. To make the image more real."

She cradled the glass in her hands as if holding an injured sparrow, and took a sip. "What is this wine?" she asked as she heard the laughter of children playing in the park and felt a warm breeze come through the window and caress her shoulder. "I've never tasted anything so enchanting." Though alcoholic beverages had held no interest to her before, this wine was a life changer.

"It's from the vineyard of Romanée-Conti. Considered by many to be magical. Let's hope it can add some of its magic to our picture."

The artist took a seat at his drafting table and shaved his graphite pencil with a razor blade. Moments later, he put the pencil to the parchment and outlined the shape of the girl's head, the swan-like neck, the wide shoulders, and the pear-shaped breasts caressed by the silken garment. Then he moved down to sketch the tight waist, the hips, and the long legs, before moving back up to the arms, and the hands holding the glass of wine. Next, he worked to capture the features of the face. Though not classically beautiful, they evoked an aura of strength and sexuality he'd yet to see in one so young. The glow of that aura intensified when the model was bathed by the rays of the late afternoon sun as it wove its way through the branches of the horse-chestnut trees lining the streets of Paris. Marciel was relieved that though the girl had shown an assertive personality, she said nothing to interrupt his focus. She didn't prattle on about the high cost of bread, the increase in automobile traffic, or badger him to add a few extra francs to the agreed upon fee.

While working to recreate the sparkle of her green eyes, Marciel felt the beginning of a strangely familiar sensation. It started with a quickening of the pulse, a heightening of mood, and an increase in energy. After perfecting the shape of the plump and rosy lips, he stood back to look at the drawing. The eyes in the face seemed to penetrate his soul, filling him with a newfound lust for life, as they sent his creative juices flowing like the lava from Mount Vesuvius. He now thought that Paris was never so beautiful and became confident that the German people would vote Adolf Hitler out of office before the lunatic could gain any more power. After staring at the sketch for several minutes, he grabbed it from the table and ripped the paper in half, which caused the girl to startle.

"What's happened, *monsieur*?" she asked with a furrowed brow. "You seemed so intent on your task. Did I somehow spoil your drawing?"

"You spoiled nothing," he said as he crumpled the paper, threw it into the waste bin, and set a blank canvas on his easel. "I'm ready to paint."

# two

---

**Terroir** *n.* environmental factors (soil, climate, sunlight, terrain) of a vineyard that gives the wine made from its grapes its unique characteristics

*"Bonjour, mademoiselle. Crémant? Vin Blanc?"* the cute man in uniform asked me from behind his service cart on the TGV, France's high-speed rail system.

"Now this is the way to travel!" I told him. *"Crémant, s'il vous plaît!"* Having only studied Spanish in high school, I was glad I could at least say 'please' in French as I handed him eight euros for my glass of sparkling wine.

*"Merci. À votre santé,"* he answered with a smile. After I took a generous sip of the bubby, he gave me a wink and refilled my glass to the top.

*"À votre santé* to you, too." I raised my glass in the air.

Three weeks after Michael Van Ness put the nix on my idea to take Waterhouse in a new direction, I flew into Paris' Charles de Gaulle airport. Twenty-four hours later, I was on a train traveling through France's Côte de Nuits on my way to the Beaune station, where Julien LeMont would meet me and drive me south to Beaujolais and the domaine that had been in their family for six generations. I took another sip of the *Crémant* and toasted myself for—in the three days I had after serving out my time at Weatherhouse—saying my goodbyes, getting international cell service, exchanging two thousand dollars for fifteen hundred euros, and stuffing several weeks worth of clothing into two duffel bags.

After checking out of my hotel that morning, I had only two hours to shop for my harvest wardrobe of work boots, work shirts, a sun hat, a raincoat, a sleeping bag, and plenty of bug spray. And, *ah oui*—I had allowed myself to splurge on three glorious sets of bras and panties I'd spotted in the window of a tiny lingerie shop before boarding the train. Though I didn't expect to have any use for them during my harvest adventure, I couldn't resist the beauty of their handwoven laces and delicate embroideries. Plus, they were *damn* sexy.

My dad had no problem with my decision to quit my job and leave New York. Maybe he was just glad to have the apartment to himself without me around to judge him. I could only hope that being alone would make him miss my mom and had my fingers crossed that the separation would be a good thing for their marriage.

After dreading the goodbye visit to my mom in Larchmont, it surprised me to find her much more relaxed than when we'd last spoken. She credited the change to a class she was taking in something called Audiogenic Therapy, that supposedly helps its students compartmentalize and ultimately banish stress. Though it sounded like New Age hocus-pocus to me, if it helped her calm down, I was all for it.

Sitting on the cushioned seat of a railcar that was silently gliding across the French countryside, it seemed like a lifetime ago that I'd typed numbers into a computer for hours on end in that always over-air-conditioned office building. My stomach fluttered as I drank in the views of vibrant green vineyards that seemed to go on forever and tiny ancient villages that looked like they belonged in a storybook. I tapped the photo button on my cell to share the scenery with the seventy friends who followed me on Instagram, but the shots were mere blurs.

•   •   •

*"Gare de Beaune,"* the conductor called out several hours later as the train pulled into the station in the ancient town of Beaune. After stepping onto the platform, I pulled up the photo of Julien on my phone that Sara had sent to help me spot him among the crowd waiting to retrieve arriving passengers. "Just so ya know, mister," I told the image as I enlarged it with my fingers. "This body is off limits

for your grape-stained hands." Zooming in, I got an up-close look at the guy's "I'm cool as hell" smile with his "bet you can't wait to kiss me" lips and his baby-blue bedroom eyes.

"*Bonjour! Bonjour!*" A masculine voice called out from behind me. I turned to face the most gorgeous guy I'd ever seen. "*Vous êtes Madame Goodyear, oui?*" He pulled out his cell to make sure I was the same girl in the photo that I'd sent to Sara so that Julien could recognize me.

*Madame? Why so formal?* I wondered while I tried to peel my eyes from his face. "Yes, I'm Samantha. *Bonjour*, Julien." I held out my hand for a shake. He gave a slight bow, took my hand, and kissed the top. Such a proper gentleman . . . *not!*

"*Ravi de vous recountrer, Samantha! Parlez-vous français?*"

"Errr . . . I *parle* only *un peu*," I said, pinching my fingers together.

"That's no problem. You can help me practice my English," he said with a way-too-adorable French accent. "Here, let me help you with your bags. And I hope you've brought some warm clothes. *Nos matins . . . Excusez-moi!* Our mornings have been chilly."

•  •  •

When I climbed into his army-green Range Rover for the hour ride south to the domaine, a low whine from the back seat surprised me. "Oh! You have a doggie! Boy or girl?" I reached behind me to pet a large yellow dog, but she shied away from my hand.

"*Femelle.* And I have no excuse for Stella. She does a good job in the vineyard chasing the rabbits and deer, but she is what we call, *un chien à un homme,* a one-man dog."

Growing up in a house filled with sofas not meant to be sat on, where the only pet allowed was a Siamese cat who despised people, I had to satisfy my love of dogs by playing with those of my neighbors and friends. Not giving up on this one, I leaned toward her and gently ran my fingers through her coat.

"I bet I can make you my pal, Stella. And hey, I play a mean game of tug o'war."

"And how was your journey?" Julien asked. "The flight, no problem? Paris was good?"

"The flight was on time. Paris is still beautiful, though there wasn't much time for sightseeing on the . . . on the . . ." I lost my train of thought when I got an up-close look at the guy's olive skin, mop of shiny black hair, and thick, dark eyelashes. ". . . on the flight in." *Cut it out, Sam. You're not gonna be another notch on this guy's bedpost!*

"My brother and *maman* tell me you have a fantastic palate," he said, focusing more on the road and less on my stuttering. "They say you're joining our harvest to learn our techniques, both out in the vineyard and down in the cellar, no?"

"No . . . I mean . . . yes! Yes!" I said as my heart began to race. "I learned a lot about wine as a kid from a great-aunt of mine. And I've always been a bit of a cork dork. Having wine dinners with friends, hanging out in Spence Walker's shop, reading all I could online. And now that I've quit my job in Manhattan, I hope to get the chance to work my way up in a winery somewhere. After this year's harvest, that is. And I can't thank you all enough for allowing me to join you for it." He looked over at me with those blue eyes—the bluest I'd ever seen. I wondered how many hundreds of women had been seduced by those eyes.

"It's our pleasure, Samantha. *Maman* has only great things to say about Spencer, so any friend of his is a friend of ours. And she insists you stay in the château where you can make yourself at home." Though the offer was alluring, I didn't want to impose on a woman I'd only met once.

"Oh, no, not necessary. I've got my sleeping bag and am happy to bunk in with the other workers. I'll thank Sara when I see her, but I'm here for the real harvest experience."

•　　•　　•

An hour later we reached the cru Beaujolais region that produces the finest grapes in the province. My eyes feasted on views of vineyards and tiny villages on hills sloping up to Mont Brouilly, a mountain topped with a dormant volcano.

"Our domaine is part of the Côte de Brouilly region, named for Brulius, a lieutenant of the ancient Roman army and the first to plant vines here," Julien told me as we turned off the main highway and onto a road that ran up the mountain. "The plants sit on the side of the volcano that blew millions of years ago, leaving us with the perfect terroir for growing grapes—stony dirt from the lava on very well-drained slopes and sunshine all around. The grapes we grow in Beujolais are called Gamay, a cross between Pinot Noir and an ancient white grape. In the *Moyen Âge*, a tyrannical duke exiled the Gamay from Burgundy, forcing the grape to grow in this stone-laden soil. But as you see with the dog, the mutts are the strongest. The Gamay is easier to grow than the Pinot, and more tough to fight disease."

*As you see with the dog? Oh my God, you're cute! But sorry, Monsieur, that ESL phrasing won't get you a pass into these too-tight pants!*

"Here we are, Samantha. Welcome to Château LeMont," he announced as we pulled up to a stately mansion surrounded by vineyards.

The house, as I'd later learn, dated back to the 1600s. It was graced by a burnt yellow exterior of ancient brick, with majestic arched entrances, and a series of black slate turrets rising high above the roof. Separating the house from the winery, was a sprawling courtyard filled with wild lavender, lemon verbena, purple cauliflower, and golden summer squash.

"Henri and I live at the other side of the property in an ancient concierge house we've restored. And please, Samantha, you're not one of the hired hands on the payroll. So I'd like you to think two times about my *maman's* invitation to host you at the château."

"Think two times? Oh, think twice! No, really, I'm good. Just point the way to my quarters. And please, let me carry these." I tried to free my bags from the guy's tanned and muscular arms, but he wouldn't release them.

"I'll take you there," he said while he walked toward the courtyard. "The workers sleep in an attic over the cave."

I'd soon learn that the cave meant the winery, where Julien tugged at a rustic wooden door and held it open for me to enter. When I stepped through it, the old stone walls had a wonderful musky aura, and the wood and iron presses and fermentation tanks posed a stark contrast to the gleaming steel equipment I'd seen in the wineries I'd toured in Santa Barbara and Sonoma.

"Wow, these old machines are wonderful!" I said as I ran my hands over one of the ancient presses and thought about the hundreds, maybe thousands of vintages it had crushed through the centuries.

"Though many domaines in the region changed over to modern machines years ago, my *grand-père* believes the old ones are best. When the sales rep from entreprises that make the stainless visit to convince us that their products are easier to clean, are faster to operate, and will enable us to elevate our production, he holds his ears and shakes his head. The old man is stubborn, but he has his reasons. And many of the winemakers my age now agree he is right."

We walked down a long stone hallway that led to another room with walls covered by what had to be thousands of bottles stacked up to the ceiling.

"We call this our façade wine cave," Julien said as I looked up at the oddly constructed tower. "These bottles are the domaine's lower end wine that were put here in 1940 to hide the door to our deepest cave. The cave that stores our most precious wine."

"Wow . . . 1940. World War II. They were hiding wine from the Nazis!" During my train ride to Beaune, I read accounts of Hitler's armies pillaging French wineries after the Nazis invaded the country, and how winemakers got creative in hiding their stocks of wine behind false walls, burying bottles in their gardens, even sinking them below water in fish ponds.

Julien pointed to a small door tucked in a corner with an old rusted padlock hanging from it. "At age eleven, my *grand-père* Gaston constructed a new entrance to our cave by tunneling through the earth. His *père* and many men of the surrounding regions had been forced into labor or to fight with the German army, leaving the women, the old men, and the children to work the vineyards, make the wine, and protect their caves. Many of our neighbors lost all of their wine in raids by Hitler's soldiers. We were lucky though—the Nazis never came here."

"And what happened to Gaston's dad?"

"Executed. Killed for refusing the orders of his Nazi commandant to shoot civilians."

"Oh, my God. What a horror. Your poor great-grandfather. But Julien . . . the war in Europe ended in 1944. Why's the real door still blocked?"

"Because every day Gaston worries that this could happen again. He insists that we keep the cave hidden."

"I don't blame him." Though Hitler's reign of terror ended seventy-some years before, the sight of those towers sent a chill through my body.

"Now, about your sleeping space." He pointed toward a narrow alcove with a roughly constructed staircase. "Really, Samantha, this won't be for you."

"I'm sure it'll be just fine. Show me the way." I followed him up the creaking wooden steps and entered a barnlike attic. Between pine slats that served as a floor, I caught glimpses of the winery below.

"There's a toilet and shower for the women to the left, and another *salle de bains* for the men to the right." He pointed to the rows of metal cots divided by a wall that only reached halfway to the ceiling. "Here is where the women sleep. The men are on the other side. You can see it's not the Hôtel Plaza. So I hope you've changed your mind."

"Well . . . eh . . ." Hearing strange men snoring and farting across the attic during the night made Sara's offer tempting. But if this would do for the other workers, it would do for me. "No, really, this works great," I said as I took my bags and set them down near a cot.

"As you wish," Julien said with a shrug. "And I hope you have a *bon appétit* for the first dinner of harvest." With that, he left me to settle into my new quarters.

### Montmartre, Paris June 1936

Vivian pulled the robe around her and stood up for a stretch. She was nearing the end of her sitting for Marciel Duprée. The painter had been working furiously throughout the afternoon and into the evening. Though he'd barely said two words to her, she was pleased that he wasn't one to bark at her to change positions or throw his brush in frustration like some artists she'd sat for had done.

"I'd like you to look," Marciel said as he stood back to study the canvas. His words stunned her. On her trip to use the water closet, she didn't dare overstep her bounds by stealing a glance at the work in progress. Now this man . . . this creative genius . . . was suggesting that he valued her thoughts on his art. She took a deep breath and slowly walked to join him at the easel.

When her eyes landed on the painting, the young woman she saw was both familiar and strange. She felt a sensation similar to when she'd heard a recording of her own voice. It sounded like someone else, but she knew it was her. Lounging by the window, with the city of Paris behind her and that glass of wine in her hand, the woman on the canvas had a hunger in her eyes, but a satisfied smile on her lips. She was beckoning, yet unapproachable. Both innocent . . . and guilty as sin. "It . . . it looks like you've seen into my soul," Vivian said. "Like you've unearthed every good and every wicked thought I've ever had. It's as beautiful as it is frightening, *monsieur*." As she spoke, she felt a weakness in her knees that worked its way up through her thighs until it settled in that spot that no man, not even her fiancée Enzo had ever touched. Now that spot ached with a craving for the man beside her. As her body pulled toward him like a magnet, she heard his breath get heavier and she could sense his heart beating through the walls of his chest. The two turned to each other. His hands went to her shoulders, slid down her body, and made their way under the robe. Then he whispered the words that made her spirts soar.

"I've found my muse."

# three

---

**Decant** *v.* pouring wine from a bottle to a more open container to let it take in the oxygen that helps to release its aromas and flavors

While I was unrolling my sleeping bag, the sound of a chugging motor roared through the attic window facing the road. Looking out, I saw a rusted van that had curtains on its back windows pull up in an enormous field. I'd read that migrating gypsies from Romania and Bulgaria received subsidies from the French government for working harvest and wondered if this vehicle was a gypsy caravan. When it stopped, a woman passenger gave a long lingering kiss to a man in the driver's seat who had bright red dreadlocks. When the woman stepped from the van, the man honked his horn and drove off.

I went into the bathroom to take a much-needed pee in an ancient, very low toilet that had a metal seat and a tank above it with a chain hanging down. It took me a few minutes to realize that I had to pull on the chain to flush. With that accomplished, I took a shower from a rusted spigot before I wriggled into my skinny black jeans, stepped into a pair of black suede boots, and pulled a flowing boho-style shirt over my head. After towel drying my hair, lining my light green eyes with a pencil of smoky grey, and adding a dash of lip gloss, I was good to go. When I walked out of the bathroom, I came face to face with the woman I'd seen through the window. She looked to be in her late twenties and had long platinum hair with jet black roots. Dozens of bracelets on each arm set off a series of cha-chings with every move she made.

"*Bonjour!*" the woman exclaimed, her eyes roaming from my boots to the top of my head, and back down to my chest. "*J'aime l'apparence de cette chemise paysanne sur une poitrine si plate.*" When she spoke, I saw the flash of a rhinestone stud in her tongue. She sounded as if she was complimenting my appearance, so I attempted to thank her.

"*Merci. . .* but . . . *pardon, parle* minuscule *français,*" I said, with a cheerful smile and again, those pinched fingers.

"Ah, an American!" she scoffed in a heavy eastern European accent. "I was telling you I do like the look of that peazant shirt on zuch a flat chezt." It took me a moment to catch her drift, and when I did, my smile vanished. "It must be nize to have clothez hang on your perzon like that and not worry about having too much of . . . what do you Americanz call them? Titz and azz?" She pointed to the voluptuous rack she'd wrestled into a spandex tank top, then turned sideways to display an ass that rivaled Kim Kardashian's in size. "Oh, pleeze do exkuze me. I'm Fifika Antonoff. And you are?"

"Samantha Goodyear. It's . . . um . . . nice to meet you," I lied, still reeling from the insult. Though my breasts were a far cry from the cannons she had on display, I'd never heard anyone refer to my chest as flat.

"Nize to meet you az vell. Might be you one of those juzt here to 'experienze' harvest?"

"Well, yes. You could say that. I'm not being paid like the other workers. Why? Do you have a problem with that?"

"No problem, just azking kweztion." She set her duffel down on a cot and tugged at the zipper. "There are two kindz that come here: gueztz and hired hand. I come to work for money. You look more like first-class flyer than hired hand."

"Well, now you've met a third kind—a guest who wants to work as hard as a hired hand."

"How very nize! I know ve'll get along juzt fine," she said as she pulled clothing from the duffel.

"Sure," I muttered as I made an escape through the attic door.

"Here she is! My Larchmont homie!" Sara called out from the vegetable garden when I entered the courtyard. "Welcome to Château LeMont!" She fluttered toward me like a young ballet dancer, pulled off her gardening gloves, and gave me a hug. "Here . . . sit." She patted the ancient stone wall lining the courtyard. "How was the flight in? You and Julien found each other I trust?"

"The flight was smooth and on time, and we found each other with no problem."

"And I hope you're not serious about staying in that dormitory up there."

"I'm all settled in. It's just fine. And by the way," I said, remembering Spence's parting words to me. "Spence asked me to apologize to you for his rudeness a few weeks ago. He seemed pretty upset with himself for behaving badly."

She lowered her head. "I guess he told you about our history."

"He did. It was hard on him to see you again after so long." Streaks of crimson spread across her porcelain cheeks. "Oh, I'm so sorry!" I covered my mouth with my hand. "Did I say too much?"

"No. Not at all." She grabbed my arm to reassure me. "It's fine."

I repositioned my butt on the stone wall and forced a smile. "Anyhow, thank you so much for—"

"He still looks good, doesn't he?" she interrupted. "When I first met him, he was *gorgeous!* A surfer boy. Hot body, shiny blonde hair, eyes that crinkled when he smiled. Had a great mind too. He'd already absorbed a world of knowledge about wine from working in that shop." A faraway smile crossed her lips. "We both loved life in the city—visits to the MoMA, those old screwball comedies at the Regency, dinners with friends—"

"Sounds like you two were made for each—"

"But he was young, I was young and thought of myself as a bit of a rebel. During my semester at the Sorbonne in Paris, I took a day trip to Beaujolais to visit this domaine. Denis, Henri and Julien's dad, spotted me from the vineyard and came over to give me a personal tour." She rubbed her thumb over a ring set with an emerald-cut diamond that looked too large for her slim finger. "Not long after, I accepted his marriage proposal. My parents thought I was crazy by marrying into such a different culture. Maybe I was." She nodded her head toward her husband who was roasting a pig over the fire pit for that night's harvest dinner.

"Must have been quite a change from Manhattan," I said.

"It's a different life, for sure. No traffic jams, views that go on forever, and this château." She looked up at the mansion towering over us that was worthy of a spread in *Architectural Digest*. "It's a big life for sure. But it's also ruled by traditions. I had to quickly become fluent in French. Denis has good English, but his parents who live with us don't speak a word of it. So he insisted that we only speak French in the house."

"Wow! Total immersion! Sounds intense."

"Yup. It wasn't easy trying to fit into a household and culture so rooted in its ways. It still isn't." She grabbed my hand in hers and looked into my eyes. "So it's nice to have a visitor from my neck of the woods."

With her husband now headed our way, Sara called out to him. "Denis, say *bonjour* to our visitor from America. From my hometown, no less!"

"*Bonjour*, Miss Goodyear, and welcome!" When he took my hand, I couldn't help but compare his rough and thickened farmer's hands to those of Spence, that poured the world's finest vintages with the elegance of a master pianist.

"Thanks, Mr. LeMont. What a wonderful place you have here."

"I picked good ancestors," he said with chest thrust forward.

"He means he landed in the lucky sperm club," Sara said with a wink.

"You made the right choice by coming to Beaujolais, the home of the Gamay," he said with pride. "Did you know that our grape was once treated like a bastard child here on the Côte? That barbarian Phillippe the Bold banned the vine from Burgundy to make more room for its arrogant cousin, the Pinot Noir."

I felt Sara's elbow in my ribs. "He gives this lecture to anyone who'll listen."

Denis tipped his head toward his wife. "She doesn't share my passion for this land. But I thank her every day for giving me sons that do." He bent down and grabbed a handful of the rock-encrusted dirt, and let it slip through his fingers. "This soil . . . created from lava that flowed from a volcano millions of years ago, forces our vines to fight to survive where the Pinot Noir wouldn't stand a chance."

"Okay, enough with the preaching, Denis." Sara was getting irritated. "Your troops are marching in." She pointed to the harvest workers that were arriving. Some came together by van, some in cars, and some in motor homes they parked in the field. Many preferred to pitch tents rather than sleep in the attic. Denis went over to greet them. He appeared to know most, welcoming them with jokes and handshakes. There was a group of local professional harvest workers, others came from different nations in Europe. Some came for the money, some to share the camaraderie, some to enjoy the beauty of the area, and all to eat the food and drink the wine.

"*Bonjour, Monsieur LeMont!*" a familiar voice called out to Denis.

He turned with a smile to answer the greeting. "*Ah, la femme en noir est revenue!*"

It was Fifika. She was marching out of the winery in stiletto heel boots and a tiny black dress that hugged and separated each of her breasts and each cheek of her buttocks. She held her head high, aware that she'd caught the eye of every man in sight.

"Oh, *crap!* That Romanian woman is back," Sara told me. "I asked my husband to strike her from this year's e-vite list, but did he listen? Nooo."

"She sure left a bad taste in my mouth when we met," I said.

"I'm not surprised. Denis thinks she has valuable skills, but I think she's trouble."

Wine was being poured from jugs into glasses lined up on a table for the arriving harvest workers. Julien was setting up speakers for the music that would play from his cell. The guy had to be aware of how ridiculously handsome he looked in a pair of old jeans, a navy-blue T-shirt, and beat-up Topsiders with no socks. Sara called him over and gave him a basket with two knives.

"*S'il te plaît, Julien, j'ai besoin d'un peu d'ail sauvage pour la salade.*"

"*Oui, Maman.* Grab a pour of wine and come help me, Samantha," he said. "My *maman* is asking for some wild garlic to add to her salad." He whistled for the dog to follow. "Stella, *viens ici!*"

On that balmy summer evening, I was tempted to email Michael Van Ness a thank-you note for rejecting my plan that would never have stood a chance, anyway. Had he given me any encouragement that it might be considered, I'd be sitting under the fluorescent lights of my ice-cold cubicle at Weatherhouse filling out tax forms. Instead, with French love songs floating in the air, I was walking through a field bursting with purple, yellow, and silver thistles, with a glass of wine in my hand.

"Have you ever tasted wild garlic, Samantha? Here you can eat it right from the earth. Come see." Julien took my glass, set it on a nearby rock, and motioned for me to kneel with him next to a bed of delicate white blossoms with dark green leaves. He pulled a few of the plants from the near-black soil, shook off the loose dirt, and peeled the outer skin away from the onion-like bulbs of each stalk. "Take a bite." He held the shiny orbs close to my mouth.

"Ehhh . . . no thanks. I really don't want to reek of garlic when I meet my fellow workers for the first time."

He chomped down on the plants and chewed for a few moments with eyes closed. "Ummm . . . a bit peppery, a bit sweet," he said with the same impish smile I'd seen in that *Paris Match* photo on Cameron's phone. "May I?" He put his hand on the nape of my neck.

"What are you doing?" I asked as he gently pulled my nose in toward his mouth.

"I'm sharing some local lore with a visitor. So, tell me . . . do you smell any garlic?"

I inhaled deeply, slow and long. Instead of garlic, my senses were met by an alluring mix of pepper and tea tree toothpaste from his mouth, along with scents of sandalwood soap, wine, and a hint of musky sweat that rose from his chest.

"You smell like a guy who spends hours in a winery."

"That's because I do. But no garlic?"

"No garlic," I answered softly as my body melted toward him and my pulse quickened. *Stay back, Sam—he's dangerous!* Before I could pull away, he stood up.

"Not only does it not hurt your breath, it's good for the heart and helps to prevent colds," he said, as if giving a dissertation to a class on the flora of the Mont Brouilly region. While I fought to suppress my awakening desires, my thoughts were distracted by a barking Stella, being teased by a chirping chipmunk scooting back and forth on a nearby log. Julien grabbed her by the collar.

"*Stella, mauvais chien! Va-t'en à la maison!*" The dog slunk away.

"Don't scold her, Julien. She's a good girl." I stood up, snapped a dry stick from a tree, and tossed it in the air. "Stella, fetch!" The dog took off after the stick and brought it back with tail wagging. I grabbed it before she dropped it for a second toss, then wiggled it while she growled playfully and held onto it. "No, it's mine!" After a few more tosses, I joined Julien in cutting the stalks of the plants until the basket was full. The three of us went back to where the welcome dinner would be served.

André, the cellar master, was pulling the pig off the spit as the onions and potatoes roasted below in the drippings. Sara took the garlic from Julien and chopped the bulbs and stalks into her salad. Julien's eighty-something-year-old *grand-père* Gaston walked from table to table, refilling wine glasses and chatting with the new arrivals.

During the harvest season, domaines in France often serve as hosts to their favorite wine writers, distributors, retailers, and restaurant owners that serve their wine. Julien led me to a table of such guests, where a middle-aged man was talking to a more than middle-aged woman. "Dalton, meet Samantha Goodyear. Samantha, this is Dalton Holby. He owns the Manhattan restaurant, Little Gem."

"Great to meet you, Dalton!" I told the man. "I'm a huge fan of Little Gem! A gang of us were there last week. Those rock shrimp tacos and porcini mushrooms are killer!"

"Yes. The summer crowds have really put a burden on chef and staff," he murmured dryly.

"And say hi to Phyllis Turnball," Julien told me. "She's the wine writer for *Palate Press* in London."

"Great to meet you, Phyllis! I really enjoy your reviews! My great-aunt wrote a column on food and wine that was syndicated in the States."

"How nice," she responded before she turned back to Dalton and rekindled their heated debate about the controversial use of sulfur dioxide during the winemaking process to protect against oxidation and bacterial growth.

Julien shrugged his shoulders and guided me to a seat beside a fellow who looked closer to our age. Stella plopped down under my chair. "Benson Doyle, say *bonjour* to Samantha Goodyear. She's here to learn all she can about making great wine. Samantha, give a *salut* to Benson. He's the assistant winemaker for Ashton White out in Napa." I knew that Ashton White owned the hugely popular Ultraviolet wine brand.

"Nice to meet you, Benson," I said, hoping for more than a cursory nod.

"It's great to meet you, Samantha!" He rose from his chair and held out his hand for a shake.

"It must be exciting to work alongside one of the hottest winemakers in America," I told him.

"It is. Ashton's a talented guy in the cellar and a genius at marketing. But if you really want to learn to make great wine, there's no better teacher than this *ami*." He gave Julien a pat on the back.

"*Merci*," Julien said, taking a bow.

"No, *seriously*. I worked harvest here while I was studying winemaking at UC Davis in Northern California. At school, they taught everything from a scientific standpoint; the biology of the fruit, the chemistry of the fermentation, and so on—very clinical. Though it gave me an excellent base, they couldn't teach me the soulful part of the process. But Julien showed me that the science should come second to the art. And that making great wine is about learning to trust your instincts. Not just going by the book."

"What Benson means, is that a lot of the big wineries, they try to, as you say . . . fiddle . . . with the wine's levels of alcohol, the acidity, the sugar, and the oak, just to sell the most bottles of wine they can. But our goal here is only to help the wine to achieve its *grandeur* as nature planned. We don't force it to be what it's not by slaving over numbers made up by sales and marketing *génies*."

"I know all about being a numbers slave. That's why I quit my job."

•　　•　　•

"*Da Da Da spuneti! Ha ha!*" a woman's voice rang out as the wine continued to flow and the laughter from the hired workers at the next table got louder. I spotted Fifika, sitting with a retired couple from a farming village outside of London, a dentist from Prague, and a jeweler from Belgium.

"It might be good politics to sit with my bunkmates for a few," I told Julien and Benson as I strolled over to the other table and took a seat. "Hi, everyone!" I called out through the party chatter. "I'm Sam from New York City. This is my first harvest, so I hope I don't slow you guys down tomorrow in the vineyard."

"No worries there, Sam." The husband of the retired British couple extended his hand. "I'm Archie, and this is my wife, Beatrix. This is our tenth harvest here, and I'll warn ya that snippin' those vines can give ya a bit of a fit if ya don't—"

"Here she iz," Fifika slurred from across the table. "She's the von who can't dezide if she's guezt or vorker! How nize she vants to sit with us if only for few minutz. But how iz it that the youngezt LeMont seems to get all the time vit her that he vants?"

"That's enough from you, Fifika!" chided Archie, who leaned over and cupped his hands to my ear. "Those gypsies sure know how to drink. But no worries. That Fifika is all foam and no beer."

"Fifika may be in her cups," bellowed the dentist from a few seats away. "But I've worked five harvests here. And she's right about one thing." He fixed his gaze on Julien's dad, Denis, who was sharing a laugh with a buxom Polish woman on the buffet line. "The LeMont men *do* get whatever they want."

•　　•　　•

The August Beaujolais sun didn't think about setting until half-past nine. While dusk was dimming the lights for the next act of the evening, groups of Julien's friends wandered over. These twenty- and thirty-somethings belonged to the new generation of winemakers from ancient domaines in the region. They all had good English and strong bodies from the clean air, the organic foods, and their physical work in the cellars and out in the vineyards. And their passion for winemaking was a joy to witness as they discussed that year's grape crop, new winemaking techniques, and the upcoming crush of harvest. I couldn't help but compare their positive energy to the tension generated by my team at Weatherhouse as we sat in our meeting rooms and readied for month-end reports, quarter-end reports, year-end reports, and the upcoming crush of tax time.

"*Bonjour*, Samantha! I'm Sophie," said a young woman with fiery dark eyes as she held out her hand for a shake. "My family's domaine is the next one over. Julien tells me you're from the States. New York City, no less. Aren't *you* lucky?"

"Nice meeting you, Sophie. Yes, I am lucky. And so are you to live in France!"

"I am. But your country has Beyoncé, Matthew McConaughey, Barneys, LA, Silicon Valley, and Coachella!"

"And yours has Burgundy, Bordeaux, Champagne, Chablis, and Beaujolais. What a beautiful place to be a winemaker."

"Beautiful, yes, but we choke on our layers of traditions and restrictions. Our laws limit where our grapes can be grown, how many vines we can plant, how we must prune and train them, how much alcohol our wine can have, where our cellars can be located, yada yada yada. Sometimes I wish I could go to the States and be free to make whatever kind of wine I want, the way I want it."

"*Bonjour!* I'm Sophie's sister, Lizette," interrupted another young woman with the same dark eyes. "Don't mind her. She believes the grass on the other side of the ocean is always greener." She gave me a knowing wink. "But tell me, how is our Beaujolais bad boy treating you?"

"If you mean Julien, he's been the perfect gentleman."

"Well, the night is still young," Lizette said, as she watched Julien give a welcome hug to an auburn-haired beauty who'd just arrived. "You know you've got to keep your eye on that one, don't you?"

"I've been told."

• • •

By midnight, Julien's family and friends had drifted away while the harvest workers continued to party. After two days of travel and logging only a few hours sleep since leaving Manhattan, I was crashing. "Good night," I called out to Julien.

I'd only taken a few steps before I felt his presence behind me. "I'll walk you back," he said.

My heart beat faster. *Stop it, Sam! Didn't you hear what Lizette just called him?* "Thanks, but not necessary. Have a good night," I said as I sped up my pace.

"It is necessary. It's very dark. You could trip on a rock. And we can't afford to lose one of our most promising workers before harvest even begins." He offered an arm, and we walked along the vineyard heavy with grapes. The big round harvest moon hung over the top of Mont Brouilly, pouring a river of light on the endless rows of vines running up to the volcano. Above our heads, a white owl emerged from the attic roof, circled in the air, and began a silent dive in our direction.

"*Faites attention!*" Julien called out as his arm went around my shoulders and drew me close while the bird swooped near us to seize its prey.

"Someone's getting a late-night snack!" I said with a nervous giggle as jolts of electricity ignited in my belly. When we reached the door to the winery, I assume he'd offer some lame reason to escort me inside. *A real cellar rat could lurk? I could trip and break my neck on that dark stairway?* While I gathered my resolve to refuse the incoming pass, I felt his fingers on mine as he lifted the back of my hand to his lips. A second later, he released it and gave a chivalrous bow.

"Sleep well, Samantha. And tell me, what is *Monsieur* Goodyear doing while you're away for so many weeks? He must be lonely."

I stared at that beautiful face with my head cocked. "Monsieur Goodyear? Who?" Then I realized that Spence must have given Henri an earful about my family problems, and the story made it to France. "Oh! You mean Greg! You heard about that drama, huh? Well, I'm sure he's happy to have the place to himself."

Julien furrowed his brow. "Well . . . goodnight then," he said, then turned and walked off.

"*Dormez bien*, Julien!" I called out, not sure if I was relieved or disappointed to see him leave. I trudged up the stairs to the attic, brushed my teeth over the cracked porcelain sink, and slid into my sleeping bag on the cot. Before my head hit the pillow, I was fast asleep. It must have been the jet lag that woke me up around three a.m. Or maybe it was the voices. Below the snores that echoed through the dormitory, whispers rose from the winery through the slats in the floor. Then I heard giggles and the familiar cha-chings from that stack of bracelets. I looked over at Fifika's cot and saw it was empty.

### Montmartre, Paris June 1936

Vivian opened her eyes and sat up in the bed. The morning sun streamed through the window and a recording of Josephine Baker singing *J'ai Deux Amours* was playing on the phonograph. Marciel was standing at the easel with a paintbrush in hand, his deep voice belting out the lyrics in time with the singer. "*C'est Paris, Paris tout entire, Le voir un jour!*" Laughing at the sight, she marveled at how different the artist seemed from the man she'd met the previous day, and her heart swelled knowing that she had played a role in his transformation. She wrapped her arms around herself and relived the glorious moments of their night together. The sensation of his hands on her body as she stared at the painting. The excitement she felt when he'd swooped her off her feet and carried her to his bed. His lips on her breasts that ventured down past her belly. And his surprise upon discovering that her body, the body that had so inspired him, had yet to be savored by another. Knowing that, he was gentle, and took care to ensure that her yearnings were satisfied.

But now, she faced the arduous task of ending things with Enzo. Though this good man would always have a place in her heart, she knew that she would never feel the unbridled desire for him that she now felt for Marciel.

It had been one year since she'd stepped off the gangplank of the *SS France* after a seven-day journey across the Atlantic. The fare cost half of the five hundred dollars she'd saved by working nights as a seamstress for a dressmaker in her Brooklyn neighborhood. Once in Paris, she found a room at a boarding house near the *L'Académie des Beaux-Arts* and enrolled in a sculpture class at the school. Having tried without success to sell her art at street fairs, her remaining funds were rapidly depleted. It was fortunate that her teacher, Phillipe de Chanel, supplemented his income by supplying life models to painters and sculptors. The first artist he sent her to required her to sit on a table without a stitch of clothing. She found it torturous. No one besides her mother, sister, and the midwife who delivered her into the world had ever seen her nude before. But she soon learned that being comfortable in her own skin made the artist comfortable, which was key to a successful sitting. During these sessions, she found that she had a love and talent for styling both herself and the setting to create the mood that the artist wished to achieve. She also found another love—a young American banker named Enzo. Three months after they'd met, he asked her to be his wife. He promised to love her and provide for her with one request—that she stop taking off her clothes for other men. She had honored his wishes until Phillipe had made her an offer she couldn't refuse. It was to sit for one of his most promising former students, Marciel Duprée.

"*Bonjour, ma muse,*" Marciel said as he came to the bed and gave her a soft kiss on the lips. "I've almost finished the painting. When it's dry, I'll take it to *mon ami* who works at a *galerie* along the Rue Chauchat. I'm certain this one will sell."

"I'm sure it will," Vivian said as she reached out to brush his hair away from his eyes. "Perhaps I should take a scissor to this mop before you present it?"

"Perhaps you should. But first, tell me about those wicked thoughts you've had—the ones I unearthed." He lay down beside her, put his arms around her waist, and pulled her to a seated position over his hips.

# four

---

**Library Wines** *n.* wines stored in a winery's cellar for future generations to open

"Good morning, *Madame*, and how did you rest?" Julien asked me. His eyes were the same shade of blue as the sky behind him as he stood by a long table filled with cheeses, charcuterie, sausages, baguettes, éclairs, croissants, homemade jams and butter, pitchers of juice, and jugs of wine. Still half asleep, I blinked my eyes to help them focus.

"Morning, Julien. I slept well, thanks. Need some coffee to warm up, though." I rubbed my hands together with a fervor. "And to wake up. I think I'm still on New York time. What are we, six hours ahead here?" The thought that it was one a.m. back in Manhattan made me feel even more groggy.

He held out a steaming cup of café au lait. "Jet lag is always the worst on day two. You'll be on *français* time by tomorrow."

"I know, but the pick is today, and I want to enjoy every moment." After a few sips, the caffeine provided a welcomed jolt. I looked into the cup of coffee with hot milk. "Hmmm . . . I taste rich body, creamy textures, smooth flavor with a hint of chocolate, and a smoky finish."

"Seems *Maman* and Henri were right. The woman's palate *c'est très bien!*" Julien said with an approving wink.

"*Allez! Allez! Allez!*" Thierry, the domaine's vineyard manager, was calling for the pickers to assemble, which only left me time to grab a few bites of bread and cheese from the table.

"Well, I'm off. Wish me luck!"

"*Au revoir*, Samantha! And be sure to find the bunch stem before you slice."

"Aye, aye, *capitaine!*" I gave a salute and joined the workers that were hiking up the trail to the vineyard.

•   •   •

The temperature dropped and the fog seemed to thicken with each step up the mountain. When we arrived at the starting point of the pick, we were each given an empty basket and a pair of pruning shears, before we lined-up at the head of our assigned rows.

"*Un . . . deux . . . trois . . . commencez!*" Thierry called out, sending us to the first vines in our row. Within moments, the air was filled with the rapid snips that buzzed like bees as the pickers moved in unison from one vine to the next with a military-like precision.

"Bunch stem, bunch stem, bunch stem," I said under my breath with a rising panic while I shuffled through the vines to locate the stalk, or bunch stem, that Julien had shown me on his phone the previous evening. After a series of slices that only produced mangled vines, I found the correct stems that, when snipped, sent those tightly packed clusters into my gloved hand. When we came to the end of our rows, we would give our filled basket to a waiting worker for an empty one. They would dump the grapes into bins on the back of the carts that the domaine's two horses, Adèle and Jacques, would pull down the hill to the winery.

The workers had warned me that the low Gamay vines were tough on the back if one stooped while picking, so I opted to do squats to perform the task. Before I was halfway through my first row, I was feeling the burn in my thighs. But the pain was a small price to pay for the pleasure. Because from where I stood on the side of the mountain, the views of vineyards, lakes, châteaux, and farms on the surrounding hills made me feel like I was floating on a cloud during a beautiful dream.

At noon, Thierry's bellow of *"A la soupe!"* sent our legion on a march back down the mountain to the courtyard. I joined the line at the serving table, grabbed a plate and utensils with purple hands, and feasted my eyes on enormous platters of short ribs, cheesy potato croquettes, spinach and onion quiche, homemade cornbread, grilled shiitake mushrooms, and Sicilian eggplant. Sara was wheeling a wagon from the kitchen filled with her hand-crafted blackberry tarts and chocolate éclairs, while *grand-père* Gaston saw that wine, both red and white, continually cascaded from jugs into glasses. After loading up my plate, I grabbed a seat next to Julien and Benson, who both spent the morning in the cellar to meet the bins of grapes as they arrived from the vineyard.

"So, how'd you do on your first day of harvest, Sam?" Benson asked while he mopped up the remnants of his meal with a slice of that chunky, kernel-laced corn bread.

"It was the best workout I've had in months! Guess I'll have some sore muscles tonight," I said as I nibbled on a short rib. But the combination of heat and exercise had killed my appetite, and I put the meat down after a few dainty bites.

"Enough picking for you, *belle femme*," Julien said, as he attacked the first of two éclairs on his plate. "You're spending the rest of the day in the cave with me."

I shifted in my seat as Henrí's warning replayed in my head. "With you? *Just you?* Won't there be others?"

"Yes, they'll be others," he said with amusement. "Many others. We can't empty the bins, destem, and load sixty tons of grapes into the tanks by ourselves."

"Right . . . *of course!*" I said, feeling like an idiot. "But won't my picking team get pissed if I bail on them?"

"Your team will be too drunk to miss you. The productivity in the vineyard grinds to a stop after a heavy meal and too much wine. There's really no point in them working at all. We'd be just as well to send our *vendangeurs* to the beach."

•   •   •

While the afternoon picking crew made their way up the mountain, Julien handed me a pair of waterproof, slip resistant, steel-toed winery work boots. My apprenticeship began by joining the cellar crew at the sorting tables to pick out rotten grapes, sticks, snails, and leaves from the bunches of harvested grapes as they rolled along a conveyor belt. We followed that process by rubbing the clusters over a screen on top of a large tub to release the berries from the stems before loading the grapes into wooden tanks where they would begin the fermentation process.

While the assembly line regimentation in the vineyard inspired daydreams, the energy in the cellar was invigorating. Julien was the author, the director, and the star of his production that moved like a well-choreographed Broadway performance. Though he could easily play the part of the pampered prince, no task was beneath him as he lifted bins, dragged vats, climbed ladders, and moved barrels with a forklift.

"You do excellent work," he told me after the cellar crew had wrapped their tasks for the day and I was giving the floors a final mopping. I soon learned that ninety-five percent of winemaking involves sanitizing the floors, walls, and equipment to kill any bacteria or virus that could make its way into the wine.

I wrung the mop out into the bucket of grapey water, brushed some blonde ringlets away from my face, and looked up at him with tired but hopeful eyes. "Really? *Ya think?*"

"I do," he said with a reassuring smile. "But I want you to do more than work during this harvest."

"But . . . this isn't work! Accounting is work. This is *fun!*"

"And you have plenty of more fun ahead of you here. Next week, you'll join me and the other guests on our field trips—a harvest tradition. Monday, we'll visit some of our neighboring wineries here in Brouilly. Tuesday, we'll head to Rhône Valley, and Wednesday, Bordeaux. On Thursday, we'll visit Domaine Romanée-Conti in Burgundy, where *mon ami* Pierre D'Ubre will take us through the vineyard and, if we're very lucky, might even let us taste some of the world's priciest wine from the barrel."

It all sounded amazing. Too amazing. And that made me wonder exactly how this reputed *coureur de jupons* would expect me to repay his kindness.

•   •   •

Those first few days of harvest flew by like a speeding train. At the end of the week, the vineyard workers were gathering in the courtyard after the day's pick. I was standing over the winery sink scrubbing the purple stains from my hands and freeing the particles of grapes from beneath my fingernails when I heard the familiar cha-chings of bracelets. It was Fifika, on her way to the attic. She spotted Denis, who was up on a ladder checking out the grapes in a tank. After the two shared a giggle, she whispered something to him in French, and he nodded. I looked at Julien, who seemed to take no notice.

"We have an hour before dinner," Julien told me. "A good time to take you down to our deepest cave."

"Your *deepest* cave?" I looked around at the other workers. "Who else is coming?"

"No one. Just you. For a quick lesson."

My spine tensed, and my stomach did backflips. *Here it comes. A quick lesson. Is that his term for a quickie? Make an excuse, Sam. Tell him you're tired. Tell him you've gotta call your boyfriend.* "Actually, Julien, this isn't the best—"

"*Papa, peux-tu ouvrir la cave?*" Julien called to Denis. "*Mon père* is the keeper of the key."

Denis came down from the ladder. "*Oui, Julien.* And how did you find your first week of harvest, Miss Goodyear?" he asked me as he pulled the key to the cave from his belt.

"Oh, I *loved* it! It just flew by! I've seen many winemaking videos. But to make wine for real is—"

"Ah, ah, ah!" Denis wagged his index finger at me. "We do not *make* the wine. We are only the guides that provide the means for the grapes to achieve their glorious destiny with the least interference from us." He walked through the stone archway to the façade cave, bent down at the small door in the corner, and opened the lock.

"*Merci Papa.* Come with me, Samantha," Julien said, as he crawled through the opening. "No worries. Nothing in here will bite you."

My heart was pounding as I gingerly stepped through the doorway and crept behind him along a narrow stone passage lit by a series of flickering light bulbs. *Maybe just one brief kiss. Or even one long, lovely kiss. If he tries anything else, I'll put a stop to it.* I knew I was courting danger. But I could almost feel the pressure and taste the sweetness of those beautiful lips against mine. When he climbed from the passage into the cave and put his arms around my waist to help me down, the scent of fermenting wine on his skin was intoxicating. For a moment, our eyes met. But instead of pulling me closer, he stepped away to reveal the interior of the cave.

"*Nous voilà,* Samantha. This is where my ancestors and I convene." He pointed to row after row of stone shelves holding what had to be thousands of bottles. Mold, some of it in the form of tiny mushrooms, was growing everywhere—on the bottles, the walls, even hanging down like stalactites from the ceiling. The dampness, the cold, and the smell of the earth worked to permeate my lungs, leaving me no doubt that this was an ideal environment for wine to age to its finest hour.

Julien pulled a bottle from one shelf and scraped some mold away with his pocketknife. "Here is one of the first wines created at Château LeMont." He handed me the bottle. "Every year we put forty bottles of each *cru* that we make down here, for our family only, to drink when we have big events occurring in our lives—marriage, grand anniversaries, births, and deaths."

It took a moment for my eyes to focus on the bottle's ancient label dated 1838 that had the same illustration of the château as the label I'd seen in Spence's shop. "Wow! It's so old," was all I could say as I held the relic in my hands.

Julien took the bottle and handed me another one. "When I was born, *mon père* chose this 1840 *Cuvée Speciale,* a blend of our finest red grapes at the time. It was made by *Grand-père* Gaston's *grand-père,* Louis LeMont, who bought the one-hundred-acre domaine in 1835 from government auction. *Maman* wrote in her tasting notes on the *cru* that 'the wine is much like the nouveau *bébé.* It has a deep-red color, very ripe flavors of black currant and blueberry, and lots of spice.' She attached the notes to the bottle that stands with the other empty ones on the shelf in the *salon* of the château."

"These bottles are so precious. And how wonderful to have this kind of history," I said while running my finger across the ancient *Cuvée*.

"The auction houses in Paris and London call each year to ask us to put these wines up for sale. Even a small portion of this cave would bring in many millions of euros. But Gaston says that selling these bottles would be the same as selling our ancestors' souls." The tremor in his voice told me that though Julien had a love for beautiful women, his primary passion would always be for the dynasty of Domaine LeMont.

### *Montmartre, Paris June 1936*

The morning showers blurred Vivian's views of the barges, push tows and sightseeing boats that made their way up and down the Seine while she sat at the tiny bistro table waiting for Enzo. He was returning from a business trip to London, and the two had planned to meet for *pain au chocolat* and Camembert omelettes at their favorite breakfast place on the banks of the great river. But now, the lump in Vivian's throat kept her from taking even a sip from the cup of expresso in front of her.

The rain was coming down hard when she finally saw Enzo leap from the running board of a bright green taxi and onto the curb of the Boulevard Saint-Germain. He pulled his trench coat above his head to begin a sprint through traffic and over puddles of water to make his way across the street. When he arrived beneath the blue and white stripped awning of the café, he spotted Vivian inside, and his rain splattered face lit up with a smile. Though several years younger than Marciel, he looked far more the adult with his pencil mustache, closely cropped hair, bowler hat, and dark wool suit. Vivian couldn't help thinking that if life with Enzo would have been a first-class journey on a steam train, loving Marciel will be like peddling a unicycle on a tightrope. Aware that her youth and high spirits would all too soon be a distant memory, she'd forgiven herself for allowing her desire for excitement to win out over her need for comfort. But that didn't make the conversation that she was about to have with this good man any easier.

"What's wrong, my love?" Enzo asked when he arrived at the table and saw her face, sticky with tears. "I trust you didn't take in that horribly sad *Blue Angel* again at the picture show. Miss Dietrich is a terrible role model for young women."

"No, I didn't go the movie theater, Enzo. I did something else. And I'm sorry. I didn't want it to happen. But it did."

"Didn't want what to happen?"

"I . . . I . . . I betrayed you."

"Ah! Don't be so dramatic, *mon amour*. There's nothing you could do that would—"

"I'd planned to stop modeling. To abide by your wishes. And I understood how you felt. I did. But my professor, Phillipe, the one who connects models to serious artists who can't pay the high fees . . . he asked me if I'd like the chance to pose for a very talented painter. Of course, I said no. But when he told me the artist was the same one whose works I'd admired at *L'Académie*, I agreed to do it. And then—"

"Don't say anymore, Vivian," Enzo said, holding his hand up to silence her. "Just *don't*. But *do* enjoy your breakfast." He stood up, threw five francs on the table, and walked out the door head-on into the rain.

# five

---

**Blind Tasting** *v.* tasting wines without knowing facts about them, such as vintage, appellation, varietal

Two weeks after the start of harvest, Julien drove his guests and me north to Burgundy's Côte de Nuits, to visit the vineyards and winery of Domaine de la Romanée-Conti. Over the previous week, we'd traveled south to the Rhône Valley, famous for Syrah, and west to Bordeaux to taste Cabernet, Sauternes, Malbec, and Merlot.

"Welcome to Vosne Romanée," Julien announced when the Range Rover pulled up in view of the ancient stone cross on the perimeter of the historic vineyard. "Pierre, the winemaker, just texted to say he's on his way to greet us."

I'd already learned that Phyllis Turnball, the wine critic, and Dalton Holby, owner of Michelin-starred restaurants, were both on the reserved side, and as the two were important fans of Domaine LeMont wines, Julien was eager to make these trips memorable for them. Though they both appeared nonplussed, Julien's friend Benson Doyle and I both found it hard to control our excitement at getting the chance to tour the winery and the vineyard once owned by royalty, that was still the source of the best, the rarest, and indisputably the most expensive Pinot Noir in the world. We had our fingers crossed that the visit would include a taste of the domaine's wine. Even a thimble-sized sip would be a once-in-a-lifetime experience.

Julien motioned for me to step aside from the group as we waited for Pierre to join us. When we were out of earshot from the others, he spoke in a low voice.

"I'm not worried about how Pierre will behave with the other guests. But I must warn you about him, Samantha. He is known to be *excentrique*. His father was the winemaker here for many years, and now Pierre makes the wine like no one else could."

"Yes, I'm sure he does. I can't wait to meet him! Does he speak English?"

"Not a word. And don't be surprised that he is very French."

I looked up to see a tall, slightly stooped gentleman come out of the winery. Julien introduced Pierre D'Ubre to the others in our group, who each got no more than a faint nod. I wondered what I could say to the man in my limited French that could hold any interest for him.

"Samantha Goodyear, meet Pierre D'Ubre," Julien said.

"*Bonjour, enchantée,*" I said, extending my hand but resisting the urge to curtsy. The man took my hand in his.

"*Je suis toujours heureux de faire la connaissance d'une belle femme,*" he replied before he kissed the back of my hand.

"Pierre said he is always happy to meet a beautiful woman," Julien told me.

*Hold on! Did Julien just say I'm beautiful?* I looked at him, stunned, but soon realized he was only translating Pierre's words.

"Oh . . ." I looked down with an awkward smile. "Well . . . *merci!*" I said to Pierre as the group began the walk up the hill toward the legendary vineyard.

When we reached it, I wondered how such a small piece of land, only about four and a half acres, producing a mere 6,000 bottles, or 450 cases a year, could so dominate the wine world in terms of price. I'd remembered reading that just three bottles of the 1990 vintage of Romanée-Conti wine had sold for $72,000 three years before. Julien translated as Pierre told us that the vines were planted by the Romans, acquired by monks in the thirteenth century, and purchased in the 1600s by the French royal Louis François Ier de Bourbon, Prince de Conti. Along with adding his name to the wine, the prince took it off the market for the sole consumption of himself and the guests of his palace before the French Revolution brought that nation's monarchy to its knees.

The small, yet-to-be-harvested grapes on the vines had enjoyed a long growing season that, as Pierre explained, adds complexity to wine by allowing the clusters to simmer and ripen slowly in the soft sun. When I put a few of the tiny jewels in my mouth and bit down, I knew that the fruit inside was unlike anything I'd experienced in Beaujolais.

After entering the ancient winery, Pierre directed us to an underground cellar with a low ceiling, gravel floor, and a rough wooden table and chairs for tastings. It seemed rustic compared to the big wineries I'd seen in Napa or Sonoma, where the average bottle might sell for fifty dollars, as compared to the ten thousand dollars that a new vintage of Romanée-Conti fetches. When Pierre motioned for us to take seats at the table, we held our breaths before a cellar worker arrived with a glass decanter and poured a small barrel sample of the wine for each of us. I wondered out loud if, since the annual production of the wine was so small, Pierre had foot-stomped the grapes.

After Julien relayed my question to Pierre, the man kept his eyes on me, while he gave his reply.

"*Oui. Je foule les raisins. Je les foule nu parce que ça me fait sentir que mille belles femmes aux cheveux jaunes caressent mon corps.*"

I looked to Julien for a translation, his chin resting on his fists as he struggled to re-phrase the winemaker's words.

"Uhhh, Pierre says '*oui*' and that he, well, how might I convey this . . ."

"Pssst . . . Julien," I interrupted in a whisper. "Give us an exact translation, *please!* We're hanging on every word Pierre says!"

Julien took a deep breath. "He says he stomps the grapes while naked because it makes him feel like a thousand beautiful yellow-haired women are caressing his body."

While the slightly hard-of-hearing Phyllis Turnball asked Dalton Holby to repeat Julien's words, Pierre nodded, still staring at me. I returned his gaze with a polite smile and fidgeted in my seat. Noticing my unease at the winemaker's fixation, Benson gave me a sympathetic wink. But he fast saw the benefit of that fixation when Pierre signaled for his assistant to fetch more wine for us to taste.

Spence, who had sampled the wine on several occasions, had described the Pinot Noir with terms like "fine stony minerality," and having "a complex variation of spices." But when I touched the liquid to my lips, I had no words to describe what I was tasting. To merely call it wine would be like calling the Mona Lisa a painting, Beethoven's Fifth a tune, the Sistine Chapel a building, or a Stradivarius a fiddle.

Pierre spoke again and Julien translated by saying, "Because he is enjoying the beauty in the room, Pierre has *un cru très spécial* to share with us." The cellar worker returned with a bottle that looked to be a hundred years old. The label and capsule were worn and discolored, the glass green and thick. Julien asked Pierre to tell us a bit about the wine. After a moment's silence, he looked at me and spoke.

*"Ce vin peut ressembler à une très vieille femme. A l'extérieur, elle est ridée et fanée."*

"This wine may look like an ancient woman," Julien translated, now talking louder for Phyllis Turnball's benefit. "On the outside, she is wrinkled and faded."

*"Mais sous l'extérieur ruiné, vous découvrirez que les années lui ont appris à vous donner le plaisir jusqu'à ce que vous imploriez la miséricorde,"* Pierre continued.

"But beneath the crumbling exterior, you'll find that the years have taught her how to pleasure you until you beg for mercy." As Julien spoke, he looked at Pierre to see where this was going.

*"Jusqu'à ce que le pénis éclate avec mille orgasmes,"* the winemaker exclaimed, his voice deepening, and his arms rising toward the heavens.

"Until, um, you erupt with a thousand or . . . or . . ." Julien said, his normally olive complexion now purple. ". . . or maybe we should just allow the wine to speak for itself."

Either unaware, or not caring that he had been censored, Pierre whispered something to Julien.

"And here is more good news!" Julien said, relieved to change the subject. "Pierre tells us that Samantha has inspired him to bring back an ancient tradition of the domaine. In keeping with that tradition, if one of you can guess the vintage of the wine he just described, he'll have another *cru très spécial* brought out for you to taste."

"Marvelous!" the usually dour Phyllis Turnball called out in anticipation of the upcoming challenge. The cellar worker gave everyone a small pour from the timeworn bottle, the year of the vintage hidden by his fingers. When the wine entered my mouth, no less than a dozen separate flavors opened, one after the other. Some seemed familiar—butterscotch, caramel, cassis, anise, burnt sugar, hazelnuts, and nutmeg. But there were others that gave me a feeling of déjà vu—like I'd tasted them in another lifetime.

When the last drop left my palate, the essence of the wine continued to linger in my soul, somehow inspiring the memory of my Aunt Vivian, who'd once told me that she'd tasted her first glass of Romanée-Conti in the year 1936, when she sat in that Montmartre garret posing for the painting that hung in her co-op. The painting that portrayed her holding a glass of wine by an open window on an evening in June.

"1934," I called out. "This wine was barreled in September 1934 and released on the open market in the spring of 1936," I said, trying to sound like I knew what I was talking about.

Pierre looked at me as if I were an idol of worship that he had reached after a year-long journey. When he nodded that I was correct, applause and war whoops filled the room. The wine critic looked at me through her half-frame glasses, wondering how I could have arrived at that answer. Though it was only a guess, no one was complaining about getting the chance to taste more of the world's most famous wine.

The next vintage was poured from a bottle with no label to give any clues of its year. And when Pierre thrust out his normally hunched shoulders with pride, I knew we were about to be blown out of the water.

On the nose, it was intense, exotic—I could even say it was sexy. On the palate, I tasted truffles, anise, rosemary, lavender, and mint. The finish was spicy and went on forever. I'd learned at a lecture given at Spence's shop that the 1945 vintage that marked the end of Nazi terror for France had proven to be the most valuable of all the domaine's wine. It was also the last vintage made from the original vines dating back to 1585 that were torn out in 1945 because the phylloxera insect that had devastated the French wine industry had severely damaged the vineyard. In 2011, just one bottle of the 1945 Romanée-Conti fetched $120,000 at Christie's Auction House, setting a world record auction price for a single bottle of red Burgundy.

"1945!" I called out. "It's a 1945!" I was right again.

·   ·   ·

"'Cause I got friends in low places,
    where the whiskey drowns and the beer chases my blues away.
    And I'll be okay."
With Julien at the wheel, Phyllis Turnball, Dalton Holby, Benson Doyle, and I had been serenading ourselves with the tunes of Garth Brooks, Willie Nelson, and Johnny Cash on the ride back to Beaujolais. The thrill of tasting the world's most famous wines, along with the amount of wine we tasted, had put us all in a singing mood. All of us, except for Julien. Pierre followed up my correct guess on the '45 vintage with several more rounds of tastes, and our designated driver had limited himself to just a few drops of each.

After Julien let the other three guests off at the château, he pulled up at the winery where I would run up to the attic and dress for dinner. "Hey, Julien . . . lemme ask you something," I began. "Does Pierre . . . does Pierre ever use terms that aren't related to sex when he describes wine?"

"Not in my experience," he said. "I just hope he didn't make you too uncomfortable today."

"Oh, no . . . well . . . yes, maybe a little. But then he tasted us on that amazing wine. The world's most famous wine! That was a life-defining moment for me." I reached out to touch the strong, beautiful hand on the steering wheel. "And you made it happen, Julien."

He shut the engine down and turned to me. "No, you made it happen, Samantha. Pierre put on that dog and pony show for you and you only." He brushed a lock of hair from my face. The moment I'd been waiting for had come at last. Those lips on mine . . . that delicious kiss. Instead, his jaw tightened as he turned back away and started the engine. "Best not be late for dinner."

.    .    .

The late-setting harvest sun was painting the sky and surrounding mountains a heavenly shade of pomegranate pink as that night's harvest dinner segued to dessert. "Time for some gallivanting at ole LeMont!" Archie, the retired Brit, called out from his seat in the courtyard. "How 'bout a bloody ace game of charades?" Cheers and shouts met the suggestion from the tables of workers who had bellies full of food and wine.

Julien walked off to help himself to his mom's crêpes suzette. Dalton Holby and Phyllis Turnball, both slightly drunk and slightly combative, were now in a heated argument over the increasing trend of including stems during fermentation to add complexity to Pinot Noir and Syrah. Still under the influence of that day's tasting marathon, I had little appetite for dinner, but was enjoying the selection of wines that Benson had brought over from Napa.

"This Cab is scrumptious," I told Benson. "They sure have some tasty wines in Napa, huh?"

"They do. You east coasters seem focused on French wines. But Northern Cal has some great terroir too. And some great winemakers. Here, try this rosé." He splashed some pale-garnet-colored liquid into a fresh glass. "All organic and made by a young couple who farm the vineyard themselves."

"I've really had enough for one day. But maybe just a taste," I said as I picked up the glass and took a sip. My phone dinged. I'd sent a group text to Spence, Stephanie, and Cameron about the amazing visit to Romanée-Conti with a list of the wines we'd tasted, and a tidbit about Pierre's kooky admiration of me. Now Cameron had a question:

**Cameron:** How r u handling the passes from that other amorous Frenchman?

**Samantha:** No passes. Hasn't looked twice. Not sure if I'm relieved or insulted!

**Cameron:** Hard to believe. Perhaps the brother gave u bad info?

**Samantha:** Could b. Or maybe I'm just not his type

I took another sip of the rosé and looked up at Benson. Studying his face for the first time, I decided he was somewhere between nice-looking and handsome. With the wine encouraging my curiosity, I leaned in close. "Hey, Benson . . . what's the story with Julien? Is he really the ladies' man that his brother says he is?"

"For sure. No, actually . . . I should clarify that." He sat back in his chair and took a long sip of the wine. "He does very well for himself, but only with women who don't have a problem with guys who're athletic, talented, well-educated, speak six languages, and have heaps of old money."

"But . . . would he qualify as a skirt chaser?"

"He's a guy, isn't he?" He tipped back his head and drained his glass.

"I see." I gave the glass of rosé a swirl, took another sip, and mulled over a new concept. Julien had not shown the slightest bit of interest toward me—because he had no interest in me.

"Finish up your dessert, mates!" Archie bellowed, as Julien came toward us with a generous portion of Sara's chocolate concoction. "And get ready to rumble!"

Benson topped my glass off with more of the wine as he and the other guests stood up from the table. "You two have fun," he said to Julien and me. "We three are bidding you *bonne nuit.*"

"And a *bonne nuit* to you lovely people!" I called out a bit too loud as I held up my glass in salute and took another swallow. "What a day we had, huh?"

"It was a royally superb day thanks to you, Sam," Phyllis Turnball called back, as she staggered away from the table.

The chatter from the other groups got louder as the workers readied themselves for the start of charades. "A LeMont tradition,"

Julien told me. "The game is a favorite of the workers. Do you want to play? It's only . . ." He glanced at his watch. "Ten past ten."

"Why not? I love charades!" I said, vaguely aware that after Benson's pours, my pleasant buzz was bordering on inebriation.

"Listen up here, mates!" Archie called out as he started sliding chairs around to create a makeshift stage. "It's a royal battle between the sexes! Women on one team, men on the other. Who's first?" He pointed into the crowd. "Ah! Here we are! Go for it, Anastazja!"

The buxom Polish woman stood up, put her hands together, and opened them to signify a book.

"*Livre!*" the crowd called out.

"It's a book!" I cried, excited for the game to begin.

Anastazja put her hand on her forehead as if she was searching for something.

I jumped to my feet, a bit unsteady, and shouted, "Search! Seek! Look for!"

"*Chercher! Voir! Surveiller!*" another woman yelled. Confused, I looked around me.

"*Recherche!*" Archie's wife Beatrix stated with authority while Anastazja gave her two thumbs up.

"The search," Julien said, nudging me with his elbow.

"I already said that!" I told him.

"*La Recherche De L'Absolu! Honoré de Balzac,*" Beatrix shouted, as she jumped up and down in celebration.

"*The Search for the Absolute,* by Balzac," Julien said, elbowing me again.

"They play in French?" I asked with my face locked in a pout.

"They had to pick one language. Years back, they voted to keep the game in French."

I attempted to cover his mouth with an unsteady hand. "I know, I know, don't tell me . . . another LeMont tradition."

Julien took my hand in his. "Samantha, I think you had too much tasting, even for playing in English. How about we take a nice *marche* around the vines?"

He stood and tried to help me up. Before my butt had left the seat, Fifika jumped to the stage. Wearing a chartreuse-colored dress sized for a seven-year-old girl, she strutted and puffed out her chest like a proud bird.

"Firzt, I muzt apologize to you all," she told the crowd. "I ordered thiz drezz online, and they sent me two sizez too small." She ran her hands up her torso. "I hope you do not mind if it'z too tight."

Most of the men, Denis included, clapped their hands and whistled their approval. Fifika made a fist with one hand and cranked her other hand in a circular motion.

"Film!" the women in the group called out. Fifika nodded her head in the affirmative as she pulled a man to the stage, guided his hands toward her breasts, then pushed him away.

"*Venez! Venez!*" a woman shouted. Fifika shook her head back and forth to signal that the answer was wrong, now leading her very willing assistant along behind her.

"*Soumets!*" another woman called out. Fifika jumped in the air and clapped her hands to signal that the answer was correct.

"*Ne nous soumets pas à la tentation!*" Beatrix called out. Fifika gave a fist pump to signal victory.

"*Lead Us Not into Temptation*," Julien translated. "The men can't touch the women in this game," he said with a wink.

"Even though they're dying to," I said, folding my arms against my chest like a defiant child. "I'm going to bed. Or as I should say, I'm going to cot." I rose out of the chair but collapsed back onto the seat. "Oops . . . I'm a tad tipsy."

"Bed is a *bonne idée*, young lady." Julien stood again and offered his hand. "But you'd better stay at my château tonight. You're not safe by yourself." I took his hand and teetered back and forth before he steadied me with his arm. "Let's collect your things from the attic. I have an empty guest chamber waiting."

•   •   •

Julien carried my duffels, with Stella trailing, as we walked toward the house he shared with Henri on the other end of the property. It was close to midnight, and a giant moon and a million stars lit the way for us while the cheers from charades were slowly drowned out by a chorus of crickets. "That Fifika is one exhibitionist," I said, still furious with the woman for the insult she'd hurled at me when we'd first met. "I muzt apologize to you all." I wiggled my butt back and forth. "I ordered thiz drezz online, and they sent me two sizez too small." I slid my hands down my torso and thrust out my chest. "I hope you do not mind if it'z too tight." I spun around to face Julien with hands on hips. "Time to talk turkey, *Monsieur Coureur de Jupons*. Is she the type of ride you're into? Ginormous headlights? A ton of junk in the trunk?"

Julien looked at me and scratched his head. "I don't know what this is all about, Samantha. But we need to get you up to bed."

"Sure. But first, tell me why you haven't given me a second look. Are my boobs, or lack of them, the problem?" I walked backwards while stretching my pink v-neck top tight against my chest. "Fifika said they were flat. You agree? Wait. I'll make this easier." I pulled the top over my head to reveal one of my lacy, new push-up bras from Paris. Thinking I was playing a game, Stella ran circles around the two of us while she let out a string of sharp howls.

Julien's eyes locked on my breasts, now beautifully plumped and rounded with the aid of that garment. "Samantha, please! Put your . . . put your sh—"

"C'mon Julien, spit it out! Are these the problem? Or am I too old? Too young? Too short? Too tall? Too thin? Too fat? Ah, too fat! *That's it!*" I tried to grab the roll of belly fat I'd accrued during my tenure at Weatherhouse to punctuate the revelation. But without those daily Krispy Kreme donuts and with the abundance of physical work I'd been doing over the past few weeks, the iota of flesh I could snare between my thumb and index finger snapped back taut against my abdomen.

"Careful there!" He grabbed my arm to prevent me from backing into a stone wall.

I stopped and turned around. Behind the wall was a miniature stone castle with a tall round turret. The top of the turret had an arched window that looked like what Rapunzel would let her hair down from for the handsome prince to rescue her. "Oh, wow! That is so cool," I said while I pulled my top back over my head. "Please tell me I'm not so drunk that I'm seeing a castle instead of a tract house!"

"It's no tract house," Julien said as we walked to the entrance. "Le Petit Château, as we have always known it, goes back to the Middle Ages—the first house on the domaine." He pushed the massive iron and wood door open and guided me inside. The stone exterior continued throughout the interior walls of the house and formed a staircase that wound its way up three more stories. Threadbare Indian rugs, gothic church pews, and an ancient painting that depicted Le Petite Château in a bygone era, graced the space.

"This place . . . it's dreamy! And these antiques . . ." I steadied myself on the back of a chair. "They look like they've been here forever!"

"They have been. When the old caretaker of the property died, Henri and I worked together to restore it. We had the modern furniture hauled away. Everything you see had been locked for centuries in the basement. We pulled the pieces out and had a grand time putting them back where we guessed they had been."

I twirled around and took in the scene of the ancient rooms and the furniture. I'd been a swap meet junkie in Manhattan but had never come across any pieces as shabby chic as these. "I love this place, I do," I said. Now I was feeling very happy and still very drunk. "And I think you're brilliant and beautiful." I threw myself against his chest and wrapped my arms around him. "Even if you have absolutely no interest in me."

He slung one of my arms over his shoulder and steered me to the staircase as my knees buckled. "Keep walking, Samantha. You have many steps to the top of the tower."

"Just like Rapunzel," I muttered as he guided me up the winding staircase.

•   •   •

When I opened my eyes, there was a tiny bird with blue wings and a red chest sitting on the ledge of an open window warbling a tune to its mate. A contented smile was plastered across my face as I enjoyed a long luxurious stretch in the middle of a big cozy bed. But the smile vanished as flashes of my behavior from the previous night hit me.

There was a knock at the door. It opened a crack and Stella rushed in, jumped on the bed, and licked my face.

"Good morning," Julien said as he walked into the room. "And how did Rapunzel sleep?" With his hair still wet from his morning shower, he looked like a *GQ* model in his work boots, worn jeans, and faded sweatshirt.

Peeking out from behind Stella's neck, I was surprised he was so cordial after I acted so badly. "Errr, good morning, Julien." I looked down and noticed that I was only wearing my top, bra, and the lace panties from Paris. "So, you brought me in here last night, did you?"

"I had to tote you up the staircase and put you to bed, so I knew you were in for a long sleep."

"And my clothes?" I looked around the room and saw my jeans neatly folded on a chair and the boots standing upright on the floor.

"I pulled off your boots and the denims. You'd already undressed yourself on the walk, so I didn't think you'd mind. And I hope your Greg won't either."

"Greg? Greg Goodyear? Why would he mind? I'm twenty-five-years old and long out of the house."

"Out of the house? Are you two apart?"

"Apart? No, he moved in with me when he and my mom split up."

"*What?* You married your *stepfather?*"

"No! What are you talking about? I'm not married to anyone! And Greg is my father! What made you think I was married? I don't even have a boyfriend."

"You mean you're single?"

"Yes, I'm single! Why, what—"

"Good old Henri!" he said with a shake of his head. "Up to his old tricks. He told me you were reluctant to come here because you didn't want to leave your husband."

"What? That's *crazy*! Is that why—" Realizing I was now fair game, I backed away in the bed. "But hold on! Just 'cause I'm single doesn't mean I'm one of your little groupies who're ripe for the picking."

He leaned in close and looked at me with eyes that the morning light had turned a lovely shade of lavender. "What are you saying? What's this about groupies?"

"Henri said you're known as a *coureur de jupons*—a man whore, who takes full advantage of the groupies that follow your nation's young winemakers."

"So, Henri told you all that, did he?" he asked, standing back again. "That's absurd. A total lie! Where are these groupies? Have you seen me with them?"

"No. I've just seen you working."

"Because that's what I do—work. And trust me, groupies follow rock stars, screen stars, pro athletes. Not winemakers."

"Maybe, but your neighbor Lizette seemed to agree with Henri. She called you their Beaujolais bad boy."

"She's called me that since I was eight years old, when I started the engine of our tractor and jumped off before it rolled down the mountain into her family's vineyard."

"Oh, wow, you *were* bad! But what about that photo of you and those hot blondes in *Paris Match*?"

"*Paris Match*? Hot blondes? Ah, yes! Zelda, Tess, and Anabelle—my cousins! Triplets, who live in Marseille—aged fifteen going on twenty. We were celebrating Gaston's eighty-five years at a restaurant last Christmastime. Wherever did you see that photo?"

"Errr . . . my friend Cam found it online before I came out here."

"So . . . Henri told you I was a man-whore and told me you were married. If I know my brother, he wants to have a chance with you when he returns home."

"I guess that's why he urged me to stay past Beaujolais Nouveau Day." I looked at him in disbelief while slowly shaking my head. "So . . . oh my God!" I giggled. "You thought I was married! To a Greg! All this time! Is that why you haven't even looked at me?"

"I've looked at you," he said as he sat down on the bed, put his hand on the back of my neck, and pulled me in closer. "But I thought you were a happily married woman. Or at least a married woman. Guess we've had what we call *un défaut de communication,* or a failure to communicate."

"*We sure have!*" My voice went six octaves higher from nerves, and I could hear my heart thumping. "So . . . what do we do about it?"

"I have some ideas," he said as he touched his mouth to my neck and gave it some nibbles, while that newly washed hair tickled my ear. I closed my eyes to savor the essence of his body against mine when a *ding dong ding dong ding dong ding* rang out in the room. It was my alarm. Set as usual for seven a.m.

"Oh, crap . . . I almost forgot!" I slid away from him and sat up. "Today's the old vines vineyard pick! And I can't miss this one!"

"I know you can't. I'll take you up there myself." He pulled me back down on the bed. "Just spare me thirty seconds for a kiss."

• • •

Thirty seconds became two hours. At close to nine o'clock, the two of us were hiking up the mountain with hands intertwined while Stella ran ahead of us to the old vines vineyard. The morning haze had burned off and the sky-high views from Mont Brouilly seemed to go on forever. Invigorated by the hike and from the total euphoria of the morning, I never felt happier and more alive. Though I'd enjoyed sex with the only two other guys I'd been intimate with—my college boyfriend, and a law student I'd dated for a few months in New York—making love with Julien had taken me into a whole new realm of emotional and physical pleasure. But that wasn't the only reason for my improved mental and physical state. The labor and the healthy foods of harvest had made my body strong and toned again. And even more important was that working in an industry that I was passionate about had made the anxiety and panic attacks that had plagued me since college become a distant memory. The vial of Lorazepan I'd refilled before leaving Manhattan remained unopened in my duffel.

"These old vines are the most highly prized of our domaine," Julien said when we reached the side of the vineyard that was yet to be picked. Some over a hundred years old, the plants had thick gnarled bases that looked like tree trunks. He bent down, picked up a handful of the soil, and opened his palm to reveal the bits of mottled blue stone sprinkled throughout the granite and the volcanic rock. Though the guy got his physical beauty from his mother, I could see the passion for the land that he inherited from his father. "See the tiny bits of blue?

That's the diorite from the volcano." He pointed to the top of the mountain. "The closer you get to the crater, the more diorite in the soil, which means more drainage and less water for the vines. So being the highest on the mountain, the old vines produce the most concentrated and flavorful grapes of all."

Julien took my hands in his. "And now, I have something to share with you." He picked a cluster of the grapes from a vine, pulled off a berry, and placed it in my hand. "Put it in your mouth and bite down." When I did, a burst of sweet flavor was followed by bitter tannins from the skins and seeds that made my mouth feel dry. "Keep it there in the mouth," he instructed. "And tell me if the taste changes." For a moment, nothing changed. Then it hit. The bitter taste of the seeds was erased by a flash of the most glorious, the most ethereal flavor I'd ever experienced. When Julien saw the reaction in my eyes, he took me in his arms.

"But where . . ." I looked up at him. "Where did that taste come from?"

"It comes from the vines speaking to you. Because, like me, you have what we call *le cadeau*, or in your language, the gift. That second burst of sweetness after the bitter is the old vines telling us it's time to harvest their fruit. The hydrometer used to measure sugar levels might say it's too early, but I would know different. My father and my *grand-père* Gaston do not have *le cadeau*. But my *grand-oncle* Albert had it and helped me to find it when I was very young. He showed me that picking when the grapes are truly ready makes the wine taste like magic."

•   •   •

The workers were halfway through the pick. Julien and I passed Fifika who was dumping baskets of grapes into bins, her stack of bracelets jangling with each move of her arm. She spotted us and walked over to Julien, sending Stella into a barking frenzy.

"Stella, no!" I grabbed the dog by the collar. "Sorry, Fifika!" I was so deliriously happy that morning I'd have been polite to Genghis Khan. "The bracelets must scare her."

"Is no problem. Come to me, my leetle puppy." She bent to offer her hand to Stella, and the barks turned to growls. Fifika pulled her hand back and turned toward Julien. "I have a kveztion for you, Mezter LeMont. I have asked this kveztion of your *père*, and he told me it is fine with him if it is fine with you."

"What is it?" Julien asked.

"I vant to know if I can verk here after harvest is over—for a few more months to take care of the horzes. The mare is with de foal and needs good care. In my country, I vork at a horze farm since I vas a little girl."

"*Oui, bien!* I would agree but must first check with my *maman*."

When we walked away, I turned to Julien. "Do you think Sara will want Fifika to extend her stay? She doesn't much care for her from what I've seen."

"The woman is a good worker. And she's right that Adèle will need special care. It can be dangerous for a horse her age to foal. It's bad that Thierry let her get . . . how do you say in English—knocked down?"

"Close," I giggled. "Knocked up."

"*Maman* surprised me with the horse when I was ten. I used to gallop her for miles and jump logs and hedges around the region. She was brave and took her best care of me. Now I want to have someone who knows horses tending to her. Someone to call the vet when her time is near and be on hand when the foal arrives. I'm sure *Maman* will agree to that."

• • •

"Don't you two look happy!" Sara said as she took a seat at the lunch table next to Julien while we feasted on grilled corn, poached chicken, and purple asparagus glazed with butter. "Love is in the air. I was hoping for that."

We looked at each other and smiled through our chomping. "Just don't tell Henri," Julien said as he put down the bare cob and moved on to the chicken. "Better yet, tell him. Let him feel foolish for telling those lies about me to Samantha."

"He exaggerated when he spoke about you. I'll give you that," Sara said.

"*Exaggerated?*" I looked at Julien.

"Please, *Maman*, don't get me in trouble with my new girlfriend."

"My lips are sealed," she said as she gave him a playful jab with her fist.

"I hope you're fine with some more news," Julien said. "Fifika has offered to stay past harvest to take care of the horses. She says she knows much about their care. I like that plan with Adèle being in foal."

"I don't know, baby. That woman annoys me."

"I say give her a chance. If anything happens to that horse, I couldn't bear it."

"Alright. A chance. If she proves to be indispensable, she can stay on. If not, she leaves with the others." Sara turned to me and smiled. "And what about you, Sam? What are your plans after harvest?"

"She's going to stay with us through Beaujolais Nouveau Day," Julien said.

"I *am?*"

"You are. When is it this year, *Maman*? The twenty-first of November?"

"Sounds right," said Sara.

He took my hand. "There's plenty more for you to do here. If you're serious about making your own wine someday. Preparing the vineyard for the winter, topping off the barrels, tasting the wine to check against bacteria. Plus, I want you to learn how we get our wine to market."

"Sounds like I'll be busy through Beaujolais Nouveau Day," I said, looking from Julien to Sara. But what I'd be doing after that, I had no clue.


*Montmartre, Paris June 1936*

Vivian used her palms to smooth the hips of the seated female form that she was creating in her sculpture class. Though she loved working in clay, she wished that the life models, who were students working off tuition that read and smoked cigarettes during the sitting, would strike more inspiring poses and make use of the props in the studio's costume box. She'd often circumvent their laziness by sculpting a chunky necklace into her creation, or a pillbox hat adorned with feathers. But on that day, Vivian just wanted the class to end so she could pay a visit to Marciel, who she hadn't seen since their one and only encounter. The stress of breaking off with Enzo had caused her monthly curse to arrive a week early. And she didn't dare pay her new love a visit while encumbered by the elastic belt that kept a sanitary napkin affixed to her private area. With that mess over with, she now ached for the painter's touch.

•   •   •

After climbing the three narrow flights of steps to Marciel's garret, Vivian heard the music of Josephine Baker floating through the door. She pushed it open a crack, and saw the artist at his easel, working at that same fervent pace that told her he was creating another work that had the power to set her soul on fire.

"I've returned to you, my darling," she sang out as she walked through the door. "Did I come at a bad time? I'm not one to interrupt such talent at work."

"Hello, *Vivienne!* Where have you been?" he asked. "My heart has cried out for you. But I have wonderful news! Come and see what you've started." He stepped away from the canvas to give her a look. The painting was of a nude woman. A strange woman.

"Who . . . who is this?"

"Allegra. Lovely, isn't she? Though two decades older than you, time has aged her to perfection." He pointed past the painting where a naked woman with long, dark hair and cat-like eyes reclined on the chaise with a glass of Champagne in her hand. "You've brought me good fortune, *Vivienne!* The *galerie* sold your portrait! *Mon ami* displayed the piece in their window. They sold it that same day to a fine gentleman for fifty francs! It's more than enough to pay Allegra's fee and my rent for the rest of the year."

"Oh . . . oh . . . oh, I see," Vivian stammered.

"Stay with me tonight, *mon amour!*"

"Tonight? Oh . . . oh, of course I will!" she said, breathing a sigh of relief that things hadn't changed between them. "For a moment, I wondered if you still wanted me!"

"Yes, I still want you," he said. "And to add even more fun, Allegra will join us in our bed! *Plus on est de fous, plus on rit!* Or as they say in the States, the more the merrier! And I promise that she doesn't snore as loud as I do."

Vivian stood frozen, sickened by the artist's perverse suggestion. "Na . . . na . . . no . . . no, I don't. I don't think so," she said, as she backed away from Marciel before she hurried out the door and scrambled down the stairs.

•    •    •

Acids from Vivian's stomach rose to her throat as she made her way through the tourists that fill the streets of Paris in June. For the first time since she'd crossed the Atlantic, she longed to be back with her parents and sisters in the safety net of the world she grew up in. A world where men and women only lay down with those they'd married or had plans to marry. When her tears dried, and her ability to reason returned, she shifted the focus of her disgust from Marciel to herself. She was a fool to think this Bohemian artist, a bachelor and grown man, would commit himself to a girl he barely knew. And she was a fool by yielding to her sexual yearnings and destroying her chance for a life with Enzo. Though her body would never pulsate with desire for him the way it had for Marciel, Enzo was a good man with a promising future who adored her.

With tear-filled eyes, she looked up at the enormous white domes of the Basilica du Sacré-Coeur, the Byzantine-style church that towers over Paris from its perch atop the hill of Montmartre. She'd read in the city's guidebooks that two thousand years before, the ancient Romans had built monuments dedicated to their gods Mercury and Mars on that same site. She shuddered, knowing that whatever supreme beings had now claimed that site as their own would laugh at her naïveté.

# six

---

**Fruit Bomb** *n.* industry term for a high alcohol, high sugar, overly ripe wine

"I'm not that impressed with this Ultraviolet Merlot, Benson. I taste the black cherry and currants on the upper palate, but the fruit is way overripe. Did your boss have you throw that canned grape concentrate into the mix?"

"Yes, he did, Miss Turnball," Benson admitted.

Phyllis Turnball had been tasting a bottle of Ashton White's wine that Benson had brought over from Napa. Though the London critic wasn't a fan, the last five releases of the brand had earned 100-point scores from the most powerful wine critic in America, Regis Preston, whose reviews appeared in *Wine Snob Magazine.*

"I'm sad to say your American critic loves these sugary wines that California cranks out," Phyllis continued, speaking in an amplified voice because of her hearing impairment. "It also helps that Ashton White has been spending his entire advertising budget on ads in Preston's magazine."

"It's fine to criticize Regis Preston, but let's not pick on Benson," Julien told Phyllis. "He doesn't enjoy adding all that sugar to the wine. But he needs to eat."

Julien and Sara were hosting a bon voyage dinner in the dining room of the château for Benson, Dalton, and Phyllis on the last night of their visit. The room's massive cherrywood dining table held platters of pulled pork, wild rice, baked bread, French heirloom squash, Tuscan kale, purple tomatoes, and umpteen bottles of wine. My contribution to the meal would be an airy hazelnut mousse with dark chocolate, cream, eggs, expresso, salt, and sugar, that I whisked, beat, and folded under the watchful eyes of Sara and Gigi the cook.

"I have a question for you, Phyllis," I said to the wine critic. "How do you think California wines compare to the wines from out here?"

"Two different parts of the world, with different styles of winemaking. Here in France, the goal is to make a wine that reflects the vineyard and the history of the domaine. Aside from having a few great smaller production wines, California is the land of monster wineries hell-bent on appealing to the widest consumer base." She put her arms around several other bottles that Benson had brought out from Napa and pulled them toward her. "But change may come there, thanks to younger wine drinkers who know a tricked-up brand from one that reflects its origin."

I turned to Julien, who was sitting next to me with his arm slung over my shoulder. He gave me a knowing wink and rubbed my arm. It occurred to me that no matter where I went to make my wine or how much acclaim my wine achieved, finding success as a winemaker would mean nothing without having him by my side.

"So, tell me, Dalton," Sara said to the restaurateur in her low melodic voice. Her husband had opted out of the dinner to catch a soccer match at a local bar. "What are your favorite Manhattan restaurants? We used to be regulars at Tavern on the Green and the Oyster Bar at Grand Central." She cupped her chin in her palms and had that same look in her eyes that she had when she told me about her relationship with Spence. I was certain she was speaking about him when she used the term we.

"Those classics are all still there," Dalton said. "But Asian is huge these days."

"I love Asian food . . . so healthy and pure. With none of those heavy meats and sauces the French are famous for," Sara said with a touch of regret in voice. I noticed that she'd consumed a lot more than her usual two glasses of Burgundy, and I wondered . . . if she had the chance to do it all again, would she still choose this life? She lived in a castle fit for a queen, had two hardworking sons, and a thriving family business. But there was a sadness about her. She elbowed me. "I need a break before dessert," she whispered. "Let me show you our *salon*. You and Julien always hang out in the kitchen or dining room when you're here." I followed her down the hall and past the grand staircase through an arched entry into the cavernous living room with huge Persian carpets, buttery-soft leather sofas, life-sized sculptures, and a gallery of paintings on the walls.

"Did *you* collect these paintings, Sara?" I asked her. "Spence mentioned that you studied interior design in college."

"I did. With a minor in art history. And yes, I found these. Some at galleries, some online, some at thrift stores. Most are Parisian oils from 1900 through 1940. It was such an exciting, innovative time in the world of art."

"It must have been glorious to live in Paris before the war," I said. "A moveable feast, as Hemingway called it." After studying the dizzying array of styles and techniques, my eyes rested on a nude. "This one reminds me of an oil that my late great-aunt left me." I pointed to the painting. "She posed for it. Worked as a life model in Paris in the 1930s. A guy she'd been engaged to bought it from a gallery. The artist was an unknown. At least, to me. It's a pretty cool-looking piece though."

"If you have a shot of it on your phone, I'd love to see it," Sara said, brightening at the thought of checking out a new old painting.

"I don't. But I can ask my dad to snap a pix. He's moved out of the house in Larchmont where my mom still lives and in with me. I hope it's short-lived, but their marriage has been touch-and-go for a while."

"I'm sorry about that, Sam. Family problems are no fun."

"Yeah, they suck," I said, feeling a twinge of my old anxiety creeping through. In need of a distraction, I walked over to the room's massive stone fireplace that had a carving of the family crest in the center with a lion on a feudal banner—the same design that was on the label of the domaine's wine. Over the mantle stood several rows of empty LeMont wine bottles, each with a tiny leather drawstring bag affixed to it by a delicate gold chain. "This must be the collection Julien told me about. Wine made by his ancestors, opened to celebrate family milestones. Can I look?"

"Please do. This is the one LeMont tradition that tells me I'm a part of this legacy. Whenever I pass by these shelves, they remind me we're all just one small link of a long chain. And that love is the only thing that matters during our blip of time on earth."

"Amen to that," I said while scanning the rows of bottles that dated back to the 1850s. Each one sat on a wooden stand with a brass plate engraved with the name of the person, or people it honored, and the date the wine had been consumed. A small sheet of paper was rolled up in each of the bags. My eyes settled on the year 1984.

"1984 . . . Henri's birth date?"

"Yes," she said.

I looked at the next bottle in the row. "1992 . . . Julien's birth. He told me about your tasting note. Pretty sweet." I looked at the next one.

"Marie Louise Plumet. Died in 1990. Who was she?"

"She was the unmarried sister to Julien's *grand-mère*, Céleste. Born and raised in a wine dynasty like this one but joined her sister here when Céleste married Gaston. She saw me as an outsider—didn't think I belonged on the Côte. Maybe she was right."

The next bottle in the row had the date 1996. I read the name on the plate. "Zelda Parker LeMont. Died in 1996. Was she another aunt of Henri and Julien?"

"No, she wasn't their aunt. She would have been their sister," Sara answered, her voice soft. "1996 was the year my daughter Zelda should have been born."

"Your daughter?"

She picked up the bottle from the stand with care, gently slid the note from the bag, and unrolled it. "My tasting notes on the wine were right on. It was a sparkling white produced in 1928—the only year that vintage was made. Mildew destroyed the vines the following year. I wrote that it was as bubbly, as bright, and as beautiful as my new baby girl was to be. But she was not to be." She slowly replaced the note and returned the bottle to the stand.

"Oh, Sara, I'm so sorry."

"I've told no one the truth about this. Couldn't tell the boys. Didn't want any 'I told you sos' from my parents. The neighbors might have put two and two together, but never said a word about it."

"Are you sure you want to tell *me*, Sara?" It worried me that the wine had loosened her inhibitions. But she kept right on talking.

"We were coming home from a neighbor's Christmas party. I was in my sixth month. It was late. Denis had been drinking heavily. Being pregnant, I hadn't touched a drop. I begged him to let me drive, but he wouldn't hear of it. The roads around here aren't lit and can be tough to navigate even while sober. I asked him to slow down several times during the ride and breathed a sigh of relief when we turned onto the road leading to the château. Seconds later, he drove us head on into one of those massive oak trees. Denis didn't have a scratch, but Zelda and I weren't so lucky. The impact brought on a miscarriage that marked the end of my fairytale."

### Montmartre, Paris June 1936

Walking at a furious pace with no destination in mind, Vivian put her hands over her ears to block the incessant beeping of horns and the screeching of tires that muted all other sounds in a city ill prepared to handle the hundreds of thousands of Citroëns, Renaults, and Peugeots that had taken over its streets. After her visit to Marciel's, she felt as if someone had stabbed her in the gut with an iron sword. Tortured by a painful combination of revulsion and heartbreak, she knew she could no longer stomach posing nude for artists, which meant that she'd soon have no way to pay for her room and board or even continue her classes at *L'Académie*. Perhaps her parents had been right by saying she had her head in the clouds when she told them she was moving to France.

Upon reaching the banks of the Seine, she looked across the river to the Île de la Cité and the Conciergerie prison where the French revolutionaries held Marie-Antoinette. Vivian couldn't help but compare herself to the young queen who had once believed she could rule the world before her own world came crashing down. While thoughts of that beautiful head being sliced off at the guillotine two centuries ago sent shivers down her spine, the chime from the 700-year-old clock on the prison tower brought her back to the present. She realized she was late meeting a good friend who worked at a dress shop on the Boulevard Saint-Germain and needed help in selecting the perfect ensemble for some very tough customers.

. . .

"This is atrocious, Mummy!" Vivian heard a young woman cry out when she entered Le Jardin Chic boutique. "We came here to find something *au courant!* Something splendid! This is 1936 Paris! Not turn of the century Nottingham!"

"We'll find something that pleases you, *mademoiselle,*" Vivian's friend Odette assured the young customer as the shop girl exited the dressing room, her arms piled high with frilly gowns of various pastel colors. Seeing that Vivian had arrived, Odette rolled her eyes at her and mouthed the word "Help!" Aware that her fellow boardinghouse resident was struggling to pay off her husband's loans from law school, Vivian knew it was crucial for Odette to satisfy these clients and keep her job.

"Well, I think that dress is just grand, Victoria!" the girl's mother insisted as she followed her daughter out of the dressing room.

"I don't want grand! I want ravishing! Sultry! Alluring! Cecil Hortense will be at the affair, and I won't catch his eye for a bloody moment if I'm entrapped in this thing. It . . . it makes me look like an English granny!" Victoria said, accenting her words with a stomp of her foot. When she saw Vivian, she pointed to her. "This girl agrees that it's awful! Tell them it's awful," she commanded while looking down at the white organza high waisted dress she had on with its full skirt, enormous puffed sleeves, and a neckline so high that it seemed to choke her.

"Where is Madame La Farge?" the girl's mother asked as she glanced at her diamond and platinum banded wristwatch. "She promised to meet us by four o'clock."

"Madame Le Farge extends her apologies to you, Madame Leon," Odette said, appearing as if she was about to burst into tears. "She had hoped to be here today to assist you, but she had to extend her buying trip to Milan and won't return until tomorrow. She entrusted me to help you ladies in your selection."

"You haven't helped us so far," Victoria cried out. "You've done nothing but wasted our time."

Sensing Odette's rising panic, Vivian put a reassuring hand on her friend's arm and shuffled through the boutique's rack of gowns. When the perfect one caught her eye, she swept it off its hanger. "Have you seen Carol Lombard in the picture *My Man Godfrey*, Victoria?" she asked the girl while affecting a crisp French accent. "It's hilarious! Mademoiselle Lombard plays an enchantingly beautiful socialite who hires a vagabond as her family's butler. But little do they know that the man is richer than they are! It's all heaps of fun, and Mademoiselle Lombard looks like a Greek goddess in a silk slip dress just like this one." Vivian held the emerald green garment toward Victoria and stroked the shimmering fabric. "But this piece may be too risqué for the affair you're planning to attend."

Staring at the gown, Victoria's petulant frown transformed into a look of wide-eyed wonder. "Oh, no, it's not too risqué. It's not too risqué at all," she said as she took the dress from Vivian's arms and held the flowing fabric against her body. "I'm sure this will do just fine." She hurried back into the dressing room, clutching the garment, with her mother trotting behind.

"Here let me help you, *mademoiselle*. These slip dresses can be quite a bother to get into," Odette said as she joined the two women behind the curtain. In less than a minute, the girl reappeared with chin held high and gave several slow twirls in front of the store's large mirror.

"It's just splendid!" she cried with a wide grin while turning sideways to admire the way the sleeveless and near backless garment with the plunging neckline hugged every curve of her voluptuous young body.

"Oh my, I don't know if that's suitable for a girl your age," the girl's mother said, wringing her hands together. "It's very form-fitting and shows so much skin. People may not take kindly to a seventeen-year-old-girl in something that revealing. Maybe try another—"

"No worries at all! This should keep tongues from wagging," Vivian interrupted, as she grabbed an oversized silver scarf with an emerald-colored fringe and placed it around the girl's shoulders to create a more modest look. She then selected a sequined evening bag with a gold chain and handed it to the girl. From the store's window display, she took a silk beret sporting white ostrich plumes and set it at a tilt on the girl's head. "Now with a pair of matching silk pumps, you'll be the belle of the ball, and still look the proper young lady."

"Oh, I do love it all, Mummy!" Victoria said, striking a series of poses in front of the mirror. "Cecil Hortense will go positively gaga when he sees me. You must let me have it! You must!" she cried, as Odette held her breath while waiting for the woman to respond.

"Well," the mother began. "I'm sure these items are all steep." She circled her daughter and examined the price tag that hung from the back of the dress. "Very steep! But you look lovely in them, Victoria." She looked at Odette. "Please wrap them up for me and put them on my account. And thank you, young woman," she said to Vivian. "You have a special talent for styling fashion. Even if the French accent is less than genuine."

# seven

---

**Armagnac** *n.* France's oldest brandy, once believed to heal wounds, embold wit, instill bravery, prevent senility, reduce flatulence, and restore the paralyzed member

It was the second week in October. Harvest at Domaine LeMont was officially over. The harvest workers had taken down their tents, leaving the field rutted and muddy as they drove off in their cars, trucks, motorhomes, and campers. Having been relieved of their bounty, the miles of vines looked eerily stark. Thierry, the vineyard manager, was teaching me the methods his crew would use to aerate or "earth up" the soil to protect the roots from the rigors of winter. Despite the chill in the air, beads of sweat dripped from my forehead as I furiously thrust my spade into the earth to work the soil. When my phone dinged with a text, one glance at the screen sent my heart beating even faster.

**Julien:** Pack an overnight bag for Paris. Pick u up in 1 hr

"Yes! Yes! Yes!" I cried out, causing Thierry to put his rapid-fire assault of the clumps on pause to find the cause for my celebration. Though I was obsessed with every aspect related to the creation of wine, the exodus of those heading back to city life over the past few days had given me the urge to feel some urban energy and check out some fantastic clothing stores, if only to window shop.

•   •   •

"I needed this! How'd you read my mind?" I asked Julien, while the two of us headed down Mont Brouilly in the Range Rover.

"Everyone needs to change out their scenery every so often." He took my hand and gave it a kiss.

"True, but who would want to change out this scenery?" I asked, as I feasted my eyes on the panoramic views from the car window. The rolling hills, mountains, and valleys that were an expanse of green two months before were now aflame with the reds and burnt umbers of autumn. With our duffels in the back and a chill in the air, I felt like a college girl again, leaving my home in Larchmont after the long summer break and driving to upstate New York through the vibrant-colored foliage of the Adirondack Mountains.

That's when the realization hit. I did feel like I was leaving home. Domaine LeMont was the closest thing I had to a home. And though our love was new, Julien and his family had made me feel like one of their own. Sara shared recipes passed down by the domaine's women for generations, Denis always had a new story about the struggles of the Gamay grape, *grand-père* Gaston continued to give me pointers on the cleaning of his old machines, and *grand-mére* Céleste used every opportunity to get me conversational in French. On her daily visit to the winery to bring Gaston his coffee and croissant, she would barrage me with questions like: "*Que porte l'avocat sur sa tête dans les chambres?*" (What does the barrister wear on his head while in chambers?) or "*À quelle heure le chef pâstissier met-il les pains au four?*" (What time does the pastry chef put the buns in the oven?)

"The end of harvest is a good time for a break," Julien told me as we headed north. "And I've been wanting for you to see Paris."

"I *have* seen Paris. I've toured the Louvre and every other museum, ridden down the Seine in a boat, climbed the Eiffel Tower—"

"You've seen Paris the way a tourist sees it. I want you to see it like you live there."

· · ·

"This is so cool," I cried out when Julien guided me through the doors of the historic and legendary shopping mecca, Le Bon Marché Rive Gauche, the store nineteenth-century novelist Émile Zola once called the "cathedral of modern commerce." One look at the beautiful people inside, the fabulous items on display, the stunning design of the place, told me that this was where the hip Parisians shop. There were indoor steel bridges that stretched up through the man-made clouds, art deco ceilings, and balustrade-crowned mezzanines. There was furniture, wine, food, jewelry, along with dazzling collections of designer clothing. All fabulously pricey.

"What size are you?" Julien asked, leading me to a display of women's swimsuits set on a sandy beach complete with palm trees and a miniature ocean.

"Hmmm . . . I was a size eight in New York." I grabbed the belt loops of my jeans and felt the extra room at the waist. "Feels like I'm back to a six, though." Julien was now shuffling through the sexy, the sensational, and the seriously expensive suits on display. "But I'm not buying anything *here*. And I sure don't need a swimsuit in October!"

"*I* am buying you a swimsuit. Choose one, *s'il te plaît*." He held them against my torso, one after another, without even glancing at the price tags. "You will need one tonight."

"Tonight? Are you kidding? You're not!" But even if I would need a suit, I didn't want him to pay the €300 the store was asking for those minuscule pieces of fabric. As a compromise, I selected the most economical suit in the bunch—a red, one-piece Speedo priced at €35 euros.

· · ·

We followed up our shopping excursion with a visit to a wine bar near the Moulin Rouge to meet some of Julien's friends from college. If it wasn't for Bob Dylan, Fats Domino, and Amy Winehouse blasting through the speakers, and the hundreds of wine bottles lining the walls, the place could have passed as an elementary school classroom. There were rows of shiny red tables with chairs. A chalkboard on the wall had that day's selection of wines available by the glass; a New Zealand Cab Franc, a Spanish Palomino, a South African Chenin Blanc, a Chilean Barbera, an Italian Impigno. I was excited to see an Armagnac on the board, a brandy produced in Gascony, where my Aunt Vivian and Uncle Freddy spent their honeymoon after World War II ended.

"*Bonjour, Julien! Ça fait trop longtemps, mon ami! Comment allez-vous?*" A group of eight young men and women called out their greetings from a table near the bar. The men all looked sharp in their Ferragamo shoes, Apple watches, and Hermès dress shirts and slacks, while the perfectly polished women sported chic haircuts, the latest looks in office attire, and nails displaying hot new trends in French manicures. All had glasses of wine in their hands.

"Say hello to Samantha, *mon amour* from America," Julien told the group as he put his arm around me. "She's not all that sure with her French, so use your English where you can."

I met Cedric and Fabre, both medical residents at Clinique de Turin; Ava, a journalist with *le Parisien*; Claire, a financial analyst for *Crédit Lyonnais*; Michelle and Colette, attorneys for Uber Paris. Julien handed me the brandy in a tall, fluted glass, and we all sat down for snacks.

"*Asseyez vous s'il vous plaît,*" Ava instructed, as she pulled out two chairs at a table for me to sit with her and three other women. Tiny burgers, cheese croquettes, pancetta stuffed mushrooms, and other snacks began to arrive at the table.

"*Parlez-moi des vins de cette année,*" the proprietor of the bar called out to Julien as he waved from across the room.

"Maxime wants me to tell him about this year's vintages," my boyfriend explained to me. "*Le travail avant le plaisir!* Or business before pleasure, as they say in your country." He gave me a quick kiss on the side of my mouth as he got up from the table. "You can do some *femelle* bonding."

After Julien walked away, Michelle looked up at me while she peeled the roll back from one of the tiny burgers and dabbed mustard on it with a minuscule spoon. "So, it looks like you and our friend are quite serious, *oui*?"

"Well, um . . ." With four pairs of eyes on me, I took a moment to inhale the Armagnac's aromas, hoping to extract some of Vivian's courage. But the powerful vapors nearly set my nasal passages on fire. "Wow! Speaking of serious," I said as I lowered the glass below my chin to try again. "Yeah, well . . . I guess you could say that . . . despite our differences. I'm a city girl, he's a country boy. I worked for a corporation, and he grew up in a family busi—"

"There are other differences," Colette interrupted, as she gingerly used her thumb and index finger to lift a croquette trailed by strings of cheese still affixed to the serving tray. "Differences you may not be aware of yet," she added before she guided the gooey concoction into her mouth.

"We hoped that he would remain with us in Paris after *l'université*," Claire said.

"But he loves the domaine, which is why he stayed with *la famille*," added Ava, who looked Julien's way to make sure he was out of earshot. "Even though he could have had any career that he wanted."

"And any woman he wanted," Michelle said.

"He broke many hearts," Colette said as she gathered her mane of black hair and pulled it across her shoulder. I wondered if one of those hearts belonged to her.

"What is this history lesson you two are sharing with Julien's *amour*?" Cedric asked the women as he sat down with us. "We all had much growing up to do while at *l'université*," he told me. "And I now see that, unlike some of us . . ." he looked from Ava to Michelle to Colette. "My friend Julien has grown up well."

"Maybe he has," said Colette as she eyed Julien from across the room. "But some things never change."

"Like what?" I asked, daring her to finish her thought before she popped another snack in her mouth.

"It's still a very different culture here than what you have in the States."

"Of course, it is. I know that."

"Good. Just so you are aware. If you go in, you have to do it with eyes wide open."

· · ·

"Your friends had a lot to say about you and our cultural differences," I told Julien when we were on our way to what he called his family's city place.

"I'm glad you got to meet each other. We were all close at *l'université*. And now our lives have gone in different directions."

"By the way the women were talking, I got the feeling Colette is an old girlfriend of yours. Sounded like things didn't end well. That true?"

"My friends are smart and successful. But the women can sometimes be queens of drama. You must take what they say with a bit of salt."

"You still haven't answered my question."

"*Excuse-moi, mademoiselle,* what question?"

"Hmmm . . . seems I'm not gonna get an answer. Then maybe you could tell me why I need a bathing suit in October?"

"You're about to find out."

A few minutes later, we drove up a hill and through a wrought iron entrance to a neighborhood of stone houses set on rolling green hills. Julien parked in a driveway and escorted me up a path lined with flowering bushes and trees that led to a building that looked more like a museum than someone's home. He banged the heavy bronze knocker against the door. A woman with grey hair and an apron tied over a black and white garment soon greeted us.

"*Bonsoir, Julien! Comment allez-vous?*" The woman turned to me. "*Bonsoir, mademoiselle.*"

"Samantha, this is Simone."

"*Bonsoir,* Simone," I said with a smile.

"*Votre chambre est prête,*" she told Julien.

"*Merci.*" He turned to me. "We'll put our bags in our room."

"You might have mentioned that your family's city place was a mansion," I told him as we walked up the wide, winding staircase that split off into two sections on the second floor of the building.

"Sorry," he said with a shrug of his shoulders. "I didn't want you to think I am a spoiled rich boy."

"I know you're not spoiled." I took his hand and gave it a squeeze. "Spoiled boys don't work from dawn to dusk, spend hours teaching newbies like me, and stress about the well-being of a middle-aged horse."

Though the structure of the city place spoke of timeless grandeur, sections of the carpet were frayed, the drapes torn, the mahogany floors chipped and scratched.

"Our family spent many happy times here when I was small. You can see it's much in need of restoration." He pointed to the faded wallpaper that had scenes of ladies and gents being ferried in horse-drawn carriages. Sections of the paper had peeled away to reveal hand-painted flowers, birds, nymphs, and cupids that covered the walls in a prior century. "The house is part of the LeMont family trust set up by my *grands-parents*. It was once owned by the House of Bonaparte and acquired by my ancestor Louis LeMont prior to his purchase of the domaine. *Maman* says she'll take on its *rénovation* for her next project. But I don't think she has that kind of interest anymore."

"Seems like bringing this place back to its heyday would be a blast for Sara." Looking down at the parlor below us, I pictured little girls in petticoats doing cartwheels and boys in silk breeches playing jacks while a young lady played a minuet on the room's grand piano. And I couldn't help thinking that renovating that house would be a blast for me as well.

•   •   •

After settling into our bedroom, Julien had us change into our swimsuits. I assumed there was a hot tub on the property. We went back down the stairs with towels over our shoulders and entered a paneled room complete with a pool table and a bar that Julien said was salvaged from a retired ocean liner. When we entered the next room, I was floored by the sight of an enormous indoor swimming pool, its rippling water illuminated by sparkling underwater lights.

We frolicked in the pool like a pair of dolphins, swimming over, under, and around each other. We chased one and other through the water, and even played some Marco Polo until I pulled myself out and collapsed onto a chaise lounge. I towel dried my hair while Julien continued with his laps. He swam with a liquid-like form that sent the long muscles of his back rising and falling with the stroke of each arm. At midnight, there was a faint ringing from under his towel on the chaise. When I grabbed his phone, I saw six missed calls from Sara.

"Julien, your mom's been calling! Must be important! I'll call her back!" While I waited for her line to connect, Julien climbed out of the water and took the phone from my hand.

"*Qu'est-ce que c'est, Maman?*" He walked in circles with the phone to his ear. When he clicked off, his face was drained of color. "It's Adèle. And it's serious. We've got to go back to the domaine tonight. My horse is dying."

•     •     •

On the drive back from Paris, Julien filled me in on Adèle's plight. Because of her advanced age and the number of foals she'd delivered, the vet had warned Thierry that the horse must not have another pregnancy. But Thierry had neglected to separate the mare from the stallion when she came into season. It was later determined that there was another problem: Adèle was pregnant with twins. Because a horse's anatomy usually allows for the delivery of only one foal, the grueling labor could easily end in death for all three equines. And as Fifika had shown her experience with horses, the plan was for her to alert the vet when the mare showed the first signs of labor. It was bad timing that the vet had another emergency that night in Saint-Amour and wasn't expected before one a.m.

We reached the stables at three in the morning. Sara, Thierry, and Fifika were there, but still no sign of the vet. There was some good news: one foal, a filly, had made it out safely on her own and was taking her first wobbly steps in the stall. The second foal was yet to be born. They had tied Adèle down for her own safety, and she was whinnying and thrashing about, as a mare's instinct is to ready her newborn to run with the herd to avoid death from predators.

"The unborn foal must be backwards," Sara cried into the phone after reaching the vet. "The mare has been struggling like this for over an hour! Please tell us what to do! She's in agony! Should we take a gun and end it?"

"Give me the phone, *Maman!*" Julien said. After being filled in by the vet, he gave us the news. "There is only one way. One of us must reach inside and turn the foal into the correct position to emerge or it will soon be dead." He took a deep breath. "And Adèle will die from hemorrhage."

"I vill do it," a voice called out. It was Fifika. While Sara and Julien had been speaking to the vet, she had slid the thirty plus bracelets off each wrist, scrubbed her hands in a sink, and kneeled by Adèle. She then reached into the horse's birth canal to manipulate the position of the foal. After several minutes of Julien and I holding each other tight, and all of us holding our breaths, Fifika pulled out two tiny hooves followed by the head and the body of the foal, neatly packaged in its amniotic sac onto the waiting bed of hay. Not long after, two foals were nursing from their exhausted but healthy mother. Denis LeMont had been right. Fifika had some valuable skills, after all.

### Montmartre, Paris June 1936

The summer sun was setting and the Iron Lady—the Eiffel Tower—began her nightly exhibition of lighting up Paris with the five thousand bulbs that shimmered on her metallic structure. After leaving the dress shop, Vivian strolled back to her boarding house on the Boulevard de Clichy. On the way, she passed the Marchands de Vin wine shop, and was tempted to stop in to purchase an entire case of the lovely Romanée-Conti Burgundy that Marciel had served during her sitting. A sign in the window for classes on wine tasting piqued her interest, and another promoting a tour of French wine regions ignited a rush of excitement in her belly. While she continued her walk, something in another window caught her eye. It was the reflection of a smiling young woman. That's when she realized that her success in helping Odette find the right ensemble for her customer had lifted her spirits and softened the wrenching pain she'd felt in her gut after her visit to Marciel's garret.

"Hello, Viv," a voice surprised her from behind. It was Enzo. He was standing by the front steps of her building, holding a package wrapped in brown paper and tied up with twine. "This is for you."

Vivian stared at the package that was the same size as Marciel's painting of her. "You?" she asked, certain of what lay beneath the paper. "You were the one who bought the painting?"

"It was in a window at a gallery along the Rue Chauchat. My heart leapt when I saw it. You look so beautiful. The painter is truly a gifted artist, and now I understand why you couldn't refuse posing for such talent. You didn't betray me, Viv. You were following your dreams."

"But I did betray you, Enzo. I . . . I . . ." She stopped and stared at the earnest expression on his face. *He doesn't know what else I did. He didn't let me finish what I was trying to tell him at the café.* While she wondered if she should break his heart or remain silent, he took her hand.

"The London bank wants me to manage the Manhattan branch. I've completed my job in Paris, and I want you to go back to New York with me as my wife. We can marry at the courthouse in the Palais before we leave and honeymoon on the Queen Mary."

"What? Go back? To New York? When?"

"My job starts in three weeks."

"Three weeks? But my class . . . my sculpture. I can't finish it by then. And I want to get proficient in French. Plus, there's a costume design course next semester at *L'Académie.* I've registered for it. I think I could be good at styling clothes for stores and maybe even magazine photos. There are jobs in that field. I also want to take classes on wine tasting and tour the wine regions of—"

"You zest for life is endearing, Viv. I love that about you. But you're struggling here. You know you are. You should take my offer."

"You're right, Enzo. I am struggling." She slowly shook her head in agreement. "But I've been reading the works of a man named Dom Pérignon. He was both a winemaker and a monk. He said that 'the berry that struggles the most to survive will become the most complex and interesting fruit of all'. And Enzo . . ."

"Yes, Viv?"

"I want to be that fruit."

# eight

---

**Complexity** *n.* the layers of different aromatics, textures, and flavors that work together to make a wine interesting from the first whiff through the finish

"Good morning, my beautiful American princess," Julien said, as he brought a cup of café au lait to the bed we'd been sharing at the top of Le Petit Château. Stella raced past him, leapt onto the bed and gave me a wet kiss with her nose and tongue. "*Stella, descend-toi!*" Julien commanded.

"Don't make her get down. She wants a hug," I pleaded as I wrapped my arms around the dog's neck.

"You can't drink your café with Stella shaking the bed." He put the steaming brew on the night table and sat beside me. "Now you pay the price for being her best friend."

"She's worth it. Aren't you, girl?" I took her head in my hands.

It was the third Thursday of November, known in France as Beaujolais Nouveau Day. Trucks, cars, and motorcycles had been arriving at the winery since midnight to pick up the bottles of Domaine LeMont's new wine to deliver to restaurants and wine shops around Europe. The domaines in the Côte de Brouilly region celebrate the day with fireworks, barbecues, live music, dancing, ball games, and plenty of wine. The LeMonts were hosting this year's event.

"Every year, I drink too much, and kick myself in the morning for my pounding head. I want your first Nouveau Day to be one to remember," Julien said as he ran his finger along my collarbone and kissed my shoulder. "We'll go to my favorite *auberge* in Chablis tonight. Just you and me."

"Sounds great, babe. Though why cut your favorite party of the year short? We still have time left for a getaway." But our time together was running out. I'd already spent three months at the domaine, and French law would only permit me to stay in the country for two more weeks without a visa. For the first time in my life, I felt adrift. And though I didn't want to leave Julien, we'd yet to have a serious conversation about our future.

"There's only one person I want to spend time with tonight, so the party comes second," he assured me. "We'll leave at seven this evening, reach the *auberge* at eight, have a nice dinner, and a cozy bed. Does that work?"

"Sure! Let's do it!"

.    .    .

The domaine was being readied for the party when Julien and I arrived around noon. A volleyball net was set in a neighboring field, pigs were on the fire pit, and a local band was tuning up on the flatbed truck they would use as a stage.

Within the hour, the courtyard was packed with guests, the band was belting out the songs of the Beatles, children were playing handball and hopscotch, and Julien joined some men for a volleyball game. Sara directed her kitchen crew that refilled tray after tray of French fries and sausages. The neighboring domaines had separate stations with servers offering their newly minted wines in plastic glasses. Fifika was servicing the LeMont station, where Denis could be found drinking and kibitzing with the neighbors.

Around four p.m., a thunder of cheers erupted on the other side of the courtyard. I felt a tap on my shoulder from a man with closely cropped red hair.

"*Mademoiselle, venez jouer avec nous,*" he shouted.

"Sorry. I'm American. *Je ne parle pas français*," was the best I could offer.

"Ah, no problem!" He came closer. "I said that we need another player for our team." He pointed to where a crowd had gathered. "We have five strong competitors, but we're one woman shy," he said with a European accent I couldn't pinpoint. "Will you join us?"

I looked over at the volleyball game in progress and saw my shirtless boyfriend launch himself into the air and smash the ball over the net to score another point for his team. Eager to try my hand at the other game before cheering Julien on, I nodded my head and followed the man to the far end of the courtyard. After we made our way through the crowd, he led me to two elderly men and two middle-aged women. "I'm Alain, by the way, and you?"

"Samantha," I said, excited to be a part of the action.

"Say hi to your teammates, Samantha—Jerome, Dudley, Suzette and Élise." The four nodded, but kept their eyes locked on a teenage boy who stood inside a small circle outlined in white chalk. The boy tossed a metal ball toward a smaller wooden ball, eliciting whistles and moans as the metal ball made its way to the target. When it came to a halt, a portly old gentleman bent down to measure the distance between the two balls.

"What is this game, anyway?" I called out to Alain. "Is it Bocce?"

"*Pétanque*. It's a bit like the Bocce played in your country. The goal is to throw those hollow metal balls as close as possible to the *cochonnet*." He pointed to the small wooden ball surrounded by larger metal ones. "But you can't let your feet step outside of the circle."

When I took my turn, the shots I attempted were laughably short or way too far past the targeted *cochonnet*. But I cheered like a rabid New York Knicks fan when Jerome—who looked to be pushing ninety—used careful snail-like moves to knock away our opponent's shots and snuggle his ball up to the *cochonnet* to steal the lead for our team. I looked around to give Alain a fist bump, but he was nowhere in sight.

• • •

By five o'clock, the games had ended, the band members were packing up their gear, and the stations offering wine had disappeared. When I reached into my pocket for my phone to send Julien a text, I remembered that I'd left it in the stables that morning on one of my several daily trips to play with the filly and colt I'd named Phoebe and Duncan. Whenever I came near, the twins pranced toward me with their feather-light gaits and baby-horse whinnies. Glad to have a reason to pay them another visit, I whistled for Stella, who had been romping with a few of the neighboring dogs, and the two us started off for the stables.

When we reached the hill above the stables, the setting sun was sinking in the sky, casting long shadows on the mountains coated with the muted tones of November. I spotted Adèle grazing in the field next to the barn while Phoebe and Duncan frolicked near her. Jacques, the stallion, remained isolated from the family in his corral. The tranquil scene was disrupted when the barn door opened, and Fifika dashed out and sprinted off toward the winery, sending Stella into a barking frenzy.

The stable was strangely dark inside when I entered. I switched on a light and retrieved my phone from where I'd left it. Hearing me, Adèle let out a series of loud whinnies, as she knew it was time for the three of them to come in for the night. Puzzled that Fifika had left without bringing them in, I grabbed a halter, went out to the corral, and led the mare with foals following into the oversized stall the three shared. Then I heard the snores. They were coming from another stall down the barn aisle. Then the words. Something to the effect of *"revenez mon amour,"* followed by more snoring. I crept down the aisle, peeked in the stall, and quickly averted my eyes from a sleeping bare-assed Denis LeMont, lying in the hay with his pants around his ankles.

I pounded Julien's number on the phone.

*"Bonjour, mon amour!"*

"Julien, where are you?"

"I'm in *la maintenance.* Thierry had a problem with his truck. I'm packed and ready. Are you coming—"

"Your father's in here! At the stable! In a stall!"

"What's happened to him? What's wrong? Is he hurt?"

"No, he's not hurt. But he's very drunk and very undressed. And Fifika just left him." There was silence. "Julien, are you there?"

*"Oui."*

"Did you hear what I said?"

"I did. But . . . don't worry about it. Just let him enjoy his dreams."

"What? This isn't a joke! Your father had sex with that woman! *How sick is that?* We have to tell Sara!"

"No, Samantha, we don't. What *mon père* does is his business. And his business only."

"But what about Sara? It's her business too!"

"Maybe. But sometimes it's better for a man to do what he has to do."

"What you mean, 'what he has to do'?"

"What he must do. To keep him happy. To make him feel that he's still a man. And it has nothing to do with his wife."

"I hope you're not serious! That kind of medieval thinking went out with torture racks and chastity belts!"

"Please, Samantha. Let's not discuss this any further. Go pack your things for our trip."

"Yeah, I'll pack my things. But I'm not going on a trip with you and your chauvinistic bullshit." I clicked off and tried not to retch as tears burst from my eyes. Then I remembered Colette's words in that tasting room when she told me, "If you go in, you have to do it with eyes wide open."

· · ·

"What's wrong, Sam?" Sara asked when she opened the front door to the château and saw my tear-stained face and duffel bags in hand.

"Can I stay here tonight, Sara?"

"Sure—upstairs, first room to the left. But what's going on?"

"Your husband . . . and . . . and Fifika," I stammered.

She dropped her head and gave a long sigh. "So, he's back to his old habits, is he?"

"I just know what I saw in that stable," I said softly.

"Well, now you know . . . now you know how I fucked up my life by marrying that man."

And I knew what life would be like for me if I stayed. I walked in the house and dropped the bags I'd hastily packed from the room in the tower. They landed with a thud on the marble floors and caused the entrance hall's massive crystal chandelier to shiver. I looked at

Sara, who shut the door and locked it. "When I told Julien about it, he acted like it was nothing. He acted like it was a perfectly acceptable thing for a married man to do."

"Oh, Sam—that doesn't sound like Julien. Maybe he was embarrassed. Maybe he was ashamed to have a father who treats his mother like a sack of shit."

"No . . . he wasn't ashamed. He wasn't embarassed. I just know that it's time for me to leave." There was a banging on the door. Sara went to open it. It was Julien. He looked in and saw me.

"Samantha—why are you here?" His eyes went to my duffels that were packed with all of my clothes. "What's this? What are you doing?"

"I'm flying out tomorrow night, Julien. I've been here too long already."

"No, you can't leave! I have special plans for tonight! This is about *mon père*, isn't it? Whatever he does—it has nothing to do with us! I love you!"

"I love you too. And what you said has everything to do with us. Please go. Don't make this any harder than it has to be." I picked up my bags and began to climb the stairs. "Goodbye, Julien."

"No—it's not goodbye. Let's talk things over in the morning."

"I don't know. We'll see."

·   ·   ·

There was no chance to talk things over in the morning. As dawn was breaking through the guest room window, red and white lights circled on the ceiling above my bed. I looked outside and saw three police cars in the courtyard of the château. Julien, Sara, *grand-père* Gaston, *grandmere* Céleste, and Gigi, the cook, stood with the officers. I threw on a pair of jeans and a hoodie and ran outside where two detectives were scanning the area for fingerprints. Everyone else seemed to be talking at once.

Gigi was near hysterics as she shouted, "*Un véhicule avec un moteur à tambour, près de la cave. À trois heures du matin! Je pensais que c'était un fourgon pour recueillir le Beaujolais Noveau!*" She was saying that she'd heard a vehicle with a chugging motor arrive near the entrance to the cellar at around two a.m. and assumed it to be a late pickup of the new wine.

Gaston cried, *"Les Nazis sont revenus. Je savais qu'ils reviendraient pour prendre notre vin!"* He was saying, "The Nazis have come back! I knew they would come back to take our wine!" The sight of Julien with his arms around his sobbing grandpa broke my heart. It seemed that when the old man had risen an hour before to give the wine presses another cleaning, he noticed the little door in the façade cave hanging open. He entered the hidden cave and saw that hundreds of the oldest and most valuable bottles of the domaine's wine were gone from the shelves.

The police officer, a Sergeant Phillipo, was telling Sara and Céleste that the cellar of another winery in the area had been robbed over the summer by a pair of Romanian gypsies. He pulled up police artist sketches of the two suspects on his iPad. The first was clearly Fifika, though the blonde hair was jet black, and the name under the picture was Natasha Petralova.

"This pair has a rap sheet a mile long," Sergeant Phillipo said.

"So!" Sara called out. "That woman was a *thief!* I *knew* she was trouble! My husband didn't even bother to check her references when he let her come here." She turned to Julien. "Where is Denis, anyway?"

"Probably still in the stables, *Maman.*"

"Still sleeping off his binge in the horse shit, is he?"

"I'll bring him," Julien said, as he climbed into the Jeep and drove away.

Sergeant Phillipo pulled up the second suspect—a man with long red dreadlocks. The name Boris Romanoff was beneath the image.

"That's the man I saw driving the beat-up van that dropped Fifika at the château!" I told the group. "He was too far away for me to see much of his face, but I remember those red dreads." The more I stared at the picture, the more familiar the face became. "Hey, wait a sec. Can you give that guy short hair with your software?"

"*Oui.* Buzz? Caesar cut? *Le Crop?*" Sergeant Phillipo asked.

"Try a buzz." In a flash the red dreads were replaced with closely clipped hair. "That's him—that's Alain! My *pétanque* partner! He asked me to join his team. We played together yesterday 'til around four-thirty. He just seemed to vanish before the game ended though."

"Sounds like the plan was to keep you occupied, so Miss Petravola could do her work. Any idea why that would be?" the *officier* asked.

"I usually went to the stables each day around four to visit the foals."

"And that's where my husband had sex with that woman," Sara said. "She only wanted the fool for the key he keeps on his belt!"

Within a matter of minutes, Julien returned with Denis bouncing back and forth in the passenger's seat. "Denis! The cellar's been robbed!" Sara called out.

"What are you saying? What's going on?" he asked. "That's not possible." He felt for the key. When he pulled up his shirt, we saw the belt undone with no key.

"It's not there! That thief stole the key while you stuck your dick in her!" Sara screamed. Her face was the color of the domaine's red wine and the furrows on her normally smooth forehead looked like they'd been pounded in with a hammer and chisel.

"Please, *mon amour*," Denis pleaded. *"La clé* must have fallen off during the *fête."*

"Don't bother lying! You've committed crimes against your parents, your ancestors, and even worse . . . our descendants."

Between the shouts and the cries, I heard my Uber pull up to the front of the château. I wanted to hug Sara, Céleste, Gaston, Gigi, and thank them for housing me, feeding me, teaching me. But with the chaos in the courtyard, all I could do was slip away and ask the driver to wait while I grabbed my bags. Minutes later I was on my way to the Gare de Belleville Sur Saone train station.


*Montemarte, Paris May 10, 1940*

Vivian smoothed a touch of rouge on her cheeks and gave her amber curls a final brush in the mirror of her room at the boarding house. She glanced at the stack of letters she'd received from her parents, brothers, sisters, cousins, uncles, aunts, and grandparents during the past few weeks imploring her to return home as soon as she could arrange for passage to the United States. They all had the same reason for wanting her to leave France—the unrest in Europe due to the aggressive actions of Adolf Hitler against Germany's neighboring countries. "I love and miss you all," Vivian whispered, blowing a kiss to the letters, most of which had yet to be opened. "And I know it's near time for me to come back to you. But I can't leave now. Not when my life here is finally showing some promise."

She stepped into one of the two cotton-twill skirts she'd packed in her steamer truck before her voyage from Manhattan to Paris. While reaching behind her to close the zipper, she felt butterflies in her belly and wondered what her first day as an assistant to the assistant stylist at *Vogue Paris* magazine would hold in store.

When she climbed aboard the bus that would take her to the magazine's offices on the Rue de Monceau, Vivian was surprised by the unusual amount of chattering among the riders. Sensing the agitation in their voices, she turned to two male passengers beside her, hoping that at least one of them understood English. "Has something unusual happened this morning?" she asked them.

The man next to her turned his head in disbelief. "Good God young woman! Haven't you heard?" he asked in a French accent. "The German army has circumvented the Maginot Line and marched into France. We've been invaded! If you have any good sense at all, you'll head to the travel office today and book passage back to wherever you came from."

"Don't scare the poor child, François," the man beside him said while folding up the issue of *The Paris Tribune* that he'd been reading. "Hitler's gang is just trying to send a message to England's bright-eyed and bushy-tailed prime minister," he told Vivian. "I'm sure that the Germans will slink back and go about their business in a week or so."

"Oh, you are the eternal optimist, my friend," François said with a shake of his head.

•　　•　　•

Vivian walked up the timeworn limestone steps of the palatial seventeenth-century building on the Rue Cambacérès that housed the offices of *Vogue Paris*. After entering the oversized elevator, she shoved her palm against the button to the fourth floor where she'd had her interview the previous week and been hired to perform whatever rudimentary tasks were required during the fashion shoots for the illustrious publication. She'd been instructed to check in with the floor receptionist who would direct her to the studio where the shoot for the October issue of the magazine would take place. When she arrived at the reception area that had been a bustling hub the previous week, it was empty save for the two men guiding metal racks packed with satin evening gowns, capes, stoles, hats, scarves, costume jewelery, and shoes.

"*Bonjour?*" Vivian called through an open doorway. She checked her watch. It was nine a.m. "***Bonjour!***" she called louder.

"*Bonjour!*" From a cavernous room, a woman's voice rang out accompanied by a recording of Edith Pilaf playing on a phonograph. "*Entrer! Le plaisir est ici dedans!*" Vivian followed the direction of the voice and entered the room where men were setting up lights and white screens for a photo shoot, and two gangly women with high cheek bones and chiseled noses sat under conical-shaped hair dryers. "*Où sont les robes nuisettes? J'ai dit a cet imbécile Maxine d'envoyer trois sur le rack!*" The welcoming voice she'd heard just seconds ago now sounded angry.

"*Désolé, madame. Nous ne sommes que les transporteurs,*" one of the men who'd delivered the rack of clothing told the woman, who was now stepping out from behind the hanging gowns. In her cream-colored trousers, flowing silk blouse, and with several rows of pearls encircling her neck, she reminded Vivian of a British royal on a country holiday. When the woman spotted Vivian, her thin red lips stretched into a wide smile that revealed two rows of shiny white teeth.

"*Ah! Notre directeur artistique est arrivé! Comment allez-vous? Je suis Coco Chanel,*" she said as she held out her hand.

"Coco Chanel!" Vivian gasped, her voice trembling. "Oh . . . oh good gracious! "Coco! I mean . . . Miss Chanel! I had no idea!" she stammered as she took her hand. Standing next to the celebrated owner of the House of Chanel, Vivian was surprised that the woman looked more like a tiny mouse than the bigger than life icon she'd seen in newspaper and magazine photos both at home and in Paris.

"Please, darling, do call me Coco," the woman said with a thick French accent. "With that naughty boy Adolf Hitler stirring up all sorts of trouble, I wasn't even sure if we'd have enough crew for our shoot. I've put in three calls to the magazine's editor about this, but he seems more concerned about covering the brouhaha on the border and less about my photo spread. Does he not know that fashion is what sells the magazine?"

"Well, I wouldn't have missed my first day at *Vogue*, no matter what's happening in the world out there," Vivian said.

"That's the spirit!" Coco said with hands on hips. "And I can assure you that the Nazi party isn't really as bad as all that. Things will settle down as soon as we all learn how to get along. But what do you mean 'your first day'? You are Mademoiselle Ponté, the *directeur artistique* of the magazine, are you not?"

"*Directeur artistique*? Me? Oh, no! I'm Vivian Goodyear—an assistant. Actually, an assistant's assistant."

Coco looked Vivian up and down and gave an approving glance at the way the girl's wide leather belt, ruffled skirt, and crepe blouse added a casual-chic flair to her hourglass figure. "Well, whatever you are, I can see you've got a keen sense of fashion. Now, help me select the gowns that'll make the women of France wrap themselves in Chanel for every affair during this year's holiday season."

# nine

---

**Sabering Champagne** *n.* the act of removing the top from a
Champagne bottle with a sword

"Peanuts? Juice? Soda? Care to purchase a cocktail?" the Air France
flight attendant asked me and the other passengers that were
crammed into the rows of narrow coach seats for the nine-hour trip
back to New York. I considered buying a martini to knock myself out,
but since I hadn't earned a cent over the past two and a half months, I
couldn't justify the extravagance. After paying off my credit card for
flights, hotel, food, and clothes, the twenty-five thousand I had socked
away in the bank had shrunk to twenty. And though I had no idea
where I'd be heading, Julien's friend Benson had said that a truck is a
must for any sort of winemaking job—be it for hauling bins of grapes
to the winery, last minute pickups of wine barrels, or schlepping
dozens of cases of wine from the warehouse to stores and restaurants.
And trucks don't come cheap. So instead of a martini, I opted for apple
juice. I also took the peanuts that, since I hadn't sprung for a crêpe-to-
go or any other pricey airport snacks, would have to serve as a late
dinner.

• • •

The music through my headphones blocked the snores of the man
sitting next to me and the motion of the aircraft rocked me like a cradle.

I took a pillow from its plastic bag, stuffed it behind my head, and squeezed my knees to my chest. In one of the last dreams I remembered, sheep were dotting the hills and cows were reclining in groups as the Range Rover began its descent into a valley illuminated by stars. A cobblestone bridge took us over a pond laced with water lilies to the gravel driveway of a French château covered by vines of yellowing ivy. Though I hadn't eaten for hours, the cravings I felt in my belly that were growing stronger with every passing minute weren't for food——they were for Julien. I looked up at the windows of the rooms and yearned to crawl with him under the downy comforter of that billowy bed I'd seen on the hotel's website.

Our meal at the restaurant began with a bottle of Krug Grande Cuvée that was sabered by the server with a sword that he'd told us was once owned by a Napoleonic warrior. The bubbles were vivacious, the Champagne full of herbs on the nose, with a lovely lemony fruitiness on the palate. Julien ordered us each a ranch ribeye with bordelaise sauce accompanied by pumpkin ricotta gnocchi and broiled baby kale finished with sea salt. Between sips of the bubbly, he took a shot at reading my palm. The lines in it told him that my future held beautiful children, bountiful harvests, and lasting love. Then the servers came toward us with our meals and the aromas had my mouth watering. When our plates were lowered to the table, they landed with a thunderous jolt, the lights above us blinked, and a roaring filled my head. The dinging intercom and the captain's welcome to New York's JFK airport were the rudest awakening of my life.

·  ·  ·

After clearing customs, I climbed into the shuttle for the trip to my mom's house. The Long Island Expressway was packed with early morning commuters, and my view of New York from the van wasn't pretty. Like the start of that old song my Aunt Suzie used to sing while she strummed her guitar, "All the leaves were brown, and the sky was grey." The lack of sunshine and the sad, bare trees lining the roads set the perfect backdrop for my mood. As we crossed the Whitestone Bridge and headed toward the I-95 North, I checked my phone for the latest edition of *Wine Business Daily*. The headline announced that a second historic Beaujolais domaine had been victimized by thieves. The story went on to relate the details of the robbery that I knew all too much about. Before I had the chance to finish reading it, I got a text from Benson Doyle. Though I hadn't seen Benson in over a month, I'd texted him before the flight to ask if we might have a conversation at some point about possible entry level jobs that he might come across in the wine industry. I was surprised to hear back from him so soon.

**Benson:** Hi from Napa. Owner of our winery needs bookkeeper—thought of u

**Sam:** In NYC now. Still not sure where I'm headed

**Benson:** Lemme know if interested

**Sam:** Will do

The taxi exited the New England State Thruway and made its way onto the Saw Mill River Parkway toward Larchmont, where I planned to spend a quiet Thanksgiving with my mom. Though my dad was still living in the co-op, I hoped my parents had found a good marriage counselor and were working out their issues.

When the cab pulled onto the street I grew up on, I was a bit annoyed to see more than a dozen cars parked in front of my mom's house. She knew I was coming and hadn't mentioned she'd be having her friends over for one of their never-ending bridge tournaments. I just wasn't in the mood for questions from those ladies about my failed romance with the Frenchman. But I'd have gladly traded a million of those questions for what hit me when I rang the front bell.

"Sam! Welcome back!" My mother opened the door. A pair of earphones hanging around her neck was all she had on. "I've missed you so much!" When she tried to hug me, I backed off in horror.

"Ahhh! Mom! Where are your clothes? Put something on!" I assumed that the poor thing had gone totally psycho since the split with my dad.

But I was the one freaking out when a naked, rail-thin man with a long, skinny penis dangling between his legs, and those same headphones over his ears, joined her at the door and held out his hand for a shake.

"What the—" I rocketed away from the door. "What the fuck, Mom?"

"Now calm down, Sam. There's nothing weird happening. It's all cool. This is Ron, who I met at those Audiogenic Therapy classes I told you about. Not only have the classes changed my life, they've taken my business in a new direction."

"What? Why are you naked? What's this pervert doing in our house? And what's going on here?"

"I know it looks a little crazy, and you may need a few minutes to get comfortable with this. But you'll be happy to know that I've finally found something that makes me feel like my old self again—relaxed, renewed, excited about life. Without a pill or a shrink." While she spoke, I watched Ron's bony white ass sashay into the living room.

"You're scaring me, Mom. And where's *he* going?" I asked as I gingerly crept into the hallway. "Did you start a cult?"

"No, it's nothing like that. Not at all. Ron's a survivor from the corporate sector. He designed and produced his own Audiogenic program that's helping other stressed-out professionals like us reclaim their lives. Kind of like yoga on steroids that uses audio conditioning, stretching, and body awareness, to help build a more empowered sense of self."

"Oh shit, Mom! You sound like an *infomercial!* Has this guy *brainwashed* you?" I kept my eyes on her face to avoid her nude body.

"He's freed my mind if that's what you mean. And now he's using his marketing skills to direct traffic to our website. Our classes are getting fuller by the day."

I peeked my head into the living room, where the lights had been dimmed and the only sounds were heavy breathing. When my eyes adjusted to the lighting, I saw twenty or so butt-naked adults—male and female of all shapes, sizes, and ages, wearing headphones in a variety of positions on every inch of the living room. The same room where I'd once been forbidden to sit on the sofa after the maid had fluffed up the chenille cushions.

"This is *disgusting!* And what do the Quimbys have to say about this?" The Quimbys were our super-buttinsky next door neighbors who called the cops to shut down the lemonade stand I'd set up in front of our house when I was seven years old.

"Those assholes *have* caused problems since we're not zoned for any commercial activity. That's why I've closed my shop and we're moving our practice there. The renovation should be finished this week."

"What? You *are* kidding!" But my mother was not the joking type. "You're not opening a nude workout studio in our hometown! That's ludicrous! And the Town Council will never approve it."

"Honey, half the shops on Palmer Avenue are empty. The Council knows there won't *be* a downtown if they don't let businesses reinvent themselves. Anyway, it's not a workout studio. It's a professional office. Ron has incorporated the same scientifically endorsed elements into our program that are offered by the franchises. The big difference here is that students can connect with their bodies at a faster rate if they're not bound by clothing. Our app lets them track their progress so they can customize their programs according to which moves work best to lower their heartrates."

I looked behind me where a huge naked woman had her ass in the air and her hands on the floor. "Jeez, Mom! You and Dad and your fucking apps!"

·　　·　　·

I took an early morning train from the Larchmont station into Manhattan. Spending more than one night at my mom's house was more than I could handle, so I'd texted my dad that I was on the way. I planned to take my time before making any big decisions. Benson's offer to set up an interview for me in Napa was nice, but with my bank account shrinking, it would be wise to try to get some per diem work from Weatherhouse or a temp agency that services accounting firms, before spending any more money on travel.

When the train arrived at Grand Central Station, I hopped off, dragged my duffel bags to the subway, and took the connections to the Upper West Side. Walking up the steps of the Seventy-Second Street subway, I felt the chill in the New York City air, and looked forward to seeing my dad and catching up with Spence, Cameron, and Stephanie.

"Hi, Dad!" I ran into him on the next block.

"Here's my little girl!" He gave me a half hug with a bag of bagels in his hand and a Sunday newspaper under his arm. "How 'bout if we trade." He switched the bag and the paper for my duffels. "So, I thought you were spending turkey day with your mom. What happened?"

"Dad, Mom is *wacko!* She's into a really bizarre scene with some nudist scam artist who's controlling her and their 'students' with a recording he made that gets people to strip when they listen to it through headsets. You've got to get her away from that guy!"

"As long as she's rid of that store, she can do whatever she wants with whoever she wants," he said as he opened the door to the lobby of the co-op with his key.

"That's pretty callous! She's still your wife! And I hope you're trying to make things right with her."

"Let's talk about you, honey. You look even more beautiful after your adventure."

"I don't feel beautiful, Dad. I feel awful. Because I broke up with Julien."

"Oh, baby, I'm sorry. You two looked like a real item in all those pictures you posted. What happened?"

"Things were great between us. I really thought he was the one. Then I found out he had a whole different view of commitment than I do. And honestly, after seeing Mom hurt by you, I never want to go through that."

"And I wouldn't want that for my daughter. I'm sure it was painful. But you did the right thing." We got off the elevator and walked down the hall to the apartment. When he opened the door, we were met by a fortyish-year-old Asian woman with a short sensible haircut, who reminded me of my high school librarian.

"I thought you were leaving a while ago, Deirdre," my dad told the woman.

"I thought so too but got delayed with some calls. Is this your daughter you were telling us about?"

"Yup. This is Sam. Just back from France." He held the door open for her to leave. "Well, goodbye now."

"Bye, Greg. We had fun last night. Nice meeting you, Sam."

"Nice meeting you too," I called out before the door shut.

"You met that woman on one of your hook-up apps, didn't you, Dad?"

"Yes. I won't lie to you. To be honest, I have been open to dating others since your mom and I had that problem."

"That problem was you. And don't call it dating. You're not looking to go on *dates*. You're just looking to get laid."

"I'm looking for companionship."

"How much companionship do you need?" I asked, staring at the twenty-something woman coming out of his bedroom with a mohawk on her otherwise shaved head, her ass hanging out of her shorts, and tattoos of snakes slithering down her legs.

"She looked better in her profile picture," he whispered. "They usually do."

"You are *too* gross!" I said as a wave of that old anxiety swept through my body. "I've gotta get out of here." I grabbed my purse and left the apartment.

"Sam, please! I'm sorry!" He followed me into the hallway. "I thought both of these ladies would be gone by the time I got back."

"It's not your timing. It's what you're doing that disgusts me!" I walked into the elevator and dialed my mom. She picked up when I reached the lobby. "Mom, you were right. Dad's having a field day with those apps. I'm sorry, but you need to know the truth. He must be having some midlife crisis or something."

"A midlife reawakening is what he's having. Just like I am."

"What? You're saying what he's doing is *okay*?"

"No. Because instead of using this time to listen to his mind and body to make positive changes, he's self-abusing. And if you love him, you'll find a way to get him back out here and into our classes."

"Your classes? Why? So he can check out naked women?"

"No, that's not what we're about. Not at all."

"I can't deal with you guys. Anyway, I'm thinking I'm gonna move to Napa to find a job. If I want to make wine someday, that's the place to be. I'm sorry if you think that's crazy, I *know* it's crazy. But I think it's the right thing. At least I hope it's the right thing for me to do." I braced myself for her response.

"I agree. And I admire your adventurous spirit."

*"You do?"*

"I do. And I'm sure your Aunt Viv would be proud of you for making such a ballsy move. But I also think you need to take a deep breath and try to enjoy the moment. You're young, smart, beautiful . . . and you've learned a lot about the wine business already. So be positive about what's ahead of you."

"*Wow!* Thanks, Mom." For the first time ever, her calm voice and encouraging words helped to ease my anxiety. "I agree. Aunt Viv *would* want me to go for it. And you're right, I *should* stay positive." Though those 'classes' she and Ron were holding were ridiculous, my mother *had* seemed to have reaped some benefits from them.

I texted Benson Doyle on my walk to Spence's shop.

**Samantha:** Can be out there next week. Would that work to meet with owner of the winery?

**Benson:** Hold on . . .

He texted back a few minutes later.

**Benson:** Will b fine. Text when ur in town to set up interview. Irv Wasserman 707-555-1958. BTW you're welcome to crash at my house 'til you find a place

**Samantha:** That would be awesome! Thx so much!

The idea of moving to a place I knew little about, on limited funds, with only the possibility of a job, sent my brain into high gear. I'd planned to meet Cameron and Stephanie later that afternoon at a restaurant in the East Village for a pouring of Pinot Noir from Argentina. But with only a few days to orchestrate the move, I'd have to skip the event.

"Hi, Spence!" I called out when the bell over his door announced me.

"She's back!" Spence greeted me with a hug. "Tell me all about it! I've been enjoying what you've been posting on Instagram. Looked like you studied all the basics of winemaking and more on that trip. And how are the folks at Domaine LeMont doing?"

"You mean how is *Sara*? She's fine." I didn't feel that it was my place to tell him the truth—that Sara's marriage was a disaster, and she appeared to have a lot of regrets about marrying Denis.

"I'm glad," he said with his eyes affixed to that bare wall by the register. "She deserves to be happy."

"She does. And so do you, Spence."

"I guess I do," he said with a sigh. "So, tell me, what your plans are, now that you're back? Still serious about finding your way into the wine industry?"

"Very serious. Got an interview next week for a job in Napa. You know anything about trucks? I'll need to get one at some point anyway, so I thought I'd buy it here and drive it out instead of paying to fly and ship my stuff."

"Wow! You're on the move! First you go almost four thousand miles east. Now you're moving three thousand miles west. And Napa's beautiful. I've spent time there on those distributor junkets. I can help you with some contacts. But not with the truck. How 'bout your dad? He's gotta know more than me."

"Yeah, I'm sure he does. I'll see if he can squeeze me in between his hook-ups. Tell me, Spence, are all men pre-programmed at birth to cheat on their spouses? Even when the marriages are somewhat solid?"

"I don't know about other men. All I can tell you is—in the thirty-five years since meeting Sara, I haven't looked twice at another woman."

•　　•　　•

"Napa? You don't know anything about Napa," my Dad said when I came back to the co-op later that afternoon.

"I know the wine from Napa generates more revenue than wine from any other place in the country. So I'm thinking that's where I have the best chance to find a wine-related job. But I'm clueless about buying a truck. Plus, I only have $15,000 to spend. Can you help me find something that doesn't have a gazillion miles on it and has a big enough bed to hold bins of grapes?"

"I can try, honey. But you just came back. Now you're going off again? And if this has anything to do with those women this morning, I'm sorry. It was a one-time event."

"Really, Dad—I am *so* grossed out about that threesome you had last night. I don't even want to think about it."

"Then don't. Just put it out of your mind." He grabbed a coat from the rack. "Tell you what . . . I'm off to the gym. When I get back, I'll order us some dinner and we'll spend some time on Craigslist. How's that?"

"Okay. But no more women tonight. Please?"

"Pinky promise," he said as he held out his pinky to lock onto mine.

•   •   •

"So, your ex-boyfriend turned out to be living in medieval times, your mom's a head case, and your dad's intent on nailing every woman between eighteen and eighty in Manhattan. I see why you've had a bad week," Cameron said after I'd updated him and Stephanie on the past four days of my life. They'd stopped by the co-op to welcome me back before hopping the subway to their wine tasting.

"Harvest did look wonderful from your posts though," said Stephanie. "All of us at The Box thought about you every day. Out there in the fresh air, while our brains got more and more numb. There's a hiring freeze on now, so they haven't replaced you. Favia's having us fill the void."

"Oh, bummer! I feel terrible about that, guys!"

"Not your fault," said Cameron. "Hey, I love these chairs." He rubbed his hands on the old worn leather of the arms. "And that art deco standing bar is pretty cool too. You're taking these pieces with you, I trust?"

"Oh yeah! These are my treasures. Aunt Viv and Uncle Freddy found them in France. My dad can get some of that industrial-sleek stuff he's into. Unless he moves back with my mom. Not much chance of that happening though."

"Hey, that Vivian was quite a beauty in her day," Stephanie said as she admired the painting of my great aunt that hung over the mantle.

"The woman whose visage and form displayed complex traits," Cameron said. "Hmmm . . . I see innocence . . . and guilt. Demureness . . . and spunk."

"I see determination and strength," said Stephanie. "Almost like the wine is empowering her."

"I'm sure it was," I agreed. "She was drinking what was, and still is, the best wine on the planet."

"Speaking of wine, are you sure you can't join us for the tasting?" Cameron asked me. "We can catch a cab downtown if you're short on time—my treat."

"Thanks, but no. I've got mountains of dirty laundry and need to find a truck pronto." The apartment's intercom buzzed. I went over and held down the button on it. "Yes?"

"Hom and Chailai for Mr. Greg."

"Hom and Chailai? Oh great! I'll buzz you in. Guess my Dad ordered Thai from the treadmill—he loves that uEAT.now app," I told my friends as I pushed the button to allow the delivery person entry from the outside. "And he'll kill for anything with peanut sauce." When the doorbell rang, I pulled the door open to two petite Asian women holding black bags. "Hi, ladies. I'll run get my credit card." The first woman stepped through the doorway.

"Mr. Greg?" she called out in a singsong voice. "Are you here?"

"No, he's not. You can leave the food with me." I noticed that their bags looked more like overnight bags than ones to keep food hot.

"Hey, where *is* the food?" I asked while Cameron and Stephanie came out from the living room to see what was going on.

"The food? The food?" the first woman asked with a giggle and looked at the second one who was still in the hallway. "We're the food! I'm the main course and Chailai is the dessert!"

"No! No! He promised!" I grabbed my phone and called my dad. He sounded out of breath and I could hear the treadmill whirring in the background. "Dad, tonight's hook-ups are here. I thought they were delivering Thai," I said as I looked at my friends and mouthed *what the fuck*?

"That couldn't be right, honey. It's a mistake. Put one of the ladies on the phone." I handed my cell to the one called Hom.

After a few words in Thai, Hom pulled her cell from her pocket, tapped the screen, and put my phone back to her ear. "Mix up! Mix up! Ah, next week." She handed my phone back to me. "Sorry!" she said as she stepped out the door. "Goodbye," Chailai called out as the two women walked back down the hallway. I looked at Cameron, then at Stephanie. They both looked at me and turned to each other. If we hadn't started laughing so hard, I might have cried.

### Montemarte, Paris May 10, 1940

The photo studio of *Vogue Paris* was a flurry of activity. Coco Chanel barked orders at Vivian and the photo crew while she pulled dress after dress from the racks for the two models to slip on before she nipped, tucked, hemmed, and tugged at her creations. After several hours of styling the desired look for the holiday spread that was slated to appear in the October issue of the magazine, she positioned the women around a Christmas tree for the first shots of the day.

"Well, what do you think?" Coco asked Vivian after dozens of flashbulbs popped from the photographer's Rolleiflex camera. "Do I have something here? Will our photos set women's hearts on fire and inspire them to wear only Chanel gowns to their Christmas galas?"

For a moment, Vivian hesitated. Though the gowns on the two women were beautiful, the photos would not have stoked any flames in her heart had she been flipping through the pricey magazine at the newsstand on the Rue St. Germain. "Well, the fashions are lovely," Vivian began. "But . . ."

"But what, my dear?"

"But . . ." Vivian hesitated, not wanting to offend the couture legend and get fired on her first day on the job.

"Speak your mind. I won't bite. We know the women who buy Chanel are older and in a higher economic sphere than most girls your age. But they do want to emulate your youth and attitude. So tell me what you don't like here."

"It's not that I don't like what you've done, Mademoiselle Chanel. It's just that I think you can do something better. Something different. Something that catches people's eyes and helps them to forget the problems of the world."

"Go on," Coco said.

"Well, that Christmas tree is nice. But we need to add some fun and spice. These are glamorous gowns, not church attire. Think screwball comedy—Irene Dunne in *The Awful Truth*, Barbara Stanwyck in *The Lady Eve*."

"My style tends to be more conservative," Coco said with head cocked in thought. "But I do like what I'm hearing. Maybe it's time I shake things up a bit."

"How about some photos with Santa?" Vivian asked. "Naughty but nice girls in red and white satin gowns sitting on his lap? Tickling his long white beard while tempting him to a plate of cookies?" Vivian eyed the chubby photographer's assistant. "Would there be a Santa suit in the costume closet by chance?" she asked the photographer.

Coco took a closer look at Vivian. "I believe we could use three models for the photo. And it seems that the prettiest one is right before my eyes."

# ten

Tannin *n.* a naturally occurring compound found in the seeds, stems, and skins of grapes that adds bitterness, astringency, and complexity to wine

I left Manhattan on Thanksgiving morning. Cameron and Stephanie had each invited me to spend the day with their respective families, but with a four-day trip ahead, I needed to get an early start. While the dawn was breaking over the Hudson River, I was driving under the waterway through the Lincoln tunnel. Hitched to the back of my truck was a U-Haul trailer packed with my clothes, furniture, the portrait of Aunt Viv, and the case of wine she left me. I got lucky with my truck. There was an ad on the board in the laundry room of the co-op for a lemon yellow and cream 1957 Ford pickup with only thirty thousand miles on it. The elderly Italian gentleman in apartment 8B had kept the vehicle in the building's garage since the late 1960s and probably hadn't driven it much more than once a year. It was priced at 25K, but he agreed to sell it to me for seventeen, thanks to the beautiful bottle of Sangiovese I handed him when he'd answered his door.

By two p.m., the I-80 West had taken me through New Jersey, Pennsylvania, and into Ohio. Memories of past Thanksgiving dinners of roast turkey, honey-baked sweet potatoes, and chestnut stuffing with my family had my mouth watering and my heart aching as I exited the highway at Strongsville, Ohio. A cruise through the town eventually brought me to a fast-food franchise known as the Big O Diner that had a sign on the window advertising a $6.99 super-sized turkey dinner. Inside, the hostess led me past a maze of booths packed with super-sized patrons before she sat me at a table for two with a super-sized laminated plastic menu. After placing my order, I checked my Facebook site. The first post was a photo of my mom and her partner in nudity announcing the upcoming grand opening of Larchmont Audiogenics. The way my mom was nestled in the guy's arms left me no doubt that the two had become a couple. I followed that bad news by deleting all the twenty plus emails Julien had sent me over the past several days. My fingers trembled as I moved on to the task of deleting the collection of selfies I'd taken of the two of us — on top of an old rusted out tractor in a field at Domaine LeMont, standing with Pierre in the vineyard of Romanée-Conti, lying on the bed with Stella. Then I stopped at a dozen or so that sent a ripple of longing through my body. We'd hiked to the top of Mont Brouilly to an ancient chapel said to protect the surrounding vineyards from disease. When I was about to take the shot of us standing together with the valley behind us, Julien surprised me with a passionate kiss that kept my thumb locked on the photo button.

*"Why couldn't you have been horrified? Dismayed? Disapproving of what Denis did?"* I hissed at the pictures, causing a boy at the next table to elbow his mother and point my way. Then something occurred to me. Julien had never promised me anything. He hadn't promised me a future, and he sure hadn't promised that he'd be any more faithful to me than his father had been to Sara. I realized then what the dentist from Prague had meant on that first dinner of harvest when he said, "The LeMont men *do* get whatever they want."

"Are you okay, honey?" asked the server with a perfectly coiffed bun of orange hair when she arrived with my plate of pressed turkey smothered in gravy, two scoops of mashed potatoes, three slices of canned cranberries, and a sprig of parsley.

"Yes . . . I'm okay," I lied as I dabbed at the tears rolling down my cheeks with a napkin. "But I'm not hungry right now." I pointed to the meal. "Maybe there's a stray cat or dog outside you could give that to."

After four and a half days on the road and three nights crashing at motels, I crossed the state line between Nevada and California where the traffic slowed to a crawl. When I neared the exit, I could see cars slowing down before they sped up and continued down the freeway. I was horrified when I saw the cause of the hold up. A dog was cowering in terror on the shoulder of the ramp. It would have been far easier and safer for me to continue on with the flow of the traffic, but I couldn't shake the thought of how terrified Stella would be if she fell off one of the LeMont trucks and no one stopped to rescue her.

Ignoring the blasts of horns sounded by the other drivers, I worked my way into the right lane, pulled over onto the shoulder, and with the engine idling, opened the passenger door of the cab. I could see the dog's ears prick up as it began to slink toward the truck. When I put my two fingers in my mouth and gave a piercing whistle, it picked up speed, and almost flew through the open door.

"What kind of dog are you?" I asked as I pulled the door shut. "You look like a Dr. Seuss character." The dog, a female, was tall and skinny, with a coat that looked more like grey hair than fur. A cowlick of the stuff stood straight up before curling over on the top of her head. "I think I'll call you Seuss." Now, I was on my way to a strange place, with three thousand dollars to my name, no permanent place to live, only the possibility of a job, and a stray dog to feed.

On Route 80, I passed Sacramento and nondescript, mini-mall-laden towns with uninspired names like Vacaville, Fairfield, and American Canyon. "What the hell was I thinking by coming out to this wasteland?" I asked Seuss when I pulled into a service station to fill up on gas. Exhausted from whatever ordeal she'd endured, the dog was fast asleep on the seat.

When I turned onto Highway 29 toward Napa, the scenery morphed from superstores to rolling green hills and vineyards set against blue skies with puffy white clouds. While my friends on the east coast were already dreading the prospect of another tough winter, it was a balmy seventy degrees outside. On a grassy bank off the freeway, a bronze statue of a man ferociously pressing grapes told those driving by that this place was all about wine. I passed one of the world's top printers of wine labels and a company that specializes in corks on the road that led into downtown Napa where Benson lived. Before heading to his house, I needed to pay a visit to an animal hospital to have Seuss checked out and entered in a lost dog registry. To get to the nearest clinic, my phone sent me a mile up a road known as Silverado Trail, a thoroughfare I would soon know well. Lined with giant, medium-sized, and small boutique wineries, the Trail winds north through the towns of Yountville, Oakville, St. Helena, and Calistoga as it offers travelers breathtaking views of vineyards, forests, and surrounding mountains with huge outcroppings of boulders running up them like staircases for giants.

When I arrived at the parking lot of the clinic, Seuss leapt out of the car and gave me my first good look at her. She came up to my waist and bounced with each step she took, as if her legs were made of springs. I was okay without having a leash because the dog stuck to my side like glue. After proclaiming her healthy, the vet said the odds of reconnecting with the owner were slim. He saw too many unwanted dogs being dropped on freeway ramps.

"Who would dump a sweet girl like you on a freeway?" I asked her on our way to downtown Napa. After consuming a bowl of dog food, she sat in the front seat like a lady being ferried about by her chauffeur. While I followed the directions to Benson's house, I wondered how a guy I only knew casually would react when I arrived for what could be an extended stay with a U-Haul packed with furniture and a dog as tall as a small horse.

I turned onto the town's Main Street, lined with charming turn-of-the-century houses, stone buildings, a historic hotel, and an old brick mill set on the banks of the winding Napa River. In the center of town, looming over every other business and residence in sight, stood the Victorian mansion that's home to *Wine Snob*, the publication featuring the reviews of critic Regis Preston, who, with a mere flick of his pen, could make or break a wine brand's chance for success.

When I parked my truck in front of Benson's tiny Victorian house, my vehicles easily spanned his home and those on either side of him.

Seuss joined me as I climbed the steps and knocked on the door. "Welcome to Napa!" my host said as he flung the door open and gave me a hug. "Whoa! Who do we have here?" I'd texted Benson to let him know I was close but had neglected to mention the dog.

"Hi, Benson! Hey, I am *so* grateful to you for putting me up. And I hate to ask for another favor, but—"

"The dog? It's no problem!" Seuss sat down and offered him a paw to shake. "Hey pooch, what's your name?"

"Oh, thank you, Benson! Thank you so much! She was stranded on a freeway ramp, and I couldn't leave her there! I'm calling her Seuss, and I'm sure she needs a bath. Is there one of those U Wash Doggie places around here?"

"There is, but I'm happy to wash doggie in the back yard with the hose and some shampoo while you unpack. Did you bring a lot of—" He looked out at my truck with the U-Haul attached to it. "Stuff with you?"

"Errr, I did bring a lot, and I've got to return the U-Haul today. But I can stash the furniture that's in there in one of those self-storage units if—"

"No, not necessary," he insisted. "I'll move my truck to the street. You back the trailer into the driveway, and we can put your furniture in my garage."

"Oh, Benson, no! I don't want to impose on you like that!"

"It's no sweat. Just give me a minute and I'll help you back up your truck." He grabbed his keys from a table and went out to move his car.

•   •   •

After Benson filled his garage with my furniture and the moving boxes, I carried my duffel bags in the door and gasped. The playhouse my dad built in our back yard when I was a tot was larger. His living room held only a sofa, a shelf overflowing with books on the science of winemaking, and a TV on the wall. The kitchen and bathroom were both the size of those on a one-man sailboat. I poked my head in the bedroom and was puzzled as to how the guy was able to squeeze his bed into the space. But I was in no position to turn down the offer of a free place to live until I found a job.

"This looks nice and comfy," I said, flopping down on the sofa. I was hoping that the power of suggestion would enable me to sleep on a piece of furniture narrower than the cots in the attic at Domaine LeMont.

"Now, Sam," he began. "I'm fine sleeping out here. You're my guest, and I want you to take the bedroom. The sheets are clean, and you deserve a good night's sleep after driving cross country."

"Absolutely not. Seuss and I will be very cozy on your couch." I tried to push down on the cushion of the sofa for emphasis, but it refused to budge.

Benson sat down next to me and took my hand in his. "And hey, Sam . . . Henri was out here a few days before Thanksgiving to promote their new wines. He said it turned into a real shitshow out there after the big party, with the theft and all.

"Yeah, a real shitshow," I agreed.

"He also said things didn't work out for you and Julien. Just so you know, I'm sorry about that too. You guys seemed like a great couple." He put his hand on my shoulder and gave me a pat.

"Thanks, Benson." Though his words brought on another round of tears, it was a relief to get the inevitable conversation over with.

"Hey, c'mon," he said, handing me a tissue. "Great things are in store for you out here. Let's walk over to the local diner when you're ready. People tie up their dogs on the patio and can keep an eye on them from the booths inside. It's sort of a social thing for the canines."

"Sounds fun. Seuss and I would love that."

• • •

"I'm delighted to make your acquaintance, Ms. Goodyear! I think our facility will be just what you're looking for."

I'd texted Irv Wasserman to set up an interview for the bookkeeping gig that Benson had told me about. Irv was the manager of the custom crush winery called Napa Juice, where winemakers pay a fee to make their wine. On the Monday morning following my arrival in Napa, I was dressed in a suit, silk blouse, and heels, while trying to ignore the kink in my back from sleeping on Benson's sofa, and hoping to succeed at selling myself as a good candidate for the position. Though I was overqualified for a bookkeeping job, working at a winery was the opportunity I needed to learn about the business. But from the way Irv was pitching the facility to me, it was clear he thought I was looking for a place to make wine instead of looking for a place to make money.

"We have a full support staff to help prepare your fruit as it comes in from the vineyard and provide whatever services your wine requires until it goes through the bottling line." The tall, lanky man pointed at the roll-up, floor-to-ceiling doors wide enough to allow trucks filled with bins of newly picked grapes to enter the building. He then led me through the pristine facility, from the cavernous barrel room where hundreds of barrels of fermenting wine were stacked in neat rows that went up to the ceiling, to the equipment room with its gleaming stainless-steel wine presses and tanks.

"I've just returned from harvest at a domaine in Beaujolais," I told him. "The press and tanks were made of wood, and the mold in the cave was welcomed and even prized. A world of difference from what you have here."

"They're still in the Dark Ages of winemaking over there," Irv said with a dismissive tone. "These days it's all about keeping the grapes and wine bacteria-free. We offer state-of-the-art wine production in a sterile environment. And of course, these steel tanks are easier and take far less time to clean than the old wooden ones."

I didn't mention what Julien, Denis, and *grand-père* Gaston had to say on the subject. The three of them had insisted that the wooden tanks and presses are far gentler on the fermenting grapes than the steel, which minimizes unwanted influences of bitter tannins from damaged seeds, skins, and stems, and results in a higher quality wine. But I knew better than to argue with a prospective employer.

"Wow! This sure is a great facility, Mr. Wasserman."

"Please, call me Irv. And you might not know that the famous vintner Ashton White makes his wine here. I must say that the man is a total pleasure to work with."

"I've heard a lot about Mr. White from his assistant Benson Doyle. In fact, Benson and I spent time together in—"

"Yes, yes," he said, more interested in roping a new client than in anything I had to say. "We're pretty much at full capacity right now. But I may be able to get creative and find a way to squeeze you in. By-the-way, you haven't told me the name of your wine yet."

"Well, that's because I don't . . . I don't have a name . . . or a wine," I began. "I think there's been a mix-up. I'm not here as a client. Not yet at least. I moved to Napa to make wine, but right now I'm here to interview for a bookkeeping job. Benson told me you had an opening?"

In a flash, the eager-to-please smile vanished. "Oh, for Christ's sake, lady. I have a business to run. What Benson *should* have told you is that I don't have time to give tours to every—"

"I have a degree in accounting and spent three years at a major New York firm. I can handle all your client billing, your bookkeeping, accounts payable, taxes, and payroll."

"Hmmm . . . well . . . seems like you can sell too. Be here tomorrow, nine a.m. Five hundred a week. We're slow lately, so that's all I can pay."

"I *can* sell, and if you up it to six, I'll help with your sales and marketing efforts."

He stared at my face before giving my accounting attire a once over. "Five-fifty and you're hired. And keep that Barbie-goes-to-the-office look going, doll. We need to work every angle to snare potential clients."

Though I bristled at the man's comment, I kept my mouth shut and extended my hand. I was in wine country now and happy to have a job. And I doubted that any of the area's wine cooperatives had the same anti-harassment policies that the big four accounting firms followed to a T.

• • •

Irv had pointed out the empty desk in what would be my office before I'd left that evening. When I arrived for work the following morning, it was covered with piles of unpaid invoices, some of them more than a year old. There were stacks of handwritten notes on services rendered to clients, and overdue city and state forms that had to be submitted for the winery to even remain in operation. My first step was to sift through the mess and put it into some kind of order. I was glad when I spotted Irv coming toward my office at nine-twenty, as I needed his approval before I could cut checks to accompany the most overdue forms.

"Samantha! I need you to come out here now," he called from the winery's tasting room, which abutted the office space.

"Coming, Irv," I said, running out as fast as my stiletto heels and vintage Chanel pencil skirt would allow. Irv was waiting for me with a white paper painter's mask, rubber gloves, and trash bags.

"Here, take the bags and put these on, please." He gave me the items. "We had a rodent problem in the barrel room last week. Javier, our janitor, put traps around, but hasn't been back to collect the dead rats and mice, so I need you to do it. You've got to be fast, 'cause a photo crew from *Wine Snob Magazine* is coming in forty minutes to shoot Ashton White for Regis Preston's review of his new release. And grab a dustpan and broom from the janitor's closet down there on the right. We can't have any traces of rat shit on the floor either. This place has to look clean as a whistle!"

"Ah, sure, Irv," I said as I started off for the closet. Along with the dustpan and broom, I grabbed a hat and one of the canvas jumpsuits the janitors wore. I piled my hair under the hat, put on the mask and gloves, and stepped into the jumpsuit to prepare for the nasty job ahead. With the clock ticking, I hurried out of the closet in my heels with the cleaning equipment in hand.

I let out a scream when I came upon the first victim adhered to one of those glue board traps, but was thankful that this creature and the others I later found were all dead. In less than thirty minutes, I removed all traces of the rodents and their excrement from the shiny concrete floor without vomiting, and was on my way out the door at the back of the building. While I was tossing the bags into the dumpster, the ground under my feet vibrated. Moments later, the roar of an engine and pounding rap music exploded through the morning air as a bright yellow Lamborghini convertible screamed into the parking lot. When the car stopped, I recognized the man behind the wheel as Ashton White from pictures I'd seen of him online.

"Samantha!" Irv was calling to me from the barrel room. I hustled back inside, ready to obey the next order.

"What now, Irv?" I could see the muscles in his jaw twitching. On the other side of the room, the photo crew was setting up their lights for the shot, and the director was pointing to some wine barrels high on the metal shelves.

"We need to do some shuffling, so Ashton's barrels are prominent in the shot. And we have to do it fast, since he'll be walking in here ready to roll any minute now."

"Do some shuffling?" I wasn't sure how I could help. The barrels weighed 600 pounds each.

"You know how to drive a forklift, don't you?"

"No, Irv, I don't. Sorry." I cocked my head and smiled. "They drove the forklifts in Beaujolais on the wrong side of the aisle, so I never could get the hang of those things. *Ha ha!*"

"That's not funny! Not funny at all!" A tide of purple rose from his neck to his face as he banged the top of a barrel with a fist. "*Everyone* who works at a winery knows how to run a forklift!" He looked at his watch and drummed his fingers on the barrel. "Okay, well there's no one else here, and these people can't see the six-foot-four head of the place sandwiched inside a goddamned forklift. So I'll show you how to run it."

"Show me how?" The vehicle's menacing iron prongs seemed to point right at me. "Don't you need a license to operate one of those?"

"Unnecessary. If you can drive that truck of yours, you can drive one of these. Just hop in, and I'll walk you through it."

I gingerly hoisted myself into the compartment, sat on the black plastic seat of the vehicle, and tested the brakes with my high heels.

Still wearing the gloves, hat, mask, and jumpsuit, I looked like the Terminix man in Manolo Blahnik.

"Turn the key and push the start button," Irv instructed. That part was simple. "Now hit the switch on the side to back up." Again, easy, as the vehicle moved backward to the sound of "beep, beep, beep".

"That's enough!" He held up his hand like a street cop. "Now, push the black knob forward, and slowly accelerate toward the second rack of barrels over there." He pointed to a stack of barrels towering above three men that were setting up lights for the shoot. Ashton White was now in the winery, looking totally cool in his worn jeans, white cotton shirt, and work boots as he chatted up a woman in a houndstooth suit who I assumed to be one of the *Wine Snob* marketing executives.

"Okay, stop!" Irv commanded. "Now take the lever marked Fork and pull it up. Keep pulling, keep pulling, keep pulling. Stop!" The fork was now reaching a good twenty-five feet in the air. "Okay, now press the Forward button on the lever. Stop!" The fork was now under a barrel that Irv wanted moved. "Push the Raise Fork button." I obeyed, and the fork raised the barrel a few feet off the rack. "Now slide the knob left." Again, I followed his instructions, but the jerk of the fork caused the barrel to hit the side of the rack and it started to roll off the prongs. "I mean right! Right!! RIGHT!!!" But it was too late. The barrel rolled another inch and toppled off the edge of the shelf. "Jesus Christ!" he screamed. "LOOK OUT EVERYONE! BARREL DOWN!" The enormous cylinder dropped like a bomb onto the concrete, where it exploded on impact, shooting sixty gallons of red wine into the air and flowing across the floor. Irv's warning had sent Ashton, the *Wine Snob* executive, and the crew running, which allowed them to escape with their clothes, shoes, and the camera unstained. There was an eerie quiet for a good ten seconds, until I heard a lone voice from the other side of the room.

"You idiot! You absolute moron!" It was Ashton. He aimed his tirade at me while he walked toward us. "Was that my barrel, Irving?" He sounded like he wanted me shot on sight.

"No worries, Ashton." Irv called out. "It was Curtis Payne's Merlot. None of your barrels got touched." Curtis Payne was a kindly old man who was bad at paying bills and even worse at making wine. "Benson's coming in now. He can finish the job and the show can go on as planned," Irv assured his biggest client with a nervous giggle.

Benson sprinted into the room. "Good morning, everyone!" One look at the scene told him what had taken place. "Don't worry about it," he whispered to me as he came near. "I'll show you how to run this thing tonight." Happy to be incognito, I scrambled from the forklift, tiptoed past Ashton and the photo-shoot crew, and made an escape back to my office.

. . .

It was the Saturday morning after my first week on the job. Though my boss was a horror show whose winery seemed to cater only to Ashton White, I was making some money and learning the ropes about making wine in Napa: what kinds of licenses were required to sell wine for public consumption; which vineyards would be best to source grapes from; where to buy corks and glass; where to have labels designed and printed; and how to get wine bottled, stored, and sold. And though there was still much to learn, my experiences in Beaujolais and my lessons from Julien had made me feel confident and at ease in the winery. I also had Julien to thank for the introduction to Benson, who was enormously kind to allow Seuss and me to sleep on his couch until we found a place of our own. And that's what I was searching for as I wound up the hills and through the vineyards of the region in Napa known as Carneros. I had an appointment with a Mr. Marshall to see a cottage with the address of 6 Twisted Vine Lane that I'd found on craigslist. When I got close to the top of what looked like the area's highest hill, I turned onto a road as instructed by my phone and stopped at a mailbox marked with the number six. The front of the property was spooky. A pair of rusted old gates hung open with a "No Trespassing" sign that had a faded image of a ferocious dog. I inched my truck through the gates toward a two-story farmhouse that looked to date back to the 1800s. The structure's green paint had worn off in sections, and any landscaping that once adorned it was long dead or gone. There was a smaller house in the back of the property that I assumed to be the cottage listed for rent. Behind that, a lone horse grazed in an overgrown field. Seuss and I got out of the truck, but before knocking on the door to the main house, I peeked in a window of the cottage. If it looked as creepy as the rest of the place, we'd get back in the truck and I'd call Mr. Marshall to say thanks, but no thanks.

When I reached the cottage, I held my hands up to the glass to block the light from the outside and peered in. Through the maze of cobwebs, I saw a cozy room with a stone fireplace, wooden floors, and an old pine table and chairs. I felt a tingling in my gut as I pictured myself sitting by a fire with Seuss while I studied books on the science of winemaking. But the tingling morphed to a stab of fear when a voice startled me from behind.

"Just what do you think you're doin'?" the voice bellowed. I wheeled around to see a man who looked to be in his late seventies wearing overalls and a plaid shirt. He had long hair and a scraggly grey beard that didn't mask the nasty expression on his face. Seuss, who had been off in the field searching for deer and rabbits to chase, ran back toward us, bared her top teeth, and emitted a threatening growl.

"Hi . . . hello . . . I'm Sa-Sa-Samantha," I stuttered. *Samantha Goodyear?* My name didn't seem to ring any bell with him. "You must be Mr. Marshall. **Seuss!**" I called the dog in fear that she might charge the man. *"Viens ici!"* The command that I'd learned from Julien seemed to work, because the dog immediately sat down in silence. "We spoke this morning about the cottage for rent?"

"I'm not Mr. Marshall, and there's no cottage here for rent," he snarled.

"What? I saw the ad for it on craigslist. I called and spoke to the owner—a Mr. Marshall." I checked my phone to read the number to him. "707-555-5602? Isn't this 6 Twisted Vine Lane?"

"Nope, wrong number, wrong address. This is 6 Twisted Vine Road, so you and your dog best be goin'."

I looked at the address I'd punched into the phone. It was 6 Twisted Vine Road. "Yikes! I'm sorry, sir. I entered the wrong address and my phone sent me here. C'mon Seuss! **Seuss!**" The dog had returned to the field in hot pursuit of a jackrabbit. "Oh my gosh, I'm so sorry, she doesn't have any manners yet!" I called back to the man as I ran after her. "I found her just last week on a freeway ramp. Seuss! Seuss! Come here, girl . . . please!" The faster I ran, the faster Seuss ran, thinking the race through the waist-high grasses in the field was a wonderful game. Then I hit something hard with my foot and fell flat on my face.

"Just what in the name of tarnation do you think you're doin' by storming onto my property, spying through my window, and runnin' through my vineyard like it's a racetrack?" the man bellowed as he lumbered toward me. "Don't you have the sense you were born with, young woman?"

I pulled myself up and reappeared from the long, thick grasses. "Your vineyard?" I looked around the field. There were no vines in sight. I thought the poor guy was suffering from some form of dementia.

"That's what I said. May well be the finest Pinot Noir vines in all of California."

It occurred to me that along with being crazy, the man could be dangerous. I decided it would be best to humor him until Seuss and I could make a quick getaway.

"They look mighty fine, sir!" Playing along, I took a handful of the tall weeds and looked at them with approval.

"What planet are *you* from? Those are weeds, woman. They covered up the vines years ago."

I pushed some long grasses away and saw that what I'd fallen on was a gnarly grapevine with a bark-covered base as thick as those of the old vines vineyard at Domaine LeMont. When I took a few steps and bent back more of the grasses, I could see there was truth to the old man's rantings—there *was* a vineyard, or at least the remains of a vineyard, there. And as with the vines at the domaine, these had grown without trellising, which gave them the look of small trees. It was early December, and though most of that year's grapes had dropped to the ground weeks before or been consumed by animals, a few shriveled clusters remained on the vines.

I plucked off a few of the tiny grapes and held them up to the man. "You mind?"

"Why not? Ya already act like ya own the place. Might as well help yourself to my fruit. Go on then." He stood and waited for my reaction.

I popped them in my mouth and sucked on them. Because they hadn't been harvested, the sugars had been allowed to ripen slowly under the weeds and the canopy of leaves on the vines. They had an intense sweetness, and a heightened level of flavor that I could only compare to the clones of Pinot Noir I tasted at the Romanée-Conti vineyard. The look on my face told the man I was well aware this was very precious fruit.

"These grapes! They're luscious! But why are they covered by weeds?"

He looked across the field, then back at me. "Ya really wanna know, or are ya just humorin' an old man?"

"I *really* want to know."

"These vines once made a great wine." His posture softened and his scowl faded. "They go back to the 1930s. Brought here by a French businessman—a kin on my mother's side named Claude Darnay. Didn't like what he saw happenin' with the political stuff going on in Europe and a fellow named Adolf Hitler, so he came to the US and settled in San Francisco." He turned and looked out at the field. "Bought the house and the land to grow grapes and make wine. Didn't know a lot about either. But he knew that this slope faces the rising sun and has perfect drainage for vines. So he sent for the finest clones of Burgundy's Côte d'Or and had 'em planted here. Always said this place reminded him of home."

I looked up at the surrounding mountains dotted with lakes, farms, and vineyards. "I can see why," I told the man. "I almost feel like I'm back on the Côte myself."

He stared at me with eyes squinted for a few moments, then continued. "Claude Darnay built a winery here and imported a fellow from Burgundy to make his wine. My parents tended the vineyard, and I worked right alongside 'em. That is, 'til I was fourteen, and the two of 'em died in a car crash."

"Oh, how tragic! I'm so sorry!"

"It was tough. But Mr. Darnay took me in like I was the son he never had. Slept in a little room at the back of that house." He pointed over at the long-neglected farmhouse on the property. "When he died, he left the place to me—the vineyard, the winery, the house."

"Wow, nice!"

"Wasn't worth near then what it is today. It happened that the winemaker fella had a daughter—a real peach of a gal named Emma, who grew up making the wine with her dad. Later on, the two of us got married, and she kept on makin' Darnay wine just the way she'd been taught. Delicate, but with lots of flavor. We picked the grapes before the sugar got too high, with enough acid to allow the wine to age. Wine critics loved us. Our scores were always in the mid-nineties. 'Til 1988, that is, when that fat cat SOB Regis Preston joined *Wine Snob Magazine* and started tellin' Americans how their wine should taste— heavy, with all nuances of flavor erased by sky-high levels of sugar and alcohol. Those were the wines he scored in the nineties—the ones that pair great with those thick steaks he consumes. Since our wine wasn't his style, he dropped our scores way down. And our sales dropped right along with 'em."

"I've heard a lot about Mr. Preston. He seems to wield a big stick in this town."

"Sure does. Folks buy wine based on the scores from that *Wine Snob* rag. To stay afloat, Emma and I had to pick the grapes late the next year when the sugar levels were over the top. We ended up with a high-alcohol, big, fruity wine with low acid that couldn't age worth a damn. It broke our hearts to do it, but Preston scored our new wine high, and we were back in business. That is, 'til the hundred-year fire roared through and took the winery in '96." He pointed at a concrete slab next to the field. "Not long after, Emma died. I never did have it in me to rebuild." His sad eyes rested on me for a moment. "My Emma had blonde curls like yours when we first got married. Came down to her shoulders, just the same. But the grey was comin' in good by the time she passed."

"You've sure had your sorrows here, sir." I took another look at the beautiful mountains surrounding us. "But this must have been a wonderful place to live and make wine."

"We all loved livin' here back in the day. That old house over there was always full of life with my boys and the kids from neighboring vineyards runnin' through it. We had barbecues, harvest parties, a shared fruit-and-vegetable stand. It was a real community. We plowed the vineyards and pulled the carts full of grapes with our horses—they were always workin'." He looked over at the horse with the serious hay belly grazing in the field. "Old Delilah out there doesn't know what to do with herself since she lost her job."

"The mare sure looks like she needs some exercise," I said with a sniffle as I thought of Adèle and her precious little twins.

"The neighbors are all gone now. Sold out to *them*, and moved away, like most everyone else 'round this part of the valley."

"Them? Who're they?"

"*Them*—the big wineries," he barked. "The corporate giants. They ripped out the old vines and put in their genetically engineered, disease-resistant plants synthesized in the lab at the U of California. Supposed to produce more tons of fruit per acre. Trouble is, those grapes don't taste anywheres near as good as what Mother Nature makes. And those folks *prefer* to wait until the sugar levels are nice and high to pick, so their wine tastes just the way Regis Preston likes it. My ten acres are the only ones left here they haven't gotten their paws on. That Galileo Winery over there has been breathing down my neck since they swallowed up Hanna Morgon's vines ten years ago. But I'm not sellin'. Even though my grapes may never again see the inside of a bottle. I've just left them alone since Emma left me. Don't bother to water or do anythin' to maintain. But they just keep on getting better every year. Almost like they're tryin' to lure her back."

"So, you . . . you live here all by yourself now?"

"Yup. My twin boys are grown with families of their own. They're after me to sell the property. And they want me to junk those old machines." He pointed to the gigantic pile that was sitting on a concrete foundation and covered by tarps. "That's what's left of the winery. Most of the structure burned to the ground, but it spared those old pieces that came over from France. Don't much matter though, 'cause I have no use for them. But I'm just not ready to have them hauled away. Not yet."

My curiosity about what was lying under those tarps got the best of me. "Would you mind if I looked?"

"Sure, if you want to see some relics even older than me." He started toward the pile. When he reached it, he scraped layers of leaves, twigs, and bird droppings from the tarps before he pulled them back to reveal an ancient wine press and tank. Though the wood looked sorely in need of conditioning, the structures appeared to be solid. The man looked like he was waiting for me to laugh out loud at them.

"I think I know just the thing that would make those old machines look almost new again."

· · ·

"The old man was so cranky when he saw me snooping around his property. I thought he was going to grab a shotgun to chase me away!"

"He must have scared you shitless!" Benson leaned forward in his seat at the bar of The Cellar, a wine industry hangout in downtown Napa. I'd been filling him in on my morning visit to 6 Twisted Vine Road.

"Yeah, I was, at first. But then he softened and shared his story. I think it was because my hair reminded him of his dead wife's." I pulled away a fistful of my unruly yellow curls that I hadn't had trimmed since my days at Weatherhouse. "Good thing I didn't have time to get a cut and blow-out before going over there." I released the locks, and the curls sprang back toward the others.

"That's gotta be Hal Pritchett you were talking to. The man's a local legend out here. Had one of the last small wineries in that northwest corner of Carneros. The area's still known as the golden triangle for Pinot and Chardonnay, 'cause of the way the ocean breezes come through there off the San Francisco Bay."

"Yeah, the guy . . . Hal, I never did catch his name . . . told me those hills and valleys were all once planted with vines from Burgundy. Said the big corporate wineries tore out and replanted most of them."

"Yup, and no one seems to know if Pritchett's vineyard even exists anymore."

"Believe me, Benson, it does exist. I ran straight into it." I rubbed the bruise on my leg that still smarted from the crash. "Hal told me he and his wife made some amazing Pinot Noir from those vines. But when Regis Preston took over as America's wine messiah, they were forced to pick late to get decent scores from him."

"Tell me about it. I'm an expert at that game," Benson admitted. "Every wine I make for Ashton has one goal—to get a high score. My boss always has me tell the vineyard managers from wherever he sources his grapes to pick when the sugar levels are sky high, so I can make the sweetest and highest-alcohol wine possible."

While we were chatting, I spotted three men walking into the bar. I recognized two of them as the grandsons of the winemaking icon Peter Mondial, who had teamed up to create their own wine that was a favorite with millennials. The other man was Ashton White. The hostess at the door was visibly gushing as she welcomed the trio.

"Crap—your boss is here." I was still stinging from the way Ashton had railed at me after the forklift fiasco.

"Don't worry about him. His moods have been all over the place lately. And he's usually too focused on himself to dwell on the day-to-day dramas at the winery."

Ashton looked toward the bar and said something to the two other men before he walked our way. "Hey, Benny, what's up? You get those samples of the new Merlot out to Preston?" Then he looked at me. I wanted to duck under the bar. "Well, hello, beautiful!" He cocked his head and flashed a hundred-watt smile, then pointed at Benson and sat down next to me. "I hope you're not interested in this asshole."

"And why would you care?" I asked.

"Excuse me, Mr. White," a waitress interrupted. She was holding a tray with a bottle of Champagne and a fluted glass. "For you," she cooed, as she placed the glass in front of Ashton and filled it with the bubby. "From the four ladies at the corner table." Ashton turned and gave the group of twenty-somethings a salute as they giggled and blew him kisses.

When he turned back around, I wondered if he knew I was the same "moron" who'd knocked the barrel down during his shoot. "So . . ." he leaned close. "What's *your* deal? You an actress? Model? Fox News anchor?" He snickered at his wit.

"None of the above. But thanks for the compliment—I *guess*." I realized that because of the mask and hat I'd been wearing in that forklift, he had no idea that he'd seen me before.

"Hmmm, I'm always fascinated by a woman of mystery." He set his finger on his chin. "FBI? CIA? KGB?" His wavy blonde hair and turquoise eyes that crinkled at the corners when he smiled almost made me forget what a jerk he'd been. "And do you have a name? Or only a number? Ya know, like 007?"

"My name's Samantha. And until this past summer, I was with one of the big four accounting firms in Manhattan."

"So there's a brain inside that beautiful head. Now, I'm really in love!" He was beginning to annoy me.

"I moved out here last month. Just doing the books for a winery right now. I'd like to make my own wine someday."

"I like that plan, Samantha. And might you have a last name?"

"Uhhh . . ." Wanting to remain anonymous in case he heard my name pop up at the winery, I glanced at a label of a wine displayed on the bar. "Lafite . . . Samantha Lafite."

"Lafite? Well, then you're in the right business for sure. Hey, how about I buy you some dinner? We can join my friends for a powwow on winemaking. Benson won't mind, will ya, Benny?"

My phone dinged with a text.

**Irv:** GET TO WINERY ASAP / ALARM WENT OFF AND YOU NEED TO RESET!

"Whoops, gotta run. Problems at work. Nice meeting you." Saved by the bell, I grabbed my purse and flew out of the bar.

### Montmartre, Paris October 1940

Intent on avoiding any contact with the pair of laughing Nazi soldiers crossing her path, Vivian walked down the steps of *Vogue Paris* as the sun set over the occupied city. The city of lights was dark with despair under German military rule as the Nazis persecuted Jews, arrested suspected members of the French resistance, censored news outlets, and clamped down on sales of food and other basic goods.

After descending on Paris like locusts, the members of Hitler's army, with their tall boots and rifles, seemed to be everywhere—marching up the boulevards, drinking and dining at the cafes, dancing in the clubs, and cavorting with whatever desperate women would sleep with the enemies to gain favors. Vivian had been shocked by the rumors circulating among the staff at the magazine about Coco Chanel. Word had it that she had been cohabiting with a German diplomat at the city's Hotel Ritz, the preferred place of residence for the upper echelon of the Nazi military. Vivian often recalled the designer's words that "the Nazi party isn't really as bad as all that", and the girl could only hope there was some truth to that statement.

The November edition of the magazine featuring the House of Chanel's holiday gowns that Vivian had styled and appeared in had hit the newsstands, and the photos were everything she'd hoped they would be—sexy, fun, and gorgeous. The bad news was that the editors had suspended publication of the magazine while France was under siege, which meant that Vivian's time in Paris would soon be over. It had been five years since the seventeen-year-old girl with dreams of finding success in Paris had left her home and family. Now, this twenty-two-year-old woman with solid experience as a stylist for the publication that dictated fashion trends for women in the French and English-speaking world would return to the States, where she hoped to get a job at the American branch of the magazine. The Nazis had already halted ocean liner travel from Paris, so she would go to London by train to board the *RMS Queen Elizabeth* for passage home. She'd already shipped back a trunk packed with clothes, wine, and the nude of her painted by Marciel, that she prayed her prying mother would not remove from its wrappings.

When Vivian reached her street, she saw a crowd gathered near the entrance to her boarding house where a German army van waited on the curb. *"Qu-est-ce que se passe?"* she asked her landlady, who stood on the front steps of the building.

*"Les Nazis les prennent,"* the distraught woman uttered.

"Taking them? Why?" Vivian asked in horror as she saw soldiers escorting her friend Odette and her husband Abe from the building. "Odette! Abe! What's happening?" she called out.

"Don't you know, young woman?" a man with a Scottish accent asked Vivian. "They're arresting Jews who do any kind of business here. Doctors, lawyers, bankers . . . even artists!"

"But Abe is an excellent lawyer. And an honest man," Vivian said. "He hasn't done anything wrong! I'm sure he'll be able to plead his case."

"Plead his case where and to who?" the man said. "They've shut the courts. You can bet those poor souls will be shipped off with the rest of the Jews to those camps we've been hearing about. Where no good will become of them."

# eleven

Malolactic Fermentation *n.* a stage in the fermentation process, usually of red wines, where harsh-tasting malic acid converts to softer-tasting lactic acid

"May I help you, miss?" the owner of Napa Spirits asked me. I'd stopped by the town's local liquor shop on the Sunday morning after my conversation with Ashton at The Cellar.

"Ah, sure . . ." I was scanning the bottles of French liquors on the shelves. "I'm looking for something called Marc de Beaujolais. It's sometimes used to clean—"

"Right here," the elderly man said as he pulled a bottle from a bin marked Half Price Spirits. "Haven't sold one of these since the nineties." He cocked his head and squinted, forcing his beady eyes to sink even deeper into the thousands of wrinkles on his face. "But this isn't something a pretty girl like you should drink."

"It's not for drinking. It's for cleaning a wooden press and tank for a man named Hal up on—"

"Sure, Hal Pritchett—poor guy. Glad to see he's got a visitor. And no charge for the bottle."

When I got out of my truck at 6 Twisted Vine Road, I worried that Hal would think I was stalking him by showing up again so soon. But when I spotted him out near the field sweeping years of debris away from his old wooden tank and press with a broom, I knew he'd appreciate my visit.

"Good morning, Hal!" I called out as Seuss and I ran toward the ruins of the winery.

"How d'you know my name?" he asked with his back to me as he rubbed the wood of the old pieces with a rag.

"A friend of mine in the wine business knew about you. He told me you're thought of as a local legend around here."

"A local lunatic would be more like it."

"No way," I said, looking at hair that hadn't seen a comb or scissors in years. *Recluse, loner, oddball, maybe—but not lunatic.* "Hey, I brought you something that the winemakers in France use to clean their wooden presses and tanks." I held the bottle of the Marc de Beaujolais out in front of him.

"I've heard about using this, but never tried it." He took the bottle, screwed off the cap, sniffed inside it, and took a swig. Then he poured some of the liquid on the rag and rubbed it into the wood of the old wine press in a circular motion. "Claude Darnay got this from a dealer in Burgundy," he said with his back still facing me. "Said it had squeezed over fifty years worth of grapes through its basket before he'd bought it, which means it was already an antique when it came over. And that was near ninety years ago."

I could already see the transformation of the wood in the places he'd rubbed. "Wow, that's cleaning up nice. I'm Samantha Goodyear, by the way." Though I didn't expect him to respond to my introduction, he turned around and offered his hand.

"Pleased to meet you, Samantha. And thanks for the Marc de Beau."

"It's my pleasure. I spent this past harvest in Beaujolais, where they used old presses like this. I'm excited to see their natural beauty restored. And I admire the French for treasuring their old vines and wish more people here felt the same way. I think it'd be criminal for the big corporate guys to rip yours out."

He stared at me for a moment. "So, you came by here the other day 'cause you needed a place to live. That still the case?"

The question sent my heart racing. My eyes fell on the miniature version of the big house. It was only a few miles from Napa Juice, and the giant property would be ideal for Seuss. Plus, the furniture that was holding Benson's one-car garage hostage would be right at home in that cottage.

"Are you serious?" I asked as my knees began to buckle.

"I stopped making jokes a long time ago, young lady."

"Then yes, it's still the case! Oh Hal, please . . . trust me . . . Seuss and I will be great tenants. We're extremely quiet. No parties, no noise." Now in hot pursuit of a rabbit, Seuss let out a series of ear-splitting barks. "**Seuss, shush!**" I yelled, before turning back to Hal. "You'll never even know we're here."

"Well, *that* might be a confabulation of the truth. But if that cottage works for you, you're welcome to move into the place. We'll work out a price that's fair."

"Wow! Fantastic! Thank you so much! And you can rest easy knowing I won't trouble you with any nervy requests." I looked across the historic property and pinched myself to make sure I wasn't dreaming. When my eyes settled on the weeds covering those amazing old vines, I couldn't resist asking the question. "Hey, Hal, I was wondering . . ."

"Wonderin' what?" he asked with eyes narrowed and head tilted.

"Wondering if there's any way you'd let me . . ."

•　　•　　•

"I've got some terrific news!" I told Benson in our booth at The Cellar after ordering a veggie burger and spinach salad. Having spent the day helping Hal clean his tank and press, I was famished.

"I need some terrific news. Let's hear it," Benson said.

"I asked Hal Pritchett if he'd consider letting me use the grapes in his overgrown field to make my wine this year. And he didn't say no!"

"But he didn't say yes, *did he?* No way would the old hermit agree to anything as communal as sharing his fruit with someone else. Even someone as cute as you."

"Gee, thanks." I blushed. No, he didn't say yes—not exactly. But I did my best to convince him it'd be a win-win for us both. His vineyard would produce incredible wine again, he'd be getting those weeds whacked away, and his horse would get exercise by pulling a plow. Plus, I'd give him fifty cases of what I know could be some of the best Pinot Noir in all of California. And if I end up making money out of the project, he'd get half of the profits."

"Wait a sec." Benson screwed his face up in disbelief. "You're going to weed, prune, plow, and harvest a ten-acre vineyard by yourself? Along with having a full-time job?"

"I'll work nights and on weekends from dawn to dark to get that vineyard into shape, if that's what it takes. Those grapes are worth it."

His face relaxed into a smile. "Well, you've got a helper here, Sam. If you want one. Something tells me that somehow, someway, you're gonna make a killer wine. And I'd love to be along for the ride."

"*Wow!* That would be wonderful, Benson! But I can't ask a winemaker of your caliber to help me for nothing. You've gotta get something out of it too."

"I would get something. The chance to be aligned with a wine that has a great story behind it. And I'm willing to take a bet on its success. But this would be a crapshoot for you too. Anything can go wrong with a single vineyard project like that; spoilage from bacteria, the fermentation can get stuck, adding too much sulfur, not adding enough sulfur, oxidation could ruin—"

"Right. Julien went over all those potential problems with me. We even dealt with some of them. But aren't you pretty slammed right now with your cool job?"

"Cool job? You still think it's cool? Like I started telling you last night, it isn't. Not anymore."

"I'm sorry to hear you say that."

"That London critic was right when she blasted me for making shitty wine."

"Hey, c'mon now, Benson. Don't be so hard on yourself!"

"I should be hard on myself—for selling out. It's no secret in the industry that Ashton's coasting on his 100-point scores from Preston. Five years ago, Ultraviolet was Napa's hottest new wine, with a mile-long waitlist on the website. But more and more kids of our generation are turning their nose up at the over-sweet reds and whites that their parents guzzle. And considering Ashton's problem, I don't think he's capable of evolving his brand to keep up with that growing customer base."

"Problem? What problem? He looks perfectly healthy to me."

"The problem is the stuff he's putting up his nose. That's why his mood swings are all over the place. Ashton's hooked on coke, and it's turning his life and business into a train wreck. Plus, it's making my job near impossible. It's always hard to get any answers from him, 'cause he rarely shows up at the winery anymore. Seems like all he cares about is keeping his scores high, chasing hot women, and snorting the best stuff he can get his hands on."

"That's crazy! The guy's got everything! How could he risk losing it all by doing drugs? You've gotta do something, Benson. Have you thought about staging an intervention?"

"I've mentioned that to Irv, but he's afraid if we do something like that, news of the problem will leak out. And Irv doesn't want any bad PR that could taint Napa Juice. So I'm just trying to keep Ultraviolet going. Other than that, my hands are tied. But they are free to help you uncover some of the oldest Pinot vines in Napa and make some amazing wine. Even if Regis Preston hates it."

"Okay, cool! I'd love to have your help with the project."

"But you'll need more than grapes to make wine. You need a facility to make it at—"

"Yup . . . I'll try to negotiate some kind of price break from Irv. Of course, this all hinges on Hal agreeing to let me use his grapes. And hey, I've got some other good news for you!"

"I don't know if I can handle any more good news," Benson joked. "What is it?"

"You can have your couch and garage back! Seuss and I are moving into Hal's cottage this week. The paint may be peeling, but the toilet flushes and the shower works. And I can't thank you enough for having us."

Benson's smile faded. "You're moving out? You don't have to do that. It's fun having you. Hey, like I said before . . . how 'bout I take the couch and you take the bedroom? That's no problem."

"No way, Benson. You've been a total sport putting up with us. We're not kicking you out of your bed!"

The server brought our plates. Benson pushed his burger to the side. His soft brown eyes looked straight into mine. "Please, Sam, I want you to have the bedroom . . . because . . . I *really* enjoy having you around."

His words caught me off guard. I'd been so busy enjoying our easy friendship that I hadn't even noticed his feelings for me had changed. "Holy smokes, Mr. Doyle! I hope you're not getting a crush on me," I said. His cheeks reddened. It was strange to see a guy blush.

"Can you blame me? You're a damn amazing woman. Smart, brave, and pretty fucking beautiful—to forgo the superlatives."

"Hey . . ." I took his hand and gave it a squeeze. "Please don't make things between us more complicated than they need to be. You know I'm just coming off a roller coaster ride of a bad romance. And I'm just not ready for another go at it." That sounded corny, but it was true.

"It wouldn't be a roller coaster ride or a bad romance with me, Sam. I know I'm not filthy rich or movie star handsome. And my parents don't own a domaine in France."

"It wasn't about that." I pulled my hand away from his. "It wasn't about his being rich or handsome—or even about that domaine," I began, my voice shaking. I looked down at the paper placemat under my plate and made precise tiny splits between the curves of the outside edges. "It was about the way he made me feel when he touched me. About the joy that seemed to flow from every cell of his body when he taught me." My eyes rose from my paper shedding project to meet Benson's stare. "About the way he made me believe that I could make a great wine too someday."

Benson gently took my hand in his. "Okay, I get it—you really loved him. But now, you're here. And he must have said or done something awful to make you run off the way you did."

That stung. It felt as if the thin scab that had formed over my wounded heart had been ripped away. I realized that no matter how much I tried to convince myself otherwise . . . I'd never get over Julien LeMont.

.    .    .

"Sam! Get out here please! Now!" Irv sounded annoyed as he called to me from the winery's tasting room. On a Monday morning, I had a slew of emails from clients and vendors that needed responses. The harsh tone of his voice confused me, since I thought I'd been doing exceptional work for the man. In the few weeks that I'd been at Napa Juice, I'd set up an accounting system in QuickBooks, had billed and paid all current and outstanding invoices, and filed the government forms needed for the winery to stay in operation. I'd even scouted out some potential new clients that were stopping by that week for tours of the facility.

"Coming, Irv!" I leapt from my desk and dashed out to receive his command.

"Ashton just showed up out of nowhere. He wants to pull a sample of his Syrah after Benson and one of the cellar workers do a pump over on one of his tanks. Problem is, Jose and Pablo both called in sick today, so I need you to help. Benson's in there waiting for you. Here, put this on. It'll keep you from inhaling the fumes." He handed me another one of those white paper painter's masks from The Depot.

"Okay, sure! Love to help, Irv. But I've gotta warn you . . . I've never done a pump over. In Beaujolais, we did all that stuff manually."

"And now you're in Napa, so it's high time you join the twenty-first century. So march those shapely legs down to the tank room, please."

To prepare for what I knew would be a messy job, I traded my heels for a pair of sneakers from my desk and grabbed a janitor's jumpsuit, a hat, and a pair of gloves from the cleaning supply closet to keep my hair and clothes from being sprayed with red wine.

After suiting up, I entered the tank room and joined Benson for the task of pumping wine from the bottom of the tank and shooting it with a hose into the top of the tank to force down the thick cap of skins, pulp, and seeds that the $CO_2$ from the fermentation push to the surface. Benson had already secured the hose to the valve at the bottom of the tank and was hoisting the nozzle end in the air with a pulley when I walked into the room.

"Hey, Sam!" he called out. "Ready to build up those biceps? Climb up on the catwalk and I'll hoist up the hose." Before he could give me more details about the task, Ashton walked into the room.

"Okay, men, let's make this quick." He must have assumed I was one of the all-male cellar workers. "I need that Syrah sample when you're done with this. I'm meeting that little shit wine critic from the *LA Times* at The Red Shed in an hour. He's up here to name the year's best bets for the December *Food and Wine* supplement. Only gave me a 92 on last year's vintage. So if he doesn't score this stuff higher, be sure to cut him off my 100-point Christmas basket list, will ya, Benny?"

"Will do," Benson assured his boss. He opened the valve and climbed up to join me on the catwalk, where we both bent over and directed the nozzle toward the top of the cap. Within seconds, the wine from the bottom of the tank shot out with a force that made me fear the hose might fly out from my arms.

"Hey, Benson," Ashton began. "What's with you and that Samantha Lafite chick from the bar the other night? Whoa, she is hot!"

"Samantha Lafite? Who's . . . oh Sam! Yes, she's a very bright young woman."

The repetitive pounding of the spray hitting the cap as it pushed the mass down into the foaming mixture was making me feel dizzy. Still, I kept my eyes glued to the pulsating liquid to avoid being recognized by Ashton.

"You're not banging her, are you?" Ashton asked Benson, while he made some snorting noises as if he needed to blow his nose.

"Ahhh . . . oh, wow!" Benson said, trying to change the subject. "Oh, wow, Ashton, wow!" He was almost yelling. "The aromas coming up are stunning! I'll bet this wine will be—"

"I don't care what you'll bet," Ashton snapped. "And I don't give a flying fuck about the wine. I'm asking you about that girl."

With my face still frozen in place, I considered ripping the mask off to reveal myself to the man before he made any other inappropriate remarks about me. But the longer I continued to stare into the tank, the dizzier I became, as the wine inside spun in one direction, and the area around the tank spun the other way, before they almost seemed to switch directions. Then the pounding started. It was coming from deep inside my skull, giving me a countdown to get out of there fast by making my way down the catwalk and out of the room.

"So, what's the deal, Benny? Are you banging her? 'Cause if not, I'd love to get in her—"

Ashton's words were drowned out by a pounding in my brain accompanied by extreme nausea. I tried to elbow Benson in the ribs to help me, but the thrusts of the hose made it impossible for me to move my arms close enough to get near him. The last thing I remembered was my hands flying away from the hose and the cap of the wine spinning toward me.

•   •   •

"Sam? Samantha? Please wake up!" The siren of an ambulance rang out in my ears. I could feel the motion of the vehicle as I lay on the gurney. On one side of me a hunky EMT was adjusting the oxygen mask over my nose. Benson was on my other side. I felt the warmth of his hand on mine. "Just keep breathing, Sam—in and out, in and out." I opened my eyes. "Are you okay?" he asked. "Please tell me you're alright!"

"Wha . . . what happened?" My head was foggy, my vision was blurred, and my voice was a throaty rasp.

"*You're awake! Thank God!*"

"Benson, *please*, just tell me what happened."

"We were doing a pump over in the winery. Ashton was making some comments about you. He seemed pretty coked up. And of course, he had no idea it was you behind that mask. In a flash you fell forward and did a nosedive into the tank."

"Did I? I remember seeing the wine in my face, but that's it."

"I jumped in after you and pulled you to the top, but you were out like a light. The fumes from the $CO_2$ coming up were just too strong for those flimsy painter's masks that Irv hands out for pump overs and for cleaning the tanks. He knows he was violating codes by not supplying the proper gear and feels terrible about what happened. Plus, he's terrified you'll sue."

"*I'm sure* he is," I mumbled before slipping back into my slumber.

• • •

When I awoke again, I was in a hospital room. A huge arrangement of roses and a smaller one with lilies made the cramped space smell like a florist shop. Benson sat in a chair with his cell to his ear.

"Yes, Mrs. Goodyear, the doctors say there was no harm done to the lungs or the nervous system. She'll have a nasty headache when she wakes up, but that's all. Uh-huh, this is one of the dangers in the wine cellar. If fact, there've been several reports of deaths in the area over the years from people being overcome by the buildup of $CO_2$ from the fermenting wine in the tanks. That's why all wineries require that two people do these pump overs. Sure, I'll have Sam call you as soon as she wakes up. Okay, take care Mrs. Goodyear. Bye." He put his cell on the table and slid his chair closer to me. My eyes were open, and my brain felt like it was about to crack my skull in half.

"Hi there," Benson said.

"Ha . . . ha . . . ha . . . hi to you too. And th . . . th . . . thanks for filling my mom in. She's wa . . . wa . . . way more than I could handle right now. *Ouch!*"

"I figured as much. How's your head?"

"Besides . . . besides feeling like it's about to burst, it's great."

"Here, let me help." Benson leaned toward me and put the oxygen mask over my nose. "The doctor said you should keep using this to flush out any remaining $CO_2$ from your organs. So take a nice deep breath. In . . . out. In . . . out."

After following his instructions for several minutes, a steady throb of blood pumping through my head replaced the exploding brain. I grabbed a section of my hair and gasped. "Jesus! What's this?" The blonde had turned purple after soaking up color from the wine.

"I like it," Benson grinned. "You look like a character from one of those anime cartoons I used to watch as a kid."

"Oh, *lovely!*" I rolled my eyes. The memory of the conversation taking place before I'd blacked out came floating back. "Hey, Benson, there's not a lot of concern about sexual harassment in the workplace here in Napa, huh? Or is it not considered sexual harassment if the harasser doesn't know the harassee is in earshot?"

"Don't know. I just hope Ashton'll realize he's out of control after this. When we carried you out into the fresh air, he was mortified to see it was you behind that mask. And he was furious with me for not shutting him up in there. Though God knows I tried. He brought those flowers in here himself." I looked over at the enormous arrangement of red, yellow, and white roses on the table. A note affixed to the bouquet by a white silk ribbon had the hand-scribed message:

> *The world's biggest asshole wishes you a speedy recovery.*
> *Love, Ashton White.*

"Whoa!" I shivered at the sight of it. "Looks like a funeral arrangement."

"The smaller one is from Irv." Benson pointed to the lilies in a clear glass vase. A plastic spike held a note typed by the floral company with the message: *Get well soon. Sincerely, Irving Wasserman.* "First, Irv worried about a lawsuit. Now that he knows you'll be okay, he's terrified you'll tell any reporters who may show up here that you weren't wearing the proper gear for the job. It'd make the winery appear unsafe. Could even result in a hefty fine. He asked me to encourage you to tell the folks from the *Napa Register* that you fell because you tripped and lost your balance. But you do whatever you feel is right. Irv's down at Napa Valley Vintner's Supply loading up on respirators right now."

"He doesn't have to worry. I won't rat him or the winery out, provided he tightens up his safety standards, and provided he gives me a super sweet discount on the use of his facility for my wine project.

Ouch!" The exploding brain returned. Benson put the mask back over my nose.

"C'mon, Sam. In . . . out. In . . . out."

"Got it, Dr. Benson," I said as I slowly inhaled and exhaled. "And in case you're wondering . . . this wasn't what I had in mind when I decided to *get into* wine."

### *Montmartre, Paris October 1940*

A pair of Nazi soldiers used their rifles to shoo the crowd of onlookers away as the German military van drove off with Odette and Abe locked in the back. Reeling from the shock of the arrest of her dear friends, Vivian stood on the curb until traffic obliterated the vehicle. She now realized the true scope of the evil that had descended upon Paris and scolded herself for ever feeling blue about things that were absolutely paltry when compared to what the Jews and the other citizens of France were now up against. She wracked her brain in search of a way to help the doomed couple. For a moment, she considered taking a bus to the Gestapo headquarters in the Hotel Majestic to plead for their release. But as she trudged up the staircase of her boarding house, she knew her efforts would prove futile.

When she entered her room, now empty save for the bottle of wine she'd planned to drink with Odette and Abe before leaving Paris and the few items of clothing she hadn't shipped home, she lay down on the bed. A few moments later, she sat up with a start and said, "Coco!"

• • •

From her fifth-floor window that overlooked the Jardins du Trocadero, Vivian watched the October sun as it sank behind the Arc de Triomphe. She knew she had to look like someone special to gain entrance to the Ritz, much less to convince the desk captain to announce her presence to Coco Chanel at the hotel frequented by the likes of Katharine Hepburn, Ernest Hemingway, and the Duke of Windsor.

She darkened her light red brows with an eye pencil, waved a wand of mascara over her lashes, gave her cheeks a rosy glow with rouge, and slid shiny red color over her perfectly plump cupid bow lips. With tortoise shell half combs, she secured her auburn curls away from her face, and let the rest of her hair tumble around her shoulders. She then studied her countenance in the mirror, much like the art director of a fashion magazine would study a model's face before it gets photographed. There was no room for vanity in her mission. On that evening, her beauty would be used as a tool to save the lives of her friends. It was unfortunate that the best clothes she had were the ruffled skirt and lace blouse she'd planned to travel in, and as she grabbed the bottle of wine from the nightstand, she prayed that her face would be enough to secure her passage through the revolving doors of Paris' most exclusive enclave.

· · ·

*"Je me fiche que vous soyez Madame de Pompadour. Vous ne pouvez pas entrer,"* the woman at the door of the Paris Ritz barked at Vivian, telling her she didn't care if she was Louis the XV's beloved mistress, entrance to the hotel was restricted to guests and members of the German military. Believing that she was now helpless to save her friends, Vivian walked away from the rambling, sixteenth-century building on the Place Vendôme that just months before had been annexed as the headquarters of Hitler's air force.

*"Mademoiselle!"* a voice called out to her from behind. She turned and saw a twenty-something-year-old man in a doorman's uniform following her. "I heard your American accent. I'm from the States too," he said, not wanting to let her out of his sight. "I apologize that they turned you away. Hotel security has heightened since the German officers have made base here. But you sounded like you have an important reason to gain entry."

"I do. I need to pay a call to one of the guests. Can you help me?" Vivian asked.

"I'll try my best," he said, aware that he could be fired on the spot for breaking hotel protocol. But he couldn't refuse those pouting lips and emerald eyes. "You've got to enter the way the Hollywood film stars do. They slip in through the service entrance in the hotel's rear, mostly to stay unnoticed. Meet me there in five minutes." With that, he jogged off to open the door to an arriving taxi full of Nazi officers.

Vivian hurried around the back of the hotel, clutching the bottle of wine. Keeping her head down as if she were a starlet not wanting to be recognized, she pushed the door open and entered the service area of the building where she heard the ding of an elevator.

"Welcome to the Ritz!" the young doorman said as he stepped from the elevator into the otherwise unoccupied hallway. "Fredrick Branson at your service. I'm heading back to Connecticut next week where a real job awaits. Had enough of these Germans. So I don't care if I get sacked for letting you in."

"Thanks, Fredrick," Vivian said with her chest heaving from both anxiety and the walk. "By the way, I'm Vivian—Vivian Goodyear. I'm heading out myself soon. Going to London and then on to New York. I'm here because some friends of mine are in serious trouble, and I'm hoping that Mademoiselle Chanel's man friend can help them. Please, Fredrick, can you get me up to his room?"

"It's not a room—it's a suite. A suite fit for royalty. I peeked in a few times when I delivered his uniforms from the cleaners. It's on the third floor—number 310. Take the staircase so you won't be discovered," he said as he led her down the hall.

"Thanks, again! Wish me luck!" Vivian said as she hurried toward the stairs.

"And how can I find you back in the States?" he called out.

"Ring me up at Tennyson 4-4766."

# twelve

---

**Noble Rot** *n.* a fungus that affects certain grapes, causing them to shrivel as they achieve heightened flavors and sugar content

"Hal, that looks great!" I called out the window of my Ford pickup as Benson and I arrived at 6 Twisted Vine Road on the Saturday morning following my stay at Napa's Queen of the Valley Hospital. Hal had just finished painting the outside of the cottage a soft shade of green.

"Well, I can't let a beautiful young lady live in an eyesore now, can I?" he asked, with brush in hand. "I saw the piece in the *Register* 'bout your dive into that tank of fermentin' Syrah. You don't look any worse for the wear though."

"Not the kind of publicity I was looking for. But yeah, I'm okay, thanks. Now that I've gotten the purple out of my hair." I parked the truck with the trailer in front of the cottage. Seuss jumped out and ran to the field in search of rabbits to chase. Benson went to the trailer and started hauling out my furniture and the other possessions I'd wrapped in moving blankets before leaving Manhattan.

"Hal, this is my friend, Benson Doyle. He's the winemaker for Ashton White, over at Napa Juice, and he's kindly offered to work with me in the vineyard and even help me make the wine. That is, *if* you decide to let me use your wonderful grapes."

"Beautiful place you have here, Hal! It's great to meet one of Napa's true pioneers!" Benson said, holding out his hand for a shake.

"That so?" was Hal's only response while he ignored Benson's hand and held the door for me to enter the cottage. I mouthed "sorry" to Benson, then stepped inside my new home. Hal had given it a good cleaning and was now painting the interior. The wide-plank floors and wooden wainscoting on the walls gave the place a cozy feel. A pile of logs sat by the fireplace. The little kitchen had a miniature gas stove and what looked to be the first electric refrigerator ever invented. The bedroom window faced the field. I hoped that in a few months, I'd awaken each morning to a view of a vineyard.

"Okay, Hal, first things first, let's talk about rent. I want to pay you a decent price." But in truth, I couldn't pay much. I had two thousand dollars left in my bank account. My salary, still a mere five-hundred-fifty a week, barely covered my food and gas. And I hadn't even calculated what a winemaking project would cost me. Still, I didn't want to take advantage of the man. "How about seven hundred a month? I know you could get more, but I'll be honest, I—"

"Consider it done," Hal said. "Who knows? We could be partners, and I wouldn't want my partner goin' bust." I crossed my fingers with the hope he was considering letting me use his grapes. But I didn't dare press him on it.

•    •    •

The sun was going down as Benson and I finished arranging most of the furniture in the cozy space. While Hal put the last strokes of paint on the living room walls, I unwrapped the painting of Aunt Vivian and held it up over the fireplace.

"Hey, Hal," I called out to my new landlord. "Would you mind helping me hang this? I've got a nail and hook taped to the back of the canvas."

He took the painting from my hands and stared at it. "Goodness! Put some clothes on, young lady! You could catch your death of cold!"

"Not to worry," I said as stared at the image with fondness. "It was summer in Paris when she sat for it. That was my Great Aunt Vivian. She loved wine too."

"Well, I'm no art critic, but this is one beautiful painting of an exquisite woman. Is this about where you want it?" Hal marked the wall with a pencil.

Benson came into the house with a long piece of furniture balanced on his back and leaned it on its side. "Here's this standing bar that's been sitting in my garage," he said as I cut the ropes and removed the blankets tied around it. We stood the piece upright. I rubbed my hand on the smooth cherry wood that brought back so many sweet memories from my childhood. "Aunt Viv served her favorite wines to her guests on this while she gave me small tastes." I looked at the case of wine she left to me that was on the floor. "Told me that if life ever gave me sour grapes, to open this case and enjoy the wine—said it would somehow make things better."

"You can store that box in my underground cellar. It's always around fifty-five Fahrenheit," Hal said. "I'll take it down there for you. Want to grab a few bottles of what we made back in the days before we worried about scores. You two up for some tasting?"

"Are we up for tasting wine from *your* vineyard? *Hell, yes!*" I said as Benson's eyes widened, and he held two thumbs up.

"Great. And that old bar looks like the place to do it," Hal said as he picked up my case of wine and took it back outside. Benson and I went out to the U-Haul to carry in the wooden stools that matched the bar. After a few minutes, Hal returned from the cellar with six bottles of Darnay Pinot Noir in his arms.

"Have you got a bunch of glasses?" he asked as he lined the bottles up on the bar. He pulled a corkscrew from his pocket and started to open them. I unpacked my wine glasses and set them out. "And you'll both need somethin' to spit into," Hal added.

"I've got just the thing," I said, as I held up two crystal spittoons. "Picked these up at the Paris airport before boarding my flight to New York. I knew they'd come in handy."

Hal put six glasses in a line on one side of the bar and six glasses in a line on the other side. He poured wine from the first bottle into

Benson's and my first glass. Then he poured wine from the second bottle into our second glasses, and wine from the third bottle into our third glasses, and so on down the line until Benson and I each had six glasses of wine in front of us with the corresponding bottles in the center.

"Now both of you please taste the first wine and tell me about it," Hal said.

I swirled a 1985 vintage around in its glass to let it meet the air after so many years in the bottle. After breathing in its aroma, I took a sip and waited for the liquid to go from the top of my mouth, then over my tongue to the lower palate, before swallowing it. While tasting several wines, most people spit them out after trying them in order to stay sober enough to continue with the tasting. But I wanted to experience every drop of this vintage. "It doesn't have a lot of fruit," I said after taking another sip. "I taste cooking herbs . . . maybe thyme and sage, and it still has a decent amount of tannin." Julien had taught me that though tannins can add bitterness and dryness to wine, they also add balance, complexity, and structure, plus they help to keep the taste of the wine lingering after it leaves the mouth. "It seems to have aged beautifully, which suggests there was a lot of acid and not much sugar in the grapes when you picked."

"Sam's right about the sugar being low." Benson said. "That tells me you picked the grapes early. I bet you had a cold spell with a lot of rain before harvest and had to pick hmmm . . . around the second week of August to keep the grapes from getting mold. Believe me, from a guy forced to make wine from grapes with high sugar levels, I find this to be a total pleasure."

"You do seem to know a good bit about winemaking young fella," Hal told Benson, while offering his hand for a shake. "Hope there're no hard feelin's for my bein so ornery when we first met."

"No hard feelings at all, Mr. Pritchett," Benson said as his hand met Hal's.

Hal then looked at me for my thoughts on the second Pinot Noir — a 1988 vintage. "This one's distinctly fruitier," I began. "It lacks the range of flavors that the first wine had and seems higher in alcohol." I checked the level of alcohol, which is required by law to appear on the bottle. Instead of spitting out the wine, I swallowed it quickly to continue my report. "Yup," I said. "Thirteen percent alcohol. The '85 had twelve percent. That tells me you picked the grapes later in the season when the sugar levels were higher. Or, a heatwave before harvest could have caused the sugar levels to rise earlier than usual."

When I put my nose on the glass of the third wine, it gave me an essence of sweet red cherries. On the palate, it was pure, like fine china, with a red fruit tartness and baking spice on the finish. I happily swallowed this vintage and helped myself to another pour. It wasn't until Hal asked Benson to tell him about that year's harvest that I realized why he was giving us this quiz. He wanted to make sure we knew what we were doing before entrusting us to make wine from his beloved vineyard.

"Hey, this is a great assignment, Hal," I said as we continued to enjoy the wine and give him our thoughts on the other bottles.

When we finished the tasting, Hal helped himself to a generous pour of the '85, took a sip, and swished it around in his mouth. "This is my favorite vintage of all. It's the most delicate and aromatic of all these wines on the table, though it's still well-structured with layers of interesting flavors, which is how a Pinot Noir should be. By the way, I like what I'm hearin' from you two." He turned to me. "You're welcome to use my grapes for your wine, young lady." He raised the corners of his mouth to form what could almost pass for a smile. "I know Emma would give her approval, same as me, if I could ask her. And help yourself to the rest of these open bottles—I switched to beer a long time ago."

"Thanks, Hal, you're the best!" I cheered as I splashed more wine into a glass to make a toast. "I promise I'll make the kind of wine this vineyard was destined to produce. Forget about going for scores and forget about trying to please Regis Preston." The three of us held up our glasses and touched them together in unison. "Forget about going for scores . . ." Hal chimed in, as we gave our glasses another clink. ". . . and fuck Regis Preston."

•    •    •

"We did it!" I screamed while I jumped up and down when Hal walked out of the cottage. "We did it, Benson! We convinced him to let us make wine from the best Pinot Noir vines in Napa! Maybe the best in the world!"

"No, you did it, Sam. You convinced him. I just watched you do it." Benson got up from the stool and flopped into one of Aunt Viv's comfy leather chairs.

I grabbed one of the open bottles that Hal had left on the table, took a swig from it, did a *tour jeté* learned in my kindergarten ballet class, and collapsed into the other chair. "It was all worth it, Benson! Everything! Quitting Weatherhouse, going to France, spending my entire savings! It was worth it because I'm gonna make an amazing wine!" I took another sip from the bottle, leapt into the air, and executed another *tour jeté*. The propulsion from the move sent me flying, bottle in hand, onto Benson's lap. "Sorry! I'm kinda rusty." I took another swig from the bottle. "Here—I didn't mean to hog it all." I tipped the bottle up to pour some wine into his mouth, but it dribbled down his chin and neck, and onto his shirt.

"That's good, Sam—thanks." He gently guided my hand with the bottle away. After the mess I made on him, he was being way too tolerant of my silliness.

"Why are you so kind to me, Benson? You're just way too darn nice." Drinking too much wine had me very happy, but now it made me sad. "You let me and my dog sleep on your couch when we had nowhere else to go." I wiped a tear from my eye with my finger. "You stayed by my side in the hospital. You carried my great-aunt's stand-behind bar in here on your back. And now . . ." I pulled up the tail of his shirt to wipe another tear away. "You're going to help me get this wild mess of a vineyard into shape. I don't deserve it."

He put his arm around my shoulder. "And why not?"

"Because I don't . . ."

"You don't what?"

"I don't feel the way about you . . . that you feel about me. So I don't deserve you."

I laid my head on his chest while he took the empty bottle from my hand and set it down on the table. "Sure, you do." He took a lock of my hair and curled it around his finger. "You're the bravest, smartest person I've ever met. And I don't expect you to love me the way I love you. Like I said, I'm not the triple threat of talent, great looks, and big money that Julien is."

"Triple threats are overrated. Anyway, I think you're quite easy on the eyes." I ran my finger over his chin, and for the first time noticed the cute dimple in the center. It felt kind of nice to be snuggling up to him, since I'd had nothing close to a flirtation with a guy in months.

"No, I'm not in Julien's league—or yours." He took my face in his hands. "When I saw you that first night at Domaine LeMont . . . the light from the candles was dancing on your skin . . . and I thought you were the most beautiful woman I'd ever seen."

Listening to his words, I inhaled the wine I'd spilled on him along with the musky scent of his sweat from carrying my furniture. The aromas reminded me of Julien, and the excitement I'd felt with him on that very first night in France when I tasted that wild garlic. When Benson pulled me closer for what would be our first kiss, I melted into his arms, closed my eyes, and took a long deep breath to fill my lungs with the essence of his body.

He pulled away from me. "What're you doing, Sam?"

I exhaled with eyes closed. "Hmmm . . . I'm imagining that I'm smelling wild garlic."

"Wild garlic? Like they have all over France?"

"Yeah . . . the stuff that grows like crazy in the fields of Domaine LeMont." I inhaled again and gave him a dreamy smile. "It's so . . . so aromatic."

He stared at my face for a few moments, before he rose from the chair with me in his arms, carried me into the bedroom, and placed me down on the bed. A few moments went by before I opened my eyes to see him walking from the room.

"Good night, Sam. Sleep well."

"Hey, where're you going?"

"I'm not the one you're thinking about. And I can't pretend to be Julien LeMont."

### Montmartre, Paris October 1940

"Le service au chambre est arrivé, mon amour," a man's voice cried from the inside of Coco Chanel's suite when Vivian rang the bell.

"Sorry, but I'm not room service," Vivian said when the door was opened by a tall, well-built man with a square jaw who looked to be in his late forties. He wore a velvet smoking jacket and had a silk ascot around his neck. "I'm Vivian Goodyear. And you must be Mr. Dincklage."

"I am. And how can I help you?" asked the man who spoke with a heavy German accent.

"I worked with Mademoiselle Chanel at *Vogue* magazine, and would like to make a request," Vivian said, her voice trembling. "I'm confident she'll remember me. But I'll start by giving you this nice bottle of Burgundy."

"How kind! Do come in," the man said as he motioned her through the door and took the bottle of Romanée-Conti from her hands.

"Oh, thank you, sir," Vivian gushed, relieved that the man was so cordial.

"My pleasure. Mademoiselle will be meeting an associate in the lounge before I join her for dinner. But let's see if we can delay her from her shop talk to speak with a lovely young *fräulein*," he said with a wink. He guided her to sit on one of the long white sofas in a room that had an ornate marble fireplace, Persian rugs, and crystal chandeliers hanging from the ceiling.

"Speak with whom, my darling?" Coco said as she entered the room looking sharp in a white tweed skirt, a matching collarless jacket, and a scarf with the interlocking C's of the Chanel logo.

"Vivian Goodyear, Mademoiselle Chanel," Vivian announced as she rose from the sofa with heart pounding in fear that the woman would be angered at the disturbance. "Remember me from the *Vogue* shoot? It's been a few months."

"Yes, I do! I couldn't forget our *directeur artistique* and super model extraordinaire!" Coco exclaimed, as she walked up to Vivian and grasped the girl's hands. "The editorial pages you styled and lent your beauty to are smashing! And I'd love to make an offer to make use of your talents both behind and in front of the camera just as soon as our great nations begin to respect each other's needs. But until then, I've followed *Vogue's* lead and shut the doors to the House of Chanel."

"Thank you, mademoiselle, and I'm sure you have good reasons to put your business on pause. And though I plan to return to the States in a few days, I'd love to work with you at some point. But I'm not here to ask for a job. You see, the Nazis have arrested some very dear friends of mine . . . Jewish friends. And I'm worried they'll send them off to one of those awful camps we've been hearing about." She looked over at the German with a smile. "And I've heard Mr. Dincklage is well-connected to the German government, so I'm wondering if he could help them out with their situation. I can assure you they didn't do anything illegal. They're good people."

"I'm sure they are," Coco said as she dropped Vivian's hands. "But you must let the new government do their work and give these people a fair trial. And though Dinky has a heart of gold, if he pulled strings for some, and word got out, he'd be flooded with calls by others wanting the same thing for their friends. But feel free to ask him yourself—he could surprise you." Coco sat on the sofa with the German and caressed his chest. "Under this body of steel, he *can* be quite a softie. Can't you, darling?" He smiled and whispered something to her in German before she stood up, glanced at her watch, and looked at Vivian. "I have to run. Dinky will show you out—won't you, *mon ami?* And I'm serious about making you an offer when things settle down. In fact, on your way out, stop by my table in the bar for a cocktail and meet my associate. Your pretty face will add extra glamour to the room." With that, she gave her lover a peck on the cheek and dashed out the door of the suite.

"Is what she said true?" Vivian asked the German in desperation as she watched the door close. "Do you really have a heart of gold? Because if you do, you'll help free my dear friends. They're having a child in a month. They think it's a girl, and if it is, they'll call her Estelle. Their names are Abe and Odette. Abe's an attorney—a good one. Odette sells clothing at one of the local dress shops."

Dincklage rose from the sofa and looked down at Vivian. "Is she as pretty as you, *fräulein*?" he asked.

"Excuse me, sir?"

"I'm asking if your friend is as pretty as you are."

"Well . . ." Vivian hesitated. "She's quite lovely. And more than that, she's kind, she's a hard worker, and I know she'll make a splendid mother."

"To the little Jew girl," Dinky said with a sneer that revealed two rows of yellowed, triangle-shaped teeth that transformed his once attractive face into something hideous.

*Oh my, he's despicable,* Vivian said to herself, perplexed that a woman as successful and sophisticated as Coco Chanel could be involved with such a man.

"I could submit an order of retraction to the military headquarters to release your friends," Dinky began. "But if I do, they must leave Paris upon their release, and cease all business operations."

"Yes, yes, they will!" Vivian said as a rush of relief flooded through her body. *Though he's a monster, he'll save my friends,* she thought with chest heaving.

"Now into the bedroom with you, to show your appreciation for my effort," he said as he pointed to a room down the hallway.

"What? What's this about?" she asked in shock.

"You know what it's about. I do you a favor, you do me one."

"But Miss Chanel?" Vivian asked, her voice trembling. "You two are—"

"Yes, we are," he said as he untied his robe to reveal a wide chest covered in thick grey hair. "We're best friends, we're lovers, and we understand each other completely. But when I get the chance to *ficken* a young *Muschi* instead of a fifty-seven-year-old *Fötze* I take it. And if you want me to get those kikes a get-out-of-jail-free card, I suggest you get your pretty arse onto the bed."

"Oh, no! No, please, Mr. Dinklage," Vivian whispered as she backed away from the man in horror.

"*Oh, ja!*" he said, as he took her arm and pulled her into the bedroom. "We must act fast in case my lady returns early from her meeting."

"I beg you, Mr. Dincklage! Please don't do this!" Vivian screamed while he pushed her down on the enormous bed, straddled her torso with his legs, put a hand across her mouth, and yanked at his trousers to release a monstrously large erect penis that waved back and forth above her face. Through her tears, Vivian caught sight of a kidney-shaped purple birthmark at the tip of the organ. Though Marciel was the only man she'd had sex with, she'd sketched penises of all shapes and sizes in art school, but had never encountered one with such a mark.

"Stop your fight," the German commanded as she kicked her legs like a wild animal and thought she might choke on the vomit that rose from her belly. "And tell me you want me to *ficken* you." He pulled up her skirt and pawed at her undergarments. "I'm warning you, *fräulein*, if you expect me to free your friends, you'd better lie still and welcome my *Schwanz*."

"Get off me! Get off!" Vivian hissed through her teeth. "And if you *don't* free my friends, I'll tell Mademoiselle Chanel you tried to rape me."

"Go on and tell her what you like. She'd never believe that of me," he said with a laugh.

"Oh, *really*? And what will she say when I mention that purple mark on your *Schwanz*"?

The motion on the mattress stopped, as he stood and backed away from the bed.

Vivian leapt from the mattress, pulled her skirt down, and faced her attacker. "Abe and Odette Newberg are their names. If they're not released by tomorrow at noon, Mademoiselle will know exactly how hard her 'softie' gets when she's not watching." With that she marched from the room, went out to the hallway, and took the elevator down to join Coco Chanel and her associate for a cocktail.

# thirteen

---

**Mouthfeel** *n.* the physical sensations in the mouth produced by wine, often described with terms such as velvety, meaty, chewy, chalky, abrasive

It was five o'clock on what had been a stressful Monday. I'd been on the phone with government agencies for the better part of the day trying to keep Napa Juice from being shut down by the US Bureau of Alcohol, Tobacco, Firearms, and Explosives because Irv was a year late in filling out the necessary forms to keep the winery in good standing with the Feds.

The day had a bright spot when my phone dinged with a text.

**Spence:** In Napa. Would love to see you and catch up. Do you have time to meet? If so, tell me when & where

Overjoyed at the chance to see Spence, I texted him back.

**Sam:** Yay! Of course! Be at The Cellar, 660 Main Street, say in 1 hr?

**Spence:** U r on!

At five forty-five, I grabbed my purse and skipped my way out of the building. Before I'd climbed into my truck, Benson called to me from his monster-sized red Ford pickup.

"Hey Sam! Save me a seat at the bar, will ya? Gotta stop for some gas on the way."

Remembering that we'd planned to meet at The Cellar after work, I ran over to his truck to make my apologies.

"Benson!" I screamed over the roar of his engine. "I screwed up! My friend Spence who owns a wine shop in Manhattan came into town. He's meeting me at The Cellar in a few. But hey, please join us!"

"Okay, see you there," he yelled back, as he muscled down on the gearshift to pilot the truck out of the parking lot.

Being the first to arrive at The Cellar, I grabbed a booth so the three of us could have a cozy chat. I couldn't have been sitting there for more than a minute before I saw Spence walk in the restaurant's door with a smile on his face and his arm around Sara LeMont.

$$\cdot \quad \cdot \quad \cdot$$

"So, there I was, unpacking boxes of wine, when the door over the bell rang." Spence was telling his story to Benson and me as the four of us sat in the booth. My old friend hadn't taken his eyes off Sara since they'd sat down. "I heard a familiar voice call out with, 'You need to fill that bare spot on the wall. How about three large photos? Black and whites, of course. Maybe grape vines before harvest?'" Sara grabbed Spence's arm and let out a laugh of pure joy. It occurred to me that I hadn't heard that laugh once during my stay at Domaine LeMont. "I wondered if I'd had a heart attack, and was having an out-of-body experience, where the best part of my life was flashing before me." Tears glistened in Sara's eyes while Spence spoke.

"The gravity of my impetuous decision to move to the Côte and marry Denis set in when the wedding was over. I was totally unprepared to take on my role as *la première dame du Château LeMont*. Plus, the cultural differences were a problem from the start," Sara said, her eyes alternating between Benson and me. "But the once fearless and adventurous feminist didn't have the courage to pack up and leave." She looked up at Spence and stroked his face. "I didn't think Spencer would ever take me back after the way I'd hurt him. When my sons arrived, our family became my priority. And though Denis was good with the boys, he didn't take his marriage vows seriously."

Spence grasped her hand, held it up, and kissed it. "She was a terrific mother and an amazing wife. But that guy didn't deserve her. Not for one second."

"After my darlings grew up, my feelings of despair were overpowering," Sara continued. "There I was, trapped in a terrible marriage and so far away from my real home." She gave me an adoring smile. "But when you came to spend harvest with us, Sam, you gave me hope."

"Me?" I asked. "You mean me and my big mouth?"

"You suggested that Spence still loved me. Knowing that, I just couldn't live out my life in misery until the only thing left of me was a bottle with a tasting note tied to it on that shelf over the fireplace. The incident with that Romanian woman was the final straw. Soon after you left, I packed up my clothes, my jewelry, my photos of the boys, and booked a one-way flight to JFK."

"And she took a cab with a hundred suitcases straight to my shop," said Spence. "I had them sent to my apartment and took two weeks off while I settled her in. We retraced our steps in the city, visiting museums, watching old movies, and eating at whatever of our favorite hangouts were still around. It was pure heaven."

"Henri understood why I was leaving," Sara continued. "I'll see him often here. He spends so much time in the States. And though Julien didn't say much when I gave him the news, I know he was very upset." She gave a half-smile. "Though I almost needed a crowbar to pry his true feelings from him." She reached across the table and took my hand in hers. "Maybe he just needed more of a chance to explain himself to you."

"Maybe he did. But it's too late now," I whispered, feeling like a knife had penetrated my gut.

Sensing my pain, Benson spoke up. "Sam's going to make her own wine this year with grapes from one of the oldest vineyards in Napa, Mrs. LeMont."

Sara leaned over and squeezed my arm. "Good for you, Samantha! Seems like your experience at Domaine LeMont had some benefits."

"You're wasting no time out here!" Spence said. "Tell me about these grapes and this wine."

"They're Pinot Noir. Planted in the 1930s with French clones by a guy named Claude Darnay. Inherited in the '70s by a man, who, along with his wife, continued to produce Darnay wine until she died."

"Sure, I remember the wine," said Spence. "A wonderful Pinot. For the first few years, that is. Then it seemed to lose all of its character. High sugar levels overpowered the delicate flavor."

"Yup, 'cause they had to pick late to get good numbers from Regis Preston. But I won't let that happen this time."

"I'm sure you won't, Sam," Spence said. "Ship out as many cases as you can spare when you're ready to release. I'll make a big display of—"

"It'll still be called *Darnay*. I want to keep the history."

"Roger that! I'll design a stack of bottles in the store window with the sign, 'Darnay—a fantastic new old-vine wine by Napa winemaker Samantha Goodyear.'"

# fourteen

---

**Brettanomyces** *n.* a spoilage yeast that can ruin red wine

"I never thought I'd see this vineyard again," Hal said as he leaned on his pitchfork and stared at his vines that were now in plain sight. "But there they are, even if they look a mite unruly."

Benson, Hal, and I had been working weekends and early mornings with hoes and battery powered weed whackers to clear fifteen-plus years of weed growth from the vineyard. Old Delilah was back on the job, pulling a cart filled with weeds to a pile for burning. Now, on a Sunday in the second week of March, I was looking at fourteen thousand old vines in desperate need of pruning.

"Okay, Samantha, we're giving these guys a buzz cut," Benson said, while he went to work with a pair of pruning shears. Spring was on its way, and the vines had dozens of branches growing out of their bark-covered trunks. When Benson finished cutting the first plant back, it resembled a log with two green shoots. "Now this guy can start putting his energy into his fruit, instead of his extraneous foliage. The natural water is scarce around here 'cause of the winds coming off the San Francisco Bay. And this clay-like soil is low in nutrients. So the vines have to struggle to survive, making the grapes very concentrated and flavorful—which is what we want. We're just trying to help the plants make more of them."

While Benson was talking, Hal was a few rows over from us, heaving the mountains of cut weeds to the edge of the vineyard with a pitchfork. With his hair trimmed and a new spring added to his step, he looked like a different man from the one I'd seen on my first visit to 6 Twisted Vine Road. He'd also taken to riding his rusted military Jeep around the field to oversee the work Benson and I were doing on the vineyard.

After we pruned an entire row of vines, a BMW SUV followed by a silver Jaguar entered the front gates of the property. Two men, who appeared to be identical twins, got out of the BMW. They both looked like they'd just stepped off a golf course in their polo shirts, tailored shorts, and ankle socks under saddle shoes. A third man with a comb-over hairdo emerged from the Jaguar.

"Dad? Dad? You out here?" one twin called out as the group walked toward the field. When the men came close to where Benson and I were pruning the vines, I heard the other twin speaking to the man with the comb-over.

"One look at that entrance says the property is too much for my father to deal with, Ken. It's sad, but you'll see it's hard for him to maintain himself at this point."

"Yup, so it goes, Andrew," Ken said, his voice sympathetic. "Sis and I had to put our mom in a retirement home last summer. She begged us not to, but like your dad, she's near eighty and starting to fail."

"I've been down to the county hall of records . . ." the other twin began. He made the motion of a golf swing with his arms while he walked. "Seems dad is years behind on his property taxes. His only income now is his Social Security, and that doesn't cover his nut. My brother and I agree we should have him sell this place and find something manageable."

"Gotcha, Lucas," Ken agreed. "I've run some comps, and between the house and the acreage, we should net close to three million to put into your dad's estate. If you wait until he passes, there'll be no tax to the family. But most heirs like to sell when the market is hot, like it is now."

"Excuse me, can I ask what you're doing here?" Andrew called out to Benson and me when he spotted us in the vineyard.

"Hi!" I stood and held up my pruning shears. "I'm Samantha and this is Benson. We're working with Hal to get his vineyard cleaned up. And we're really excited about the way it's taking shape!"

"Young lady," Andrew began. "My father is a tired old man, and he doesn't have the interest or the energy to do *any* work on this vineyard. I don't know you people, and I have no idea what you're doing here, but—"

The sound of a diesel-powered engine drowned out his words as Hal sped up the slope of the hill in the Jeep. When he saw the three men, he yanked on the vehicle's emergency brake, shut the engine down, and jumped to the ground.

"Well, I'll be an orangutan's uncle!" Hal called out to his sons. "The golf course musta been empty today if you two finished your round in time to fit in a visit to your old man! I was thinkin' just the other day that I can count the times on one hand you boys have visited me since your mama died."

"Hi, Dad! Hey, you shouldn't be driving that thing," Lucas said, looking up at the Jeep as if it were about to explode. "You could blow out your knee on that clutch. And how about those cataracts? Didn't you say they were clouding your vision?"

"Great to see you, Dad!" interrupted Andrew. "This is Ken Watson from Watson Realty."

"How do you do, sir?" Ken asked with a too-wide smile."

"I'll be better when I know what this is about," Hal told him.

"It's about your plans, Dad. It's a conversation we've tried to have with you—thought a professional might have more success."

"So, you want to know my plans, do you? Well, right now, I plan to give that old wood tank and press another treatment with the Marc de Beau that young lady over there kindly brung me a few months back." Hal pointed toward me.

"C'mon, Dad, get serious," said Andrew. "Ken's here to talk about putting the house and property on the market."

"He is, is he? Okay, then, let's talk. So, Ken . . . since my boys here have taken it upon themselves to hire you to sell my house and my vineyard, it would behoove you to set me straight on the financial gains to you if such a transaction occurs."

"Well, Mr. Pritchett," Ken said as he slid his hands in the pockets of his pants and rocked from one foot to the other. "If the property sells for close to the three million we'd hope to get, the seller, you, would pay a five percent commission on the deal. Seventy-five thousand would go to the buyer's agent and to his or her firm to split down the middle. The listing broker and his or her firm, in this case Watson Reality, would also get the same.

"But . . ." Hal began. "Isn't Watson Realty owned by yerself?"

"It is, sir," the agent said.

"I see. So, you would be makin' seventy-five thousand dollars when you sell my place, while I would have the pleasure of living out my days in a foul-smelling nursing home eating boiled chicken and mashed potatoes prepared from a box of freeze-dried flakes until I croak from boredom, whereupon my boys would inherit somewheres over a million four each."

"Dad," Andrew intervened. "You know you can't afford to stay here any longer. It's only a matter of time before the County forecloses on you. We only have your best interests at heart."

"I'll tell you and your brother what's in my best interest, Andy. That would be to take your gold diggin' friend and get out of here now. Go on—git!"

Sensing Hal's anger, Seuss started barking and nipping at the heels of the three men, sending them running to their cars. "Seuss! Come back here now!" I called out.

"Don't scold the dog," Hal said. "She can smell insincerity from a mile away." He stood with his head to the ground and kicked a rock in frustration.

I walked toward him and put my hand on his shoulder. "I'm sure your sons worry about their dad living alone on this big place with no close neighbors. They don't know that I'm here watching out for you."

"Thanks, honey," Hal said with a smile. "Problem is, my boys never showed respect for this land. I gotta say, that's one thing that wasn't right about Emma. She went too easy on them. I tried to toughen them up and have them work the vineyard, but she always gave them an out . . . golf lessons, tennis lessons, music lessons. And later on, fancy colleges. She herself grew up tilling the soil, pruning the vines, picking the grapes, and workin' the cellar. But she wanted something else for them. Not sure why, though." Hal twisted the gold ring on his wedding finger round and round with the fingers of his other hand. "Always meant to ask her 'bout that. But then it was too late." He pointed his finger at me and looked at Benson. "That's why my heart damn near melted when our Sam here took a taste of the grapes in my field. To see someone so young who had the same passion we had." He shook his head. "It's just too bad my boys didn't inherit that gene."

"Hey, Hal," I said. "Do you mind my asking how much you owe on the place?"

"About twenty-five thousand on the last bill, with all the interest and penalties the County keeps slapping on. Haven't paid 'em anything since the winery burnt. The Social Security barely pays for my electric and beer."

"Hmmm, twenty-five thousand. And our deal is, we split the profits on the wine down the middle. If we sell all of the three hundred cases we're making, I'm figuring that after the costs to get it to market, we should each net around fifty grand."

"Fifty grand minus what Irv's gonna charge you for making your wine at his facility," Benson reminded me.

"Best he'll do is to cut my salary in half and not charge me anything—*if* I bring in my own tank and press. How about that, Hal? Would you let me bring *your* tank and press into the winery? I've been wanting to use those beautiful old pieces ever since I set eyes on them."

"They're all yours, young lady. I'd be honored to have them put back into service. You're also gonna need some pricey barrels to age your wine in if you want it to taste great. So you can use the twelve barrels I've been storing in the basement from the great Moreau Cooperage. They're made of the finest oak from one of France's premier forests."

"Oh, thank you, Hal! Thank you so much!" The barrels were the last piece of the puzzle for making my project happen. "And later on, you and I are going down to the County offices. I've heard they can be open to letting older homeowners work out payment plans on their tax bills."

"Yes, ma'am." Hal gave a salute as he climbed back into the Jeep and released the brake. "But right now, I'm going to give that press and tank another cleaning. Those old pieces got a ways to go before they can show themselves in public." When the old vehicle started its roll down the hill, Hal popped the clutch, and the engine fired up.

# fifteen

---

**Flowering** *adj.* stage in the grapevine's life when tiny flowers emerge

My alarm went off at six-thirty on a Monday morning in May. I rolled over in bed, felt Seuss' cold nose on my cheek, and pulled on my running shorts, tank top, socks, and sneakers. There was only time for half a run, as Benson would be arriving with a few guys in the flatbed truck he'd borrowed to haul Hal's press and tank over to Napa Juice. Before I could tie the laces on my shoes, Seuss was spinning in circles at the door ready to go.

A host of white-crowned sparrows darted through the rows of vines as we finished our first lap of the vineyard. The sun was flicking its light on the leaves that would soon provide soft shade for the berries and nourish the plants by converting sunshine to usable energy. Just a few weeks before, tiny clusters resembling buttons had popped from the shoots that had sprouted from the arms of the vines. Now, each cluster was sporting dozens of tiny flowers. In the coming weeks, the pollen from the male stamen of each flower would fertilize the flower's female ovary, which would make seeds. The flowers would then morph into grape berries to protect the seeds.

After ten laps of the vineyard, Seuss was only getting started, but I needed to get showered and dressed before throwing bananas, kale, almond milk, yogurt, and protein powder into a blender to make smoothies for myself and Benson.

When Benson backed the enormous truck up to the ruins of the old winery, Hal's chest puffed up with pride as he stood by the antiques he'd meticulously cleaned and conditioned. The press, like the one at the LeMont winery, was a good twenty feet around with an iron crank in the center to crush the grapes and force the fermented juice through the staves of the basket into a wooden tub below. The redwood tank was only four feet high, which, much to my delight, would allow for the grapes to be foot stomped.

Before we reached the winery, I'd texted Irv to meet us at the loading dock to give his approval before the crew unloaded the machines from the truck and set them up in the clean room alongside the steel equipment. When we'd negotiated our deal that allowed me to bring in the tank and press, I'd neglected to mention that they were both made of wood.

A few minutes after we arrived at back of Napa Juice, Irv's red Corvette Stingray flew around the corner of the building. "Good morning, Irv," I called out when he shut the engine of the car down. "Hope you had a wonderful weekend. We wanted to give you a look at the great antiques I plan to use here. C'mon over and check them out!"

"Antiques?" he snapped as he got out of the car and shut the door. "You said nothing about antiques!" He walked to the back of the truck while Benson and the other men pulled the tarps away from the pieces.

"This tank and press were shipped over from Burgundy in the 1930s," I began, well aware that this might not be an easy sell.

"What the hell are those?" Irv snarled. "Do you think for one second that I'd let you bring that rotten crap into my winery?"

"But Irv," I pleaded. "Winemakers at the top houses in Burgundy and Beaujolais are going back to these old wooden machines. And a lot of them never even converted to the steel. These could be a major draw for those purists who want—"

"First of all, those pieces of shit are probably infested with worms and termites! Second, we'd be a laughingstock for anyone who saw them sitting there next to my state-of-the-art equipment!"

"I understand your hesitation, Irv. But I'm sure we can come to an arrangement that works for you."

"Arrangement? What kind of arrangement?"

"If you allow me to bring in these old pieces, I'll handle the services the winery normally provides by cleaning the tank and press myself after I use them. Plus, I'll be freeing up the winery's stainless machines for your other clients. I'm sure it gets crazy here during harvest."

"All right," he grumbled. "But get 'em out of here as soon as you can," he said as he stormed back into the Corvette and slammed the door. I put my hands to my ears before the noise of the engine exploded through the fresh spring air and Irv jetted off to the front of the building.

"Quick, let's get this stuff inside before he changes his mind," I told Benson. He backed the truck up near the roll top doors to the clean room where the cellar crew helped us unload and set up the machines. I knew that the short and squatty wooden press and tank would stick out like sore thumbs next to the gleaming metal equipment towering over them and could only hope that Irv wouldn't have another hissy fit when he passed by them later that day.

# sixteen

**Veraison** *n.* stage in the grape's development marked by the onset of ripening

In the first week of September, the sugar levels of the pea-sized grapes were rising as harvest time approached. I tasted the dark purple orbs several times a day, hoping that they'd "speak" to me the way the old vines at Domaine LeMont had done when Julien handed me that berry. In the late afternoon on the third day of the month, I put a grape in my mouth and tasted the burst of sweetness followed by the bitter taste of the tannins when I bit down on the skins and seeds. Then it happened. The bitter taste was erased by a flavor even more delicious than what I'd experienced in the old vines vineyard. Though Benson and Hal, who were going by the sugar readings from the refractometer, recommended that I hold off picking for a few more days, I knew that the vines were telling me they were ready for their bounty to begin its glorious transformation.

The eight-person picking crew, made up of myself, Benson, Hal, and some guys from Napa Juice that we traded favors with, arrived at midnight and helped to light up the vines with lamps powered by rented generators. In Beaujolais, we picked at seven-thirty a.m., but in Napa's warmer climate, we needed to pick before dawn to get the bins of grapes to the winery before sunrise, as even a few minutes of heat on harvested grapes can have a negative effect on the outcome of the wine.

I met each of our volunteers with a steaming cup of cappuccino, a huge chocolate chip cookie, and the promise of a bottle of Darnay within the next year. Hal organized and directed the crew, while I led Delilah along the rows of vines as the buckets of picked grapes were dumped into bins on the cart she was pulling.

By six a.m., Benson and I were driving our trucks filled with grapes to Napa Juice. When the first bin slid through the doors of the winery, I felt like a mom looking at her new baby for the very first time. I'd gone for over a day without sleep, but the rush of adrenaline had me snapping photos of the purple beauties for Stephanie, Cameron, and Spence, and to post for my growing list of Instagram followers.

Though most California wineries do their destemming by machine, we did the process manually by rubbing them on a screen as Julien had taught me. Next, we loaded the grapes into the tank, where they sat overnight before I added the yeast that would begin the fermentation process. Then it would be time for the most fun part of all—the part I'd been dreaming about even before I'd gone to France to work harvest. It would be time to foot stomp my grapes.

Many purists like me believe that foot stomping is the best way to push down the cap of skins, stems, and seeds that rise during fermentation to lessen the effect those bitter elements will have on the wine. Foot stomping also enables winemakers to feel pockets of warmth and cold in the fermenting fruit with their feet and create a more even dispersion of temperature throughout the tank. My dive into that tank of Syrah had taught me about the dangers of inhaling the carbon dioxide that's released during fermentation. To prevent another trip to the hospital while I stomped, I made certain that the doors of the winery were wide open, and that I always had a buddy to keep an eye on me. This was never a problem. Three times a day for a week, I'd change into the red Speedo that Julien had bought for me on that abbreviated jaunt to Paris. The men at the winery were always more than happy to gather around the tank to make sure I wouldn't succumb to the fumes from the bubbling red mixture as I lifted my legs above the thick cap and pushed it deep into the warm liquid.

On the seventh day of my stomping, Benson came by to test a sample of the wine with a tool called a hydrometer that measures the sugar levels during fermentation, which continue to fall as the yeast converts the sugar into alcohol.

I could tell by the taste of the wine that the fermentation was near completion, but to play it safe, I checked Benson's hydrometer for conformation. Any lingering sugar in the wine when it goes to barrel can turn to bacteria and spoil the entire lot. "Yup, we're almost negative," I said. "I'll give it two more days before pressing." I climbed out of the tank and grabbed a nearby hose to wash off the purple juice that covered me from my navel to my toes.

"Here, I'll do that for you." Benson took the spray gun and shot the icy cold water on me while the runoff circled into the floor drain.

"Whoa! That's freeee-zing!" I jumped up and down on the concrete floor to get my blood moving faster.

"Hey, are you losing weight?" Benson asked, as he adjusted the force of the spray. "Your ribs are showing through that suit."

"You noticed, huh? That's cause I'm on half salary 'til the wine goes to barrel. Two seventy-five a week doesn't leave much for food after insurance, gas, dog food, and dry cleaning my work suits and blouses." I grabbed my ponytail that was now reaching halfway down my back. "And I still haven't gotten my hair cut. Plus, I'm three months behind on my rent. Hal insists he won't take money from me, but I know he needs it as much as I do."

"Sam, please—I'm happy to lend you whatever you need. You can pay me back after you start selling your wine. It's no problem."

"Absolutely not." I turned around so he could get my backside. "Aunt Viv always said that before borrowing money from a friend, you should decide what you need most—the friend or the money."

"Sounds like that Viv was one wise old bird." Benson turned off the hose and coiled it back up while I sat back down on the edge of the tank and scanned my body for any remaining grape skins. I noticed he was right about the ribs, which I wasn't thrilled about. But working in the vineyard had given me abs that looked like you could bounce a penny off them and legs that were strong and toned. "Hey, seeing you tread through that beautiful maceration has given me a cool idea I'd like to run by Ashton," Benson said as he checked the time on his phone. "If he ever shows up."

"Now, that's what I call a pretty picture!" A deep voice reverberated through the clean room. It was Ashton on one of his few visits to the winery since the pump over fiasco.

"Hey there, Ash," Benson said to his boss. Ashton walked a circle around me, with his eyes fixed on my body while he took several sniffs of the air. His dilated pupils and sallow complexion were signs that the coke was taking its toll.

"The last time I saw you here, you were covered head to toe," he told me. "Now, you're practically undressed—not that I have a problem with that."

"This is my first release, so I'd like to be very hands on."

"I'll take having your hands on me any day," he said with a sly smile.

I winced at the comment. "Please don't make me uncomfortable, sir. I'm just trying to make my wine."

"Sorry. I really didn't mean it that way."

"So, in what way *did* you mean it?"

"He means that we're talking about creating a new brand," Benson chimed in. "A fun rosé for next summer. We've been trying to come up with a catchy name, and you've given us one. What about *Stomp*, Ash? The label could feature Samantha here doing her thing in the tank in that red suit with the blonde ponytail. *It'd be killer!* And it won't hurt the reviews of the wine either. Regis Preston always appreciates a beautiful woman."

"Hmmm, *Stomp*, huh? It's short and sweet. Sticks in the mind. Yeah, I love it, Benny!"

"Really—ya do?" Benson asked, surprised.

"Yeah, man, in fact, that's a fuckin' great idea! Oops! Sorry, Miss Lafite, or whatever your name is."

"It's Samantha Goodyear—and sorry, but that's not my thing. I'm not into wearing a bathing suit to impress a wine critic."

"It'll be good money," Benson insisted. "And the final label won't be an exact likeness, if that's what you're worried about. The artist will create an illustration from the photo."

"I don't know . . ." I said, shaking my head, even though I very much needed the money.

"How does fifteen hundred for your trouble sound?" Ashton asked me.

"It's sounds like you're halfway there," Benson told his boss. "C'mon, Ashton, rosé's red hot right now. That wine's gonna make you a *lot* of money." He gave me a wink.

"Okay . . . three thousand," Ashton agreed, albeit reluctantly.

"Paid upfront," Benson said.

"Paid upfront." Ashton held his hand out to me.

Though the offer was tempting, I didn't want to take advantage of a guy with a drug problem. I looked at Benson, my eyebrows knitted in concern. "Are you sure about this?"

"We're sure," Benson said, nodding his head.

"Okay, then. Deal." I reached out to return Ashton's handshake.

"Deal," he said. "Call Lamberton, Benny. Try to set up the shoot for Saturday. And have a check waiting for Miss La . . . Goodyear."

• • •

"Looking good, Samantha. Can you give us a half smile? Perfect! Now how about we get a shot of you sitting on the edge of the tank? Almost like it's a swimming pool," the photographer instructed.

Sean Lamberton ranked as one of the wine industry's top photographers. Though an artist would use the photo to create an illustration for the final label that would go on the wine bottle, Benson wanted Sean to capture the nuances of my actions.

"How're we doing here?" Sean asked Benson, who was shuffling through digital printouts of the photos on the camera.

"These look great to me." Benson put the photos down and picked up his phone. "I'm still hoping for Ashton to show so he can sign off on them. Been trying to get him for the last hour. *Ashton . . . where are you?*" He was leaving a message. "*We're ready to wrap things up here. Call me.*" We waited for fifteen more minutes. "Well, I guess that's a wrap. Appears that the boss is a no-show." He rolled his eyes.

I climbed out of the tank, grabbed the hose, and sprayed off the purple juice with the icy water that left me shivering and covered with goose bumps. Sean called out for his assistant to fetch a robe for me. With his stocky build, mass of black curly hair and dark eyes, the photographer looked like he'd just stepped off the set of a medieval epic movie.

"Have a question for ya," he said in his cute Irish brogue. "I've been asked to scout out some fine-looking lady winemakers for a piece I'm shootin' for next month's style section of the *New York Times Magazine.* There'll be some photos, and a wee write-up about each lassie and the wine she makes. I'd like to send today's shots to the lad in charge of the gig to see if he thinks ya'd be a good fit. If ya'd be interested, that is."

"The *New York Times Magazine?* Are you kidding? You bet I'd be interested!" I jumped up and down, clapping my hands together as the assistant handed me the robe.

The photographer laughed. "No promises. But give me your info and I'll let ya know as soon as I do if it's a go or not."

"Sounds good to me. Hey, Benson!" I called out to my friend at the other end of the barrel room to tell him what Michael had said. "Benson!" I called out again. He turned to me and pointed to the phone at his ear.

"Benson's a busy man," I joked to Michael, who was helping his assistant pack up the equipment.

"Sam!" Benson called me over to where he was standing. I could tell by the tone of his voice that something bad had gone down. He held his hand over the mouthpiece. "I'm talking to the Calistoga cops. Ashton drove off a mountain from the 128 West last night. Another driver spotted the wreck an hour ago. He's on the way to St. Helena Hospital in an ambulance now. I've gotta go meet him there."

# seventeen

---

**Racking** *v.* task that separates clear wine from solids before wine is put to barrel

"Hmmm, let's see . . ." I said to the beefy guy in the white butcher apron. "I'll take three pounds of those skinless chicken breasts. And two pounds of sliced prosciutto. How much is the prosciutto per pound? *Thirty dollars!* Make that a half pound please." I'd been standing at the counter of the Whole Foods meat department on the Monday evening following the photo shoot. After crossing the pork and poultry off my list, I still needed breadcrumbs, Romano cheese, lemons, red onion, and arugula for the chicken rollatini and salad I'd be making Benson and myself for dinner. Benson had spent the entire weekend dealing with the Ashton fiasco and I was eager to get details on it. He'd only texted me the CliffsNotes: Ashton had been trapped in his car for hours after careening 300 feet into Calistoga's famed Petrified Forest; the winemaker had tested positive for cocaine; and he had compound fractures in both of his arms.

Knowing all that, I was almost feeling guilty about spending what I'd earned from the shoot, because the crash and the DUI were sure to cost him big time for court and attorney fees. I'd already used a portion of his check to pay Hal the back rent I owed him and was now stocking up on some much-needed groceries to fill my empty fridge and nourish my aching body. Two days before, I began moving my seven hundred plus gallons of fermented wine and grape remnants from the tank into the wooden press and squeezing it through the basket by cranking the machine's century-old iron handle. Following that job, I racked the pressed wine by letting it flow back into the tank to separate the clear liquid from the dead yeast and other solids. Next, I transferred the racked wine into Hal's wonderful Moreau barrels, sealed them with their lids, and raised them to the highest racks on the shelves—*with a forklift!* The wine would age in the barrels for a little less than a year before I would have it bottled and packaged for public consumption.

•   •   •

"Hey, girl, how was your day?" I called out to Seuss as I got out of the car in the driveway of Hal's property. When I reached the cottage, I found the envelope I'd put Hal's rent check in taped to my door with the torn pieces of the check inside. "That man is incorrigible!" I told Seuss, who barely had the energy to wag her tail after a long day of chasing rabbits in the vineyard. She was fast, but caught none, as they all had their escape routes through the fence. When we went into the cottage, Seuss plopped down on her bed for a snooze. "I know how you feel. I'm tired too, girl. But I'm looking forward to a nice dinner with your Uncle Benson."

I pulled up the rollatini recipe on my phone and heard the ding of an email. When I opened it, the animation of a white and gold envelope came forward on the screen with my name. Within seconds, a card popped from the envelope.

***Karen Langer Goodyear & Ronald James Marchetti***
*Invite you to celebrate their wedding*
*Saturday December 11th of this year at 5 pm*
*Larchmont Audiogenics*
*222 Palmer Avenue*
*New York, NY 10538*

"No! Nooo! Noooo!" My cries caused Seuss to leap to her feet and begin a series of barks at a nonexistent intruder. "How could she?" My hands were shaking so violently that it took me nine tries to tap my mom's name on my cell.

"Sam!" she answered. "Did you get the invite?"

"Mom, how could you? How could you even think about marrying that man? Wait . . . you can't! You're still married to Dad! *Aren't you*?"

"Our divorce will be final on December 8th. Three days before the wedding."

The D word shot through my heart like a hot poker. It was a few moments before I found my voice. "Mom," I whispered. "This is all too fast! You hardly know that guy. And he seemed really weird." I wished I could have told her she hadn't given my dad enough of a chance. But I couldn't. Not after knowing what he'd been up to.

"I know Ron turned you off when you met him, honey. But I'm sure you'll change your mind when you come back for the wedding and see more of him."

"More? What's left? The crownwork on his back molars?"

"Be serious, Sam. He's smart, caring, and he makes me happy. And our business is really taking off!"

"Yeah . . . *taking off!* Ha ha!"

•　　•　　•

I was putting my groceries away when Benson walked in the door. "I just got off the phone with the attorney," he told me before even saying hello. "Says he thinks he can negotiate a stint in rehab to keep the boss out of jail—which is good. The Lamborghini is toast, though. Anyway, enough about that disaster. How did ya do with your wine? Got it safely into those Moreaus?"

"Yup." I turned to him with a tear-stained face.

"Uh-oh. What went wrong?"

"Nothing. Until I came home and found out that my parents are getting divorced, and my mother is marrying some New Age carnival huckster who's gotten her into a suburban freak show. And I'm expected to go back to New York to attend their joke of a wedding. How ridiculous is that?" I grabbed a napkin and used it to blow my nose.

"Oh, Sam, that sounds *crazy*." He pulled me in for a hug, snot and all. "I'm so sorry."

"I just can't believe that creepy nudist is going to be my *stepfather*."

"What can I do to help?" He stepped back from me. "Do you want me to go with you to the wedding for moral support?"

"Who says I'm going to the wedding?"

"You have to go, Sam. She's your mother. And I'm serious about going with you."

"Do you mean that? Would you really go all the way across the country to hold my hand?"

"Sure, I would. Anyway, being a California kid, I've only been to New York City once. Would love to go back and spend some time there."

"Well, it's something for us to think about," I said as I untied the string and white paper from the chicken breasts and pounded them with a mallet. "Now let me start dinner so I can get some shut-eye. I didn't sleep but three hours all weekend. And hey, maybe you'd like to research some cool restaurants and wine bars for us to visit in Manhattan."

# eighteen

_____

**Karuizawa** *n.* rare Japanese whiskey (some aged for up to sixty years in barrel) that can sell for as much as $100,000 per bottle

My phone rang at seven a.m. on a rainy November morning. I picked it up and saw Irv's name on the screen.

"Sam, I need you to get to the winery, pronto. I just got an email from *Wine Snob*. The tasting for Ashton's Cab and Syrah is at eight a.m. I can't make it in 'til ten, so you've gotta handle getting Regis Preston the wine from the barrel."

"Sure, Irv."

"And be sure to fire up the cappuccino machine as soon as you get in and have his mug with six sugars in hand as you greet him at the door."

I leapt out of bed and into the shower, overjoyed that I'd be getting the chance to meet the powerful, the legendary, and the controversial wine critic Regis Preston. I was well aware that many people, Hal included, had nothing but disdain for the man, and felt his tendency to reward high-sugar, high-alcohol wine with high scores had damaged the quality and reputation of the California wine industry. Still, I relished the opportunity to find out if he knew something they didn't. Perhaps his rating process was more complicated than he was credited for. Whether or not it held merit, I was excited to witness his rating process firsthand.

At five minutes past eight, I saw a black town car pull into the winery's parking lot. A tall and rather frail-looking gentleman wearing a navy wool suit and round-framed tortoise-shell glasses emerged with an umbrella from one of the back doors of the vehicle. I remembered hearing that the critic was verging on obese, because of his penchant for sweet wines and thick steaks. Perhaps his high-fat, high-sugar diet had caught up with him by bringing on some devastating disease. Or maybe he'd just gone on a diet.

"Good morning, sir!" I held the door open for him as he walked in from the rain. "Here, I'll take that," I said as I took the umbrella and shook out the water in a corner of the building. "I'm Samantha Goodyear. Irv Wasserman told me to expect you. He's sorry he can't be here to greet you in person. But he told me exactly how you like your morning cappuccino." I smiled and handed him the mug.

"Thank you, miss," he answered in a near whisper. He took a sip and made an expression of distaste before he put the mug down on a nearby table. I winced, wondering how I'd screwed up the brew. *Had Irv said, "nix the spoons of sugar", instead of "six spoons of sugar"?*

"If you'll follow me to the barrel room, I'll pull your samples." I led him through the lobby. "Irv said you'd be tasting Mr. White's Cabernet and Syrah." Silence met my words. "So, do you live out here in Napa?" I asked. We entered the clean room where Hal's ancient wooden press and tank looked comically out of place alongside the other stainless-steel presses and tanks. With harvest over, Irv had been pressuring me to get them out of there, and I worried he might refuse to let them back in for my next year's vintage.

"No," he replied, eyeing the equipment while he spoke. "I live in the city." Being that San Francisco was the closest big city to Napa, I assumed that was the city he was referring to.

"Oh nice! I'm from New York City. Moved out here about nine months ago." Again, silence.

"Okay then," I said when we reached the shelves where Ashton's barrels of wine were stacked. The placement of barrels on racks in a facility like Napa Juice often depends on the ability of the brand's name to impress wine critics and potential winemaker clients. Irv had situated the thirty barrels of Ashton's Ultraviolet Cabernet in direct view of a long table with several chairs where critics often sipped barrel samples and made notes for their reviews. Because my wine had no brand recognition, he'd relegated my Moreau barrels to the very top of the racks. "We can taste in here." I pointed to the table. "Or, if it's too chilly for you, I can bring the wine into our tasting room." The temperature of barrel rooms is always below fifty-five degrees, and I assumed that was why the man was dressed for a New York winter.

"In here is fine," he said.

"Great! If you'll take a seat, I'll pull the Cab first. I know you're a big fan of Mr. White's wines." I hoped to hear a response from him that would explain his reasoning for awarding those 100-point scores. But he sat down without a saying a word, opened the leather-bound notepad he'd been carrying, and clicked his ballpoint pen to ready it for writing. Giving up on trying to start a conversation, I slid a standing ladder to the shelf, climbed up to one of the barrels, removed the plug from it, and siphoned the wine into a long glass tool known as a *thief*. I carried the thief down the ladder and released the wine into one of the wide-bowled, crystal stemmed glasses used for tastings.

He took a sip of the Cab and swished it in his mouth for a few moments before spitting it into a spittoon. After making some notes on his pad, he took a sip from a glass of the Syrah that I'd also poured for him. After spitting that out and jotting down a few more notes, he clicked the button on his pen and checked the time on his wristwatch.

"Is there anything else I could help you with?" I asked, surprised that he exhibited so little emotion for a man who had just sampled wines that he would likely bless with perfect scores. I wondered if his silence was because of the rumors popping up about Ashton's recent drug related crash, and his quiet entry into a rehab facility known for its celebrity clientele. But the critic's next question stunned me.

"What's in the Moreaus?" he asked in that whisper of a voice as he pointed up to my barrels.

"The Moreau barrels?" That he picked them out among the hundreds of others on the racks floored me.

"Yes," he nodded. "I recognize the tool work around the rims."

"That's my wine up there. It's a new brand of Pinot Noir. Actually, it's a new version of an old brand called Darnay."

"Yes, I remember Darnay."

*You do. You destroyed the brand,* I wanted to tell him. Instead I said, "The wine is still very young. Picked at the beginning of September from eighty-year-old vines, so it won't be ready to drink for a while yet." Knowing how much the critic had disliked the old Darnay until Hal picked the grapes at sky high sugar levels to please him, I had no interest in having him taste my wine and give it a terrible review before it was even in the bottle.

"I'd like to have a taste if I may." He turned to a fresh page in his notebook.

Now my hands were tied. Being an employee of the winery, I couldn't refuse to provide a sample for any wine writer, especially Regis Preston. "Ah . . . okay . . . sure." I climbed to the top of the ladder with the thief, siphoned out my beautiful ruby-colored creation from one of Hal's gorgeous old barrels, climbed back down to the floor, and released the wine into a fresh glass for the man to trash it.

"Thank you, miss." He took a sip of the wine and clicked on his pen to make more notes.

"I've gotta tell you, sir, this wine is not in your style at all," I said as I struggled to suppress my anger at the damage he'd wreaked on Hal and Emma's brand and was about to wreak on mine. "It didn't suit you thirty years ago, and it certainly won't now." My airwaves tightened, making it hard to catch my breath. "You don't . . . you don't have to bother giving it a score or troubling yourself with making any notes on it." I took a deep breath and exhaled before continuing. "My friend . . . my friend Hal Pritchett and his late wife made wine from the same vineyard in Carneros back in the 1980s. After getting some lousy scores on it, they resorted to picking the grapes late to get it high enough in sugar and alcohol to get your blessing on it. It broke their hearts to do it, but it was the only way they could stay in business. After his wife died and the winery burnt to the ground, Hal shut down production. But he agreed . . . he agreed to let me use his grapes because he believed I would make a wine that reflects the true beauty of the fruit and not give a damn about scores!" Fighting once more to catch my breath, I looked at the man for a response. *Say something, please!* But again, just silence. I sucked in enough air to continue my rant. "I'm keeping the name Darnay, named for Claude Darnay, the man who originally planted the vines of French clones in the 1930s. I even moved the original wooden press and tank Darnay brought over from France that survived Hal's fire into this facility to make the wine. You passed them on the way in. Irv was terrified that the old machines might contaminate his sterile environment, and some people thought I was crazy. But I know the wine will prove me right." With chest heaving, I grabbed the edge of the table to give my lungs a break, well aware that I'd crossed all lines of professional behavior. *Apologize, Sam, now!* "Sorry to get so carried away, sir. I get fired up about things I'm passionate about."

He looked at me and nodded while he continued to jot down whatever notes he was making before he stood up and closed the folder holding his notepad. "Thank you for pulling those samples, Miss Goodyear. Good day, then." He marched back through the winery, picked up his umbrella, and walked out the door.

· · ·

"Did Regis leave, already? How'd it go? Were there any problems? Did he love the Cab and Syrah?" Irv asked, as he flew in the door to the winery at ten a.m.

I looked up at him while carrying the used glasses into the tasting room kitchen for washing. "Yes, he left," I said, not daring to mention the tirade I embarked on while the critic tasted my wine. "I got him the samples but couldn't tell if he liked them or not. He just tasted them and left. He was super quiet. Is he usually like that?"

"No way, not Regis! He gets very pumped up when he's tasting great stuff. Especially Ashton's wine. Hmmm . . ." He cocked his head in thought. "Perhaps when he's hungover, he's less chatty than usual. That could've been it."

"He sure didn't seem like the type to get a hangover. He seemed very controlled."

"He's the type, alright. By the way, I need you to put together a courtesy basket and get it over to his office today."

"A courtesy basket?"

"It's standard practice here this time of year. At least for Ashton. Take a drive out to Embarcadero Spirits in the city. See if they've got a bottle of thirty-year-old Karuizawa whiskey for under three grand. That'll be the centerpiece. Throw in a can of white caviar, a dozen of those pricey Cuban cigars—I'll tell you where to get 'em, and a box of French truffles from The Fatted Calf. And maybe an Apple watch. Wrap it all in a basket, but don't put Ashton's name on it. Take it to *Wine Snob* and tell the receptionist to leave it on Mr. Preston's desk. He'll know who it's from. Put the bill on Ashton's tab. With a ten percent mark-up."

"That's a bribe, Irv. We can't bribe a critic! It's not legal—*is it*?"

"What you don't understand, doll, is that this is the wine business, and every point that critic awards to those wines is worth a couple hundred thou in revenue to Ashton. And with the hundred grand he's paying each month for that beachfront wellness retreat, he can't afford anymore dips in his sales. So, get busy on that basket!"

•   •   •

At four p.m. on that same Tuesday, I was making my way in heavy traffic toward Napa from San Francisco with a basket packed with the pricey goodies Irv had told me to buy for Regis Preston. It was fortunate that I had the winery's credit card, as there was no way that I could put items totaling over seven thousand dollars on my card. Prior to quitting Weatherhouse, I paid no rent, had no debt, and had a job that paid seventy thousand a year with full medical benefits and a 401K account. Less than a year and a half later, I was making twenty-eight thou a year with no benefits. I had no savings and owed several thousand on my Amex. Even scarier, was that in a matter of months, my wine would need to go from barrel to bottle, and I'd need to come up with thousands more to get it ready to sell. All I could do was pray that Regis Preston would not make any mention of my wine in *Wine Snob*. A 'thumbs down' from him would kill any chance I had of selling my first vintage of Darnay at a penny more than a break-even price per bottle.

I turned onto Route 29 North and headed into downtown Napa to drop the basket at the magazine's headquarters. After parking my truck, a look at the plaque outside the building told me that the four-story mansion topped with a deck offering spectacular views of the bay was built in the 1850s by a man named Henry MacIntyre, then president of the long-defunct Napa Wine Trading Company. As I carried the lofty basket up the wide steps of the grand entrance, I felt like a humble servant paying homage to the all-powerful wine gods of Napa.

"Good afternoon," I said, hoping that someone would hear me when I entered the lobby teetering behind the four-foot-wide and just as tall basket heaped with gifts and covered by a sheet of cellophane tied with a gold ribbon. "I have a delivery for Mr. Preston."

"Mr. Preston is no longer here," a woman's voice answered from the other side of the basket.

"What? No longer working here? At the magazine?" I fought to maintain my balance while I spun around and caught sight of a heavyset, middle-aged woman seated at the reception desk.

"You heard right. In fact, that's the third goodie basket I've had to turn away this week. Sorta too bad 'cause Mr. Preston always gave me those Cuban cigars that my husband went gaga over."

"But . . . what happened? Why'd he leave?"

"Hear no evil, see no evil, speak no evil, is my mantra." Her eyes rolled up at me from behind half-frame glasses perched just above the tip of her nose and anchored by a gold link chain that draped down below her shoulders in the front and looped around her back. "All I can say is we got a new general manager in here last Friday morning, and by Friday afternoon Mr. Preston had left."

"But I just saw him this morning. He came to Napa Juice at eight to taste Ashton White's wines."

"That wasn't Mr. Preston. That was Mr. Broadhurst. He's taken over Mr. Preston's job as the magazine's senior critic. Should be a press release about the change-over coming out sometime today. And as I told ya, this new gentleman won't accept any 'deliveries.'"

"Well, thank you," I said to the woman as I spun back around and trundled the basket out the door.

•   •   •

"No longer working there?" Irv screamed. "That's impossible! The man's been calling the shots in this town for over twenty-five years!"

"I thought there was something strange going on when he first walked in the door here, Irv. This man was rail thin—I'd heard that Preston was obese. Plus, he grimaced at the six-sugar-coffee you said to have waiting for him. And I can't conceive of this guy ever getting pumped up. Even when he's tasting great stuff."

"This could be bad," Irv said as he sat on his office sofa holding his head in his hands. "Ashton's success depends on that man's reviews. Who knows what kind of scores this other guy's gonna hand out?" He looked at the basket that was covering the large coffee table where I'd set it down. "Well, you'd better take that stuff back first thing tomorrow. I can't very well bill Ashton for gifts he didn't order and couldn't even get delivered."

"You think I can take all this back? The watch, yes, and probably the Karuizawa. But can you return three hundred dollar cigars, a five hundred dollar box of chocolates, and an eight hundred dollar tin of caviar that've all sat in my un-air-conditioned truck for three hours?"

"Just give it your best shot."

•   •   •

I woke up Wednesday morning dreading driving back to San Francisco and trying to return the perishable goods (some) and ridiculously expensive items (all) in that basket. When I picked up my phone to turn off the silent tab, I saw a stack of texts on the screen.

**Benson:** Did you check out *Wine Snob*?

**Cameron:** Have you read it yet? What a tale!

**Ned:** *Wine Snob* piece is amazing!

**Stephanie:** Wow! Unbelievable!

**Benson:** Check it out yet? Call me!!!

Assuming the messages were all referring to the changeover at *Wine Snob*, I cut and pasted this reply to them:

**Sam:** Heard about it yesterday

The phone rang. It was Benson. "Hey, did you see it?"

"Don't need to. Like I texted, I heard yesterday that Preston was out when I dropped Ashton's gift basket off." I yawned and gave myself a long, early morning stretch. "So how you doing?"

"You didn't see it then, did you?"

"See what?"

"Sam, hang up the phone, and check out today's issue of *Wine Snob*. Now."

"Sure thing, boss!" I opened my app of the magazine. The home page ran the announcement of Regis Preston's departure and the appointment of Winston Broadhurst to Senior Wine Critic, who had previously held the same position at *Decanter*, one of Europe's most respected wine publications.

I scrolled down to read Mr. Broadhurst's opening message:

*A Tale of Two Wines—by Winston Broadhurst*
*I'd like to begin my introduction to you by admitting that I accepted this position based in Napa with mixed feelings. I relished the chance to return to my homeland after being stationed overseas for more years than I'd like to admit. But after developing a passion for French Pinot Noir, it broke my heart to know that the wine I'd review here would be worlds away from what I'd tasted in Europe, because of the tendency of California winemakers to follow the rule that bigger is better in terms of alcohol, sugar, fruit, and oak. I knew these wines would not come*

*close to their French counterparts in flavor, structure, and the ability to speak of their origin.*

*But just yesterday, on a tasting outing at the wine facility Napa Juice, I spotted several Moreau barrels up on the racks and knew they had to contain something special. They do . . . a Carneros Pinot Noir, crafted from old vines with the name Darnay. Though still very young, it already exhibits subtle nuances of complexity that tell me this wine has the potential to stand up against the most exquisite vintages of France.*

*Darnay winemaker Samantha Goodyear, a former Manhattanite who cut her teeth in Beaujolais, filled me in on the history of the brand. The vineyard was planted with Burgundian clones in the 1930s by French businessman Claude Darnay. Upon his death, Darnay left the vineyard and winery to its current owner, Hal Pritchett, who released the wine commercially, but was forced to pick his grapes at high sugar and high alcohol to receive favorable scores on it. After the death of Pritchett's wife and a fire at the winery, he retired the brand. When Miss Goodyear met Mr. Pritchett just one year ago and discovered that the original vineyard continued to produce magnificent fruit, she wanted to use the grapes for her debut wine. She even brought the ancient wooden press and tank that were part of the original winery into Napa Juice, where, next to their stainless-steel counterparts, they speak of a time before winemaking was done by the numbers.*

*Though I will wait to rate Darnay until I have the pleasure of tasting it in bottle, I can assure you that this time around, the winemaker will not have to do any manipulation of what nature intended to receive an impressive score.*

"*Do you have any idea what this means?*" It was Benson again. He'd called six times while I'd been reading the article, and his trembling voice was making some high-pitched yelps.

"It means the wine is off to a good start?" One of us had to stay calm.

"It means that you have a *shitload* of work to do. If a big winery got a write-up like this from a respected critic for one of its new releases, they'd put their marketing and PR team behind it to boost upfront sales. I'll get this piece on the website and you get busy posting it on Instagram." While Benson was talking, my phone continued to ding with congratulatory messages. "You need to get labels designed, glass, corks, and I've got to finish up the website and e-commerce section." Along with possessing tremendous knowledge about winemaking, Benson also had a talent for designing websites. He'd already helped me create the site for Darnay with photos of Hal's vineyard, the wooden tank and press, and the story of the wine past and present.

"By the way," Benson said, "Broadhurst didn't even bother to include a review of Ashton's Cabernet and Syrah in the magazine. But that's no surprise to me."

"Oh, I'm sorry, Benson. I'm sure you did the best you could with the wine under the circumstances."

"Don't be sorry. This is actually a good thing for California wine. The guy can't be bought. He'll reward good wine, and Ashton will have to work again for a living. If he ever cleans up his act, that is."

•　•　•

"I was thrilled when these antiques arrived at the winery. We're even considering putting a search out for more vintage presses and tanks, as they're becoming quite the rage." When I walked into the clean room of Napa Juice after my failed mission to return the day-old cigars, chocolates, and caviar, I was shocked to hear Irv talking up the same wooden pieces that he'd referred to as 'pieces of shit' just a few months before.

"Pssst, Irv, can I see you for a moment?" I needed to tell him the bad news about the non-returns, and feared he'd hit the ceiling if I waited until those vendors had closed for the day.

"What is it, Sam? Can't you see I'm busy?" Irv whispered as he walked toward me. When the man he'd been talking to turned around, I recognized him as Steve Littauer, the winemaker with a cult-like status in the industry, applauded by wine writers in magazines, newspapers, and books on wine. "Steve is drooling over the press and tank!" Irv said. "Read about them in the *Wine Snob* piece. He's even considering making his wines here if he can use them. That would be *huge!* Between this guy and Ashton, I'd have the hottest custom crush in Napa!" He took me by the arm over to Steve. "This is Samantha Goodyear, who you read about this morning," he told the winemaker.

"Hey, Sam, great to meet you!" Steve said, as he shook my hand. "And congrats on the nice press from Broadhurst!"

"Th . . . th . . . thanks! Thanks so much, Steve!"

"I remember visiting the Pritchett place with my dad as a kid. I'd love to see how those old vines are doing after all these years. Could be one of the oldest Pinot plantings in California."

"Please come visit the vineyard any time, and take some cuttings if you'd like," I told him. "I'm sure Hal would be honored." Vine cuttings are often grafted onto rooted vines to add variety to vineyards.

"Would love to! I'll come by with my pruning shears after the winter," Steve said with a smile.

"And hey, Steve, I love your Chardonnay. We tasted it with Phyllis Turnball at Château LeMont during harvest last year. Everyone had nice things to say about you and your wines."

"Glad to hear it. You picked a great place to work harvest. I've long said that domaine produces the best wine in all of Beaujolais. 'Specially since the younger son has taken the helm."

My sunny smile vanished. I hadn't thought about Julien all morning, and it was already past nine-thirty—a record for me.

"Geez, terrible thing about that robbery there last year, though," Steve said. "Lost a lot of their library wines. Can't replace that stuff."

"Yes, it was . . . it was . . . a real bummer," I stammered.

. . .

"Why do I let him do that?" I growled at myself as I walked back in my office. "Two years ago, I'd have given anything to meet Steve Littauer. I'd have killed to get a compliment from him. Now I've let Julien spoil another amazing moment!" I grabbed my head with my hands, wondering how I could banish him from my brain, once and for all.

But as I sat down at my desk, I couldn't erase the image of that beautiful face still etched in my mind. And I couldn't ignore the cravings for his touch that permeated my body. That I continued to obsess over a guy who had never given me any commitment, and if he had, probably wouldn't have remained faithful to me, was making me question my emotional stability. More than once, I'd even caught myself scanning my phone for any pictures of us that might have escaped my deleting frenzy in that diner on the way out to Napa.

To get my mind off my still-wounded heart, I logged into my Darnay website to check out Benson's progress on the e-commerce link. When it came up, I assumed I'd gone to the wrong site. Staring back at me from the screen were thirty separate orders for upfront purchases of the wine. A dentist with a Miami address wanted three bottles, a doctor in San Francisco wanted two, an attorney in Malibu wanted six. There was even a request for a twelve bottle case from the Regional Vice-President of Weatherhouse, Steve Bowen, who had toasted me for quitting the company. The orders totaled over three thousand dollars.

"Benson!" I called him on his cell. "They're buying the wine! I have over three grand in credit card orders!"

"Told ya so!" he bragged. "People read a write-up like that and scramble to lock in their allocations. They don't want to end up on a two-year waitlist for Napa's hottest new wine."

"But it won't even be bottled for another nine months. Do I bank the money almost a year before I can ship it out to these people?"

"That's how it's done. If you keep getting orders, you'll have enough money to finish up your production and get the wine ready to sell."

"Sorry, gotta run!" The phone beeped with Spence's name on the screen.

"Sam! Terrific write-up in *Wine Snob*! I've had ten customers stop in today to ask if I can put them down for a pre-order of your wine. One of them is an Oscar-winning actress! Another's a super-hot female singer! I need to respect their privacy, but I *can* say that both ladies are very into French Pinot and excited to try Darnay. I told them they'd have to wait awhile, but they're on the list."

"*No!* A famous actress and singer? Asking for Darnay?"

"Yup! I also had a heart surgeon at New York Hospital, the speechwriter for the Mayor, and a producer for *Sixty Minutes* requesting your brand. That's one of the fun things about this business. People from all walks of life are serious about wine. Making a brand hot is all about PR, as you're finding out, so you'll want to keep up the momentum in the press."

I had another call coming in. "Thanks, Spence, talk later."

"Hey, Samantha, Sean Lamberton here."

"Hmmm . . . Sean Lamberton, Sean Lamberton . . . oh, sure. How's it going?" I asked with my head still spinning from the wine orders.

"Going well. I showed the shots I took of ya for Ashton White's new wine label to the lads at the *New York Times Magazine*, and they loved them! They want me to snap some other pictures of ya to use for the piece on lady winemakers. Can I count ya in?"

"Can you ever! Yippee!"

# nineteen

---

**Pairing** *v.* Matching wine and food that complement and enhance each other

A little more than a year after moving to Napa, I was flying back to New York to attend my mom's wedding. She'd sent me a round-trip ticket, and I couldn't hurt her feelings by not showing up. Plus, I missed her a lot. Benson was sitting in the seat next to me wired with earbuds watching some goofy comedy and laughing out loud. We planned to stay with my dad, who, I hoped to God wouldn't embarrass me by having another one-night stand show up at the co-op.

The December night sky was black when the jet touched down on the JFK runway. We packed everything we needed for the short trip in our carry-on bags, so we bypassed baggage and went straight to the arrival exit.

"Didn't you bring a coat, Sam?" Benson called out through the ice-cold wind that sent my hair flying in fifty different directions.

"No!" I shouted. "Should still be in the co-op's closet. Didn't think I'd need it in Napa."

"Here ya go." He took his warm coat and wrapped it around my shoulders. A few minutes later, my dad's silver BMW pulled up at the curb with a strange woman in the passenger seat.

"Welcome, you two!" my dad said as he jumped out of the car to help us put our bags in the trunk. "I'm Greg. Nice to meet you, Benson!" The two men shook hands.

"Another hook-up?" I whispered to my dad as Benson held the back door open for me. "At least there's only one this time."

"No more hook-ups, honey. No more dating apps. I've found a very classy lady. We're quite serious." We got into the car. "Serene, meet Samantha and Benson," my dad said as we pulled away from the curb.

"I've been waiting to meet the two people from my favorite place in the world! Hello, Samantha. Hello, Benson," said Serene, who had a British accent and looked to be from India. Something about her made me feel like I'd known her forever.

"Hi, Serene." Benson extended his hand toward her. "Thanks for picking us up." Pellets of sleet danced on the car's roof and windshield. "Especially in this weather."

"I'm happy to come along for the ride." Serene turned to me. "You look a lot like your mom, Samantha. I mean that as a compliment."

"You know my mom?"

"I do. She's lovely! In fact, Greg and I met each other at one of her and Dr. Ron's classes out in Larchmont."

"Nooo! You two met at one of *those* crazy scenes?" I looked at Benson and rolled my eyes. He shrugged his shoulders.

"They're not so crazy. I'm an analyst at Goldman's. My hair was coming out in clumps and I was grinding my teeth down at night from stress. I saw Dr. Ron's ad for Audiogenics with the testimonials and tried it out. After a few weeks, the tension that was holding my body hostage seemed to melt away. I haven't seen it since. Now all I need is a trip out to Napa for some wine tasting."

"I don't know if Sam told you, Benson, but I was in a terrible place too," my dad began. Different from Serene's situation, but I still felt like I was prisoner to my destructive behavior. Sam's mom encouraged me to try their program, and I took her up on it. It's definitely unique."

"Sure, if you're a nudist, it's great," I said.

"It's really not all that discomfiting," said Serene. "You get a robe in the locker and the lights are very dim. They've even added some partitions for the shy students."

"Sounds like they might be on to something," said Benson.

•   •   •

Benson slept on the co-op's living room couch. If he woke with an aching back, I'd feel terrible, as we'd planned an early morning power walk to lower Manhattan to meet Cameron and Stephanie for brunch. The wedding was at five that evening, so we were hoping to fit in a visit to Spence's shop before driving out with my dad and Serene to Larchmont. It surprised me to hear that my mom had invited them to the wedding, but as both of my parents were happy with their new partners and, apparently, with themselves, they'd been able to end their marriage without killing each other.

At eight a.m., we marched downtown under sunny skies to the restaurant owned by the actor Robert De Niro on Greenwich Street. When we walked in the door, my friends got up from the table to give me hugs and to meet Benson. It saddened me to see that the bags under Cameron's eyes had doubled in size and that he'd easily gained what those at Weatherhouse called 'The Box ten.' Stephanie, however, still had the face of an angel and the body of a supermodel.

"Remember all that research you did for your proposal on servicing wineries?" Stephanie asked me after we sat down to enjoy tiny cups of bittersweet espresso with lemon peels on the saucers. "Your work didn't go to waste! Favia pulled up your files for Steve Bowen, who used them to prepare a proposal of his own to submit to the firm's hierarchy. It was basically the same as the one you wrote!"

"*No!* Steve Bowen did *that?*" I asked as I gave my lemon peel a twist and dropped it into the thick dark brew. "But he said it was pointless. He said the Worldwide Operations guy Brett Newmark vowed he would never let the firm veer from doing accounting for box makers."

"That's why he went over Newmark's head in the annual meeting and pitched it to Morton Drydock," said Cameron. "The Chairman's seriously into wines. Even has a piece of a winery in Sonoma. He fucking loved the idea. Made Newmark look like a real dipshit."

"The word around The Box is that the firm's gearing up to start the new division," added Stephanie. "And Cam and I will be the first to apply for a transfer into it."

"And I'm sure you'll both get in. The brass'll do whatever it takes to keep you two if they're smart. *Wow!* So those all-nighters weren't a waste! 'Specially if they helped to make your jobs more fun!'"

"We owe you some thanks . . ." Cameron said to Benson. "For taking such good care of our Sammy here. It's nice that we don't have to worry about her being all alone on the other side of the country."

"We miss her nonstop bitching and moaning about how hard she works," added Stephanie. "But we're glad she's got a sympathetic pal to vent on."

"I guess New York's loss is my gain," Benson said as he gave me a wink. "Hey, you two have to come west for a visit. You can both camp out at my place."

*"Nooo!"* I shook my head. "You do *not* want to camp out at Benson's place. *He* can barely fit in it. The three of us can squeeze into my queen-sized bed. Just tone down the snoring, okay, Steph?"

Benson picked up the wine list. "Who's up for some Champagne? My treat."

"I knew I liked this guy," said Cameron.

•   •   •

"Well, here they are! Napa's hottest young winemakers!" Spence met me with a hug and Benson with a handshake when we walked into his shop that afternoon. Spence's Fine Wines was once again named one of Manhattan's top ten trendiest places to buy wine in the December issue of *New Yorker* magazine. While Benson went to check out the wines, I spotted some cool additions in the shop that I credited to Sara. There was a large antique map of the Côte de Nuits, along with glass jars filled with chunks from the fossilized oyster beds of Chablis, a region once covered by an ancient sea. But when I checked out that once bare wall near the counter, I teared up.

"You got them developed, Spence! The pictures you and Sara took on your trip to France!"

"That was the first order of business when she came back. I thought the film would have gone bad after all these years, but they developed brilliantly." The black and white shots that Sara had suggested when she and Spence had first met were all hanging on that wall—the establishing shot a French vineyard, the closer shot of vines with grapes, and the close-up of purple berries. "So, did you bring me a barrel sample of Darnay?" Spence asked. "I can't wait to try the wine Winston Broadhurst is raving about!"

"Just grabbed it from the co-op." I pulled out one of the small sample bottles we used at the winery from my bag and handed it to him.

"Great." He set the bottle on the bar. "Sara's at the apartment. She's eager to see you both and try the wine. You know where we live. Any chance you'd like to fetch her?"

"Sure. I'd planned to stroll Benson by some neighborhood sites, anyway. He's never been to the Upper West Side."

• • •

A few minutes later, Benson and I were walking past the historic and grand co-ops of Central Park West. When we reached the corner of Seventy-second Street, he stopped to look up at a gothic-style building with ferocious-faced gargoyles, heavy black wrought-iron gates, and tall, pitched roofs topped with spirals. "That's the Dakota, isn't it?" he asked.

"That's it. John Lennon was shot and killed right outside of those gates. My Aunt Viv never got over that."

"Just saw *Rosemary's Baby* on Netflix—Rosemary lived there. Wow! What a cool and scary-looking place."

Spence and Sara's apartment building was around the corner from the Dakota. We walked into the lobby, gave our name to the doorman, and took the elevator up to the fifth floor. When I rang the bell at 5C, the door flew open.

"Sam! Benson!" Sara sang out. She gave us both hugs. "I heard you're in for your mom's wedding, Sam! How wonderful!"

"Well, yes, and no . . ." I began. "Not too thrilled with my new stepfather."

"But she's going to give him the benefit of the doubt." Benson gave me a nudge. "Aren't you?"

"If you say so," I agreed.

"Well, I do wish your mom the best," Sara told me. "It's never too late to find true love. I'm proof of that." Dressed in worn jeans, a white V-neck T-shirt, and running shoes, she looked a million times more at home in her twelve-hundred-square-foot apartment than she had in her twelve-thousand-square-foot château. "C'mon in here for a minute and see what I'm up to." She led us from the front hall into the living room, where she'd pushed furniture away from walls that had paintings propped against them. A hammer, nails, and picture hooks were on a table. "I'm hanging these pieces I've just bought at auction. All from my favorite era in Parisian art."

"These are beautiful," I said as I scanned the row of canvases that, like the oils in her château, represented a mix of styles and techniques in pre-World War II painting.

"They are, though they're not anywhere near as valuable as the paintings you saw in the château. And hey! I got the shot of that oil painting you had your dad send me. The one you'd told me about after that farewell dinner?"

"Oh yeah! I forgot he'd sent it. That seems like ages ago."

"It was a lifetime ago, for me. And now, I'm doing some consulting for Sotheby's fine art division. I just took another look at that photo because it intrigued me. It's a longshot, but it could be something special."

"All I know is, that the guy who painted it liked wine, and that my aunt's face and form inspired him. There's a signature on it. Hard to read, though."

"Well, just out of curiosity, I'd like to have another specialist look at some more detailed shots of it. Do you know the size?"

I held my hands apart—horizontally, then vertically. "Yea-big. I don't know . . . maybe twenty by fifteen inches? And no frame. Just a canvas."

"Can you get me some close-ups? Also, a back view and a shot of that signature?"

"Sure, will do. When I get back to Napa."

•   •   •

"By the power vested in me by the laws of the state of New York, I pronounce you husband and wife. You may now kiss the bride." The string quartet struck up the recessional song and there were whistles and applause from assorted friends, relatives, and students of Ron and my mom. I was just happy that the couple and guests weren't naked. They held the ceremony in the large studio of Larchmont Audiogenics and filled it with flowers for the occasion. The success of the business had prompted the need for additional studio and office space, so when the stores on either side of my mom's original clothing shop failed, the couple took on the leases and expanded in size. An organic food market and a vegan restaurant soon opened on the block to take advantage of the increased traffic generated by the studio.

While the guests filed over to the bar, a man was handing out headphones from a basket. "Oh, no! We're not expected to strip, are we?" I asked, panicked that the event included those ridiculous lessons.

"Gosh, no," the man assured me. "These are for dancing! With the acoustics in here, music blasting from speakers could cause hearing loss. So Ron and Karen have opted for a silent disco. The playlist is only audible through the headphones."

Benson came over and gave me a nudge. "I picked Ron's brain a bit before the ceremony. The guy seems super smart. He gave me some good ideas on search engine optimization for the Darnay website. Seems to know a lot about the wine business too. Ran a hedge fund that invested in some wineries in his other life. You should give him a chance."

"You're a winemaker, aren't you?" asked a man who'd just walked into the reception room with the magazine section of the next day's *New York Times* in his hand. He opened the pages and peered at my face. "Yup, that's you. Samantha Goodyear! I wondered if you were Karen's daughter when I saw the piece."

"Oh, wow! Do you mind?" I almost tore the magazine from the poor guy's hands. "Thanks so much! I wasn't even sure if I'd made the cut!" I gaped at the pages with the story titled *Women Winemakers of Napa*, that profiled me and three other women. We each had a full page devoted to us, with our name and the name of our wine at the top. My layout featured one of the grape stomping photos, a shot of me taking a barrel sample, and walking in Hal's vineyard. A block of copy alongside the pictures told my story.

*Three years ago, Samantha Goodyear gave up crunching numbers at a Manhattan accounting firm to crush grapes in Beaujolais. After a stint working harvest, she drove from Manhattan to Napa in a 1957 Ford pickup truck determined to make a California Pinot Noir as flavorful and complex as those she discovered in France. She may have done just that. Though still in barrel, Wine Snob critic Winston Broadhurst writes that her wine, Darnay, ". . . exhibits subtle nuances of complexity that tells me this wine has the potential to stand up against the most exquisite vintages of France."*

"Mom! Dad!" I called out through the crowd. I found my parents by the hors d'oeuvres table chatting with Ron and Serene. "Mom! Dad! Look!" I held up the magazine.

"*Nooo?* Is that *you*?" asked my dad. "Oh, baby!" cried my mom as they both stared at the layout.

When Ron saw what they were looking at he gave me a thumbs up. "Congratulations on the fantastic piece, Samantha," he said as he held out his hand. "I'm sorry you saw more of me than you wanted to at our first meeting. Karen and I got a bit out of control when our business took off like that. We've toned things down here since then. I hope you and I can start over."

I shook his hand. "I'm sure we can, Ron. And congratulations to you on landing an amazing lady."

My mom put her headphones on and handed a pair to Ron. "They're playing our song, my love." She took his hand. "Time for our first dance as man and wife." She led him to the dance floor to join an assortment of people rocking out to music that only they could hear. Though it all looked very silly to me, I noticed that my mom had never seemed so happy and so relaxed in her life.

•  •  •

Benson and I were back on a plane to San Francisco the next morning. There were passengers in almost every row reading that day's issue of the *New York Times*. I spent a good part of the six-hour flight craning my head over the seats to see who was reading the magazine section. When we were exiting the plane, I spotted a man with a familiar face walking out from the first-class section. I elbowed Benson.

"Hey! Isn't that Richard Weller?" Weller, the owner of the world-renowned restaurant, The Red Shed in Napa, had created an empire for himself as the author of cookbooks and the star of his own cooking show on cable.

"That's him, alright," said Benson. "Ash and I met him a few times at his place when we tried him on some Ultraviolet varietals."

"So you know him? Please introduce me!"

"Sure." We squeezed our way through the travelers walking through the jetway. "Hi, Richard! We met at The Shed," Benson said when we approached him. "I'm Benson—"

The man turned to me. "Samantha Goodyear, isn't it?"

"Yes, it is . . . I mean . . . yes, I'm Samantha! How'd you—"

"Splendid piece on you in today's *Times*! Here we are, right this way, guys." He pointed at the sign for the baggage claim. "I'd love to put your wine on my list at The Shed when it's released, if you could spare a case for us."

"Whoa! I sure could, Mr. Weller," I answered with a somewhat shaky voice. I knew that getting Darnay into The Red Shed would be a huge plus for my brand.

"Call me Richard, please. And shoot me an email." He handed me his card. "I'll have my somme send back an order for the wine."

Benson held out his hand to him. "Good to see you again, Mr. Weller. As I was saying, we met at—"

"Hey, if you two are heading to Napa," Richard interrupted, giving Benson's hand a cursory shake while he turned to me, "I'm driving there now. Want a lift?"

"We were going to grab an Uber," I said. "But if it's not too much trouble . . ."

"No trouble at all. I need two passengers for the carpool lane anyhow."

"Well then, sure!" I looked at Benson, who, though saddened by the slight from the famous chef, was happy to have the ride.

•   •   •

"If there's one thing I don't love about Napa, it's that it's way too far from the airports. I'm not used to that inconvenience after living in Manhattan," I said as we headed out of San Francisco in the red Tesla with "SHED" on the back plate.

"But I see an upside to that," Richard said. "In Napa, we rarely see or hear any jets flying overhead, which annoys the hell out of me when I'm in Chicago, New York, LA, or almost any other big city. Besides the lack of proximity to the airports, you must be pleased by finding fame and fortune in Napa. You've gotten a great write-up in *Wine Snob* plus a feature story in the *New York Times*, and your wine's not even out of the barrel yet."

"Fame? No. A little press? Yes. But definitely not fortune, as Benson can tell you. Right, Benson?"

"Sure." He was checking out the Darnay website on his phone.

"I'm making five hundred dollars a week doing the books for a winery, and I have to use the money that's come in on pre-orders for my wine to get it to bottle." As I was speaking, Benson held the screen of his phone up for me to see what he'd been looking at. There were scores of new orders resulting from that day's *New York Times Magazine* piece. "But I have to admit that things *are* looking better all the time." A glance at my Instagram site showed that my number of followers had skyrocketed. "And how 'bout you, Richard? How does it feel to be America's most famous chef?"

"Hmmm . . ." he gave a sigh. "It feels like I've got my work cut out for me, if you really want to know the truth. Business is still good overall, but I'll be as out of date as the payphone if I don't adapt fast. You millennials are eating lighter, healthier food and are backing away from the heavy dishes with creamy sauces that chefs my age love to prepare. A year ago, I packed my wine list with big Cabs and brands like Ultraviolet that got huge scores from Regis Preston to pair with my foie gras au torchon and veal osso bucco. Now, I'm looking for more elegant and flavorful wines like Darnay, that work well with the more nutritious and simpler fare we're putting on the menu."

"It sounds like you're on the right path, chef." And as we crossed the new Oakland Bay Bridge, hailed for its clean architecture, I knew that I was on the right path too.

# twenty

**Topping Off** *v.* adding additional wine to the barrels to make up for any evaporation that has taken place

It was six-thirty in the morning when I arrived at the winery to spend an hour topping off my barrels before starting work. Because air can work its way through the wood, resulting in oxidation and bacterial growth, it's important to keep adding additional wine to the barrel as the wine evaporates.

The sun doesn't rise until seven on February mornings in Napa, and the barrel room was pitch black before I turned on the overhead lights. It would have been nice to have Benson help me with the job. I'd texted him the night before to let him know that I'd be topping off bright and early. But when he didn't show up, I wondered if he'd hooked up with the young Australian woman we'd met the week before at The Cellar, who was hoping to find a job in the wine industry.

The first step of my task was to grab a keg of my topping wine that I'd stored beneath the racks. I used the other hand to slide the ladder on wheels to the section where my barrels were sitting. I'd gotten so good at the climbing that I hadn't found it necessary to change from my heels into my sneakers for the process. After scaling twenty-five feet up the ladder, I rested the keg of topping wine on the rack and took a moment to look down the row of Hal's beautiful barrels. A wave of happiness fluttered through my belly as I thought about the string of good luck I'd had since coming to Napa. Not one to tempt fate, I reached out to knock on one of the barrels. Before my knuckle could touch it, the first jolt hit. It felt like a high-speed train had crashed into the building. My feet flew out of the rung I'd been standing on and my hands grabbed the ladder as it pounded back and forth against the rack with the force of the impact, sending my body slamming along with it. That's when the rows of barrels began their descent from the racks, erupting in a series of explosions as they landed, one after another, on the floor. I hung on with my hands, rocking back and forth with feet paddling through the air in search of another rung to support the weight of my body. Then the lights went out, and darkness encased the room. The mayhem seemed to last forever, though it was only a matter of seconds before the explosions stopped and all was still. The most intense Napa earthquake in recorded history was over.

"Help! Help! HELP!!!" My voice was raspy from terror as I called out through the darkness. With the electricity out, and the air conditioning shut down, the only sound in the cavernous room was the rush of liquid streaming from the broken barrels while the aromas of the wines rose from the oak and the concrete. Not knowing if the ladder was secure, I attempted, but failed to grab a piece of the metal racking for support. If I tried to climb down, the ladder might topple over, so I remained motionless. Hanging on that rung. Waiting for the sun to rise. Before it did, I spotted some dim rays of light streaming in at the far end of the room. Then I heard Benson's voice.

"Sam? Sam? Sam? Where are you?"

"Here, on the ladder! On top of the ladder where my barrels were! Hurry, please!"

"Stay where you are!" It was a minute before the light found its way to the rack. My arms were shaking from exertion. The ladder rocked back and forth as a ray from the flashlight traveled up my body. "I've got the ladder. Start down now." I hooked my foot on a rung, and slowly begin my descent. Before I reached the floor, I felt Benson's arms around me in the near darkness. With the flashlight in his hand, he guided me over the layers of barrels, some broken, some still intact, that were lying in a sea of red and white wine. Then the aftershock hit, and the ladder crashed to the floor, missing us by inches. The room shook, and a roaring filled my head while Benson steered me away from a barrel that was rolling across the top of the wreckage.

• • •

It was near seven a.m. when Benson pulled me out of the barrel room. The rays from the morning sun were slowly creeping through the windows of the winery. "Are you okay?" he asked as he ushered me through the equipment room and sat me on a bar stool in the tasting room. At the head of the bar, what looked to be a hundred long-stemmed glasses lay in a mountain of shards on the floor.

"I'm . . . I'm okay . . . maybe just a little bruised." Fighting to catch my breath, I felt a soreness in my chest where the ladder had been pounding against me. "I think you saved my life in there. But I am . . . I am a bit annoyed at you."

"About what?" he asked as he brushed some locks of hair away from my face.

"When you told me . . . when you told me all the things that could go wrong while making wine . . . you forgot to mention earthquakes."

"Yeah, my *fault!* No pun intended. Ha ha!"

My heart rate slowed down, and the reality of the previous twenty minutes set in. "That was crazy! The barrels . . . everyone's barrels . . . holding everyone's wine have been destroyed! The wine you made . . . the wine I made . . . it's all gone."

"Yup. 'Fraid so, Sam. That was a big one for sure. Had to be over a six. I didn't get your text 'til this morning and got here around quarter of seven. The quake hit as I was pulling into the parking lot. I saw your car and knew you had to be in trouble."

"Hal!" An icy chill shot down my spine. "I have to see if Hal made it through this!"

"I'm sure he's okay. You can bet that old guy's been through a bundle of quakes out here."

"No. I have a bad feeling. He's old and he's all alone in that big house. I have to go to him."

． ． ．

My drive through downtown Napa on the way to Carneros seemed to take forever. There was only static on the airwaves when I tried to dial in the local radio station for news. The quake had knocked out the area's power transformers, causing massive electrical outages. Traffic lights were out, and the façades of century-old stone buildings lay on the ground. Firetrucks and police cars were on the scene to rope off dangerous areas, and television news crews were covering the story of the 6.3 Napa earthquake.

When I pulled into Hal's property, the big old house looked unchanged.

"Hal! Hal!" I called out, as I ran to the front door and went inside. "Hal, are you here?" I called out again as I entered the farmhouse-style kitchen with an enormous butcher block center island and iron skillets hanging above an old gas stove. There were no signs that anyone had been in there that morning, which seemed odd, as I knew Hal was an early riser and never missed his breakfast of corned beef and hash browns. "Hal, are you here?" I raced up the stairs and stuck my head into the bedrooms. Though I'd never been upstairs, I surmised that the first two had once belonged to Andrew and Lucas, as they each had black and red checked bedspreads, and shelves that held trophies topped with miniature golfers and tennis players. One room had a collection of autographed baseballs encased in plastic stands and a poster of Barry Bonds. Another had a poster of Cindy Crawford and a life-sized cardboard cut-out of a bikini-clad Heidi Klum. Down the hallway was a larger bedroom, which I assumed to be Hal's. Near the bed, a large wall hanging lay face-down on the floor. I lifted the heavy object, turned it over, and propped it against the wall. It was a framed painting of a woman that fit Hal's description of his beloved wife, Emma. She was holding a basket filled with clusters of purple grapes.

"I can see why he loved you so much, Emma." Still rattled from my experience, I found a strange comfort in talking to the woman in the painting. Her blonde hair curled down over her shoulders just as Hal had described. From her smile, she almost appeared to be sharing a laugh with me, and her twinkling eyes seemed to look right into mine. I breathed an enormous sigh of relief when I spotted Hal from the bedroom window. "Ah, there's your husband!" He was sitting on a bench near the edge of the vineyard. Seuss was lying by his side, and Delilah was grazing on grass nearby. Relieved, I gently set Emma down and went outside to join the living.

. . .

"Hal! I was worried about you!" I gushed as I approached him. "I'm so glad you're okay."

"I'm glad too. In fact, it was quite an awakening." He was slowly nodding his head.

"That's for sure! Downtown's crazy! I was up on a ladder in the winery, about to top off my barrels when it hit. I've never been in an earthquake before. It could have killed me! Benson came in and got me out of there at the last second. And our wine's ruined! It looked like all the barrels in the winery rolled off the shelves. Some survived, but ours didn't, since they were on the highest shelf. I'm so, so sorry."

"I'm sorry too, my dear," he answered slowly. "But you'll have an excellent vintage next year, and the year after that, and for many more years to come. Because you're gonna keep these wonderful old vines safe from those bastards." He pointed to the vineyards of the big wineries that surrounded his land.

"Hey, what's this 'you'll' stuff? It's we, Hal, we! We're going to bring Darnay back to its glory days, just like we said." But something about him was off. He didn't seem like himself. "Hey, why are you just sitting on this bench? We've just been through an earthquake!"

"I'm spending time with my vines," he said. "We kinda grew up together. We've lived through a wonderful marriage, two births, a death. We've experienced love, hate, success, and failure. And you brought these vines back to life, Samantha. Emma will be so happy to hear about that. I'll be seeing her real soon now. She's made sure of it. Just have some business to take care of first. Hope she left me enough time to tend to it, is all."

"Hal, you're scaring the crap out of me." I walked in front of the bench to get a better view of him and saw a stream of dark red blood running from a wound in his head. "Oh, dear God! What happened to you?" I furiously punched 911 into my phone. The operator answered. "Send an ambulance to 6 Twisted Vine Road, Napa. There's a man here with a serious contusion on his head. I think something hit him during the quake."

.   .   .

Hal died on the way to the hospital. The EMTs wouldn't let me ride in the ambulance, so I followed behind in my car. I didn't have phone numbers for either of his sons, so I called Watson Realty. Ken Watson passed the news on to Lucas and Andrew, and the two men met me at the hospital shortly after the ambulance arrived. They were told that there was nothing the doctors could have done for their dad, due to the severe thrombosis caused by the blow to his head. When the County authorities later inspected the house to determine the precise cause of death, the blood on the frame of the painting confirmed that by falling off the wall during the quake, it made Hal the single casualty of the disaster. I told his sons that their father had seemed at peace that morning and had talked about joining their mother and telling her that the vineyard they'd loved had come back to life. Lucas gave me a hug and thanked me for being a good friend to Hal. Andrew asked me if I locked the door to the house before the ambulance left. He worried about any thefts that might follow the earthquake.

.   .   .

"I'm sorry about you losing your friend this morning, Samantha. And I'm sorry about your wine." Those were the first kind words Irv had said to me since I'd started working at Napa Juice. The man looked like he'd had the life sucked out of him, as we stood outside the barrel room. The electricity had come back on at three o'clock that afternoon, allowing Benson and the cellar workers to begin the massive job of cleaning up the destruction. Most of the barrels on the lower shelves remained intact after falling. Some were lying split open, and a portion of the wine could be siphoned out and saved. Others, especially those from the higher shelves, were total losses.

"It's a disappointment to lose my first vintage, Irv. And I'll miss my friend Hal terribly. But what really kills me is that his dream of preserving one of the last historic vineyards in Napa will go up in smoke when his sons sell that property."

"Yup, this earthquake seems to have broken a lot of dreams," Irv agreed as he looked at the devastation that covered the cellar floor. "Clients have been calling all day, and I've had to give most of them the bad news about their wine. They all had insurance against accidents at the winery, but none of them had earthquake insurance. Jacques Barrlét lost sixty of his eighty barrels of Technique. Trevor Sheen was lucky that half of his Hologram made it through. And poor Curtis Payne . . . that Merlot of his that sat in the barrel for over two years is all gone." He pointed to the barrels of Ultraviolet that the workers were rolling away from the carnage. "We're just lucky that Ashton's barrels were on the lower racks and sustained the least damage."

"I'm happy about that for Benson," I said.

"Why don't you go home, doll? You've had a long day." I slowly nodded my head while staring at the piles of broken barrels that covered up whatever remained of my wine.

·     ·     ·

The power came back on, making my drive home that evening a lot quicker and easier than the one that morning. But I avoided the downtown area where rows of vans and trucks carrying local and network news crews had set up camp to cover the earthquake. The primary focus of the reports coming in on my AM radio was the amount of wine the quake had destroyed. The damage seemed to hit in pockets. There were wineries in parts of the valley that sustained huge losses. Those in other sections didn't lose a single bottle. Though most restaurants fared well, some close to the epicenter had their entire wine cellars wiped out.

After turning onto Old Sonoma Highway toward Carneros, another problem came to mind. The several thousand dollars I'd processed in credit card payments over the last few weeks for pre-buys of Darnay would have to be returned to my customers. I'd already spent part of those funds for licenses and the standard lab fees to test the wine for bacteria. But I quickly forgot about that issue when I arrived at 6 Twisted Vine Road and saw Ken Watson installing a "For Sale by Watson Realty" sign at the front of the property. Seuss stood a few feet away from the man, barraging him with growls and barks.

"The man's not even cold yet, and you're already trying to sell his home?" I cried out through the window of my truck. "Don't you people have any shame?"

"Ah! Amanda, isn't it?" The realtor flashed that same slimy, bleached-toothed smile he subjected me to when I passed his billboards on Route 29. "The property won't officially hit the multiples until the family can get the house emptied. Andrew just wanted me to put the sign up now to get some heat going."

"That's what's on his mind the day his father dies? *Unbelievable!*"

"Hey, glad I ran into you by-the-by, 'cause Andrew asked if you had a signed lease for that cottage you're living in. If so, could you provide us with a copy, Amanda?"

"The name is Samantha, and no, there isn't any lease. Hal and I worked out our own arrangement for my living situation."

"Well, that's a beautiful thing for us! It frees the property of any contingencies. I'll check with Andrew and Lucas, but you'll probably be dealing with me on a month-to-month rental until the close of escrow. Then you can ask the buyers if they want to keep that cottage rented out. But if they do, I'm sure you'll be looking at paying a few grand a month on that cute little place. The market's getting crazier all the time out here. And, *hey!* If you have any friends looking for a property like this one, have them give me a jingle." He passed a bunch of his business cards through the window of my truck.

"Sure, I'll tell *all* my multi-millionaire friends to call you." Either ignoring or unaware of my sarcasm, he gave me a thumbs-up as I drove through the gates.

After parking my truck, I saw a screen of missed calls on my cell from my mom, my dad, Stephanie, Cameron, Spence, and Sara. I finally answered my mom's eleventh call as Seuss and I walked into the cottage.

"Sam, baby, I'm so glad to hear your voice! The Napa earthquake has been on the news all day! Are you alright?"

"It's been a fricking nightmare, Mom. I was on a ladder in the winery when the quake struck and thought I was a goner. Then my friend Hal, who owns the property I live on, died on the way to the hospital after getting hit on the head by a portrait of his dead wife. Now, his vineyard is for sale. They're talking about asking three million dollars for it, so I can't use any more of his grapes for my wine and I'll probably have to move out of this cottage. Downtown Napa is a train wreck! Oh, and hundreds of barrels of other people's wine and all the wine I made got destroyed in the quake. So I've gotta refund the money that came with the pre-orders, some of which I've already spent."

"Oh, how horrible! But I'm glad you're safe! I'd love to help you with your finances, but I'm still in the hole for the store. And after your father fired me, his firm is hemorrhaging money, so he can't help you either. But what I can do is email you some of Ron's lessons to download and study. They'll help you find that if you have faith in your mental and physical strengths, success will follow."

"Okay, whatever you say, Mom." I shook my head, amazed that my once doomsday prepper of a mother was now the eternal optimist.

•  •  •

"How're you holding up?" It was Benson. He'd called as Seuss and I were about to go for our run on the morning after the quake.

"I still can't believe he's gone, Benson. The funeral is Saturday. You'll be here, won't you?"

"Sure, I'll be there. Hal was a great guy. I'll miss him too."

While we were speaking, I looked out at the vineyard through the window. Ken Watson was talking to a man in a business suit, who I assumed was a realtor representing one of the neighboring wineries eager to purchase Hal's land. I pulled up the listing for the property on my phone and saw it's three million dollar price tag.

"It's kind of ironic," I told Benson. "Hal wanted his ashes sprinkled in his vineyard. But it'll only be a matter of months before whatever corporation buys this place destroys these vines."

"Well, I do have some good news for you," Benson said.

"Good news? What good news?"

"Hal's mighty Moreau barrels survived the quake."

"*What? Are you joking?*"

"Nope. All twelve of them made it through intact. The crew just dug the last of them out of the rubble after working all night. Cellar master Jose said he's never seen barrels that could withstand such a fall. That cooperage must use some secret ancient techniques to impart that kind of strength to them."

"*Wow, that's amazing! So there will be a Darnay after all!*" But reality quickly dampened the good news. "It's just too bad that there won't be any more after that. The brand will end up a one-year wonder and barely worth releasing. There's no point trademarking a name or doing labels and promotion for a wine that won't be around the next year."

"Well, just find a rich sugar daddy to buy you that vineyard. Then you can keep Darnay going for as long as you want."

"Sure, no prob. But first I've gotta find a cheap place to live that allows dogs."

•   •   •

Hal's funeral took place in his vineyard. His sons and their families, a few of Hal's army buddies, and some of his old neighbors came to pay their respects. Delilah and Seuss relaxed in the nearby field while Hanna Morgon, who had once lived and owned a winery next door, gave a tribute to her old neighbor. She praised Hal and Emma for their determination to preserve the family-owned vineyard and their refusal to sell out to the big corporations that, if they acquired Pritchett Vineyards, would be certain to rip out the historic French plantings, poison the soil with the toxins they used to control weeds and pests, and stress the groundwater levels by over-irrigating the new vines to get the biggest yield possible. While Hanna spoke, I spotted Ken Watson at the edge of the property having what looked to be a serious powwow with the same man that I'd seen him with the day after the quake. I elbowed Benson, who was sitting next to me. "Would you look at those guys!" I pointed to the two men. "They can't even wait 'til Hal's funeral is over to close their damn deal!"

· · ·

People were still milling around and chatting with each other when Benson and I went back to the cottage. I pointed to a pile of spreadsheets I'd laid out on the dining table. "I've been wracking my brain to see if there's any way in hell I could possibly come up with three million dollars."

"Good luck with that, Sam. Three million is a shitload of money. The only way I could come up with that much is to start with two million nine hundred, ninety-five thousand."

"Let's be serious. If I could come up with half a million for a down payment, I could get a mortgage from the Bank of Napa by using the property as collateral. My payments would be around eleven thou a month. I could probably earn five grand a month tending bar at The Cellar on nights and weekends while I worked a day job."

"That wouldn't even get you close."

"I know. So I'm thinking I could get a good-paying accounting gig in San Francisco."

"You'd be dead in a year doing that. Especially with an hour commute into the city and back. And how are you going to come up with half a million, anyway?"

"Okay . . . so . . . listen up. We only used a fraction of last year's grapes to make Darnay. And this year's harvest should have a much higher yield. What if I could secure a contract with a winery to buy half of the grapes before we close escrow on the property?"

"No way!" Benson shook his head. "No one pays in advance for grape tonnage. They pay when the grapes have arrived safely at the winery. Too many variables—an early frost, mold, drought. Buying grapes is not like ordering cardboard boxes."

"I know . . . just wishing . . . hoping there was some way to buy this place. I'm sure Aunt Viv would have fought tooth and nail for it. If she were in my shoes, that is." I gave a deep sigh and rested my chin on my hands. A call from Sara LeMont appeared on my cell. I'd neglected to return her previous calls that I'd assumed were about the earthquake.

"*Sam!* How are you holding up after that awful shaker?"

"I'm okay, Sara. But it turned our world upside down."

"Well, maybe this will help to right it. For you, at least. I forwarded the shots of the painting of your aunt you'd sent me over to our specialists here at Sotheby's. Now, I know the piece is a treasured family heirloom—"

"It is Sara. My aunt was a major force in my life."

"I'm sure she was. I could sense her strength, just in those photos. And it excited me to learn that the artist, Marciel Duprée, long dead, is very hot right now! Other paintings by him have brought in strong numbers. And it looks like your work is genuine. Forgery is rampant with prices going wild, but that signature and those brushstrokes would be hard to replicate. Is there any chance you'd consider selling it? Of course, the experts here would need to analyze it in the labs for certification before any sale."

"Sell it? Oh, no. I don't think I could ever sell that painting, Sara." Hearing my words, Benson closed in on me.

"Okay, but just so you know . . . one of our clients . . . a very serious collector, has offered two and a half million for the piece—which would net you two million three! Unless we can get them to pay our commission and you'd get the full two and a half."

"What? *Two and a half million?* That's *crazy!*"

"*Two and a half million what?*" mouthed Benson.

"I agree," Sara said. "Prices of recognized artists *are* crazy."

"I don't know . . . I just don't know," I said as I looked up the painting of my beautiful aunt with the glass of Romanée-Conti in her hand. "I don't know if I could sell Aunt Viv's painting for any amount of money."

*"Yes, you could!"* mouthed Benson.

"I get it, Sam. Plus, you'd have to prove that you're the owner of the piece, and that might be difficult."

"Ummm . . . not really. My aunt set up a trust for transferring the co-op to my dad. I think she listed the other items like the furniture, jewelry, wine, the painting, in the trust docs. And I still have her handmade list somewhere."

"Well, that's all good," Sara said. "And if you change your mind, let me know."

*"Tell her you'll sell it!"* Benson hissed in my face. I mouthed the words *"no!"* and waved him away.

"Okay. Will do. Bye, Sara." A call from my mom was coming in. "Hi, Mom."

"How are you, baby? I know your friend's funeral was today. How'd it go?"

"It was nice . . . and sad. I just got off the phone with Julien LeMont's mom, Sara. You know that painting Aunt Viv left me? The one I brought to Napa?"

"Yeah. The nude. Did it get damaged in the quake?"

"No, it's all good . . . right here . . . on my wall. I'd sent some photos of it to Sara. She's back in New York with Spence and working with Sotheby's."

*"And?"*

"Well . . . it seems that the artist friend of Aunt Viv's who did the painting was a guy named Marciel Duprée, whose works are getting big bucks. Sara told me one of their clients has put in an offer of two and a half million for the painting!"

*"What?"*

"You heard me. Before we could close on a sale, I'd have to get it back to New York so they could run it through some tests to prove it was genuine. A genuine Duprée, that is. Isn't that *crazy?* Who'd a thought Aunt Viv—"

"Oh, God! Oh Lord! Hallejulah! That's wonderful! When are you bringing it back?"

"Well . . . that's my dilemma. I don't think I *can* bring it back. I don't think I can give it *up.*"

*"Yes, you can!"* Benson hissed.

I mouthed the words *"no"* to him again. He threw his arms in the air and walked around the room. "That painting is my link to Aunt Viv. It's my inspiration."

"Are you *insane?*" my mom asked. "What if it's *stolen?* What if you have a *fire?* You already had an *earthquake!* You take that painting and march right down to whatever shipping store there is in Napa and have it safely crated. Then you get your airline ticket and fly the crated painting back here."

"First of all, Mom . . . most of the stores in downtown are still closed after the quake. Second . . . you're sounding just like your stressed-out old self."

"You're making me feel like my stressed-out old self. Let me put Ron on the phone. Maybe he can talk some sense into you."

"How about we all talk later? After you've calmed down. Gotta go, Mom. Bye."

"Your Mom's right!" scolded Benson when I put the phone down. "And what do you think your great aunt would say if she knew you lost the vineyard . . . *the vineyard that has your soul running through its soil and its vines* . . . because you wouldn't part with her picture? Tell you what! I'll find a printing place tomorrow with a scanner that can make a beautiful digital copy and mount it on a canvas. How's that?"

"Well . . . you have a point about what Viv would have wanted for me. Let's open a bottle of some very tannic wine, so I can think on it."

• • •

Twenty minutes later, I got another call. It was Ron. "Hi, Ron! How are you? I think I know what this is about."

"Hi, Sam. Your mom filled me in on your painting quandary. And I agree with her that not accepting a strong offer on it at this point in time would be madness. I have some friends in the art world that I used to do business with. I just had them check out prices on Marciel Duprée's work. Prices go wild when an artist gets hot. But they don't always stay hot. And they think two and a half million is an excellent price—but I'd try to negotiate for the buyers to pay the commission. I also checked out that property on 6 Twisted Vine Road and think three million is very reasonable. Carneros is proving to be one of the fastest appreciating regions in Napa. If you could get it for anything under asking, it'd be a good deal."

"It *is* an amazing and beautiful property, Ron. And if I sold the painting, I might qualify for a loan for the balance from the bank." Benson stared at me to find out what was happening.

"If you sell that painting, you can get a loan from me for three hundred thou. That would bring you to two eight. Anything more and you're on your own, 'cause three hundred is as high as I can go right now with what I've put into our business. I'll give you two percent interest, which is lower than the bank will do. And if you have a terrible month, you can make it up the next. I won't slap on interest and penalties like a bank would."

"Wow! You would do *that* for *me?*"

"YES!" Sensing progress, Benson gave a fist pump.

"Sure. I am your stepfather. And I've heard how hard you've worked on that vineyard and on your wine project. I'll email you an intent to loan you that money. But you've got to sell that painting as soon as possible. A bird in the hand, you know."

"Okay, Ron, will do. And really, thanks so much for your help. Bye now." I turned to Benson. "Hey . . ." my voice was shaking. "You were right about making me go to the wedding. And you were right when you told me to give Ron a second chance. Because the guy I had no use for, is now the guy who's helping to make my dreams come true."

Benson came over and held me until my body stopped trembling. I looked up at the painting of my aunt. The rays of sun that streamed into the window of the cottage were lighting up her face. For the first time, it appeared as if she was offering up that wonderful wine to me. Almost like she was giving me her blessing. "Is that Ken guy still out there?" I asked Benson.

He looked out the window and pointed to where the four men were standing in the vineyard. The man in the suit was handing an envelope to Ken Watson. "He sure is. And the guy in the suit looks like he just made an offer to him and those twins."

"Oh, shit. I better get out there!"

"Hey, Sam, didn't I hear someone say Hanna Morgon is doing real estate now? You need representation on this. Maybe you could catch her before she leaves."

I ran to where Hanna was getting into her car. After filling her in on my situation, the two of us walked to the vineyard.

· · ·

"Good day, all!" Hanna called out to the group. "I'm Hanna Morgon of Napa Realty," she said to Ken and the man in the suit. "Lukey and Andy already know me. I watched them grow up." She handed her business card to each of the four men. "My client, Samantha Goodyear, would like to make an offer on this property."

Andrew looked at Hanna. "Excuse me, Mrs. Morgon. We're close to wrapping up a deal with Galileo on this." He gave the man in the suit a wink. "I think it'd be best for you to leave us to our business."

In a flash, Hanna morphed from buttoned up professional to scolding matriarch, with nostrils flared as she wagged her index finger in Andrew's face. "Don't you *dare* try to tell me what's best, Andy Pritchett. You always *were* a brat! Never shared your toys with the other kids. Rude as all heck to their parents when they asked ya to play nice. I can't count the number of times I've wanted to wash that sassy mouth of yours out with a bar of soap 'cept your mama woulda sent the sheriff after me. Emma was a lovely lady, but she spoiled *you* rotten." I cringed, certain that Hanna was about to blow any chance I'd have of making an offer. But Andrew just stood there with his head to the ground, while Hanna turned to Ken. "Now, we'd appreciate it if you'd give us a few minutes to write something up."

"Mrs. Morgan," the realtor for the winery interjected. "My clients have wanted this land for a long time, and I intend to close this one." He shook hands with each of the three men. "We feel we've made a reasonable offer, gentlemen. It's an all-cash deal and we're fine with a thirty-day escrow. Look forward to your call," he said, revealing teeth that resembled a row of Hotpoint refrigerators. He marched off with a step that exuded confidence.

A wave of panic swelled up within me as I looked from one twin to the other. A film of tears covered my eyes, and my larynx vibrated when I spoke. "Can you guys at least give me a chance to get in an offer? I love this land every bit as much as your dad did."

"This is business," began Andrew. "Your profession of love won't work with—"

"I say, give her a chance, Andy," interrupted Lucas. "And being ninety seconds older and the executor of dad's estate, I'm asserting my seniority." He leaned in close to his brother. "Mrs. Morgon's right. You always *were* a brat."

"*Whatever*," Andrew said while he tossed a rock into the vineyard.

"Thanks, Lukey!" Hanna gave the more amenable twin a quick kiss on the cheek. "Just give us a minute!"

Hanna and I hurried to the cottage. I didn't want to overpay, but I didn't want to lose the property by bidding too low either. The broker had me write out a check for ten thousand that I'd have to ask my mom or dad to cover to keep it from bouncing if it got deposited into escrow. I then googled and printed a standard real estate offer form. Hanna thought a reasonable offer from Galileo would be two million seven hundred and fifty thou, so at her suggestion, I typed out $2,800,000.00 in the "amount of offer" box. In less than ten minutes, Hanna and I were presenting our bid.

"What happens to old Delilah here if Galileo gets this place?" I asked the twins as Hanna handed the envelope with my offer and check for the deposit to Ken. "And how about your old house and the cottage? What happens to those?"

"The house and cottage will probably get demolished and sold for salvage," Andrew told me. "We haven't talked about what happens to Delilah yet. It may just be time to put the old girl down."

"That would be awful," I said, looking over at the mare who was happily grazing in the field. All I could do now was to wait for Ken to tell Hanna which offer, if any, the twins would accept. I went back in the cottage to email Sara with the news that I'd be willing to sell the painting.

# twenty-one

---

**Rudy Kurniawan** *p.n.* the world's most famous wine forger, sentenced to ten years in prison for making and selling millions of dollars in counterfeit wine

On the Friday after Hal's funeral, I flew back to New York for the auction house to verify that the painting of Aunt Viv was a genuine Marciel Duprée. During my absence, Benson had a digital scan of it printed onto a canvas that he hung back over the fireplace of the cottage. It didn't have the textures or vibrancy of the real thing, but it was still a beautiful image. I returned from Manhattan on Sunday afternoon with two and a half million in my bank account. Because the painting was an inheritance, the money I earned from it was tax free. That evening, I got a call from Hanna.

"Bad news, Sam. Galileo had upped their offer to two million nine."

"Oh, crap, Hanna!"

"Crap is right! But Lucas said if you could match Galileo's offer within close of business on Wednesday, they'll abide by their father's wishes and let you have the property at that price. They would need a thirty-day escrow, however."

"Wait . . . what do you mean about their father's wishes? And how do you know they'd give it to me at that price?"

"One of my old neighbors told me. An attorney named Larry Holmes, who did the legal stuff for Hal. He was out of town for the funeral, but said he'd called Lucas last week to tell them their father had set up an appointment for the day after the earthquake to change his will and leave the property to *you* instead of them! That's when Lucas told him he'd give it to you at two million nine."

"*What?* Hal was going to disinherit his sons and leave all this to *me?*" I had to think for a moment. "But maybe . . . maybe that's what he meant by what he said to me after the earthquake. Said he had some business to take care of before he saw Emma. Guess that didn't happen. *Oh, wow!*" The realization of what Hal planned to do for me sent a rush of emotion through my body. "But I wouldn't take their inheritance from them anyway. No matter what Hal wanted."

"I still believe if you could get that property for two nine, it'd be a steal."

"Maybe. But my chances of getting a hundred grand from a bank in thirty days are slim to none. Sorry, Hanna. It's just not going to happen."

"I'm sorry too, Sam."

· · ·

I called Benson to give him the bad news. An hour later, he came in with a bag of groceries to make me a consolation dinner at the cottage. I was searching the real estate listing for rentals. The earthquake had made a slim rental market even slimmer.

"I brought an Austrian wine, a new red that Ash's distributor is carrying," Benson said, taking the bottle from the bag. "The grapes are Zweigelt, from a village just south of Vienna. Something different for us to try."

I got up from the table and headed for the door. "I thought we'd drink something else. That okay?"

"Sure, Sam, whatever." He followed me out to the side of the big house and through a door on the ground. I navigated my way down a series of stone steps and pulled a string that dangled from a light bulb in the cold underground cellar. There were rows of cases of wine with the name Darnay and the years of the vintages written in marker on the sides of the boxes. On top of some boxes was the case of wine from Aunt Vivian that Hal had been storing for me.

"Here it is." I picked up the case.

"I'll get that for you." Benson took the case from my arms. I shut off the light, and we climbed the steps.

"Aunt Viv said I should open this case when life gives me sour grapes," I said as we entered the cottage. "I think this qualifies."

Benson put the wine down on my table. I cut the yellowed packing tape on the carton with the blade of my corkscrew and pulled out a bottle from the center. "It's a Château Siran 1970," I said, handing the bottle to Benson.

"Ah, Château Siran!" he exclaimed. "One of the oldest domaines in Margaux. Once owned by the grandparents of the artist Toulouse-Lautrec. I heard the château has an amazing museum filled with ancient winemaking tools. The wines are good, but nothing special. You can pick one of these old vintages up for about . . ." He scanned his phone for the price. "Fifty-seven dollars."

I took the bottle to the kitchen counter and sliced off the silver tin capsule that covered the cork. Benson pulled the flaps of the box away to inspect the other bottles. "Hmmm . . . four of these have maroon capsules," he said, as he pulled one of them out. "Let's see . . . this wine is . . . is . . . *holy shit!*"

"What happened?" I turned back to look at him.

"Romanée-Conti 1934! That's what happened! I'm holding a bottle of fucking Romanée-Conti 1934 in my hand!"

*"What?"* I raced to the table as he pulled out the other four bottles that had the same maroon capsules and time-worn labels with beautiful scripting. *"No!"* I took the bottle in my hand and stared at it, wondering if my eyes were playing tricks on me.

"You've got five of them here!" Benson said as he googled the price of the vintage. "These bottles are going for over twenty-five thousand bucks each! Do you know what that means?"

"I do! Thank you, Aunt Viv!" I said, looking up at the digital copy of the painting.

"If you could get that, or close to it, you'll be home free!"

"Maybe Spence can help. What is it, six o'clock? It's only nine in New York. I'll try him." I called Spence on his cell.

"Sam! What's up?"

"Sorry to bother you guys so late. Remember I'd once mentioned that Viv had left me a case of wine?"

"Sure. The sour grapes wine."

"Yup . . . well . . . seven of the bottles are Château Siran. The other five are Romanée-Conti 1934! Can you get them sold for me, Spence? If I could net anything over a hundred grand on them, I could still buy my friend Hal's property!"

"Wow, that's very cool news! And I do hate to be a killjoy, but selling those old bottles isn't so easy anymore. Ever since the notorious Rudy Kurniawan flooded the market with counterfeit wines, collectors are wary. You have to prove the bottles aren't fakes, that they've been stored properly so the wine hasn't spoiled, and you have to prove ownership. Did you check the box for a receipt?"

"A receipt?" I turned to Benson. "Check the box! Check the box!" He pulled an envelope from the bottom of the case and unfolded the paper inside.

"We found something, Spence." Benson put the paper in front of me. "It's written in French . . . from Marchands de Vins, Paris. It looks like it's listing the purchase of five bottles of Romanée-Conti for five francs, dated November 16, 1936. There's a signature on the bottom— it's my aunt's."

"Excellent—those merchants are still around. They should be able to verify the receipt. I know Marchands de Vins keeps accurate records. And you, as your aunt's heir, can prove ownership. But that's only part of what you need to get them sold. Text me some pictures of the entire bottles. Then hold them up to a light and get shots of the fill lines. Also, some shots of the bottoms, so I can get an idea of the color of the wine. It should be nice and clear, and ruby in color. I also need to see the amount of sediment in those bottles. Some is okay, but they can't have too much breakdown."

·　　·　　·

Spence thought the photos of the five bottles looked great, which also showed that they'd been stored properly. He was able to get confirmation from the Paris wine merchants that Vivian Goodyear had purchased the bottles in November of 1936. By Wednesday of that week, a billionaire wine enthusiast in China that Spence did business with had wired one hundred twenty-five thousand into my bank account, and I had the bottles shipped to Hong Kong. Thirty days later, I closed escrow on 6 Twisted Vine Road.

# twenty-two

---

**Finish** *n.* the flavors that remain when the wine has left the mouth, often described with terms such as savory, sweet, bitter, complex, acidic, long-lasting

"Please understand that Mr. Wasserman didn't intentionally avoid renewing his license this year, and he's happy to pay any penalties he's accrued." I was on the phone with the Alcohol and Beverage Control Commission when Benson popped into my office. He was rotating his finger in a circle to get me to wrap up the call.

"Hey, what's up?" I asked when I clicked off.

"What's up is that I've got two tickets to The Napa Valley Wine Auction this Saturday night at Mondial Winery in St. Helena! They sent them to Ashton, 'cause we're donating another barrel of Ultraviolet like we do every year, but he's got one of his Narcotics Anonymous meetings and can't skip it per his deal with the courts." Ashton had completed his three-month stint in rehab in March. Benson and Irv were keeping their fingers crossed that he could stay clean. "How 'bout it? Wanna go?"

I knew that the auction was one of the industry's biggest charity extravaganzas, that raised millions of dollars each year for the Napa community by offering wine donated by the area's vintners for guests to bid big bucks on. The part of the evening that brings in the most money is the barrel auction, where the winning bidders receive their purchase after the wine in the barrel is bottled.

I jumped up from my desk and gave Benson a hug. "You're asking me if I want to go to *the* industry event of the year? *Hell, yes, I want to go!*" But I also knew that I wouldn't feel comfortable taking up an expensive spot at a charity event when I couldn't afford to bid on the auction items. After acquiring 6 Twisted Vine Road, I'd spent whatever I had left from the sale of the Romanée-Conti to pay the closing costs and taxes on the property. Plus, Hal's house needed extensive work before I could even think about moving out of the cottage. "I'd feel better about going if I could make a donation. And I *would* love to find a way to honor Hal. Hey, do you think I could donate a barrel of my wine to the auction in his name?"

"Sure, you could," Benson said. "I've got the contact info of the lady in charge of all that. I'll send it to you."

"Thanks! Now, I've got another problem."

"What's that?"

"I have absolutely nothing to wear. I checked out last year's photos. That event is glitzy! But I shouldn't be buying anything."

"Oh, c'mon, Sam. Every smart accountant has some mad money tucked away for a rainy day. Or a good party."

.   .   .

"I have a feeling we're not in Kansas anymore," I told Benson as we pulled into the valet parking line at the entrance to Mondial Winery.

"Let's just hope they don't tell us to park out in the cornfield," he said as he looked toward several acres of weeds where the winery's heavy machinery was stored. Benson's ginormous pickup truck looked totally out of place in the line of stretch limousines, Italian sports cars, Teslas, Jaguars, and Bentleys. When we walked up to the grand entrance of the building complete with guards in uniform, it felt like we were on the red carpet of the Academy Awards. I wore a black cocktail dress I'd found online that crisscrossed at the back and showed a bit of cleavage in the front, and Benson looked great in a black vintage blazer, cowboy boots, and a skinny checked tie. A row of photographers took pictures of us, and waiters offered glasses of champagne from a tray. It seemed as if every major player in the California wine industry was at the event, from local legends who'd built and ruled the big wineries, to makers of trendy boutique wines. There were owners of hot restaurants, along with wine critics for the *New York Times*, the *San Francisco Chronicle*, the *Los Angeles Times*, *Wine Spectator*, and *Wine Snob*. Many of those attending were just serious oenophiles. I'd spotted players for the San Francisco Giants, the Golden State Warriors, and even heard someone say they'd seen Johnny Depp in the barrel room.

"Hi, Samantha, remember me?" a voice called out.

It was Chef Richard Weller. "Sure! How could I forget my airport driver?"

"I'm looking forward to getting your wine on the list at The Shed. How'd those Moreaus hold up during the quake?"

"They were superheroes! My wine would have been toast without them. I'm just sorry for all the other folks who lost so much. Hey, Richard, you remember Benson Doyle? The assistant winemaker of Ultraviolet?"

Richard offered his hand to Benson. "Sure. Ultraviolet, *huh?*" The chef didn't seem to recognize Benson, but immediately clicked on Ultraviolet. "Horrible about your boss's accident last year. How's he doing?" Though the circumstances of Ashton's crash had initially been well-contained, rumors that he'd tested positive for cocaine at the time were spreading throughout the industry.

"The boss is doing well," Benson told him. "His new church is keeping him busy. He's singing in the choir and he's met a nice lady deacon. Seems like the two of them are serious."

"Singing in the church choir? A lady deacon?" I asked after Richard had moved on to another conversation.

"It's just some bullshit story that Irv made up to protect Ashton's brand," Benson said. "When distributors and restaurants get even a whiff that a winemaker is into drugs, they back off quick. Sales are already in a slump with all the rumors flying around."

"Samantha!" It was Steve Littauer. "Hey, I saw your barrel down there in the cave and took a taste. Seems to me you've got what they refer to in France as *le cadeau*, or the gift. You harvested those grapes within hours of the perfect balance of sugar and acids. And the wine is exquisite!"

"Thank you so much! Wow! I am honored to get a compliment like that from the great Steve Littauer!" He gave me a thumbs-up and moved on.

We followed what seemed like a tidal wave of guests down a musky tunnel to the winery's vast underground cave where dozens of barrels of wine donated by Napa vintners were available for tasting. A sign telling the story of the wine accompanied each barrel. We spotted Ashton's barrel of Ultraviolet Cabernet, and then found my barrel. A sign on it gave this information:

Lot #398
*Darnay*
Pinot Noir
Pritchett Vineyard, Carneros / French clones 118 / Planted 1933
Aged 12 months in Moreau Barrels, French Oak
Winemaker: Samantha Goodyear
Donated in Memory of Hal Pritchett

I chatted with several guests who were sampling various wines, while Benson talked up Ashton's wine to people who were tasting from the barrel of Ultraviolet. Out of the corner of my eye, I saw a man in a dark suit standing near my barrel. It took a moment for me to recognize him as Winston Broadhurst of *Wine Snob.* Though Broadhurst had written a rave review of Darnay when it was very young, it was still possible that the way it had aged could disappoint him. My stomach did a backflip as a server used a thief to slip a taste of my wine in a glass for him. After he took a sip, I waited for him to spit it out in a nearby spittoon. But when he took a second sip, I mustered up my courage and approached him.

"Hi, Mr. Broadhurst!" I extended my hand. "It's Sam Goodyear. Remember me from Napa Juice?"

He peered at me through the thick lenses of his glasses. "Yes, my dear, I remember you," he said in that familiar whisper. The roar of hundreds of guests drinking and socializing in the cave forced me to read the man's lips to understand him.

"Thank you for writing that terrific piece about my wine," I said, in a near shout. Then I locked my hands behind my now rigid body as I dared to pop the big question. "So . . . how do you think it's coming along?" I stared at his mouth, awaiting his answer.

"It's developing beautifully, as I knew it would." He rotated the wine in the glass and took another sip. "You *do* plan to stay with that vineyard for your next year's vintage, I trust?"

"I plan to keep making wine from my vineyard for as long as I have the strength in my body to stomp those grapes, Mr. Broadhurst!"

A small crowd had gathered around us to meet the renowned former critic of London's *Decanter*, who had dethroned Regis Preston at *Wine Snob*. The way he cradled his glass in his hand made it clear he'd given my wine his blessing, which made those in the crowd eager to get a taste for themselves. Among them was Morton Drydock, who I instantly recognized as the chairman and founder of Weatherhouse Accounting.

Before I could introduce myself to Drydock, a bell signaled that the barrel auction would begin in ten minutes. Event organizers directed the sea of guests away from the barrels and gave numbered paddles to each potential bidder. When the lights dimmed, they encouraged us to take our seats in the rows of chairs facing a podium. Penelope Mondial, a granddaughter of the legendary Napa wine industry pioneer Randolph Mondial, took to the microphone.

"Good evening, friends," she began. "We thank you all for joining us tonight for Napa Valley's annual fundraiser that has enhanced the health and well-being of our community for over thirty-five years. During that time, the barrel auction has raised over twenty million dollars for families in need. Now, I'll turn the mike over to our auctioneer Harvey Brimstone. So, open your wallets and indulge your palates with the incredible wines donated by the Valley's most acclaimed vintners."

After a burst of applause from the crowd, the auctioneer took to the podium. "Cheers everyone! Are you *ready to rumble*?" he bellowed. The crowd replied with a mixture of applause and whistles. "Okay, then, let's *do* it!" Brimstone shouted. "The first of our wines in barrel is a Whistling Leaf Pinot Noir from Coombsville, crafted by winemaker Matthew Corrina. Do I have an eight thousand dollar bid?" A paddle rose from the crowd. "There it is, eight! Now nine, will ya give me nine?" Another paddle rose. "There it is, nine! Now ten, will you give me ten?" The bidding continued for several minutes before the gavel came down on a final bid for twenty thousand dollars, which elicited more applause and whistles. "Next, we have a barrel of Ultraviolet Napa Valley Cabernet, crafted by Ashton White. Do I have a bid of eight thousand dollars? There it is, eight! Now nine, will ya give me nine? There it is, nine! Will ya give me ten? There it is, ten!" The bidding for Ultraviolet went on until the gavel came down at twenty-six thousand, which, though a far cry from the fifty-six thousand that Ashton's wine had gone for two years ago at the same event, was still a large amount of money for the twenty-five cases of wine the winning bidder would receive. A glance at the handout told me that my wine would be next, causing my stomach to contract into a tight knot.

"Why did I do this?" I whispered to Benson as my chest heaved with abbreviated breaths. "No one really knows my wine yet. What if it doesn't sell at all? How embarrassing would that be?" He gave my hand a squeeze and patted my arm. I slowly inhaled and exhaled. "Well, if it doesn't, it's not the end of the world. I can't expect these people to buy a wine that hasn't even been released, when they can bid on these other big names."

"Just stay calm, Sam. It'll be okay. I promise," he assured me.

"Next up . . ." the auctioneer began, "a barrel of Darnay Pinot Noir sourced from Pritchett Farms in Carneros crafted by winemaker Samantha Goodyear. The wine is being donated by Miss Goodyear in memory of her friend Hal Pritchett."

I curled up in my seat and held my hands against my ears. "Nobody's going to bid. This is *so* humiliating."

"Do I hear eight thousand?" the auctioneer asked. "Do I hear eight thousand?" He looked around the audience.

"*No*, he *doesn't*. Let's just go home, Benson. *Please!*" I reached for my handbag and readied myself to rise.

"Ah, there it is, eight!" the auctioneer said.

"Thank you, God!" I cried, as I looked toward the ceiling of the cave and sank back in relief.

"Now nine, will you give me nine? There it is, nine!" Brimstone called out as someone else raised a paddle. "Now ten, will you give me ten? There it is, ten! Now eleven, will you give me eleven? There it is, eleven! Now twelve, will you give me twelve? There it is, twelve! Now thirteen, will you give me thirteen? There it is, thirteen! Now fourteen, will you give me fourteen?" I pinched myself to make sure I wasn't dreaming. Then I wondered if I'd heard wrong, and they were bidding on a different wine until Benson gave me an 'I told you so' elbow in the ribs. Five or six paddles continued to rise as the bidding went from twenty to twenty-five to thirty thousand dollars. When the auctioneer got to forty thousand, paddles 199 and 288 continued to rise like ducks in a shooting gallery as the auctioneer's chant got faster and faster and the price of the barrel got higher. When it passed fifty, the chatter of the crowd got louder as many of the guests rose from their seats to get a glimpse of the dueling bidders.

"That's Morton Drydock holding up 288," a man a few seats away said to the woman sitting next to me. "The guy's a total wine geek. He's loves a good Pinot, and he's famous for bidding up prices at these charity things."

"I can't see the person behind paddle 199," someone else said.

I nudged Benson. "This is *crazy!* Who could that other person *be*? And why would these people want to pay so much for *my* wine?"

"Because they saw Broadhurst taking multiple sips and spending time with you. They know you've got an exciting new release and they want to own a barrel's worth of the first vintage."

"There it is fifty-seven! Now fifty-eight, will I see fifty-eight?" the auctioneer chanted as the dueling paddles kept rising. "There it is! How about fifty-nine, will I see fifty-nine? There it is! How about sixty? There it is!" Paddle 199 went up. "How about sixty-one? Will I see sixty-one?" The murmuring stopped, and the room fell silent. "*Sixty* thousand dollars. Going once. Going twice." The gavel came down on the block. "Sold to number 199 for *sixty* thousand dollars!" A collective gasp echoed through the audience. "Folks, you've just witnessed a barrel selling for a *record* price at the Napa Valley Wine Auction!" I sat in disbelief that *my* wine had earned sixty thousand dollars to help needy families. "Is Miss Goodyear with us here tonight?" the auctioneer asked. "If you are, please stand up."

"*Stand up? Me?*" I looked around, wondering if the whole thing was happening for real.

"You," Benson told me, as he took my arm and guided me out of my seat. There was a burst of applause along with whoops and whistles from the audience. Benson looked up and smiled at me. I bent down to give him an enormous bear hug for all of his help and support.

"Now, will the winning bidder please stand up?" Brimstone asked. "And let's give him or her a hand for his huge contribution to the families of our community!" When the bidder stood up to thunderous applause, my heart began to pound so hard, I thought it would crack a rib. The bidder was Julien LeMont.

"The Napa Valley Wine Auction organizers thank you for your generosity, sir!" Harvey Brimstone said to Julien, who gave a friendly wave to the crowd. One glance at that gorgeous face made my body go limp. He looked my way and gave me a wink.

"Wow, you must really have a thing for that wine!" the auctioneer told Julien. "And I can see why you love it so much!" He pointed to me. "She's pretty!" The audience laughed at the remark. "But don't tell her husband." The auctioneer was pointing to Benson. "Or is that her boyfriend? He looks like the jealous type!" That got another laugh as I shook my head in protest. "Next on the block . . . a barrel of Poe Chardonnay from the Sonoma Coast."

I saw Julien stand up and walk through the aisle toward the exit of the cave with his brother, Henri, following. "I have to thank him," I said to Benson as I got up from my seat. While slowly making my way through the rows of chairs, I was filled with conflicting emotions—a rush of adrenaline at seeing him after all this time, anxiety at the thought of finally speaking to him, and a flash of long-simmering anger over that attitude of his that destroyed any hopes I'd had for our future. When I finally reached the lobby of the winery, I spotted Henri standing at a bar with a glass of wine in his hand. Julien was nowhere in sight. "Henri! Henri! It's me, Samantha!" I called out. "Where's Julien? I have to thank him for what he did!"

"Ah, Samantha! Its been too long. And now you're making your own wine!"

"Yes, I am. But please . . . where's Julien?"

"It's too bad that you missed him. My brother left just a few minutes ago."

"Left? What do you mean, he left?" I looked around the lobby in a panic.

"He flew in yesterday to join me on my sales trip. I had an extra ticket to the auction, and when we saw your wine listed on the program, he joined me here tonight and to explain himself to you once more. To tell you he was very embarrassed and very ashamed by the actions of our *père*. And that he never had the chance to convey his sentiments."

"Embarrassed? Ashamed? But I just assumed from the way Julien acted . . . by what he said . . . that he thought what Denis did was fine. That's why I left him."

"It sounds like you and my brother had, what we call in France, *un défaut de communication.*"

"A failure to communicate. I guess we did."

"Julien bought your wine to win you back. But when they announced that his old *ami* from harvest is now your boyfriend or maybe even your husband, he knew it was too late."

"Benson's not my boyfriend. Or my husband. We're just friends. Oh my God! We *have* failed to communicate!" Tears spurted from my eyes, and I felt my throat constrict. "Can you help me find Julien? Please! I have to see him."

Henri pulled a plastic key card from his pocket. "Tomorrow he goes to New York to see our *maman*. But tonight, you'll find him at Villagio *Auberge. Chambre trois deux deux.*"

"Thanks, Henri! Thanks so much!" I took the card, gave him a kiss on the cheek, and ran back to the cave to make my apologies to Benson.

·   ·   ·

I crept back to my seat while the auction continued. "Benson," I whispered. "I've got to get to the Villagio. Julien thought you and I were a couple, so he left here without even saying goodbye!"

"It's okay, Sam." Benson forced a smile, but he wouldn't meet my eyes as he handed me the valet ticket for his truck. "No prob. I'll Uber it home. I'll stay at your place to take care of Seuss in case you don't get back tonight. Just go!" Though I felt terrible leaving him in the lurch, I knew I'd never have another chance to make things right with Julien.

I made my way to the entrance of the winery, where I gave the valet the ticket. A few minutes later, with the keys in my hand, I scrambled up into the Super Duty F350-XLT—no easy feat in my heels and figure-hugging gown. When I took the wheel and started the engine, I realized that my '57 Ford pickup was more like a go-cart compared to this monster. Not knowing that the truck had over four hundred horsepower, I jammed the shift into first, stepped on the gas, and rocketed out of the parking lot with a cloud of black smoke trailing behind. Three minutes on the road seemed like three hours before I turned onto a street that led to the tiny and beautiful town of Yountville. I was lucky to have dodged a speeding ticket as I flew into the parking lot of The Villagio Inn and Spa, where I parked the truck with my heart racing, and scurried past ancient-looking statues, olive trees, and fountains to reach the rambling Mediterranean-style building.

"Good evening. And how can I help you?" asked the gorgeous young woman in a crisp grey suit at the front desk.

"Which way to room 322?" I held up Henri's key card.

"Staircase on the left. Third floor."

I bounded up a staircase and raced down the hallway in search of 322. When I reached it, I pounded on the door. "Julien! Julien!" When there was no answer, I waved the card over the electronic lock, and the door opened. I walked into the bedroom where a carry-on bag sat on a chair. "Julien? Julien? Are you here?" I called out again before noticing that the glass doors to the terrace were open. Walking through them, I looked out at the hotel's pool, and saw someone doing laps by the light of the moon. The power of the wake behind him made it clear that the swimmer was a man with a liquid-like form that caused the long muscles of his back to rise and fall with the stroke of each arm. "Julien! Julien!" I was sure it was him. But with his head below the water, he didn't hear me, and kept on swimming. I ran out of the suite and down the stairs to a door that led to the back of the hotel, pulling my shoes off along the way. It was past ten o'clock at night, and there was no one else besides the two of us in the pool area. Hoping that my black strapless bra and black panties could pass for a bikini if anyone else came by, I pulled my dress over my head, tossed it onto a lounge, and dove into the pool. From under the water, I saw muscular arms stroking and long legs kicking, and swam toward them like a seal. When I reached the man I still loved, I wrapped my arms around his powerful chest, never wanting to let go. Not knowing who or what had grabbed him, he almost flew into the air. But when he realized it was me, he relaxed, and we held each other in our arms with our lips locked together, slowly sinking to the bottom of the pool.

"I've dreamt about this . . . so many times," I said with chest heaving when we finally came up for air.

"So have I," Julien said as he held me up from the water and stared into my eyes. "But why are you here? The man who ran the auction said—"

"Benson's just a friend. Nothing more. And I'm sorry for running away like that." I reached out to touch the beautiful wet features of his face. "I should have listened. I should have given you a chance to explain."

"It's okay, *mon amour*," he said softly, as he caressed the back of my neck. "I should have been honest about my feelings. Honest about the pain *mon père* has brought to my family. Instead, I chased you away." We dog-paddled to the edge of the pool and climbed out of the water. He wrapped a towel around me and held me tight, as we went into the hotel and climbed the stairs.

"I'm so proud of you, Samantha, for making such a *bon* Pinot Noir. I took a taste from the barrel when I first arrived at the auction," he told me as we walked down the hallway. "It's a *formidable* young wine from ancient vines, and you picked at just the right time, as I knew you could do. In six months more, it will be even more complex, more vibrant, and more *délicieux*."

"I know it will. And getting your stamp of approval means the world to me. You were my teacher. And I have so much to tell you. So much has happened in my life since I left France," I said as we reached the door to the room and went inside.

"Which gives us so much to talk about in the morning." He picked me up and carried me into the bedroom where the towel slid to the floor.

•  •  •

The sun streamed through the woven bamboo window treatments that covered the doors to the terrace. I sat up in the king-size bed and looked down at the gorgeous man sleeping beside me. A breeze coming in through the open doors made the morning light dance on his mop of shiny black hair. I ran my fingers down his back and pressed my lips to his sun-kissed skin, sending a series of shivers throughout my body.

Two eyes as blue as the ocean opened and looked up at me. He slung an arm around my waist and pulled me closer as he rolled on top of me and kissed my lips.

"Remember our plan to go to the *auberge* in Chablis on the night of the Beaujolais Nouveau *soirée*?" he asked.

"I remember. I've dreamt about how amazing that trip would have been for us."

"But you don't know just *how* amazing it would have been."

"What do you mean?"

He got up from the bed, opened the blinds, unzipped his carry-on bag, and fished around in it until he pulled out a small satin box. "The only person who knew what I had planned at the *auberge* was my *grand-mére Céleste*," he said as he fell back on the bed, took my hand, and put the box in it. "And I'm certain she did not tell you." Stunned, I looked at his face. He nodded for me to open it. When I did, I gasped. It held a ring with an intricate filigree band and a sparkling emerald-cut diamond surrounded by smaller diamonds and rubies. "Céleste gave me this ring that once belonged to her *maman*, to give to you. I was taking you to the *auberge* to ask you to be my wife. And to promise that I'd always be faithful."

I sat and stared at the ring with my mouth open. "Oh! Oh wow! Oh Julien! If I'd only known! How could I have been so wrong? How did everything fall apart for us?" I held the box to my chest and tears rolled down my cheeks. "We lost each other, and you lost your wine!"

"But only for a while. The wine is back, and you have returned to me."

"The wine is back?"

"*Oui.* The police found all of it in a storage locker traced to Fifika and her accomplice. The condition of the wine looks to be good. So my family's tradition will continue."

"Oh! How wonderful!"

He reached for my hand. "And you will be a part of that tradition." He took the ring from the box and slipped it on the finger of my left hand. But it was too small and refused to go further than the knuckle. "It's no problem. Our family's jeweler can make it to fit you," he assured me, as he kissed my finger, and held up my hand. "*Elle est La Première Dame du Château LeMont.*"

"*La Première Dame?* Hold on there, Julien." I felt my spine stiffen. "Wasn't *La Première Dame du Château LeMont* your mother's title? I'd be taking Sara's place?"

He gave me a wry smile. "If my *maman* ever comes back to us, you and she can get in the arena for a *match de boxe* to see who keeps the title."

"All kidding aside, Julien, I don't think I'm able to take that position. I'm making three hundred cases of wine here in Napa. I have a ten-acre vineyard and an eighty-year-old house that needs a ton of work."

"And now, you'll be *la première dame* of a domaine that's making twenty thousand cases of wine in Beaujolais, has two hundred acres of vineyards, and a six-hundred-year-old château that also needs a ton of work."

I thought of Sara in the booth at The Cellar, when she said she couldn't live out her life at that place until the only thing left of her was a bottle with a tasting note tied to it on a shelf over the fireplace. While I stared at the ring on my knuckle, her words echoed in my head.

"Our children will inherit our gifts for picking grapes and our love for the vineyard," Julien said as he kissed my belly. "They will continue our traditions, as I am doing, as *mon père* has done, and as *mon grand-père* and his *père* and *grand-père* before him have done."

"Our kids will continue our *traditions*?" I squirmed, moving my torso away from his lips. "Kids who grow up on vineyards don't always want to stay in the wine business. My friend Hal raised his kids on a vineyard, and they didn't want any part of it."

"Not our *enfants*. They and many generations after them will work to keep Domaine LeMont one of the finest producers in Beaujolais."

"Forget about kids. What about right now? I have a life here, Julien. Can't we make this work for both of us? Maybe visit each other every few weeks? Or what if we alternate our time between France and Napa? I know of another winemaking couple. She's American, he's French, and they—"

"Domaine LeMont is *my* life, Samantha. *Mon père* and *grand-père* have earned the right to rest, so I have no more time for travel. If you love me, you will love me for who I am, and who I must be. And I need to have you by my side." He guided me back down on the bed, ran his fingers across my chest, and kissed my neck.

My eyes drifted out the window where a host of white-crowned sparrows were flitting through the air. I thought about my new crop of grapes, that were well into the veraison stage, and would be ready for harvest within the next two weeks. I was eager to taste them, as I'd done every morning, while their sugar levels continued to rise, and their acid levels continued to fall. The ring had been constricting the flow of blood through my knuckle, and my finger throbbed. I pulled away from Julien and sat up in the bed.

"A year and a half ago, I would have stayed by your side in a heartbeat." I tugged at the ring until it released from my finger, then placed it back in the slit of the satin cushion and snapped the box shut. "But I've made a new life for myself out here. And I'm just not ready to give that up."

•   •   •

I was getting the hang of Benson's truck as I drove back down the Silverado Trail toward home. It would only be a matter of time before

I'd need to trade out my truck for one that would fit the needs of my growing production. The vineyards on both sides of the Trail were lifting their leaves to soak up the morning sun that would warm their ripening berries. When I pulled through the gates of 6 Twisted Vine Road, the fog was rising from the surrounding hills and Seuss came bounding out from the vineyard to greet me. Before opening the truck's door, I took a quick look at three emails that had dinged on my phone since I'd left the hotel. The first was from the artist who was creating a label for my wine and had sent me the first draft of his design for my approval. The second was an invitation from Steve Littauer and his wife Maggie, for their annual "Kick off the Harvest Season" barbecue they'd be hosting on their vineyard property the following weekend. The third was the Sunday edition of *Wine Business Daily* with the headline, *Darnay Pinot Noir Sets off Record Bidding War at This Year's Napa Valley Barrel Auction.* I looked out at my vineyard and waved to Benson, who was pruning the excess growth from the vines. After changing from my dress and heels into my jeans, flannel shirt, and work boots, I'd head out to join him.

# the end

# about the author

Linda Sheehan has lived in New York and Los Angeles where she wrote and produced commercials and trailers for movies and television. She now lives in Napa, California where she's the co-owner of Poe Wines that makes highly acclaimed Chardonnay, Pinot Noir, Cabernet, Rosé, sparkling wines as well as an organic grapefruit vermouth awarded 95 points from *Wine Enthusiast Magazine*. *Decanted* is her second novel. Besides indulging her passion for great wines, she is an avid horseback rider and golfer.

# note from the author

Word-of-mouth is crucial for any author to succeed. If you enjoyed *Decanted,* please leave a review online—anywhere you are able. Even if it's just a sentence or two. It would make all the difference and would be very much appreciated.

Thanks!
Linda Sheehan

Thank you so much for reading one of our **Women's Fiction** novels.

If you enjoyed the experience, please check out our recommendation for your next great read!

*City in a Forest* by Ginger Pinholster

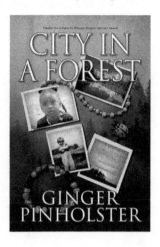

Finalist for a *Santa Fe Writers Project Literary Award*

"Ginger Pinholster, a master of significant detail, weaves her struggling characters' pasts, present, and futures into a breathtaking, beautiful novel in *City in a Forest*."

*–IndieReader*

CPSIA information can be obtained
at www.ICGtesting.com
Printed in the USA
FSHW011336280321
79924FS